SHALASH
THE IRAQI

Shalash the Iraqi

Translated by Luke Leafgren

Foreword by Kanan Makiya

SHEFFIELD – LONDON – NEW YORK

This edition published in 2023 by And Other Stories
Sheffield – London – New York
www.andotherstories.org

1 3 5 7 9 8 6 4 2

ISBN: 9781913505646
eBook ISBN: 9781913505653

Editor: Jeremy M. Davies; Copy-editor: Jane Haxby; Proofreader: Bryan
Karetnyk; Cover design: Tom Etherington; Cover painting: Faisel Laibi
Sahi, *The Coffee Shop*, 2015; Typeset in Albertan Pro and Syntax by
Tetragon, London. Printed and bound by CPI Limited, Croydon, UK.

And Other Stories gratefully acknowledge that our work is
supported using public funding by Arts Council England.

Support for this book, including its translation from Arabic,
has been funded by the Makiya-Kufa Charity based in London.

CONTENTS

INTRODUCTION

Who Is Shalash the Iraqi?

I first met "Shalash the Iraqi" in Paris in the summer of 2006. An odd place for two Iraqis who don't speak French to meet, chosen in part by circumstance (roughly halfway between Cambridge, USA, and Baghdad, Iraq), but also because the chronicler of the ever-so-endearing residents of city block number 41 in Madinat al-Thawra needed to visit the cafés and city haunts of Jean-Paul Sartre. And that is how we spent our first week together, walking Sartre's streets and talking about an Iraq that had descended into sectarian strife the previous year, just about when Shalash started posting the daily blogs that made him so famous among Iraqis that it seemed no conversation between them, anywhere in the world, could be conducted without some reference to one of his stories.

Alas, I cannot tell you much more about "Shalash the Iraqi." Not even his name. All I can say is that he is the author of some eighty posts written in colloquial Baghdadi dialect between 2005 and 2006. Oh, and I can say that he is a polymath who at the time of our first meeting was much taken with the French intellectual life of the 1960s and '70s (Sartre, Foucault, Derrida)—as indeed was typical of the small group of Iraqi oppositionists operating then in Baghdad as an Eastern European-style samizdat collective.

I myself had an Anglophone education alongside my official Arabic one, and never could make head or tail of anything Derrida wrote. I was therefore flabbergasted not only by the fact that Derrida and Foucault were known, but being hotly debated during the 1990s in the privacy of at least some Iraqi homes and cafés in Saddam Hussein's Baghdad. Shalash introduced me to those circles inside Iraq, hitherto completely unknown to those of us exiles outside the country so preoccupied with opposing the Saddam regime. And, as I soon discovered, a delightful novel called *Baba Sartre* (*Papa Sartre*), written by the gifted Iraqi writer Ali Badr, captured the fascination with Sartre inside those circles, among whom Shalash was by far the leading light.

Another of Shalash's many gifts is his ability to recite from memory all of Saddam's speeches, in exactly the tone and register that they had been delivered; the difference being that when Shalash recited them one could not help but collapse in paroxysms of laughter, whereas laughter in general (not only while Saddam was delivering a speech) was foreign to the Iraq that Saddam built. I envied Shalash his prodigious memory, as any fellow writer would; and whereas I had only written about the Iraq—Iran war, he had served on its frontlines for eight grueling and exceptionally cruel years. Those are two entirely different ways of "knowing" war. To "know" the biggest war of the post-Independence "Third World," and still be able to make people laugh, is a blessing granted to very few.

But again, alas, I cannot tell you much more about who Shalash really is, because the identity of the person who created this fictional alter-ego must, for the security of his family and friends, remain a secret, even today, sixteen years after he abruptly stopped writing his stories. The fear this time does not derive from some brutal dictator or the all-pervasive organs of a security state; it derives from the anarchy that Iraq fell into shortly after the toppling of Saddam Hussein in 2003.

The morning after Saddam fled Baghdad on April 10, 2003, Iraqis found themselves in a state of deep anxiety and confusion. They had learned only too well the rules underlying survival in a semi-totalitarian state. But they did not understand waking up overnight to find themselves in a world with no rules.

By the late 1990s many of them could see that another war was brewing, but they assumed it would end like the last one, in 1991, with a bruised dictator still very much in power. Even when American troops were on the outskirts of Baghdad, and in spite of all the rhetoric about freedom and democracy, they never in their wildest dreams expected a foreign occupation. When it came, it was a total rupture with their past, in the form of a new beginning to which they had not contributed and yet in which they were now expected to serve as principal actors. In such conditions, it was easy to imagine that American incompetence was deliberate; that every Iraqi who popped up on the public stage was either a fool, an opportunist, a carpetbagger, or someone else's stooge. And, to be sure, some of them were all these things at once.

Shalash writes about such people. He created a constellation of villains and other characters who pop up again and again in his stories, all of which center around one small neighborhood in Thawra City, a sprawling Shiite suburb of

17

Baghdad containing roughly half of the city's population of eight million strong. Featured are bumbling Imams, suddenly politicized thugs, vain and venal politicians, and fanatical militiamen who switch allegiances at the drop of a hat, carpet-baggers descending like an army of cockroaches from all corners of the world to make a quick buck.

In the course of doing so, Shalash made anxious and worried Iraqis laugh. They hadn't laughed much in the previous thirty years. In fact, it was dangerous to so much as crack a joke. Humor had landed many an Iraqi in jail, and worse. But it turns out that laughing was a kind of tonic to the unfolding craziness, especially after that craziness evolved into civil strife between 2005 and 2007. Laughing was, even more importantly, a safety valve, a form of sorely needed solace.

However, just as abruptly as they had burst onto the scene, and right when the sectarian killings were at their peak, the anonymous writings stopped. When I pressed Shalash, who had revealed himself to me that same year, to explain why he had given up on giving us more of Shalash's stories, he told me he just didn't know how to be funny anymore.

*

The Palestinian cultural critic, Salma Khadra Jayyusi, has written about humor and irony in Arabic literature:

> With only a few exceptions, modern Arab writers . . . wrote in the romantic or realistic tradition, in the tragic or heroic mode, they favored a serious tone and a direct approach. The comic apprehension of experience, burlesque and parody,

double meaning, the picaresque, the ironic and sarcastic, were
not easily adopted, and the richness of both classical Arabic
and Western literatures in these modes was rarely utilized . . .
it remains true, as one peruses the vast panorama of Arabic
literature, that the tragic spirit is more spontaneous with the
Arabs, while the heroic, so muted in modern Western literature, is even more constantly alive in their hearts.*

Standard written Arabic, in which most literature is written,
is a poor halfway house between the classical language of
the Qur'an and the multitude of spoken local Arabic dia-
lects. No one speaks it on a daily basis, although everyone
understands it; it is the language of newspapers and radio
broadcasts; the language of politics and speechifying that
does not know humor. In fact, all feelings are strangers to
this kind of Arabic, which is what makes it so ineffectual
in the fictional mode. But Shalash was deploying sarcasm,
wit and irony; in order to make people laugh at the newly
installed Iraqi political elite, he had to write in the way that
ordinary Iraqis speak, not listen to speeches or read newspapers. In this sense, Shalash is a very different kind of Arabic
writer. For one thing, his use of an already "minor" dialect
is peppered with phrases and expressions used primarily in
Thawra City itself. His language feels, from an Iraqi point
of view, deeply authentic, and deeply hilarious—things that
most literary writing in Arabic has a great deal of trouble
achieving.

* Salma Khadra Jayyusi, "Introduction," in Emile Habiby, *The Secret Life of Saeed: The Pessoptimist*, translated by Salm Khadra Jayyusi and Trevor LeGassick (London: Zed Books, 1985), pp. viii–ix.

19

There is a drawback to this authenticity, of course: it is "local" almost to a fault. Shalash's humor is not always a movable feast. His writing makes for uphill work to the prospective translator, being difficult at times for even non-Iraqi Arabs to follow. Marvel then at the easygoing, raffish, faux-naïve, rollicking tone of Luke Leafgren's English-language Shalash—a remarkable achievement, and the fruit of many, many days and months working with Shalash himself, and with other Iraqis too: devotees of Shalash who were familiar with his language and Thawra City's range of idiomatic idiosyncrasies.

I have said that Iraqis found—and find—Shalash hilarious. Who were the Iraqis laughing at? Themselves. That is the deeper source of his achievement; the beating heart of his "Iraqiness." It is impossible to laugh at "Imperialism" or "Zionism" or "Arab Reaction"—the subject matter of Saddam's officially sanctioned cartoonists and storytellers. Real laughter comes from the inside; it is an eruption from the belly, not an emanation of the brain. Instinctively, Shalash understood that; one laughs and loves at the same time. And what is it that Shalash loved? Iraq: the very thing that the political elite installed by the American Occupation were falling over themselves to forget. They chose to govern in the name of their sect or ethnic group, or as stooges for the Islamic Republic next door, never as upholders of that collective abstraction, that multiethnic mosaic of groups and religions held together in our imaginations by a name: Iraq. It is those very same factions, with their false and foreign allegiances pilloried by Shalash, that the youth of Iraq rebelled against in 2019; and they did so in the name of Iraq, toppling perhaps *the* most sectarian government of post-2003 Iraq, and *the* most beholden to Iran's Revolutionary Guard. Shalash's writings were the forerunner to those protests.

Shalash's "Iraqiness" is not jingoistic patriotism, but the kind of intimate, defensive, and profoundly personal "love of place" that George Orwell talked about, and that Jill Lepore tries to understand in a recent book (*This America: The Case for the Nation*). The writer calls himself Shalash "the Iraqi," even though the word *Iraq* appears very rarely in his stories. He did not need to belabor the word; love of Iraq is implicit in all his writing, in every character he created, be she a housewife wrestling with her neighbor over a draft of the constitution, or a new user of the internet, trying to learn the mysteries of "Google Earth."

At the time, Iraqis turned en masse, in a fever of urgency to Shalash's stories. True, there were only 25,000 users of the internet there in 2003. But that posed no impediment. People were printing them out, copying them longhand, memorizing them, talking about them, sharing them, telling and retelling them, plagiarizing them, and bombarding Shalash with questions and opinions about them by way of the email address he always provided for his readers at the end of each post.

"Ordinary people" loved Shalash, but we all know that politicians are less than ordinary. Sad to report, none of Iraq's crop of new powermongers had a sense of humor—with one notable exception. I have it on good authority that a Kurd, the fat President of the Republic, Jalal Talabani, whose prodigious banquets are themselves pilloried in one of Shalash's posts, was a fan. Talabani was the butt of some of Shalash's jokes, but Talabani liked to laugh. It seems no one else in Iraqi politics did.

Of such delicious ironies is this remarkable collection of stories made. That should be reason enough to make them available to an English-reading public. But there is another reason. For thirty years the West has only known Iraqis through wars, occupations, Saddam Hussein, and the brutal nature of the Ba'ath regime. Throughout that period the word "Iraq" has appeared in newspaper headlines week after week, even replacing the former primacy of the Arab–Israeli conflict in the public's imagination. Perhaps it is time to know the inhabitants of that sad and troubled land in a new and more human way.

KANAN MAKIYA
October 2022

PREFACE

Greetings, dear reader! Who could have guessed, when I first sent these observations to a friend to post online almost twenty years ago, that anyone outside of Baghdad would care what I had to say? I was writing for my fellow Iraqis at a time when we were rebuilding and dreaming and suffering, and I used the language and the people and the places of our everyday lives. But now that my stories have traveled so far from home, perhaps I can set the stage for you?

You'll find your new friend Shalash reporting from Thawra City, the suburb of Baghdad that takes its name from the Arabic word for revolution. This area is composed of seventy-nine sectors, or blocks, each of which contains a thousand houses made up of exactly a hundred and forty-four square meters. Thawra City is the largest suburb in the Middle East, with more than three million residents. But you're more likely to have heard of it as Sadr City, named for one of the most powerful religious families in Iraq, whose scion, Muqtada, plays an important role in the tales you will soon read. Of all the people you'll encounter here, you've probably heard the most about a guy named Saddam Hussein, and maybe his sons Uday and Qusay. But there are other names in what follows—the names of religious, political, and cultural figures—that may be less familiar. If you are curious, you can learn more via that most remarkable tool, the internet, which made its way into Iraq after Saddam's fall, soon before I began writing. Still, let me lay out some few general details before we begin—some background that you might find helpful, starting with our religion, which appears on almost every page of our lives.

According to the religion of Islam, God chose Muhammad as his Prophet and sent him a holy book, the Qur'an. After Muhammad's death, Muhammad's followers disagreed over who should serve as caliph. This conflict was the origin of the split between the Sunnis and the Shiites: unlike Sunnis, Shiites believe that Muhammad's nephew and son-in-law, Ali ibn Abi Talib, should have filled that role. What's more, Shiites—among whose number we might include almost all the residents of our beloved Thawra City—revere the entire household of the Prophet, especially Ali and Ali's sons, Husayn and Hasan, both of whom were killed, along with most of their immediate families, at the Battle of Karbala (680 CE): a massacre that we commemorate each year during the festival of Ashura. One of Husayn's sons was spared, and he and ten of his descendants—together with our beloved Husayn—are believed by the largest branch of Shia to form the Twelve Infallible Imams of Islam. Their tombs are important shrines for Shiite pilgrims. The Twelfth Imam in that chain, however, known as the Mahdi, is believed to have gone into hiding to avoid being murdered, and he is expected to make a miraculous return one day to purge the world of injustice.

No small number of Muslims trace their lineage to Muhammad and Ali, and they wear black turbans and are honored with the title sayyid. But it is the Islamic theologians who play an especially important role for Shiites, because believers are expected to follow the guidance of the religious clerkship in all matters, large and small. That clerkship is dominated, on the whole, by five major families, named Sistani, Hakim, Sadr, Kho'i, and Haeri. These families, based in both Iraq and Iran, wield immense religious and political authority, and have often competed with each other for bigger slices of the same.

When Saddam Hussein came to power in 1979, he and the Ba'athist Party consolidated power, often by killing or exiling anyone who might stand as competition, including the abovementioned theologians. While Ali al-Sistani lived quietly in Iraq largely by avoiding political affairs, the leader of the Hakim family sought refuge in Iran; and as for the Sadr family, Muqtada's brothers and father were assassinated. Members of opposition political parties moved to the US, the UK, or Iran, while the Kurds were able to carve out a measure of autonomy in the north thanks to a no-fly zone enforced by the US and the UK. Everything changed after Iraq was invaded in 2003. With Saddam out of the way and in hiding, Abdul Aziz al-Hakim came back from Iran, backed by a militia largely composed of Iraqi exiles called the Badr Brigade. Muqtada al-Sadr was supported by his own militia, the Mahdi Army. Ayad Allawi, Ahmed Chalabi, and Ibrahim al-Jaafari were just a few of the exiles who arrived from the US and the UK to play roles in the new Iraq.

After disbanding the Iraqi Army and outlawing the Ba'athist Party, the US official who oversaw Iraq from May 2003 through June 2004, Paul Bremer, set in motion a plan for a new democratic government. Bremer worked with the Iraqi

Governing Council (which had a new president each month to satisfy all the parties and factions), which was replaced in June 2004 by the Iraqi Interim Government. Elections were held for the Iraqi National Assembly in January 2005, and that Assembly confirmed the Iraqi Transitional Government, which took power in May 2005. In October of that year, Iraq voted in a referendum to approve a new constitution. Then, in December, elections were held for a permanent government, which took power in May 2006.

And if you should find any of that a little confusing, well, think of how we must have felt—especially when there were multitudes of political parties, ethnic groups, and religious leaders vying for control of the territory and its natural resources. Violence between the groups and against the US and other foreign troops was a common occurrence, especially when al-Qaeda began operating in Iraq and fomenting sectarian violence through suicide bombings against the Shiites.

It is for you to imagine, dear reader, what it was like for a person to wake up one morning to find American tanks driving through the streets of their already exhausted city. Without warning, people we had lived among for our whole lives were turned into historical figures, pulled this way and that by the orations of religious men, whose photos our neighbors carried and whose names they chanted. That's what happened to me. I found myself a stranger in my own country, as bewildered as if I were suddenly thrust into the set of a movie about the Prophet of Islam in the early years of his ministry. Yes, my country vanished from the map after the invasion, and it was a bitter shock. But the real shock was when the people with whom I had spent my whole life became strangers. That realization is what drove me into the street, laughing with bitter pain. And that was the moment in which these writings of mine were born, writings that my readers took more seriously than I ever could have imagined. And so I lived those first years under cover, writing under a pseudonym and afraid of violence at the hands of the same people I had loved since I was born.

SHALASH THE IRAQI
Probably somewhere in Iraq, 2023

You Want a Bottle of Arak?
A Missed Call's All It Takes

When you pronounce the Arabic word *al-'abeed*, slaves, as
a'ibeed (so, dropping the initial *laam* and voweling the letter
'ayn with an I sound instead of an A), you get the slang word
used in Thawra City for people with dark skin, of whom there
are many in the neighborhood of Gayyara. They get special
treatment here. Respect. No, really! People step aside to
let them by is what I'm saying. First because the story goes
that they're especially fearless and ferocious when they get
into fights, which is often, since fights are always breaking
out in this crowded city. But also because they're the ones
who put our city on the map. Take the Fiori soccer team, for
instance, which was the most famous sports team we had,
back in the day, and if you wanted to play in the nationals,
that was your first stop. We all remember Bashar Rashid,
who played internationally and then got executed by the old
regime. And there was Ali Hussain, and . . . too many to list.
All of them a'ibeed.

But look, it's not just sports. They've had a hand in
every cultural institution in Thawra City. We all remember
Falayful's *shadda*, and the one led by the artist known as
Alexander the Great. (For those who don't know the term, a
shadda is a band that performs at weddings and other festive
occasions.) And there were so many famous singers that won
our hearts, people like Abade Al Amare, Hussin Albasry,

Abd Rambo—who changed his name to the far more pious Abd Rabo, meaning "Servant of his Lord," after he became a religious poet, writing poems to our revered Husayn and declaring his loyalty to the Sadr family. Of course, the a'ibeed also invented dances like the *bazzakha* and the *khawshiya*, and without them, who would ever have thought to bring us break dancing?

People like to say that the a'ibeed don't join political parties or get too pious. But they preserve our culture in an even more important way by opening coffeehouses and rattling the cups all day long after being trained by our local sheikhs in the traditions of tribal hospitality. And everyone knows that while they won't take any shit from outside their community, inside it they live together in a truly admirable peace.

What I'm leading up to is that the a'ibeed of Thawra City probably wouldn't have had a whole lot of racial discrimination to worry about even if the list of their accomplishments went no further. But the major reason they get so much respect here has to do with what they did for the city at the end of the '90s. Each month of Ramadan, when Saddam's religious revival was in full swing, the a'ibeed community played a heroic role, inscribed forever in the pages of glory, by secretly providing Thawra City with all the arak, gin, vodka, and cold beer we needed. They would put the liquor in big plastic bins with blocks of ice and go door to door to quench the city's thirst—or, anyway, the thirst of those citizens of the city who didn't see it as a holy month of fasting so much as a month when alcohol was particularly hard to get. It's true that prices went up a little, but they were taking a risk for which we held them in the utmost reverence.

Now, with Ramadan standing sullenly at our door once more, we drinkers remember with longing the days of the a'ibeed and their glorious service to their fellow citizens! But, what's this? It seems the a'ibeed have insisted on demonstrating their liberty once again. They've set about knocking on the doors of the customers to inform them, on the QT, that the goods in question will again be plentiful this year . . .

Knocking on doors, you say? Can't they get with the times? But of course! They've stocked up on burners and have provided their clientele with emergency phone numbers in case any should be seized by a sudden, pressing need for liquor. When Irhayam, the distributor for our particular block in Thawra, visited our house unexpectedly last night, he said, "It's easy, Uncle Shalash. A missed call's all it takes. Just dial and hang up, and the bottle will be in your hands within minutes." I thanked Irhayam and stored his number in my mobile under the name "Abu Wagafat," the Bedouin nickname for someone who always has your back.

And what a lovely surprise it was, ladies and gentlemen, when I saw Irhayam himself, this very day, on a sectarian religious TV channel, speaking clearly and distinctly: "I congratulate the holy Hidden Imam (may God hasten his noble appearance!)—I congratulate the high religious clerkship, with Sayyid Ali al-Sistani at its head (long may his shadow stretch!)—and I congratulate each and every son of the Iraqi people, on the occasion of this first night of the blessed month of Ramadan. May God renew it with every blessing for us and for you."

Ramadan kareem, my brothers: a generous Ramadan. Now you know the true origin of the blessing!

Hassoun the Dane Spends His Vacation
in the Nation's Heartland

My neighbor Hassoun just got back from Denmark. He's staying with his family here in Thawra City. The first person to report on his reappearance was Khanjar, that meddlesome son of a meddlesome man, saying "What?! He shaved his mustache right off!"

All us neighbors crowded together inside Hassoun's place, turning this novelty inside out with our stares. Some of the women called out blessings upon the Prophet Muhammad and the Prophet's household so that Hassoun would be protected from the evil eye; others took this opportunity to find fault with his fancy clothes and his new, pretentious way of talking. "Look who's gotten too big for his boots," said one.

That wasn't what interested the men and the older boys, though. They were waiting for Hassoun to finish with all the welcomes and all the see-you-soons so he could spill his guts to them about his sexual adventures abroad—for Hassoun had undoubtedly indulged himself with plenty of young Danish women, not to mention Danish divorcées, as the spirit had moved him.

Whereas all Hassoun could think about was how miserable he was to have come home. He was in agony, let's not mince words. There was the climate—the temperature here felt simply lethal to him now. And then the filth of it! He couldn't bear sitting anywhere dirty, and the house wasn't exactly clean. There was no way, absolutely none, that he could reuse cups or dishes that hadn't been washed. Anything less than what he'd gotten used to in Denmark was unacceptable. Likewise, he had a throbbing migraine from the constant roar of the generator. But he could hardly admit all that; he could hardly say anything without being cut short: "Hey, who do you think you are, anyway? Why do you keep blabbering on about this Denmark? What, you think we haven't been around the block a few times ourselves?"

Khanjar—that despicable son of a despicable man—led the charge. He couldn't wait to find something to hold against Hassoun. He brooded there like a knife in his side. Every so often he would say something like, "Hassoun, you're not the only one who's traveled, okay? We took a trip to Iran to see the shrine of the Eighth Imam once, remember? And we've been to Syria to visit the tomb of Zaynab bint Ali. And in a few days, we're even going to go to Turkey!"

Luckily, Hassoun's aunt, Umm Jabbar, was there too. She was a nice lady who worked at the government food bank in some official capacity. She had a sense of how much Hassoun the Dane must be suffering, particularly as she was used to dealing with cheeses. Yes—as it goes with cheese, so goes it with men. Umm Jabbar could as easily judge the worth of a man as compare Egyptian cheese—with which Saddam used to poison us during the days of the sanctions—to the soft, delicious Danish cheeses that Hassoun now resembled. That's what prompted her direct request, delivered in an imperious tone: "Come along, then, all of you! Let the boy get some rest! You're killing him! Nephew Hassoun, go to your room. Relax a little, take a nap."

Hassoun couldn't believe his luck. He obeyed: got to his feet, hitched up his jeans, headed off into the next room. But back he rushed in alarm only a few seconds later.

"What's wrong, my son?" asked his mother, reaching up to caress his face. "In the name of God, the merciful, the compassionate, what's the matter, my child?" But Hassoun didn't so much as look at her, just stood there stock still, his mouth hanging open. "What's wrong with you, child? Speak!"

Hassoun could only point mutely toward the room he'd so quickly vacated. His mother of course rushed over to find out what on earth had so spooked her son. Hassoun's sister-in-law and a few other women I didn't recognize accompanied her.

Hassoun's mother grasped the problem at once. She came back and laughed in her son's face. "What's wrong with you, child? Why so scared? That's only your brother's rocket launcher and your brother-in-law's old machine gun. The other stuff, the explosives, rifles, and grenades, those are all ours. Look, child, we've all joined Muqtada al-Sadr's Mahdi Army, didn't you know? What, you never heard about the Mahdi Army in Denmark, my dear, sweet child?"

This was one blow too many for poor Hassoun. Here he'd come to visit the home of his honorable family only to find that they'd become a detachment of fifth columnists while he was away! And yet, even still, Hassoun allowed himself to be convinced to stretch out on the bed and close his eyes for a bit amid all those guns and bombs. His mother tucked him in with a beauteous smile upon her face.

At which point the well-wishers saw the fun was over and decided to leave. I'd like to report some of the comments I heard as people passed me at the door, intending to go their separate ways:

"It's no wonder he was shocked. He's probably never seen a gun in his life. The boy's been a draft dodger as far back as I can remember."

"Give him a break, guys, he'll come to his senses eventually."

"Hey, it's not like the Danes don't kill people like anyone else. They know plenty about guns over there. Denmark even had troops in the attack on Al-Suwaira in the '91 war, remember? But what can I say, Hassoun's always been a bit . . . you know."

"The way Hassoun jumped! Like a cat at the dog pound!"

"Hassoun off to Denmark while we're stuck here being eaten alive by bugs. Sure as hell didn't see *that* coming."

But that rat and son of a rat Khanjar didn't leave with everyone else. He stuck around Hassoun's house, trying to ferret out information, since he still hadn't gotten answers to his many questions . . . questions like:

"How many dollars did he bring back?

"How long's he going to stay?

"Does he support Sadr? Or is he with Sistani?

"Is it true he's going to marry a local girl and take her back to Europe with him?

"Is it true he's already married an old Danish widow?

"Will he be visiting the shrines of the Imams while he's home, particularly Al-Kadhimiya Mosque, or is he going to spend the whole time drunk?

"Is he spending his whole vacation with family, or is he going to move into a fancy hotel at the first opportunity? That's what Farhan, the quilter's son, did when he came back last year from Australia . . ."

But that's only a sampling! That rogue and son of a rogue Khanjar had plenty more shots in his locker, and no intention of giving up till he got what he was after. For that reason, among others, Khanjar held firm despite all the hints from Hassoun's mother and sister, increasingly brazen, that it was past time for him to get going. Khanjar pretended not to notice. Pretended to be deaf and blind both.

Meanwhile, it transpired that the crowd who'd left the Hassoun house hadn't gone home either. They were still outside, standing around, burning for news from their spy, Khanjar, who was taking so long to come out. It took till long after half the rooster slaughtered for Hassoun's arrival had flown down his gullet for Khanjar to come out for an audience, smacking his awful lips and sucking his greasy fingers. He made no statement apart from a single sentence delivered in passing:

"Uncles, don't tell me you really fell for Hassoun's theatrics? The weapons in that room are actually part of a crooked deal with the Danes. Our very own Hassoun the Clean-Shaven brought them into the country with the intention of hand-delivering them to the minister of defense, Hazim al-Shaalan, as part of al-Shaalan's latest profiteering scheme."

Plans to Populate Thawra City, Prepared by the Office of the Sayyid

As for myself, I've never traveled in my life, and till recently I never even gave any thought to taking a trip. Who, who could really abandon the country of his birth, go willingly into exile, and become a foreign agent of Iran, the US, or the UK, like every other one of our politicians these days? Besides—why travel when my Thawra City is soon going to become paradise? Our very own neighbors, Salim Manati and Razzak al-Shaykh, were elected to the new National Assembly this year, and they've taken an oath on the honor of their brothers that they're going to turn Thawra into nothing less than a new Switzerland.

On top of that, Sa'd Hitler—the ancient director of Muqtada al-Sadr's office who was born in the days of the Third Reich's support for Iraq against the British and so got saddled with a rather regrettable name—has declared, "Just let those infidel Americans show up here! They'll see that Thawra City is a hundred times more lovely than Kufa!"

"You've been very patient," said the president of the neighborhood council. "Just be patient a little longer, and—I swear by the Seventh Imam—Thawra City will become a dream!"

And Qasim Ta'ban, the city's chief of police, said, "From now on, the police won't carry weapons on their patrols to every corner of the city. They will be true police, serving the city's residents, and every kind of bribe and shakedown will be prohibited."

37

Seeing as these are official statements issued by the highest-ranking administrators of our city, to cast any doubt upon their sincerity would be completely out of the question.

Further information was, however, provided by Khanjar the Kiss-Ass and son of a Kiss-Ass, who, as usual, provided commentary on their proclamations in a parallel press conference convened on the corner of our street. He clarified that the Office of the Second Martyr (God bless Muqtada's father, murdered by Saddam!) intended to enact a plan that could be summarized as follows:

First, they're bringing in the most competent ex-Soviet engineers they can find, with the goal of optimizing the city's residential spaces. Each private house will from now on be provided with one hundred and forty-four square meters of floor space, a swimming pool, a game room, and a miniature shrine to Husayn with a fancy sound system for Qur'anic recitations.

Second, they're bringing in workers from the Baltics who, in the thrall of the thrust of their natural Nordic urges (his dirty word, not mine, with God as my witness!), will plant trees in all our open spaces, trees that will become the lungs of our new city, giving everyone fresh, clean air. And these green spaces will of course be equipped with modern playground equipment (the kind we see on European game shows) and will be called Muqtada Disney.

Third, an Ecuadorian company is taking charge of setting up the largest Husayniya hall in the world, with an area of four square kilometers, starting at Fellah Junction in Block 55 and extending to the intersection of Fellah and Muzafar. Its purpose will be to create an open-air venue for conducting the Friday prayers and hearing the sermons and lectures of the Sayyid leader, Muqtada himself, as well as live commentaries by Muqtada's spokesman, Abdul-Hadi al-Daraji.

Fourth, there will be a partnership with Mexico for the goal of developing the city's marketplaces. The Mexicans will come in to build us new stores with glass windows, furnished with surveillance cameras and air-conditioning, which will run even in the winter! Each shop will be designed to accommodate the goods being sold. For example, there will be crystal tanks for the binny fish, carp, sardines, and stromateus. As for the groceries, they will have mechanical rotating shelves that will display the full range of produce to the honored customers, who'll need only to press a button to have a kilogram of cucumbers, carrots, eggplants—whatever they want!—dropped into their shopping cart.

Khanjar added, "And permit me to offer an apology to the shopkeepers in the al-Arwa, Jamila, and Ariba markets for the fact that the aforementioned plans will do away with them entirely. On account of the many crimes of the Ba'athists during the sanctions, the old produce markets will be transformed into vast halls with artificial snow for downhill skiing, designated for residents from Iraq's reconstruction zones. As for the Maridi Market, it'll be allowed to keep its name, provided that it focuses on electronics—computers, printers, DVDs, and such. It will be our own little Maridi Silicon Valley."

Next Khanjar came to sports clubs and recreation centers. He declared that Fellah Street, the main drag running down the middle of the city, would be set aside for processions commemorating Husayn. A Spanish company specializing in parades and bullfights would develop the street in order to provide it with a grandeur appropriate to those occasions. The color black would no doubt predominate amid these new, permanent decorations, but certainly red (for blood) and green (for the banner of Husayn—peace be upon him!—which was carried by his brother Abbas ibn Ali until his dying breath at the Battle of Karbala) would also feature.

Khanjar wrapped up his remarks by saying, "Nor has the office of Sayyid Muqtada (God bless him!) forgotten the pious women of Iraq, for he will have special sidewalks paved on every block of the city and set aside exclusively for their use, the better to ensure that their character, their independence, and their modesty will remain inviolate. These sidewalks will be forbidden to any male over the age of four."

Khanjar left it at that, which is to say without having clarified for us any other aspects of the plan, for example those relating to schools, hospitals, cinemas, theaters, cafés, hotels, and recreation centers. We all made sure to write down our questions and save them up for the next visit to the block from our city's two representatives to the National Assembly, Razzak al-Shaykh and Salim Manati—those paragons among the world's parliamentarians.

All of us, that is, except for those few who for some reason seem to prefer to go into seclusion in their homes in order to wait for the revelation of the Hidden Imam, the Lord of Time himself: may God hasten his appearance, damn his enemies, and make his children victorious!

Plato's Block

As you may or may not know, a block in Thawra City is a square residential division of a thousand homes. On the map, the eighty or so blocks that comprise Thawra City resemble each other like so many peas in a pod. So let me invite you, as my guest, I make you my guest to take a closer look at ours. Our block has more philosophers than Athens ever had. Our block has more politicians than all the countries of the European Union. Our block has more radicals than the Irish Republican Army; more priests than the Vatican; and more gangs, petty thieves, and armed robbers than all the mafias of Italy. Our block has more civil-society organizations than appeared in all of Iraq after the fall of the regime; more political parties than Latin America; and more noble and exalted descendants of the Prophet Muhammad than the actual number of people residing in said block.

There are more tribal sheikhs living on our block than there were Sheikhs of Araby before Islam—and after. We have more journalists on our block than are employed by Reuters, and more poets than Mauritania. We have more tabla players than Ataturk's Turkish republic, just as we have more singers on our block than all of Sister Egypt. Just one subdivision of our block contains more children than a whole province of China. Our block has more communists than Poland did before perestroika, and our block contains an arsenal of small arms whose combined firepower more than matches that of the bombs dropped on Hiroshima

41

and Nagasaki. Our block boasts a number of martyrs far exceeding all the martyrs of Algeria. Our block houses more political prisoners than could be found in Stalin's gulag.

Our block also has a run-down elementary school built in the early sixties. It's now a clinic that can boast more patients than medicine or staff to treat them. There's not even a single doctor, just one trained nurse, a pharmacist-by-intuition (that is, with no training), and one "nurse" whose mother was a licensed midwife and bequeathed her daughter that profession when she died. Oh, there's also the woman who mans the door—sometimes she delivers medicine, and sometimes she tries her hand at treating light wounds.

Our block has a barber, Papa Spittoon, who, with all the power outages and water shortages these days, uses his saliva as shaving cream. It works fine, okay? One way or another he'll get your beard off. And our block has a TV repairman, which makes us the envy of all the neighboring blocks, even though his expertise is limited to sending our televisions fifty years back in time. That is, he loves to watch things in black and white, and thanks to his unique brand of ingenuity, he's able to restore even color sets to black and white—and sometimes just black. And our block has a butcher who does his slaughtering on the roof and his selling in the street, and of course our block also has the Rosanna Supermarket, where you can buy all the Pepsi anyone could want—as long as you don't mind it being bottled exclusively right here in our block.

Our block has a mosque that was silent for forty years— now it's making up for lost time by constantly beating us over the head. Besides the calls to prayer, we hear chanting all year round, as if someone's a little too enthusiastic about flagellating themselves raw and bloody, as during the festival of Ashura. There are also those rushed prayers they've started conducting before the main prayers get going (such an innovation in piety!), plus religious poems, call-and-response venerations of the Prophet's martyred grandson, Husayn, and teachings from Sayyid Muqtada's office. And the mosque's antique, trumpet-like speakers parcel out weeping even on happy festival days.

Our block has a satellite-dish shop, Mahdi's Dish Receivers, which sold out of everything the first week of the month and then closed down because Mahdi got "too busy." Our block has a woman selling beans who'll also throw in a little fortune-telling free of charge if you just agree to sit at her door for a few minutes.

Our block has so many horses as to embarrass the Royal Mews in Britain, and the noble residents of our block happen to own more Afghan mules than all the farmers of Afghanistan. Our block can boast more open sewers than the city of Venice with all its hundreds of rivers and canals. Our block has more pictures of ugly turbaned men hanging on its walls than we ever put up for Saddam. And then, the apartment buildings in our block put up more flags, particularly during Ashura, than the United Nations. (Flags of every sort of color and shape, though not a single one is the flag of Iraq.)

In our block there's not even half of a Ba'athist. The sons of our block have no clue what that word even means! Our sons were never signed up for Saddam's Quds Force or for his paramilitary Fedayeen. Our sons never wore the uniform of the People's Army, and, in fact, none of us has ever in our lives laid eyes on that olive color in which party

43

comrades would strut about in the old days. In our block, we've never had one of those tribal bards who would raise streaming banners before Saddam and lead the call of "Hail, Mr. President!" According to the testimony of no less a personage than Kofi Annan, Secretary-General of the UN, our block is entirely clean of Ba'athists, and all those we used unjustly to call "comrades" have turned out to be partisans of Ahmed Chalabi or Ayad Allawi, members of the Sadr movement, or followers of the exalted religious clerkship (or perhaps one that's not so exalted). Or else we merely dreamed those fantastical creatures up for so many years. Now that the regime has fallen, we've woken up and can't find a single trace of them!

Still, between you and me, our block has lots of other things too. Secret things. And if those things came to light, believe me, the stink would be so bad that it would reach the Eskimos and make them sneeze in their igloos.

But mum's the word!

Constitutional Skirmishes on Sabiha the Threader's Street

The referendum on our new constitution is less than a week away, and now Article 41 has caused a major crisis on our street. Fakhriya, the wife of our former mayor, said the copy she received didn't include a particular article ensuring the free practice of religion, which she considered essential for guaranteeing us the rights and freedoms stipulated by international treaties. Meanwhile, Sabiha—whom everyone called the Threader, on account of the cosmetic services she offered—maintained that her copy did contain that article.

So our street divided into two factions, one-half supporting Fakhriya and the other siding with the Threader, each group waving its own copies of the constitution taken home from the local government food bank, the traditional distribution point for everything the government wanted to give us. Even as I write these words, office workers, construction workers, day laborers, porters with their carts, fancy pigeon trainers, the unemployed, and the recently laid off are all engaged in reading their constitution. Each of them grabs a copy and reads intently, as if studying for a graduation exam. Have we become a street of the cultural elite? What can you do!

Anyway, Fakhriya is insisting on her position, and Sabiha is insisting upon hers. Yet a constitution, as is universally known, couldn't possibly be voted upon without at least a complete consensus as to its contents. The crisis came to a head when Umm Hasan, who claims descent from Ali, announced that she had numerous reservations regarding the draft, among which was the lack of emphasis on the clear role of the religious clerkship, and that de-Ba'athification must necessarily include a purge of all former mayors, who used to report on anyone who was trying to dodge their military service—a capital offense. This point, as will be obvious, touched Fakhriya, the ex-mayor's wife, very deeply. Fakhriya started convening extensive discussions each day after breaking the Ramadan fast. As soon as sundown brought the fast

45

The agent in charge told her, "Fakhriya, where've you been? You think there any copies left? People swarmed on us like seagulls!"

At that, Fakhriya went straight to the house of Salim Manati, who together with his companion Razzak al-Shaykh comprised the two most corrupt parliamentarians in the world. Fakhriya demanded that Manati clarify, in writing, this question of the article that Sabiha was claiming had been deleted from the final text. That public servant reassured her that this omission did not affect the essence of the text because there was a paragraph within the preamble that clearly pointed to the wide application of democratic principles. She wasn't reassured, however, by Manati's words, so she went to the office of Sayyid Muqtada to learn its position. The spokesman there replied, "The constitution, along with all issues related to it, falls within the jurisdiction of Ayatollah al-Haeri, who is currently in Iran. All we are permitted to report is that, as of now, no fatwa has been issued concerning this matter."

So Fakhriya had to go home empty-handed. As she passed by Sabiha the Threader's door, she screamed at the top of her lungs, "Vote no to the constitution!" Before the sound had even died away, a response came from inside the house: "Yes! Yes to the constitution!" Immediately, all the women who were at the Threader's house to benefit from her services rushed out in a throng, like a flash mob, shouting, "Hurray for our constitution! Who are you to criticize!" Fakhriya dealt with the situation by swiftly summoning her supporters for a counterdemonstration against any constitution that did not guarantee the unity of Iraq.

Things would have gotten violent were it not for the sudden arrival of Khanjar, that precipitous son of a precipitous father, who calmed everyone down by saying, "O noble children of our street! Our new constitution, even with all its defects, is a good and healthy thing for us to have. True, it contradicts itself in places, is pretty confusing in others, and surely is no vessel for even the lowliest ambitions of our great nation. But, look—it's a constitution. It's really not so bad. It's okay! The kind of robe, as they say, that you wouldn't be ashamed to wear in public. And if it's approved, well, at least we'll be able to say we have a constitution!"

The women of our street didn't know what to make of this. For Khanjar, that dissembling son of a dissembling father, to stand up and express even this much of a clear, well-defined opinion was unheard of. The ladies of our street dispersed, heading back to their homes to spend yet another night going over the constitution with a fine-tooth comb. Meanwhile, since only I remained, Khanjar swooped down upon your poor Shalash, finding me easy prey for his flood of analyses and interpretations—of which I understood nothing. In the end, I was forced to confront him with a clear, well-defined question: "Khanjar, are you for the constitution or not?"

I have to admit, I really considered myself a genius for coming up with such a straitjacket of a question. Khanjar sat on the sidewalk and pulled me down beside him, saying, "Look here, my dear Shalash. This constitution thing isn't the Qur'an. It's just a bunch of words written by a group of villagers, religious men in turbans, and a handful of failed lawyers, half of whom are Kurds and Yezidis. Tomorrow or the day after, as soon as things get better, we'll sit down and change it at our leisure. And if we don't all agree, let everyone write a constitution of his own! It's no big deal. Come with me tomorrow, we'll go down to Amara and buy ourselves a piece of land. That's where all the oil is. The people of Amara will not let themselves be robbed yet again! So let's get in on what's finally coming their way. *Constitution, shmonstitution!* Each tribe will look for its own international importer of oil and sell to it directly. The Sawa'id tribe in Amara has already made an agreement with this French company, Total. So what I say is, bring along some money and snap up whatever you can get before the market stabilizes."

"Khanjar, truly, your words have touched my heart," I replied. "But you still haven't told me whether I should vote yes or no."

Khanjar laughed and said, "Hey man, who do you think you are, anyway? Who cares whether you vote or not? One yes from Ayatollah Sistani, brother, and the constitution is in the bag. As for Sabiha the Threader and Fakhriya, the ex-mayor's wife, their votes are nothing more than a fart in the market—you can't hear a peep over the coppersmiths clanging! Anyway," he went on, angry now, "you've got your very own copy of the constitution right here." He grabbed it out of my hands and slapped my face with it. "Soak it in water, squeeze it out, and drink up the ink! You're delusional! Are you worthy of a constitution, you arak-besotted rat-face? What, you want to become a politician?"

Thereafter, Khanjar, that so-called son of a so-called man, went on spewing curses and vulgar expressions that I simply refuse to record here out of consideration for public decency and the common good.

A Quiet, Out-of-the-Way Corner Beside
the Tomb of Sayyid Hamdillah

In the 1950s, the days when peasants migrated from the south of Iraq to the capital, they established settlements around Baghdad in their own rural style. These included districts called al-Mayzara (perhaps deriving from *al-Majzara*, meaning "the slaughterhouse") or al-Aasima (meaning "the capital"), where the newcomers lived hard lives in reed huts unfit even for animals. Among these people was a family known as the household of Sayyid Hamdillah.

Having come up to Baghdad among other migrants from his old district, he'd suffered no loss whatever of his old social standing. Like any sayyid descended from God's Prophet, the man was an object of abiding respect. When he passed away (may he rest in peace!), his body was washed inside his home before being carried off to a final resting place in the holy city of Najaf. Later, when Abd al-Karim Qasim came to power in 1958 and transported all those poor migrants to Thawra City, along with so many other "undesirables," Sayyid Hamdillah's old settlement of al-Mayzara was entirely abandoned, and its peculiar name dropped out of use.

Toward the end of the 1970s, the government put this area to use for the Ministry of the Interior complex and all its many appurtenances. The heavy machinery came to do its work, and one task was to remove all the remnants of al-Mayzara and level the ground. That is when the miracle occurred. According to the testimony of one of the workers, a guy who used to live nearby, the bulldozer stalled right in front of what had once been the house of Sayyid Hamdillah. A second bulldozer came, and then a third, but it was no use! Each broke down in the same way at the exact moment it got close to the crumbling abode where once Sayyid Hamdillah had dwelled. Finally the authorities erected a wall around the place to protect it from the bulldozers, or the bulldozers from it. The big machines were allowed to work around the house of the late sayyid so long as nothing touched it.

News of this incident—with various marvelous and fantastic details added in, the kind that wars or crises tend to breed by the score—spread fast, and from that moment on, the spot became a holy shrine known as the Tomb of Sayyid Hamdillah. People began making pilgrimages there on foot, particularly from Thawra City. Always, all along the road leading to it, you can see our mothers walking along, raising green banners in the direction of Sayyid Abu Hashim, as he was also called by those seeking his intercession, who showed him honor by using the name of Ali's grandson.

The site of their veneration led to an uproar among the cultured religious men of the city (and not only them), who said, in all frankness, "How can we have this place, where a dead body was washed, turn into a holy shrine?" Or, "What practical or religious importance did this sayyid have, such that the place of his squalor should become a shrine, when he—may he rest in peace!—was just like the rest of his illiterate generation, and when, given this lifelong ignorance, he never demonstrated any particular piety such as might now merit this dignity?"

Anyway, this talk wasn't too welcome among the departed man's family, upon whom God had bestowed undreamed-of riches. They took little time in erecting a modest green dome with a wall around the site. The government, which by this time had entered into war with Iran, took charge of paving the street leading to the shrine, and the place began to enjoy a kind of official approval after its popular support broadened on account of its reputation for fostering incredible miracles. It became revered even by the drunks of Thawra City, who would salute the shrine as they stumbled back from the Eastern Gate, to say nothing of the cars honking in Sayyid Abu Hashim's honor as they arrived or departed the city. But none of that is the point of my current story about Sayyid Hamdillah! Rather, it's that this august sayyid, whom doubters and critics proclaimed so insignificant in life, became monumentally important in death—and most important of all, in fact, to the young lovers of Thawra City, so much so that he deserves, in one way or another, to be called the "Imam of Lovers."

Yes, that's how it is! And if he's not the Imam of Lovers, he's at least their concierge, for the ladies of Thawra City have found no better excuse than the Tomb of Sayyid Hamdillah for getting out of the house with their younger sisters or an old grandmother. It's here at this shrine that all their assignations are planned, and in its porticos and all around you can hear the moans of love's anguish and the sighs of desire. That is, if some girl's sweetheart should ask her for a rendezvous, especially if he's coming home from the battlefront on a brief leave of absence, the poor girl has no choice but to wake up the following morning and call out to her grandmother:

popularity of the sayyid declined, for "If he wasn't able to save the son of his son, how could he save anyone else's children? No, my dear, it's better for us to visit the tomb of the Tenth Imam instead." But the young ladies refused to give up on Abu Hashim, and they praised and exaggerated the potency of his miraculous responses to their various offerings and vows in order to preserve the shrine as an oasis for lovers ... seeing as the social norms of the tribal city of Thawra would never allow for a reasonable replacement, what with the holy place being relatively safe and comfortably nearby, and no one being willing to permit their daughters to travel to the more distant and crowded shrines—either on their own or even in the company of a grandmother or another relative.

Still, it seems there's no stopping the dimming of Sayyid Hamdillah's star—especially when Iraq is filled with living sayyids who battle daily for our allegiance. I went myself this morning to visit the place. It was nearly deserted. Three or four old women pressed their hands against the window as they lamented the cruelty of destiny and the passing of time. By a corner of the wall sat two beautiful and anxious young women; whenever they heard a car approaching, their hearts flew off to meet it, their eyes pinned to the road.

So our oasis for lovers is drying up. It'll disappear entirely one of these decades, years, or days. Yet when all trace of Sayyid Hamdillah has faded and people no longer speak about his miracles, that's when the grandchildren will come. The grandchildren of those of us who enjoyed some scant moments of passion at the shrine will return to this place to erect a monument not to a man, or even a saint, but to love itself—a towering statue of crystal that will rise in the middle of our sprawling city, with the following inscription on its bronze base:

Here is a monument to the tears of our adoring mothers. Here is the final resting place of the poems of our ardent sons. Stay awhile and hear the sighs of the lovelorn maidens. It is not the chirping of sparrows that you hear: these are the songs of our mothers, forbidden to love. Here lie their great dreams; here their longings died; here their desires withered. As for Sayyid Hamdillah, he's long gone! You can see that for yourself. Who was he, you ask? He was the answer to the prayers of a city full of frustrated lovers. They had the greatest need—the need for an imam to whom they might express the pain of their love.

O visitors! Here, under the feet of the goddess of love, scatter flowers and mint in the memory of those passionate maidens who never plucked a rose, maidens whose days wilted like flowers during the ten lean years of the sanctions, or in the days of black-clad militias that followed.

For their sakes and the sakes of those who loved them, we have built this memorial. May love in our land never again go wanting.

OCTOBER 12, 2005

The Sayings of al-Jaafari and Khanjar's Placards

Saddam was a talkative guy. He chattered away on every occasion—or even without one. Our national television networks took it upon themselves to convey his every word to us, and since satellite channels were strictly forbidden at the time, there was no choice but to pay our leader's "tax" by lending our captive ears each time he plunged into history, geography, engineering, media, health, cleanliness, manliness, construction, mustache and hair growth, literature, the art of war, matters relating to women and children, and just about everything else.

Now, Sayyid Ibrahim al-Jaafari was our vice president under the interim government, and he became prime minister after the elections last January. As the leader of the party that derives its very name—the Islamic Dawa Party—from the word meaning to preach or proselytize, al-Jaafari is a formidable linguistic power in his own right, and he has taken possession of us, root and branch. He, like Saddam, is obsessed with the little black screen, and every so often he can't keep himself from climbing inside it to reward us all with a nice long lecture. But what the estimable fellow forgets is that the little black screen is open to anyone now, for example the trashy Saudi channel Rotana, which is just waiting in there to eat any competitor's lunch. Whenever al-Jaafari appears on our televisions sitting next to the Iraqi flag on the state-owned station Al Iraqiya, his official pulpit, in a comfortable chair not too different from the ones our former leader favored, our remote controls trade him for sexy music videos by Nancy Ajram and Laura Khalil, or some beautiful women dancing to that classic hit "He Went to Basra and Forgot Me," before al-Jaafari can get out a single syllable. Mind you, that's assuming that the frequent power outages have allowed him to enter the homes of us poor, afflicted masses in the first place.

Saddam had an army of sycophants who would gather up his every word and put it into circulation accompanied by commentary and praise. Newspapers, magazines, books, school curricula, and the billboards that lined every street, alley, lane, and dead end were filled with his pronouncements under the title SAYINGS OF THE LEADER. And, for the record, I want it noted that countless people memorized countless SAYINGS of Saddam's, word for word, if only on account of the fact that they were repeated everywhere you looked. These days, no one listens to, much less memorizes, a single sentence from al-Jaafari—for the reasons we've mentioned, but also because every single community now has their own little LEADER with his own little SAYINGS that are now almost as unavoidable as Saddam's.

Sayyid Jalal Talabani, our current president, has better screen presence. He's got a sense of humor. He's spontaneous. He has no use for gravitas; he talks in the ordinary language of everyday people. He doesn't go out of his way to sound stiff and official, and he doesn't mean for his every word to be polished and published as part of an official pronouncement. Everyone got a big kick out of it when some journalist asked him why Sayyid Ghazi al-Yawer, who was the interim president last year, didn't bother showing up for the recent ceremony to unveil the text of the new constitution. Talabani looked all over to confirm the absence of his deputy, laughed, and said, "Ghazi al-Yawer? Oh, I guess he must be out sick . . . But, look, he's behind the constitution a hundred percent!"

Whereas Ibrahim al-Jaafari, a mullah if there ever was one, talks like he just ate a few expensive dictionaries and is about to lose his lunch. Not to say that there isn't something admirable about the way he constructs phrase after phrase that sounds terrible without actually being incorrect. What they are, his speeches, is grand—but in no way related to any of the questions occupying his fellow citizens' minds. And on top of all that, the man is afflicted with an official spokesman, and, for reasons unknown, it is Dr. Laith Kubba, who projects the image of an ideal statesman, a profile more refined by far than the one offered by his boss Mr. al-Jaafari. I don't know how they convinced Kubba to take on the position of a mouthpiece, and nothing more, for a man whose only capital is his tongue.

What does my friend Khanjar think, you ask? Well, he's still living in the pre-April 9, 2003, era. He fervently believes anything and everything said by someone with the Iraqi flag on their right as they speak. So our Khanjar was puzzled by the current status quo. "Why aren't the sayings of al-Jaafari put up everywhere like Saddam's?" he kept asking. He waited and waited for the posters to appear. At last, he had to take matters into his own hands. He set about writing his own notices, in big letters, and pasting them on every corner of our block. Each of them began with "Dr. Ibrahim al-Eshaiker al-Jaafari has said . . ." and went on to immortalize such sparkling witticisms as:

Responsibility for building the state rests fundamentally on a kind of national manifestation that fortifies the elements of a man's integration with his formative parts, including his being centered upon expressions of religion, identity, and history.

Last month's martyrs, who drowned at Aimmah Bridge, form an emulative expression of what it means for a person to be a martyr, even in the very moment of their existential submersion, showing that the doors of heaven are cast wide for those who value martyrdom as the life-affirming act.

We do not have time to respond to what President Jalal Talabani has proposed. What keeps us from doing so is our daily immersion in the work of unifying efforts to administer the various portfolios that await us as a government elected by two-thirds of the Iraqi people.

What we want from the media is that they adopt the good example set by Al Iraqiya in order to achieve the goal for which the media ultimately exists, which can be summarized as an unmediated preoccupation with the daily concerns of the people, given the people's sincere belief in the message of this media.

The geographically proximate countries are a historical reality with which we are forced to coexist. In order for them not to become a burden, it is incumbent upon us to seize the reins, taking the initiative to rush along with them toward the utmost degrees of mutual understanding and noninterference in each other's internal affairs. These remarks do not necessarily apply to our neighbor Iran, which we recently visited.

This very morning, I met Sayyid Muqtada al-Sadr, and from His Eminence I heard a hard-hitting discourse about instances of dawdling with respect to the portfolio of services. Likewise, I came into contact with the pressing eagerness of His Eminence to encourage the political process in order to avert any and all dangers that would be caused by neglecting to plunge headlong into the dynamics of this process.

Indeed, Iraq is part of the international system, and any shift that occurs in the structure of that system affects, to one degree or another, the social movement toward the center and to the south of the country.

Truly, my study of medicine in Mosul, that kindly city, has imparted to me a civilizational dimension that has made me more agreeable to others, just as it has opened my mentality to be more accepting of others in their existence as cultural beings. It is from here that my flexibility toward all formulations of the Iraqi people stems.

For the sake of avoiding any neglect of religious precautions, it is necessary for each inception put forward as we chart our path to seek out the religious clerkship and listen to its relevant directions and pertinent corrections.

So now the people in our block found themselves in a serious situation. No one could leave their home without seeing the posters. How could they carry on ignoring such magnificent pearls of wisdom? They had to engage with them.

As such, people have taken to congregating around the posters as they come and go. I come to you now, live from the scene, to record for you the following comments:

"By God, but al-Jaafari can sure spin a tale!"

"What is he talking about, anyway? You can't follow the thread."

"A perfect nightingale, so beautifully he sings!"

"What's the deal? By God, I don't understand a word!"

"I value al-Jaafari as I do myself. His every word is golden!"

"Take a look at these! The wisdom of a religious seminary made available to all!"

"It's too much! He's so stupid, you'd think he was a Kurd!"

"His tongue drips with honey! God's own masterpiece!"

"Bless the hands of Khanjar for posting these miracles of rhetoric! Such wonderful initiative. By God, if Khanjar hadn't taken on this responsibility, we would all have been lost, we wouldn't have known our left hands from our right!"

"Brother, your head—could you move it just a little? I'm writing down these phrases to use in my composition for class tomorrow."

"Sweet child, could you double-check whether he says anything about our ration cards?"

"Excuse me, what's this crowd here for, are they giving something away?"

"My God, what's al-Jaafari smoking? This shit makes your head spin."

"Oh, no! We've gone back in time! To the years when we'd spend all day, every day, rehashing what our Leader said!"

"Like it or not, al-Jaafari will have to go take some lessons from Muqtada. Does al-Jaafari think it's the other way around?"

"Khanjar made a great start, but it would have been better if he had given us more."

There were other comments too, but I'm afraid we're just about out of time . . .

Mind you, that wasn't the end of it. Khanjar's initiative was soon emulated, and in the weeks that followed, not only our block but the neighboring ones too were soon festooned with placards, posters, signs, and banners bearing the remarks, maxims, and meditations of each and every one of our singular leaders throughout recorded history.

The Sheehan-Makiya Strike Outside the Sayyid's Office

Following the example of Cindy Sheehan, the mother of an American soldier killed in Iraq, Makiya al-Hasan took her complaint to the very top. After writing "Enough with your problems!" on a piece of cardboard, she pinned the sign to her chest and headed in the direction of Block 13 in Thawra City. There, she planted herself across from the office of Sayyid Muqtada al-Sadr, amid the astonishment and wonder of passersby at this new form of insanity. Barefoot boys circled around her, spelling out the word: "p . . . r . . . o . . . b . . . l . . . e . . . m . . . s."

Cars going by on Chawadir Street, one of our main drags, slowed down so their occupants could rubberneck. What was going on? they asked. And the answer was always the same: "She's crazy!"

Early in the afternoon, a family from one of the apartments that overlooked the street came down to make a donation, bringing lunch and a glass of tea for Makiya. Makiya made her excuses, saying she was fasting for Ramadan. She explained to them that she was not some homeless vagrant, she was Umm Ali: Ali being the name of her only son, who had gone to Najaf the previous year and was martyred in the battles between al-Sadr's Mahdi Army and the American forces. The news spread quickly, and people became more interested in this rather eccentric woman.

In the evening, when Sayyid al-Sadr's office was crowded as usual, three young men carrying rifles went over to Makiya and asked her to please beat it. She was, in a word, making them edgy. After she informed them that she was the mother of Ali Salman Younis, who was killed by the American troops in Najaf, one of them recognized her and said, "Ah, don't worry, dear Umm Ali: we shall be your sons! We will avenge him! Just put away this sign. For shame, auntie!"

"No, my boy! I don't want you to die. I don't want any more of you to die! All of you are indeed my children. Ali has gone, but I want you to stay, my dear."

The young men didn't fully understand what she was getting at. They went back to the Sayyid's office and told her story to the turbaned officials there. The order came back to "Leave that crazy woman alone!"

Makiya spent her night in the street, breaking the Ramadan fast with some sympathetic residents of Block 13 and Block 58—the one located diagonally across Chawadir Street from Block 13—who'd begun gravitating toward her.

There was also a group of teenage boys who took to making fun of her: "Look, it's Cindy Sheehan," they said. "She wants to stop the war! *Hay, Sheehan,*" they called out in their broken English. "*Haw ar yu? Guud eefneeng, Sheehan. How ald ar yu?*"

Two days later, Makiya had become just another street sign to most of the locals. Yet farther-flung flocks of busybodies, passing through on business, kept the doubt and suspicion simmering with their comments:

"There's something more to this!"

"An Israeli spy?"

"No, it's just the Hakim organization egging her on to get under Muqtada's skin."

"Maybe she's a Ba'athist."

"God only knows who put her up to this!"

One morning, she was visited by Falah, the correspondent with the famous green eyes from the American-backed TV station Alhurra. After Makiya filled Falah in on her primary demand to Sayyid Muqtada al-Sadr—namely, that he should preserve the lives of the poor children fighting his war—the reporter claimed to suffer a sudden equipment failure, apologized, and gathered up his things. "It's a trap," he told his team, and gave orders for an immediate retreat before anyone could broadcast a story that would get them killed.

That Makiya began to gather followers only made matters worse. For, one day, a middle-aged man came along and sat down beside Makiya. He let out a loud cry for his son, who had been killed recently during an American raid on the neighborhood of Gayyara. An old woman in her seventies came and started weeping over her husband, who had died two months before. A fat woman came, sat down cross-legged, and wept for her son who had also been killed, though she didn't know by whom. A blind woman came and sat too, not explaining her distress but just crying. Then a child in tattered clothes turned up and went to sleep in the blind woman's lap.

These people and others like them formed an open and ongoing mourning session. Journalists snapped photos from afar, not wanting to be contaminated. This was too much attention for the office of the Sayyid, and new orders came through to break up the gathering. Armed men approached and, without thinking too much about it, dispersed the gathering. Without a conscious plan, the scattered demonstrators reassembled in Picture Square at the entrance to Thawra City. A picture of the Two Martyrs—Muqtada's noble father and father-in-law—had been painted over the decades-old mural depicting the tyrant of Iraq, now that he had been caught in a hole.

Makiya's group settled in at their new location, and this time they kept their mouths shut. New hooligans collected to insult and mock the bereaved. Some carried a picture of the American, Cindy Sheehan, under which they wrote, MAKIYA THE YOGURT LADY!, mocking her for meddling in things above her station.

A group from the Mahdi Army formed a circle around the place, but they didn't interfere with Makiya or her companions, who had begun to win the sympathy of the people. The elderly man who had lost his son in Gayyara cried out to the militants, "My little children, drop your rifles! By God, you're killing us! This is America we're talking about! If China can't beat them, what do you think you can do? And what did America do to you anyway? Didn't they come and free you from Saddam's tyranny? What's wrong with your brains?"

They all pretended not to hear. Then Makiya got up and kissed them, one after the other, as though they were her own sons. "My children, go to school! Go to your families! My dear, beloved children, nobody here cares at all for you. These people are just using you."

At which one of the young men handed his rifle to his companions and slipped away. The others had no idea how to react. They sent someone to hand in the gun at Muqtada's office.

And the office was no less nonplussed. It was getting to be a real problem. What to do?

So some genius suggested gathering donations for the group: "These people want money, that's all. Saddam taught them that martyrdom means cash." Sacks of flour and sugar were brought in, along with cans of oil and other staples that were "donated" by the shopkeepers down the street in Jamila Market. But when the soldiers brought the requisitioned goods to the occupied square, the people there wouldn't touch the stuff. Indeed, the donation even drew in a few additional protesters.

Word spread to every corner of the city. Delegations from each block showed up and started sponging off the strange gathering. What I can't understand is why Razzak al-Shaykh and Salim Manati, the two dirtiest parliamentarians in the world, have yet to get their fingers in the pie!

All the office of the Sayyid could do was keep observing the situation from a distance. Sometimes some soldiers from the Mahdi Army would interfere and try to scatter the people, even beating them with canes. But you could tell their hearts weren't in it.

Then my old pal Khanjar came to see what all the fuss was about. He approached Makiya, who was a neighbor from his block. He begged her "by the soul of her son Ali" to bring an end to her useless rebellion, raising his voice so that Sadr's men could hear that he had come to perform a good deed without expecting anything in return.

Makiya just screamed at him. "And why am I seeing your face again? Has anything good come my way since the time I first laid eyes on you? Aren't you the one who hoodwinked Ali and told him to go fight in Najaf?"

"Your son is a martyr," Khanjar told her in a loud voice. "He will guide you to paradise after him."

"Any kind of paradise you're selling isn't one I want!" Makiya replied. "I want my son. I want my son. I want my son!"

So Khanjar tried another tack, leaned down and whispered in Makiya's ear, saying, "You won't get anywhere like this, Makiya—not like this! Remember Cindy! You have to go out to Muqtada's private resort on the weekend and confront him face-to-face."

"What the hell are you talking about—what *resort*?"

"It's like Bush's ranch, right? Where he met with that Sheehan woman?"

"Muqtada has the same setup as Bush?"

"No, no, it's not the same thing. But he has this big traditional house in Najaf. That's where the family spends their vacations."

"Vacations? What are you talking about, Khanjar? Where do they get off taking vacations? Have they ever given *us* a break? Just go! Get away from me! I'll only leave this place when I go to my grave."

By now there were foreign newspaper and television journalists, international delegations of feminists, more cameras, microphones, and signs bearing the phrase "Enough with your problems!" painted in English than you could count. Colorful balloons filled the skies of Thawra City.

Children in glittering clothes sang of peace, security, and freedom. Beautiful young women scattered flowers, and in the middle of this international assembly, the soldiers of the Mahdi Army threw down their weapons en masse in Sheehan-Makiya Square and, like their erstwhile comrade, simply slipped away.

"My God, the crisis is over! Praise God, we shall live in peace! Can it be true that we will finally find some relief?" Thus spoke Makiya, starting from sleep with a smile that quickly dissolved when she found herself lying in the same square beside a blind old man tenderly embracing a young orphan in tattered clothes.

OCTOBER 15, 2005

Khanjar: A Communist in the Sadrist Mode

I took Khanjar very seriously today when he told me, "On my father's soul, I'm a communist! If you don't believe me," he went on to say, "go ask Trotsky."

"Who's this Trotsky?"

Khanjar laughed. "Who else but Comrade Abu Dawud?"

This left me more confused than when I began, since there were at least four men by that name living on our side street alone and—praise be to God!—not one of them had ever struck me as resembling a *comrade*.

"Tell me, do you know what dialectical materialism is?" Khanjar asked.

"Not at all!" I replied.

"No? What a dummy. How'd you ever manage to get a degree in surveying?"

"Look, Khanjar, I didn't take that class. So what is this dialialecticalecticalism stuff? Materialism, that much I recognize. That's like how my wife loves money, yeah?"

"Let's leave aside that so-called wife of yours for the time being. Actually, her problem is *classism*."

"Come on, man! Classism, Khanjar? What's that supposed to mean? Don't make me start worrying about my wife, okay, or I'll have to divorce her to preserve my honor!"

Khanjar thought that was pretty hilarious. Once he recovered, he said, "Not at all! Your wife has nothing to be ashamed of. These are matters that far outweigh the petty concerns of you and your father-in-law. But wow, what an idiot you are!"

Then Khanjar let loose a whirlwind of words that went right over my head: determinism, capitalism, dialectics, Hegelianism, and then Marx turning Hegel inside out.

"Hey, Khanjar, take it easy! Did you eat something weird for breakfast?"

"What could I eat?" he said. "Aren't I already full on love, the revolutionary poems of Muthaffar al-Nawab and Erian Al Sayed Khalaf, my constant reading of Engels, and every word that ever came out of Lenin's mouth!"

"Come on, now," I said to Khanjar. "Are you making fun of me? Last I heard, you were in lockstep with the Sadrist movement—supererogatory prayers, the Hidden Imam, the Second Martyr, and Shibani, Daraji, Khaza'i, and Zargani. What's going on today? You've traded all that for Marx and I don't know what other lunacy now?"

I seemed to be tickling Khanjar no end today. Once his next batch of guffaws was over, he called me a dimwit and asked me if I had the slightest idea what I was talking about. "Are you for real, O Shalash? Tell me, since you have such insight, what's the difference between the Sadrist movement and the Communist Party?"

"You tell me!" I said. "It's true, I don't understand a word of all this, but aren't they polar opposites?"

"Look, genius," he shouted. "Don't both movements come from the ragged proletariat? And both are fated to struggle against the Hakim family, which has, throughout its long history, belonged to the exploitative class. Don't you know what the great Hakim said about us communists?"

"What did he say?"

"That communism is atheism and apostasy."

"True!" I said. "Communists are the unbelieving sons of unbelievers. Aren't they?"

"That's not the point! The point is that ever since Abd al-Karim Qasim overthrew the monarchy in 1958 and enacted agricultural reforms, Hakim's interests took a hit. The fifth share that he would steal from tribal sheikhs and feudalists—who themselves used to snatch it right off the shoulders of the poor peasants—flew out of Hakim's hands and returned to the peasants. So Hakim called the communists unbelievers and fought against Abd al-Karim Qasim. You know how much a fifth comes to? Millions, you say, *millions*? Not at all. It's in the *billions*!"

"And the Sadr family, what's their relationship to the communists? Don't they take a fifth too?"

"No, my boy, no! The Sadr family are all honest people.

Go and look at Sayyid Muqtada's house: he doesn't even have a couch to sit on. And they hate those pirates, the Hakims! Look at the whole neighborhood of Jadriyah! Hakim stole Jadriyah and Masbah too, just as soon as they arrived in Baghdad. I dare you to go there. As soon as you do, the Badr Brigades will hang you up by your ankles and beat the soles of your feet. Hell, they won't be content with that. They'll steal your tobacco and wipe their asses with it!"

I shifted in my seat, cleared my throat, and said, "Khanjar, don't confuse the issue. Aren't communists the ones who say, 'Religion is the opium of the masses,' or something like that?"

"Ah, bless your heart. Now you're starting to understand. Haven't you seen the drugs that are being smuggled here from the Islamic Republic next door? The opiates are the opium, obviously, the Islamic Republic of Iran is the religion, and you and every idiot like you comprise the masses!"

Not for the first time, Khanjar left me without a thing to say. I was dumbstruck that even he might suggest that the turbans were themselves somehow the opium of the masses. He took this opportunity to get right up in my face and say, "Listen, Shalash! I'm fasting for Ramadan today. After breaking the fast at sundown, I'll find you and explain capitalism, the class struggle, and historical determinism, okay? Then, tomorrow, after voting on the constitution, I'll test you on these concepts. I'll make a communist out of you yet!"

I managed to object: "Fasting, Khanjar? You're making my head spin. Are you a communist or are you fasting?"

"What am I supposed to do with a fool like you? Don't you know that fasting was a legitimate Marxist requirement before it became a religious one? Our ideals lead us

71

into solidarity with all those who go hungry. The Prophet Muhammad (peace and prayers be upon him!) was the greatest socialist of them all. And both the revolution of his grandson Husayn (peace be upon him!) and the October Revolution were gestated within and born from the very same womb of humanity's suffering—the class struggle."

Khanjar just isn't himself today, I said to myself. He must have accidentally eaten some high-ranking member of the Central Committee.

Comrade Khanjar turned his back, reached into his breast pocket, and pulled out a little red book. He set off, reading as he walked. When he reached his house, he ran smack into the door. Before going in, he made sure to turn around and give me a vicious grin.

OCTOBER 16, 2005

An Eternal Nightmare Named Jaabir

The story of Jaabir and Mahdi began in the year 1982, when Comrade Jaabir, the Ba'ath official in charge of one of the blocks of Thawra City, insisted on tearing Mahdi away from his widowed mother and his two bereaved sisters and attaching him to a division of the People's Army in order to contribute to the war against the Zoroastrian enemy in Iran.

Mahdi did his best to escape his duty. He took to varying the times of day he would leave the house. He likewise altered the route he took to his job at the nearby samoon bakery. But, in the end, he was caught despite all his precautions. Early one morning, when Mahdi was on his way to the bakery, Jaabir managed to spot him and squeezed him into a car on the spot.

Mahdi's tears and pleading did nothing to soften the heart of this Ba'athist Comrade Jaabir and his confederates. And when Mahdi lost all hope, he asked only to be given the opportunity to notify his sick mother, who had no one else to provide for her. But it was no use: the party had taught Jaabir to heed nothing but its principles. The car set off, and after a few hours, Mahdi found himself in a training camp far from his mother's anxious heart.

Mahdi's mother, meanwhile, waited up for him until late. In the end, she was forced to conclude that he had indeed fallen into the clutches of Comrade Jaabir. "This is exactly what I was afraid of, and now it's happened!" she told herself, bursting into hot, stinging tears.

First thing in the morning, she called upon her older daughter, Fatima, asking her to lead the way to the comrade's abode, which everyone knew as "The Official's House." With a timid hand, she knocked on the door, and the Official himself, Jaabir, came out. He explained to this mourning mother that their homeland needed men, but that he, due to his respect for the neighborhood where he had lived his entire life, would see that things worked out well for Mahdi. "And in a few months, it will all be over."

When Umm Mahdi, between her sobs, explained their difficult living conditions—"God preserve you, but we don't even have a mouthful of bread!"—Comrade Jaabir replied, "Verily, the country is passing through a critical, historic period, and we must all sacrifice what is most precious to the heart of Iraq for dear Saddam. We need every last good, strong man!"

In his very first campaign, the famous Battle of Shush, Mahdi was taken prisoner. He lived out his youth in a prison camp on the Iranian–Soviet border, suffering horribly. "We would get a little rice and a little bread to eat. We never had meat. We had no shoes on our feet. The weather was freezing cold in the winter. The snow would be three feet deep, frozen solid, and we would try to chip our way through it using our bowls. We heard no news about the outside world. On top of that, there was . . ." Anyway, that's how Mahdi described it later, after his return from captivity.

He'd been there five years already when, in 1987, something no one in the camp could have imagined, not even in their nightmares, came to pass. One day, a member of the High Council of the Islamic Revolution visited the prisoners in order to give a religious address. This turbaned man was named Sayyid Fadil, and he was among the closest confidants to the Hakim family, which controlled the Council. Four others accompanied this pious man, with Comrade Jaabir front and center. Yes, the same Comrade Jaabir, who, in 1985, had also been taken prisoner by Iran, but who'd proclaimed his "repentance" and denounced Saddam and the Ba'ath Party. He and the other "penitents" were plucked out of the prison camps and enrolled in the Badr Brigades.

Mahdi's head spun at the sight of him. Heaven had set Jaabir over him back in the homeland, and here in this for-saken corner of the world heaven was again apparently send-ing Jaabir against him. Mahdi turned his face to the sky and asked, "God, why is this happening?"

Comrade Jaabir recognized Mahdi and approached, saying, "Truly, God has sent me as a mercy upon you! Is it really you, Mahdi, my lifelong neighbor? Oh, Mahdi, how you have changed! Who is this ghost that I see before me? Look at all this gray creeping into your hair! But do not despair! God will never forget you! Come! I will record your name among the penitents so that you can serve among the sons of the heroic Badr Brigades. Under the banner of Imam Khomeini (God extend his verdant shadow!), we will liberate Iraq from the unbelieving tyrant Saddam (God's curses upon him!)."

Mahdi stared at Jaabir. The new outfit, the long beard. In his mind's eye, the prisoner recalled the form in which he'd last seen this wolf, when all he could speak of was duty to Saddam and Saddam's holiness, waving the banner of that hero of the people, the Defender of the Nation, Saddam Hussein (God preserve and guide him!).

Mahdi found his courage and said, "Listen, Comrade Jaabir! Aren't you the person who got me into all this? Aren't you the one who ambushed me in the street? Why are you still chasing me? Isn't it enough that my mother was deprived of the sight of me, of my support, that my sisters were all left on their own? But, okay, let's set all that aside. I can forgive you for all that. But if you try to make me a traitor, you'll see that neither I nor God will forgive you! After everything you've done, you want to put me to work as an agent for Iran? Come on! Which nation do you belong to? Whose 'official' are you, anyway? What are you exactly?"

Jaabir was unruffled. "Listen, Mahdi," he said to his unfortunate prey, smiling. "I can tell that you are sincere and honest, that you really do believe all that nonsense you just spouted. But the thing is, you're not doing yourself any favors by advertising your unfortunate sincerity. What's more, you have to know that I'm the sort of person who rises to the top wherever he might be—here, there, or on the planet Mars. God made me a leader. It's out of my hands! So I'll give you a week to think it over, and after that, you'll see what I do to you, you filthy unbelieving Ba'athist!"

Mahdi repressed his rage, which meant closing his lips tight on the spit in his mouth boiling to be let fly. He turned his face away from the despicable traitor and headed back to the communal cell.

One week later, Comrade Jaabir began holding daily torture sessions for "Saddam Mahdi," as he called him, torture that Mahdi wasn't able to relate in detail, when he came back to us, because as soon as he remembered it, the color would drain from him, his eyes would be flooded with tears, and he would even start running a fever. Then he would break out in a sweat and hide his face.

The days passed. The war came to an end. Mahdi made it home only to find that his mother had departed for heaven. Before that, though, she had lost her sight out of sorrow, while his skinny sisters were made to live on family charity. Mahdi put his trust in God and began his life anew, working in the same samoon bakery during the awful years of the sanctions. The days went round and round, Saddam's regime fell, and everything was thrown into confusion once more.

Today, at the voting center for the referendum on the constitution, Mahdi decided to vote yes. He went into the building with his hunched back and faltering steps, with his body old before its time. As he was making his way over to sign in, his eyes met those of none other than Jaabir, who was overseeing the whole center together with a group of men bearing the rings and beards of the Badr Brigades. Mahdi's spirit faltered; he nearly fell on the floor when Jaabir called out to him, "Why, Mahdi! Is it really you, Mahdi? How'd you get here?"

Mahdi gave a half-dead "yes" that rattled around in his throat and never quite escaped. He barely heard it himself.

"How are you going to vote, my Ba'athist friend?" asked Jaabir.

"Yes! I'm voting yes, and I don't care what you say! If you want, you can write it down yourself!"

"Oh, Ba'athist Mahdi! Why did you refuse repentance and go back to rot in the cages instead? Why did you not believe me when I informed you I was a leader by nature, and that you are an insect, a mere insect who doesn't know his ass from his elbow?"

Mahdi stared into the face of his eternal executioner. "And you, comrade, are a traitor. Heart and soul, a traitor!" And having spoken his piece, Mahdi disappeared and was never seen again.

Sistani's Fatwa and Salman the Enforcer

Mind you, the people most eager to vote in favor of the constitution were the ones who didn't read it, or at the very least didn't understand the first thing about it. The people who fought the hardest for federalism were those who were hearing the word for the first time in their lives, and who never bothered to ask what it meant. The people demanding religious and civil freedoms were the same ones who snatched away the freedom of others by force of arms, while those calling loudest for the right to hold peaceful demonstrations, for any reason whatever, came from the ranks of the armed militias. The most sectarian people don't themselves hold any religious beliefs, but rather have found their fathers to be devoted to a certain brand of theology and are convinced that they must have been right.

Take, for example, Salman the Deaf. Day and night, this man has been agitating for the necessity of participating in the referendum, both before the draft was amended and after. No one insists more than he upon federalism—or "fe'ralism," as he says it. Salman has participated in every demonstration at Firdos Square, where Saddam's statue came tumbling down. He first demonstrated there in April 2003, right after the invasion, when the demand was for the release of the poet al-Fartousi, a Sadr ally detained by the American forces, and he's kept at it through the latest protests that broke out just last week, a gathering for which no one, least of all its own organizers, knows the cause or the objectives.

Salman the Deaf is an odious sectarian. He looks for the arch-traitor Yazid—the seventh-century caliph responsible for the murder of Ali's son Husayn—in every face he sees in the street, and Yazid, in his view, is every individual who does not obey the Hakim family, everybody who has not joined the Mahdi Army, and everyone who doesn't stroll the mere two hundred kilometers from Thawra to Najaf every year to celebrate the birthday of the Twelfth Imam on the fifteenth day of Sha'ban. Not that Salman is a praying man; he hasn't memorized any part of the Qur'an, not even the 112th sura, which has only four verses. He doesn't know why he belongs to his particular theological sect. What's more, he believes that Ayatollah Sistani is the reincarnation of one of the Twelve Infallible Imams: Salman hasn't got the least doubt that this Sistani has a direct line to heaven, that he meets each week with the Hidden Imam, the Mahdi himself, and that if Sistani wanted to split the moon, as Prophet Muhammad is said to have done, it wouldn't take more than a wink of his eye! (Of course, when I talk about this Salman the Deaf, you understand that there are many thousands like him, across the Shiite and Sunni divide.)

On this particular day, Salman kept pounding on my door to remind me that the gates of the voting center would close at five in the afternoon, and that the opportunity to have my say would pass me by if I didn't go and vote "yes" on the constitution right away. Sistani had voted "yes," it was said, and immediately thereafter Salman the Deaf had transformed into one big resounding yes from the top of his head to the tips of his toes.

"Uncle Salman," I said, "just let me do my thing! We'll vote when we're ready. Go easy on my door!" I had to say it all twice, very loudly, for him to hear me.

"Hey, were you all sleeping? Haven't you heard the fatwa?"

"We heard it, Salman, we heard it! And we're going to go, but we have guests over. We'll go in a bit, okay?"

"You have pests? What pests? Papa Sistani says, 'Vote!'"

"God keep you, Salman! Just . . . go away. Don't worry about us. We'll be sure to vote!"

So Salman took off, and after an hour, I picked myself up and did indeed go to cast my vote. But Salman was waiting for me at the door of the voting center.

"Shalash," he said, "what are you doing here alone? Where's your family? Where are your esteemed mother and father? Where's your dear nana? That old woman's sin will be on your neck if you didn't tell her about the fatwa!"

"Uncle Salman, have you seen the old woman lately? She's got one foot in the grave already. She can't speak or hear, believe me . . ."

"Fine, let's go get her! I'll pick her up and carry her over on my back. I'll be amply rewarded in heaven! Don't you know the going rate for rewards in heaven for helping ratify the constitution? It's worth a hundred visits to the shrine of the Eighth Imam, and that's on the far side of Iran!"

Then Salman turned away, engrossed in reminding the other voters just arriving about Sistani's eternal *yes*. Speaking only for myself, and according to my own humble reading of the course of recent events, I had decided to vote yes on the constitution, especially after the amendments came through. But seeing Salman there made it all seem just as partisan as he was himself. I felt disgusted with myself for getting my hopes up and changed my mind about going inside.

But Salman somehow noticed my hesitation. How could I have known that his eyes hadn't left me for an instant? He leaped at me and said, "Hey, Shalash, what's the holdup? What's wrong with you? By God, Sistani said to vote yes. Don't you believe me?"

At that, my disgust boiled over. "Fine!" I said. "I'm not voting! I'm done!"

I guess Salman had been waiting for just this sort of reaction. He was obviously delighted that I'd provided him with this opportunity to deliver a historic oration about my character in the presence of so many of our fellow citizens. I'll take his words to my grave.

"I know you, Shalash," he declared. "How could I not know you? You hate the religious clerkship and all five of its leaders: Sistani, Hakim, Sadr, Kho'i, and Haeri. You're just a secularist—and a drunk to boot. You drink arak from a shoe! You have no shame! If you had any shame at all, your sister wouldn't be attending college with boys, now would she? You really think you're something, don't you? Too big for your britches, eh, just because you've picked up a little culture? But I've been watching you at night, and I've seen you point your new dish at the European satellites to watch porn! But that's nothing new, is it? You turned away from God long ago. But don't you fear: your day is coming, atheist! You think you can make a mockery of Sistani's fatwa like this? I'll teach you. If I allow you to take another breath, my name isn't Salman! What a tragedy, for a good Shiite boy to turn out so rotten!"

Some of my neighbors heard the ruckus and tried to stick up for me, saying, "For shame, Salman! What's all this about? Stop busting Shalash's balls already."

"Who's busting what? He told me he doesn't give a fig for Sistani!" (Of course, I never said such a thing.)

So, in the end, I was forced to go inside and vote yes despite my misgivings, just as a form of damage control, even as Salman the Deaf went on addressing the people, recounting my entire life story, even the part about my aunt Zanuba marrying a Sunni man thirty years ago.

81

The Federalism of Thawra City and Its Suburbs

In line with the wave of federalism that is crashing over Iraq these days, Thawra City and the surrounding areas decided to set up a federalist state that would include Thawra, Sha'ab, Al-Baladiyat, Mashtal, Al-Ubaidi, Kamaliyah, including the neighborhoods of Al-Amana, Habibiya, Orfali, Jamila, Talbiyah, Binouk, and even Tariq (which was formerly called Tanak).

For this purpose, a formation committee was convened, made up of representatives from the most important tribes in Thawra, as well as those that enjoyed noticeable influence here, such as al-Sawa'id, Banu Lam, Albodrag, Banu Malik, Albu Muhammad, Ahl Aziraj, Sarray (with all its branches), Kaab, al-Sudan, al-Baydan, Kinana, and Hilaf (in addition, of course, to our local politicians in the Assembly, Razzak al-Shaykh and Salim Manati).

Those assembled expounded on the importance and legality of forming this federalist state in the valley to the east of the Army Canal, which would result in benefits to those living in the aforementioned regions, numbering more than four million souls. In that way, this confederation would surpass that of the Kurdish state and any other state that might be formed in the future out of any three of Iraq's provinces—a right guaranteed by our new constitution.

Those assembled explained that Thawra City and its suburbs all float on a lake of oil. Our home has a large workforce, just as it has an independent army and a local police force that would never dream of answering to Bayan Jabr Solagh and his lethal Ministry of the Interior. Our new state would also contain a number of manufacturing regions, including Kasra, Atsh, Orfali, and the very industrious Jamila. Likewise, we take pride in our Army Canal, that singular waterway that connects us to neighboring cities in the Republic of Iraq and forms a strategic natural resource. (Never mind that the canal has been a muddy cesspool for years.)

Having agreed upon the necessity of establishing this state, the committee moved on to determining the founding principles that its local constitution would have to guarantee. A subcommittee for drawing up the first draft of the constitution came forward. Here is their text (and if you compare it with the Iraqi constitution just approved, know that its authors must have read the minds of the geniuses on our subcommittee):

PREAMBLE

In the name of God, the merciful, the compassionate

"Everyone upon this earth shall come to naught"
(Qur'an: Al-Rahman 55.26)

We are the sons of the Army Canal East Valley, a country of sayyids, sheikhs, and tribal heads, pioneers of the wilds, unemployed day laborers, and a cradle-of-civilization's worth of problems. Our land is where the first laws of the tribes were laid down, and where the most ancient methods of stealing were perfected, and it was our very ancestors who first established the principle of an eye for an eye. Upon this soil the elegists of Imam Husayn and Saddam Hussein spoke their honeyed words, and here too flourished the varied tribes of neighborhood poet-singers, brothel dancers, hired mourners, and mattress stuffers.

Recognizing God's rights over us, and in fulfillment of the will of the people, and in response to the call of our tribal leaders who direct our tribal forces, and according to the insistence of the Sayyid's office and his agents, and with the regional backing of our friends and loved ones in Al Shuala and Kadhimiya . . .

On this day of Farhat al-Zahra, when we commemorate the massacre of Husayn at Karbala, we have marched for the first time to the ballot boxes—men and women, young and old— remembering the horrors of sectarian cleansing perpetrated by the hegemonic class; inspired by the disasters suffered by the martyrs of our block; recalling the injustices we suffered when our sacred side streets were invaded by the secret service, the anti-terrorist force, the People's Army, and those enforcing the army conscription; articulating the torments of ethnic cleansing in the massacres of Maridi, Fellah Street, and Gayyara; and having endured, along with the people of Sha'ab, the Islands Neighborhood, Hosseinia, Orfali, and Tanak, the liquidation of our leadership, the violation of our symbols, and the murder of our sheikhs, together with the forced exile of all our prominent citizens . . .

We hereby proceed, hand in hand, shoulder to shoulder, to form the new state of Army Canal East Valley—without sectarian pride, without any racial or neighborhood-centric bias, and without discrimination against, or the silencing of, any faction.

We, the people of Army Canal East Valley, have taken it upon ourselves, together with all our constituent elements and parts, to affirm our freedom by choosing to separate from the people of Baghdad and the rest of those no-less-troublesome provinces of Iraq, such as Ramadi, Diwaniyah, Tikrit, Darbandikhan, Samawah, not to name names, thereby giving tomorrow the opportunity to learn from the mistakes of yesterday. Our laws will be gleaned from the best of our customs, tribal rules, and traditions, and from all the innovations that have reached us, our sayyids, and our prominent people from beyond our borders.

Our adherence to this constitution shall liberate us from Iraq and all its nauseating tribulations!

FOUNDING PRINCIPLES

ARTICLE 1. The Army Canal East Valley State is an independent and sovereign district. Its system of government shall be tribal, democratic, hereditary, and federal.

ARTICLE 2
  I. The so-called Speaking Seminary of politically engaged theologians shall be the central religious authority for the region and the fundamental basis for all legislation.
      A. No law shall be passed that contradicts the fatwas of Sayyid Muqtada.
      B. No law shall be passed that is incompatible with tribal customs.
      C. No law shall be passed that is incompatible with the basic rights and freedoms to be found in this constitution.
  II. This constitution shall in no wise interfere with the proud though poor "Easterner" identity that is held

so dear by the majority of the inhabitants of our great state, just as it shall protect and guarantee the rights of every individual to maintain their own religious creeds and practices, just as are enjoyed by the Christians found in Al-Baladiyat and Habibiya, and by the Sabian goldsmiths, wherever that sect may reside.

ARTICLE 3. The Army Canal East Valley State forms a part of the zone east of the Tigris, which is composed of diverse tribes, subtribes, lineages, and families. Its Arab population belongs to Amara in southern Iraq; its Kurdish blocks—namely, Blocks 13, 14, and 18—form part of Kurdistan in the north; and our Kawliya neighbors in Kamaliyah shall be recognized as members of the International Romani Union.

ARTICLE 4. Sovereignty derives from custom and tradition. The sheikhs are the source of authority and legitimacy, which they exercise however they may please.

ARTICLE 5. Power is transferred hereditarily through the tribal mechanisms set forth in this constitution. Sheikhs shall take turns holding the presidency of the state by alphabetical order, a matter that will be determined by a fatwa.

ARTICLE 6. The Kawliya area shall enjoy its own cultural and artistic identity, no matter how scandalous or shocking others may judge it to be. Its schools shall be exempt from the official curriculum of the state, and the residents of Kawliya shall be free to practice their own rituals and rites, which freedom shall include the right to perform ceremonies such as marriage, purification, and all the "other activities" they deem necessary for the preservation of their identity (which will not be mentioned here), with the understanding that the revenues of this unique district shall nonetheless be gathered in coordination with the state government, and profits be distributed in a manner fair to all, after deducting a share for the reconstruction zones.

ARTICLE 7

I. The state military and security apparatuses shall be composed of the Mahdi Army, the tribal brotherhood, as well as all break dancers, thieves, carjackers, and housebreakers who have reached the age of majority. The balance of power between the various units and their overall coordination shall be closely supervised by the office of Sayyid Muqtada without discrimination or silencing of any one faction. Rather than forming an instrument for the repression of our citizens, the military and security forces shall defend the state and defer to its leadership. Moreover, they shall not interfere in tribal affairs, nor will they have any role in the peaceful transfer of power from one administration to the next.

II. The formation of paramilitary groups unaffiliated with any recognized tribe shall be forbidden.

III. When necessary, conscription shall be organized by a fatwa.

(Don't ask me why the subcommittee left out Article 8. I'm sure they had a good reason!)

ARTICLE 9. Within the state, the traditional diwans of the sheikhs, the Husayniya halls, the homes of the sayyids, and any homes of the descendants of Ali that are not connected to a sayyid are to be declared holy symbols of civilization, and the government of the Army Canal East

Valley State shall be obliged to confirm and preserve their inviolability, and to guarantee the free practice of rituals therein.

ARTICLE 10. Block 79, with its currently established boundaries, shall be the permanent capital of the state.

ARTICLE 11

i. The procession of those who represent the state will be determined by a fatwa, as will the ceremonial processions of those beating and cutting themselves, insofar as that symbolizes all components of society.

ii. Badges of honor, visits during the month of Sha'ban, religious festivals, the honorific tribal names (so-and-so is the brother of so-and-so, etc.), and the colors and sizes of banners will all be determined by a fatwa.

OCTOBER 19, 2005

In Our House, There Is a Submarine. In Our House, There Is an Elevator.

Humility is considered the cardinal virtue in Zuhayra's family. Whenever her son Fadil would pass people's houses with his propane cart, he would shower them with greetings and all his very best wishes. Often, he would jump down from the seat of his cart, in his familiar clowning manner, to kiss the hands of sheikhs or sayyids or just any random old people. This habit of his didn't change much even when he exchanged his propane cart for a *sugmarine*, which is to say a "submarine," in our distinctive pronunciation, which is in turn our slang term for a modern black Mercedes.

This situation also applies to Jasim, Fadil's younger brother, who, for his part, maintained the same air of humility in *his* new submarine as he'd shown behind his own little gas cart. But, obviously, I wouldn't be writing here today if all I had on my mind were the praiseworthy characteristics of the Zuhayra family. No, no, I'm here on account of the submarines themselves, which might as well have fallen from the sky while we were sleeping.

The first one showed up one day in June 2003. The whole block woke up to the sound of horns honking, horns unlike any we'd ever heard, a ruckus followed shortly by the sight of the first submarine coming down our street, the first we'd ever seen in our corner of Thawra City. Two days later, or thereabouts, the second submarine rolled up—the first being Fadil's, of course, and the second Jasim's. Not everyone was equally impressed. In fact, most were more concerned that the brothers' two horse-drawn carts had vanished, along with their wares, whinnies, and neighs. Even the smell of propane, which once distinguished Zuhayra's house, had dispersed, replaced by that of high-octane gasoline.

"In our street, there are *two* submarines!" That's how the local kids put it, having adapted the model sentence they learned in Arabic grammar class to our unique situation. They had only a short time to enjoy bragging rights over the other neighborhood children, however, since then, without any warning, Zuhayra bought a house in the fancy Ziyouna district and moved there under cover of darkness. In recognition of which, dear readers, I ask that you grant me a little time to recount the description I received following the traditional housewarming visit that Kamil and his wife Badriya paid Zuhayra to scope out her new place and keep their noses in her business. What follows meets not only my own personal standards insofar as poetic accomplishment is concerned, but, more, I consider it an entirely objective and neutral piece of reportage.

Kamil: "Oh, wow! Like, what a palace! And what a catastrophe! Not a house, no, not at all! It's not a house, but I can't say what it is! I'm getting dizzy just thinking about it! What's going on with those windows? Those doors? All those fancy couches? And the garden? No, no! I can't believe my eyes!"

Badriya: "By the soul of your father, Kamil, give me a chance and let me get a word in! Mamma mia, the marble everywhere! Even the floor tiles are marble. And that ceiling! It was so high, you'd think you were in a government ministry! The kitchen? . . . Let's not even talk about it. I've never seen anything like that kitchen, not even in a movie, neither Egyptian nor foreign. The porcelain everywhere! The gleaming counters! The cabinet handles, which look like they might be gold or silver. God isn't stingy—when He sends down one blessing, he provides ten more besides!"

Kamil: "Honest, I got so blinded I couldn't find the way out! Hey, they even have an elevator. Yes, God's truth! An electric elevator, meaning that if Zuhayra gets a bit tired, she just presses a button, and *zip*! Now she's upstairs."

Badriya: "The bathtubs are like swimming pools! And it has this thing that people lie in . . . God, how do I describe it? It's a tub, like, but in the middle there are these holes where bubbles come out? Zuhayra says it's good for her back."

Kamil: "As for Jasim's bedroom, it might have been made for Saddam's son, Uday! I swear, I don't have the words to describe it. I would lose my mind trying to tell you. I mean, what could I say? If I went on from now till morning, I swear, I still wouldn't be done. But Zuhayra said she was going to invite the whole street, and hopefully you'll go and see it for yourself. Just please don't embarrass Zuhayra in front of her new neighbors. Put yourselves together a little when you go! Their neighbors really gave us a looking over, head to toe."

Thus concludes Kamil and Badriya's description of the house where Zuhayra now lives with her two sons and their wives, along with one child, Fadil's firstborn son. Which brings us at last to our main topic of interest—namely, where the hell did all this come from, Zuhayra?

Now, I know some of you are going to say, "It's sad how jealous you are, Shalash." While others will no doubt comment, "Why all this envy when they're just another poor family contending with God for their daily bread?" And others still among my dear readers are going to say, "What do you want from them? Aren't they good, humble people who'll sooner or later invite you to a feast in their new home?" And I could hardly deny the truth of these statements . . . But since I began this story, I'm going to finish it! And I'll do so without leaving out all the incidental and seemingly unconnected events that surrounded it, since to do otherwise would mean my losing all my credibility with you moving forward.

A few nights before the fall of Baghdad, Fadil and Jasim were hovering near the Nidal Street branch of Rafidain Bank. Their analysis of the military situation indicated that Baghdad was bound to be invaded on April 4. That night passed, however, and its uneventfulness made them some-what anxious. Not that this the delay could dissuade them. They had a plan; it was the opportunity of a lifetime; so they kept taking turns at the main door of the bank, which didn't arouse any suspicion so long as they had the cover story of manning their horses and carts.

On the night of April 8, before the American forces entered Baghdad from the direction of Thawra City, Fadil and Jasim, Zuhayra's two sons, begotten by Turki (may he rest in peace!), were sitting in the inner courtyard of the bank (along with some accomplices assembled from several other Baghdad neighborhoods). By the time Mr. Bush's Hummers crossed the Army Canal in Thawra City, heading toward the center of Baghdad, Fadil and Jasim were traveling in the opposite direction, which is to say they were on the road from the center of Baghdad back to their house in Thawra, carrying stacks of US dollars. But let me assure my dear readers that despite this apparent divergence in direction, the paths taken by the families of Mr. George W. Bush and Mrs. Zuhayra, respectively, were by no means in opposition. On the contrary, anyone with eyes in their head could see that this was a meeting of their true interests.

The sum realized must remain a matter for supposition. The financial experts on our street estimate it to have been in the millions, or even tens of millions, while Razzak the Wheelwright says that these are silly exaggerations, that the matter couldn't possibly exceed a million, or one and a half at most. There are other even more unrealistic prognostica-tions that we have deemed appropriate to ignore, given our reputation for probity.

And even all that dough didn't provoke the envy of the estimable Ghaziya, who, until the moment the city fell, had been Zuhayra's lifelong neighbor, friend, and confidant. What *did* annoy Ghaziya, and what she couldn't stop obsessing over, with or without provocation, was that Zuhayra had acquired a cell phone with a camera on both the front *and* the back. On top of that, it had "Blue-toot," as she pronounced it. Whenever the thought of the device with two cameras and Blue-toot came into Ghaziya's mind, she would start complaining about Zuhayra, now deemed "that mother of two *sarjin.*" And *sarjin*, ladies and gentlemen, isn't a treatment for stomach pains, as the Arabic word may suggest. Actually—and may God protect your ears!—it's what we in our neighborhood call the horseshit that you use to keep fires burning, and which has other names in the Baghdadi dialect. (Certain readers may know it as *sawn* or *fashqi*.)

In any case, I will soon be numbered among the most important of the invitees to Zuhayra's palace—she who has not forgotten her former neighbors, or her former life! Once I've penetrated its walls, I will report to you live, with images as well as full documentation on the reactions of the other guests. Stay tuned!

OCTOBER 21, 2005

The Street-Corner Sermon of Abbas the Drunk

Abbas finally did it. He showed up drunk. The problem is that he didn't hide his shame. He didn't go to bed. He stood on the corner and delivered a sermon. And here, ladies and gentlemen, is the text of that sermon, word for word (omitting the commentary interjected by the crowd he began to draw):

What the hell is this Ramadan, anyway? Look what it's done to me! So is it a sin for me to relax a little?! I fasted ten whole days. Isn't that enough? I say all the rest of you can go to heaven without me—I want nothing to do with it. Hopefully, the whole block will go to heaven and leave me alone. What's it to me? Hey, this nonsense is killing me! How much longer can it go on?

Let the Mahdi Army come. Not even their biggest badass can scare me! I'm the one who knocked Saddam off his high horse, remember, and I'm still here! You think I'm afraid of some pill-popping Mahdi Army? God, they don't have anybody left to fight besides drooling babies anyhow! *Pffft!*

Yes, I'm drunk! I'm *so* drunk! And it's not just me who's drunk! My friend Hamza is drunk too. He just went inside. Hey, come on out, Hamza, Mr. Crybaby! What, are you hiding? Afraid? You coward! Show yourself!

I'm gonna get drunk every day from here on in. Anyone who doesn't like it can go vote *no* on the constitution, okay? Yesterday I voted. What else do you want? Isn't this freedom?

What do you mean, What did I vote for? Well, I guess I don't remember!

What the hell are you looking at? What am I, some schmuck? You think I'm here to amuse you? I'm Abbas, Abbas Cinder Block. Don't you know me? What's gotten into you all? So everyone's turned into a believer now, is that it? What a world. You spend your lives in fear. Come on, we've lived our whole lives with people telling us, "The coyote's coming to get you! The wolf is at the door!" Because the coyote doesn't care one bit if the chicken happens to have a runny beak when it finally catches up with it. To a wolf, a chicken with the bird flu tastes just as good.

What's that? I hear you asking. How does poultry come into it? Well, I'll tell you, since I'm your entertainment for the night.

So, one day, I say to Hamza, "Did your chick lay an egg?" And he says to me, "No, she just caught a little cold." Hamza's mother, see, that chicken had a fever, for real, its forehead was all sweaty, it had the chills—the whole nine yards. Ha! They even smothered the bird with Vicks—and out popped Hamza! Brothers, if anyone sees a sneezing chick, have him go tell the mayor, and he'll get a prize from Channel Euphrates. Hahaha! Our prince of a mayor won't fall short in his duty. Oh, no! Right away he'll prick her with his lusty needle and send her to bed for some rest.

Ah, I shit on your honor, Mayor Abu Zaki!

Whenever he sees a chick with a runny beak, he tells her, "How lovely you're looking these days!" No, really! Rasmiya, the daughter of Na'im—she's ugly as sin, you know, but he tells her, "Your beauty lights up the entire block!" Ha! But this Rasmiya, *her* beak has been running since birth. She takes a step, she sneezes, she takes a step, she sneezes. "My child," I told her, "Go, clean your radiator. You're attracting too many flies!" But she just sneezes and spits on me, this runny-nosed chickadee who's promised to her cousin!

Man, the Baghdad city folk were sure right when they called you tent-dwellers a flock—though the better word would be *cowed.* Not even free-range! You're a flock of battery chickens! Truly, what are you but a bunch of chickens, yellowbellies, cowards. You didn't fire a single shot!

Show yourself, Hamza! Come on out! How much did you drink, anyway? Just a quarter bottle of arak, you say? Only a quarter, and you start cursing Muqtada, al-Jaafari, and Paul Bremer? Hey now, come on out! Don't be afraid! Nobody here but us chickens. What, you think we're gonna eat you up?

What's happened to him now? Did you evaporate, Hamza? Eh, vanished into thin air? Speaking of disappearing acts, by the way, where's Saddam? Wasn't he just telling us, "You'll never see me evaporate from the field even if the Prophet's uncle, Al-Hamza himself, shows up to scare me away!" Well, what else would you call hiding away in a hole! And doesn't that make America into Al-Hamza, the good guys in the story? I might just have to shit on your honor too, Saddam! What a joke! What a junkie, what a cheat! He must have been laughing his ass off at us, no? But then they stuck him in that white cage and the joke was on him. They locked him in and said, "You murdered a hundred and forty-eight people in Dujail in 1982!" I almost pissed myself laughing. A hundred and forty-eight? Hell, he ate a hundred and forty-eight every day for breakfast. No, really! And then he says, "I am the president of Iraq." But hey, where is this Iraq place anyway? We've got twenty presidents in every back alley—do they all have their own Iraq too? I swear, throw your shoe any which way and you'll knock down forty presidents, including the honorable president of the anti-corruption committee. The judge is satisfied, so what's it to the mufti, eh? Haha!

(Sound of a motorcycle racing by.)

Go for it, Motorcycle Man! The wind's at your back, my only friend! God, I used to have a motorcycle myself, faster than a speeding bullet. But when I went to prison, my mother sold it. Of course she did. The question is, what *didn't* she sell? The only thing she's held onto is her husband, the hajji. She could have sold him for parts, but no, she's still got every ounce of him, even the bits she could live without.

Hey! You! Don't you dare laugh at the hajji! Even the hajji's left sandal is more honorable than you, son of Tasa. *Tasa*, eh? What did your mother have to do to get a name like that, I wonder. Let's explain to our new American friends that her name means "drinking bowl," yeah? Ha! If my mother had a name like that I'd throw myself off Aimmah Bridge, just like all those poor souls who died there last month!

(*Musical interlude:*)

Your sweet love has made me see laughter and tears
Candle by candle, my life is worn away
Your sweet love has made me taste, tra-la-la-la
Your sweet love has made me taste laughter and tears . . .

(*Ends.*)

A thousand blessings on your soul, Abu Khaled, for that short piece. Now the rising star, Salah Al Bahar, steps onto the stage, and that other guy too, Ali Al-Issawi, the one who looks like he wandered into a cloud of chemical weapons. But the old songs are still best! Ah, my friends, where is the arak of yesteryear? Back then, booze was more plentiful than water, and to be strong also meant to be silent. What's happened to the world? I woke up the other day and saw

Irhayam on TV! You know, the one who used to sell donkeys? Seriously! And he had the words "strategy analyst" floating under his name in the caption box! "Strategist Abu al-Fuh," it said. Makes you sound important, Irhayam! God, how he talked and talked! And he started every sentence with "I think . . ." Ha! When did *you* start thinking, Mr. Hee-Haw?

And you know my friend Salima? Well, I saw her yesterday at the polls. What's happened to her, you ask? Good question! And it's a good thing I saw her before she saw me, you know? What could I say to her? Right off the bat she'd be, like, "What's the deal with the wedding? The wedding, eh? What's happening? When are you going to propose to me already?"

But her sister, Halima, now she's still beautiful. So beautiful, in fact, I may have to shit on her honor too. How the hell could she have fallen in love with that bicycle repairman? I can't figure it out! Maybe he pulled her up onto the bicycle behind him like that famous scene in the movie with Abd al-Halim Hafiz—was that in *Love Street*? Or *Girls and Summer*?

(*Musical interlude:*)

Something strange, tra-la-la-la
Something strange, tra-la-la-li
Something strange

(*Ends.*)

Hey, Mom, what are you doing out here? Go back inside, if not for your own sake then for Gramps and Nana's, may they rest in peace. I'm coming in now, never you fear . . . What's that you say? Some dude from the Mahdi Army is going to come by and shut me up if I don't shut myself up first? Go inside! I'd give my life for you, Mom, but leave me the hell alone, okay? It's been a long time since I've given a sermon in the street. This street of mentals, notwithstanding you and Dad of course. A whole street with not a single decent guy on it! Just people saying, "This guy's a drunk. This guy doesn't pray." They've all turned into that movie, *The Prophet*, overnight! If they want to go back to the seventh century, be my guest, but don't bring the rest of us with you!

Why, hello there, Abu Sitar, where've you been? You look pleased with yourself. You must have made some good money? Things going well, eh, uncle? Listen, in that case, I need a new pair of tires, used is fine too, in fact, if you've got any on hand, my little Abu Sitar. No? Then piss off, my friend. Piss right on off. I ask you, citizens, has there ever in the history of the world been a dealer in car tires with a shred of goodness in his soul? I doubt it! Go away, Abu Sitar! Don't look at me! You think *I'm* drunk? You know your nephew, Hamza, is also drunk and already went inside? Hamza, for shame!

Show yourself, Hamza Big-Nose! Come out, if you value your honor! I'll even tell you a joke about your uncle, Dirty Sitar . . .

(*Musical interlude:*)

Your image has slept in my eye from the day it first opened
tra-la-la-la
Your shadows have shadowed my waking hours and my sleep
tra-la-la-li

(*Ends.*)

Coming, Mother, I'm coming! Why are you always nagging me? Make me some dinner and I'll be right in.

(*Musical interlude:*)

My son, Allawi, is all grown up, now in the very first grade ...

(*Ends.*)

God, the old songs are the best. How'd they know we'd have a prime minister named Ayad Allawi? What a guy! He sent the army in against them in Najaf last year, and the Mahdi Army scattered willy-nilly. They all just ran away!

What is it, Uncle? What's happened? My dear Shakir the Barber, don't you know how to greet people, for God's sake, Mr. Goatee? Ah, I'd lay down my life for that goatee of yours! Say, do you think you could thread my beard?

I'm gonna go in and get some rest. Yeah, yeah, I'm gonna go in! And here's my family standing there waiting to scoop me up like I'm some little kid! Hey, Mom, I've been a hopeless drunk for at least twenty years now. No use pretending this is my first rodeo.

Hey, listen, all of you! I'm gonna go in. Yeah, by my own decision, I'm going inside. Not because I'm scared of the Mahdi Army. Not because I'm scared of some sayyid named Hussain, that same Hussain who spent his life in Iran and now comes traipsing back to us as though he's the hero of the liberation. That sayyid parvenu!

(*With that, Abbas staggered into his house and, even before eating dinner, fell fast asleep.*)

Asi the Thief's Blackmail and the Portrait
of Husayn (Peace Be upon Him!)

Immediately after the fall of Saddam's regime, Asi sold the truck belonging to the Ministry of Trade that had been entrusted to him to use for his job. He then set himself up as a middleman to sell other vehicles belonging to other ministries, which had likewise been entrusted to other employees, all of whom now put that trust in the market. Things were looking up for Asi! He got full of himself and started strutting down the middle of the street like the proverbial peacock, casting looks of contempt and disdain upon all passersby.

"A thief—no more, no less." That summarizes the view of my honorable neighbors toward Asi. As for his sons and daughters, they began to be called "the children of the thief" or "the robber's brood."

Finding his newfound status sullied by this reputation, Asi made a desperate attempt to buy his neighbors' esteem by building a wall across from his house in the middle of the small square that formed the center of the block. It was three meters tall and four meters wide. He brought someone in to paint a picture of Imam Husayn upon it (and peace be upon him!) in much the way a nineteenth-century Iranian portraitist might have imagined him. Asi then fenced in the picture with a cement wall, around which he planted two half-dead plants. He would go out and pretend to water those two unhappy shrubs whenever some displeasing comment regarding his sale of state-owned property happened to reach his ears. The portrait of Husayn (peace be upon him!), which for the simple-minded demanded the same reverence as would Husayn himself (peace be upon him!), was thus a wholly owned subsidiary of Asi's business, handling public relations for him and his family both. They fortified themselves behind it, as it were, almost as though Husayn (peace be upon him!), in the flesh, had taken up residence under the wing of the ignoble family of Asi.

But, simple-minded or not, the locals mainly found the wall confusing. Confusing and challenging.

For one thing, before the wall was built, the square was generally used as little more than a garbage dump. For another, Asi himself had already monopolized half of its navigable area by parking a long trailer there that he hadn't found a buyer for yet. Thus, even the more sophisticated locals, who knew that this mural of a man with bushy Iranian eyebrows and soft features couldn't possibly be Husayn bin Ali (peace be upon him!), the hero of Karbala and the Sayyid of the young martyrs of paradise, were now forced to choose between dumping their garbage in front of the putatively holy portrait or else by Asi's trailer.

People did their best to thread this needle, but since they tossed their garbage as far from the portrait as they could manage, day after day, the pile sooner or later had to begin encroaching on the territory staked out by the long trailer that had been brooding there for months. So by the time the municipal authorities decided to grace our block with a one-off visit from an actual garbage truck, the driver and the locals who gathered around him to help him navigate into the square and so finally empty a little of it out, found that the area, which was narrow to begin with and had become even narrower on account of Asi's larcenous car-dealing on the one hand and his spurious devotion to the Father of Martyrs (peace be upon him!) on the other, had become almost impassable.

The crowd went silent, working through their conflicting emotions, leaving the poor driver at a loss. How could he pull into the square without either menacing the portrait or else crashing into the trailer? He got out of his truck and went around to take a closer look so as to see if he might find a way out of the extremely trying and sensitive situation into which he had fallen. Finally, after despairing of his ability to get his truck through on his own, he asked the crowd to help him move the square's garbage by hand from its current location to the back of his trash-compacting garbage truck. The people willingly agreed, rescuing the driver from between the jaws of the dilemma into which he'd been dropped by Asi, who was watching the proceedings from his house, with his usual hauteur, without ever offering to help them carry the garbage, not even the bags his family had contributed.

This latter point provoked the resentment of one Abu Sa'dun, who took the opportunity to yell to Asi, "Hey! Come and take away your crap. We're not your servants!" This served to open the floodgates, and soon other voices were rising up from the crowd, criticizing Asi's pride and his disreputable character. His refusal to dignify this assault with a reply only increased their zeal and contempt, until curses were raining down upon him, focused in particular upon his thievery and his transformation from an ordinary sort of functionary into an egocentric monster simply on account of the money he'd raked in by flipping state-owned vehicles.

Asi has the intuition of a jackal, so he knew that matters were building toward what might prove an unsavory climax. He went inside his house and hurried back out with a pitcher of water. Squeezing himself into the square, he began—with a dramatic flourish—to water the shrubs, long dried out, which he'd planted around his mural. My neighbors—the true lovers of Husayn—gave up their litany of insults and could only shake their fists in helpless rage at this spiritual blackmail. They picked up the trash and loaded it in the truck. Then they dispersed and went their various ways.

When, later, it finally rained, in the first great downpour the sky had given them in quite some time, the water washed away the cheap paint that had been used to create what was believed to be a portrait of Husayn (peace be upon him!). One of my neighbors took advantage of this opportunity to dismantle the wall and erase all trace of it forever from the square of Asi the Thief, so that Husayn would remain, eternal and glorious, solely in the hearts and the consciences of all the free, noble, and oppressed peoples of the world, and not in the cheap Iranian dyes of a profiteer.

OCTOBER 24, 2005

Al-Hakim on "Winning with Majid"

Backers of Muqtada al-Sadr have been joking these days about the mistake his rival, Abdul Aziz al-Hakim, made during his meeting with Amr Moussa, Secretary-General of the Arab League, when Hakim said, "Omar Mukhtar is Algerian." Even people who'd never heard of Omar Mukhtar, people who don't know where to find Algeria on a map, felt as though their stomachs might explode with laughter at Hakim's ignorance. Some Hakim-family sympathizers made excuses for him on the grounds that he's been in Iran all these years and had no chance to catch *Lion of the Desert* since they prohibit TV and movies over there.

There's no question that Sayyid Hakim, leader of the largest bloc in parliament, has scandalized us in front of the nobodies and the somebodies both. It's true, he's never exactly professed an interest in geography or modern history; but, then again, nobody poked him in the arm and told him, "Come on, open your mouth and make a royal ass of yourself!"

Mind you, it's not as though the international community cares a fig for Hakim; his blunders; his extremely blinkered grasp of history, limited as it is to the timeline of the Iranian revolution and the dates of the birthdays of its exalted leaders; or his knowledge of geography, equally limited, exceeding not a millimeter beyond his own sphere of influence, which extends from Kut, passes through Najaf, and reaches as far as "holy" Jadriyah, the Baghdad neighborhood he has requisitioned for his headquarters . . . But, unfortunately for him, the residents of Thawra City heard him say what he said, and they've been laughing about Omar Mukhtar ever since.

"Omar, the mukhtar? No, that's the mayor over in Adamiyah—a Sunni neighborhood for a Sunni name. Hakim doesn't live in Adamiyah, so you can't fault his ignorance.

Now if the question were about the current mukhtar of Jadriyah, *then* Hakim would immediately know the answer . . ."

"I bet Hakim doesn't know a single Omar. Not even Omar Sharif!" Laughter everywhere. "What if Hakim were on the game-show *Winning with Majid*, and they asked him who invented the hammer. Another Omar, right? Omar El Hariri did it all . . . No, no! Omar al-Bashir!"

"Uncle, he failed geography and history, and he certainly failed civics. He doesn't know anything about anything, not even what's under his own nose."

"Okay, but how is he at chemistry?"

While everyone was having another good laugh, Inad the Philosopher, who was sitting on a couch in the back of the café, made the following proclamation: "They planted your body in the sand as a standard . . . Which rouses the Wadi by day and by night."*

Everyone turned in the direction from which this strange statement had issued. Inad wasn't known for his gnomic utterances. His title had been conferred on him for purely ironic purposes.

"Inad, where in the world did you come up with that?"

Inad drew his legs up under himself and said, "What, you never learned that back in middle school? It's from the poem written by Ahmed Shawqi to elegize Omar Mukhtar."

Everyone agreed that Inad was showing hidden depths and was deserving of wide acclaim and a seat in parliament—or else a chance to win the prize on Majid's game-show.

---

* E.E. Evans-Pritchard, "Translation of an Elegy by Ahmad Shauqi Bey on the Occasion of the Execution of Sidi 'Umar al-Mukhtar al-Minifi," *The Arab World* (London), February 1949, p. 2.

Inad thought they were being serious and said, "No, you're quite right! We've left politics to the ignorant: Hakim, Qasim al-Araji, and Ali Aldabbagh!" The thought of Ali Aldabbagh set everyone present into hysterics again.

"Right!" said one of the café wits. "That's the suck-up who goes around saying, 'I'm an expert on the religious clerkship,' but chews gum twenty-four-seven. No! He even combs his hair like Hamid Mansour, with that wave!"

"More like he's an expert on hair gels . . ."

Ah, it was such great fun to gloat over ignorant Hakim and his cronies! But then a local named Shayyal came running up, shouting, "Quiet! Stop! Not another word!"

"What is it? What's happened now?" everyone gasped.

Shayyal took a deep breath and said, "A fatwa was promulgated today by the highest authorities. From here on out, Omar Mukhtar shall be Algerian!"

Ah, and then the laughter broke out yet again, and this time it didn't stop until the predawn Ramadan meal.

OCTOBER 25, 2005

A Perfectly Legitimate Donkey

O Lord, when shall we be free of these asses? And here I'm referring to actual asses, real donkeys. Our city is chock-full of them! I don't think there's a block that doesn't have at least one donkey in it, and that's a significant percentage for the most ancient capital in the world: Baghdad, the center of the civilized world for so many centuries. How could this city allow these asses to roam at will, free and easy, and become such a common means of transportation through its streets?

Our street, in fact, has two donkeys. The first is a gentle, eminently forgettable animal, a donkey who enjoys zero notoriety on our block or with our neighbors. The second one, though, is an ass in every sense of the word, one that boasts of that most ancient lineage, stretching back through history. And, in its nature, this white donkey resembles its owner, Matar, who is married to three women due to the intensity of his sexual desire. Night and day, this donkey puts his "capacities" on display before the eyes of passersby without the least shame, without any consideration for the changes that came after 2003 in the social conditions here in Thawra City, with a rising flood of religiosity and the latest prohibitions on public singing, music, beauty salons, and any clothing so immodest as to provoke our more basic instincts. Matar's donkey couldn't care less about all that; neither does he recognize the authority of those intent on maintaining common decency in the public square, and who have no desire to see him when he is, himself, in an immodest and offensive state.

Aside from his matrimonial and hauling duties, Matar's donkey has another occupation, which is to bray every hour and on the half-hour, as though synchronized to those dubious broadcasts from Al Jazeera. The godly residents of our district are able to distinguish his braying from that of the unprepossessing donkey I mentioned because Matar's donkey's bray is louder and longer, and the end of each phrase takes on a unique musical note.

Recently, one of the many little devils who call our block home decided to have some fun at Matar's expense, telling him, "I just saw four armed men in black surrounding that donkey of yours, with an air of severe disapproval for its, uh, disdain of the sensibilities of our good citizens. Likewise," this trickster went on, "they were saying that this matter would have to be taken up by the Commission on Public Integrity."

Matar was terrified. He began circling his donkey, muttering unintelligibly and gesturing erratically with his hands, completely at a loss over what to do with the scandalous beast. He went into his house and came back with a black plastic bag, which he wrapped around the donkey's genitals, cinching them tight in an attempt to decrease the size of the problem, so to speak. In the morning, however, Matar found that the donkey had somehow freed itself of the bag and so resumed its well-known display.

It was a disaster, without a doubt, a disaster falling on the head of poor Matar, who could not do without his donkey just then. So one of his wives put forward an idea that seemed semi-reasonable at the time: "Write 'for sale' on him," she said. "That way, you'll distance yourself from any moral responsibility."

Matar agreed and painted ASS FOR SALE in big black letters on the creature's right side. Matar's donkey was the only one in the world who couldn't see what was written on its back, and it carried on with its disgraceful natural life.

A couple of days later, an elderly man, accompanied by his two sons, knocked on Matar's door. They immediately began bargaining with Matar for his donkey. As I've explained, however, Matar had no real desire to sell his donkey; it was all just a part of his wife's ploy. Nevertheless, the offer he received was appealing enough that he found himself giving in. After counting up the wad of cash and stuffing it in his pocket, he untied his donkey and handed it over to its new owners—but before they and the donkey went on their way, Matar was unable to restrain his curiosity and had to ask what was behind their paying such a large sum for such a wanton donkey.

The old man, now lawful owner of the beast, cleared his throat and said, "Listen, my son. My previous donkey was stolen right after the fall of the regime, and after an exhausting search, we found it over in Block 33 with Saddam's old nickname, 'Master of Necessity,' painted on it. When we brought it home, we did everything we could to wash those words off its back and restore the donkey to its original condition so it could do its work without provoking resentment from partisans of the deposed president. But all our efforts were in vain! So we finally set the donkey free, but had to buy another one right away because we really need one for our work. After a week, we woke up to find that someone had painted the name of one of our *new* big men on his back! What could we do? We got rid of it immediately, cursing our luck. But now that we've had elections, our government is perfectly legitimate. Under the circumstances, we thought that an ass possessed of your donkey's famous qualities and proclivities might be just the thing. It's young, eternally vigilant, and shows unflagging vigor—what better symbol could there be for our newly elected administration? On top of all that, if someone comes along and paints some official's name on its back, our new politicians will be grateful for the free advertising!"

The Republic of Funerals

Whenever Al Iraqiya cries, Euphrates slaps itself in the face. And when Al Iraqiya slaps its own face, then Euphrates pours mud onto its own head, rends its clothes, and tears out its hair. And when Al Iraqiya is the one doing that—namely, pouring mud on its head, rending its clothes, and tearing out its hair—then you can only imagine what Euphrates gets up to.

The thing is, what we're talking about here are the two new satellite channels that started up around the beginning of our current era of freedom—not about two young wives who've lost their husbands in a terrorist bombing. Channel Euphrates is Iranian—certainly as far as financial backing, programming, and personnel go—so it can abuse itself however it likes. But as for Al Iraqiya, the idea behind founding it was to create a monument to our civilization, a channel by and for the Iraqi public, not the Iraqi government. The not-insignificant amount of money sunk into it was the money of the common people; therefore, the guiding authority of the channel ought to be those same people—via parliament, anyway. That being the case, I feel I have a perfect right to object to Al Iraqiya's follies, since I consider myself to be a member in good standing of Iraq's most common people.

Yet this same station, my dear fellow viewers, transformed Iraq from a country into a funeral, a funeral full of wailing, weeping, and lamenting—as though these were things the Iraqi people needed more of. Switch on Al Iraqiya and your screen will be crowded with more turbans and melancholy beards than at a wake, to the point that Iraq has become, thanks to that channel, one long, unending Karbala massacre. The government has even imposed a curfew, the better to keep us glued to Al Iraqiya, preventing us from going out, not just to sample the night air but to finally move forward, to *go out* in the more profound sense of leaving our current states of being—miserable animals, bloodied by wars and sanctions—to become proper human beings who can live and enjoy their lives like the rest of God's creation. So it's clear that the head of our network either *won't* allow that to happen, or, worse, *can't*. How are we ever supposed to relax if our lives are an endless wake?

Oh, maybe not endless. Sometimes something entertaining does slip through the dirge, probably by mistake, but when it does, oh boy, there's hell to pay. Ali al-Wa'iz, the Baghdad representative for Sistani, our highest religious authority, hits the roof. His office immediately puts in a phone call to the president of the network:

"Hey, Habib al-Sadr, what's all this cheerfulness about? Is there a wedding going on or what? Don't you know that today is a day of mourning for so-and-so?!"

Which means Al Iraqiya immediately throws its black veil back on and begins to wail and slap itself in the face, surrounded by a team of broadcaster-mourners assembled from who knows what unemployment line. (Billy goats, nanny goats, and bleating kids, all of them—may God rot your eyes!)

Woe is us! My God, this has become the most depressive nation in the world. It doesn't even help when you change the channel to one of the commercial networks like Rotana or any of the other stations actually meant for human beings, the dejection follows you. We're like people going to their neighbor's wedding when their own house is in mourning. I can't imagine how the next generation will be shaped by these public displays of sobbing, face slapping, and ritual consolation. What sort of will to live will they have? What will push them to build, to flourish, to seek freedom? God help those who will open their eyes to find their homeland is an eternal funeral! Just like He helped their parents, when they opened their eyes and found their country to be one long battlefront . . .

And what might be the biggest disaster of all is that Sayyid al-Jaafari seems to think that Al Iraqiya ought to be a model for all other media. Now that would be a true catastrophe, even though I doubt such a plan could possibly have originated in the mind of our current prime minister, a rational man and a doctor, who made a home for his family in the United Kingdom for so many years. For that matter, I have to doubt that any of his kids would be caught dead watching that channel, except of course when their dear papa appears on screen to advise the Iraqi people as to how they should spend their day.

A few days ago, the spokesman for the theological seminary in Najaf criticized Al Iraqiya, saying, "Our school is not pleased by all this." He was referring to the national unity conference that was being broadcast live. But where was this spokesman a few months ago, I wonder, when Al Iraqiya broadcast a gathering of fifty Turkish supporters of the Hakim family, live from Istanbul? The conference lasted four whole hours, four hours of propriety and decency, as we were all forced to endure a most valuable sermon by some pipsqueak son of the noble Hakim. Just imagine, my dear friends, how much it must have cost to broadcast live for four hours! This is the news that our money buys?! As though we'd never seen a Turk before, or we were all just bursting with the desire to hear what, in his wisdom, Ammar al-Hakim, that pampered son of Iraq, distinguished from Saddam's son Uday only by the turban on his head, had to say to us.

And, while I'm asking, where's that seminary spokesman when the Badr Brigades hold their own conferences and celebrations after every new round of assassinations carried out in this Iraq of smoke and mirrors and blood?

Al Iraqiya isn't an international channel, that's true—but, as far as I'm concerned, it's not even Iraqi. Mind you, I'm not accusing it of anything shady. I'm just saying that what it broadcasts doesn't concern all Iraqis. It barely concerns all Shiites—not even 10 percent of them, I'd guess. The slapping-your-own-face-and-wailing-all-the-time segment of the audience makes up a tiny minority, yet the screaming always comes out on top.

In one of our poor markets in Thawra, all it took was one old vendor missing her right eye for the place to be dubbed One-Eye Market. Well, now we've got two channels featuring twenty-four-hour masochism, which is more than enough for us to change the name of our country from the Republic of Iraq to the Republic of Funerals, and instead of "Iraq First," let our new slogan be "Funerals First"!

Reader Emails: A Letter from My Brother, Word for Word

Dear Mr. Shalash the Non-Iraqi,

I read the article you wrote under the title of "The Federalism of Thawra City and Its Suburbs," and it didn't take me long to realize that you were poking fun at our tribal sheikhs, our symbols, our customs and traditions, and so on. I'm here to say you have no right to drink the waters of the Tigris and Euphrates. Even the sewer water of the canals is too good for you! You're some kind of a half-wit son of a bitch is all I can think. And so rude! It's clear even your family didn't want to waste time raising you right. Or maybe you never had a proper family. You must have grown up on the street, but to call you a vagrant would be to insult our honest vagrants! If you ever even belonged to a tribe, they must have cast you out long ago. And that's a big if!

How could you possibly mention those licentious Kawliya gypsies alongside our sheikhs and our sayyids unless your mother was one of them. Did she also dance in that debased music video that everyone is talking about these days, the Orange Song? But now I'm starting to wonder if maybe you're actually a Wahhabi terrorist, because you seem to hate everything that's popular and honorable. Or maybe you're a filthy Ba'athist, or a despicable atheist communist—whatever. What matters is that you're obviously a real bastard, as I've already mentioned. And if you don't know the meaning of the word, ask your mother to explain it—if you can find her.

It's not that the nonsense you write doesn't sometimes make me laugh. Sure it does. But so what. That doesn't make you a real writer. Any old son of a whore can make people laugh. Let's be serious. I urge you to leave off writing and look for some honorable way to make a living—if, indeed, you even want to be honorable. But I know the sad truth is that assholes like you don't know the meaning of that word either.

I'm an ordinary guy, okay? I enjoy a cold beer now and again. And sure, I used to get howling drunk with my friends when I was a kid. But even then we kept up our principles. We didn't pick fights and harangue people the way your Abbas the Drunk does. Yes, I laughed when I read about him, but only because of how he insisted on getting drunk out in the street.

I take no joy in sending you this note. It just seemed to me you could use some good advice. Of course you're free to take it or not. Still, what a pity I had to waste so much time to write you. You don't deserve a single word from me or from any honorable people like me, the children of respectable parents.

With God guiding my intent,

FADIL SAWADI
Sadr City

(End of letter)

Brothers and sisters, I've conveyed for you the text of this email from Mr. Fadil Sawadi in the hopes that it might provide some enjoyment . . . But I cannot fail to inform you that Mr. Fadil Sawadi happens to be my eldest sibling. He doesn't know that "Shalash the Iraqi" is the pseudonym adopted by his little brother, the one whom he stayed up late each night to take care of after our father departed to his abode of eternal rest. I testify before you that Fadil never once failed in his obligations to me, and I'm indebted to him for putting me through university. He was responsible, first and last, for my "upbringing."

This is the first I've heard, though, that my brother, Abu al-Abbas, as we call him, has also guzzled cold beer and gotten drunk, even while standing on his principles. And I can't predict what his reaction will be when he realizes his misfortune upon reading my post today. I apologize here and now if I've impugned his character in any way, though I hope that he will appreciate how I've corrected the many spelling mistakes in his message, and I ask that he please be more attentive in future.

OCTOBER 28, 2005

Dreams Can Suddenly Come True

Personally, I love girls with long hair and short skirts, provided that those attributes come as a set. Meaning, I don't like girls with short hair wearing short skirts, or the opposite, long hair and long skirts. And, while I'm on the subject, I positively hate men who wear long beards and short dishdasha robes. Those don't need those to come as a set, though, for me to hate them.

117

Sometimes I like long beards when I see one in a picture of some great genius, while short dishdashas are odious to me when it's clear a person is too poor to afford anything else.

Back in my college days, I would instinctively pursue any long hair I saw fluttering over a short skirt, just as I would instinctively flee from any long beards above short dishdashas. The hypocritical religious campaign inaugurated by our "sixty-ninth caliph," Saddam the Accursed, gradually lengthened skirts and hoisted up dishdashas. Hair gradually disappeared under hijabs, while long beards started coming out from under every rock. Where once our university was a path strewn with roses, now it became one big, stinking garbage dump of facial hair. Then the caliph disappeared into a hole, and, with him, all the short skirts and short dishdashas both vanished for good. I tend to see the former only on TV these days, and the latter I see only in the nightmares that pursue me down every street and through all the restaurants and cafés of our city.

Two nights ago I dreamed I was walking across Jumhuriya Bridge in the company of a young beauty in a short skirt and with crazy hair fluttering over her shoulders. Sadly, all good dreams come to an end, and when I woke in the morning, I headed out toward the East Gate, and from there to the neighborhood of Dora, where I work in a shop. After I'd sold enough for my daily bread, I decided to treat myself to a taxi on the way home because things had "improved a smidge, thanks be to God!" I managed to flag a cab down and, lo and behold, found my dream coming true . . .

That nice dream about the bridge and the girl? Not on your life! It was the other kind of dream. My driver had a long beard and a dishdasha that was so minuscule, so tiny, so truncated, that it could only mean one thing: its owner was an al-Qaeda terrorist who had decided he would break the Ramadan fast in paradise that very day—no doubt about it.

Now, ordinarily, even when I *do* find a cab, it's even money whether the driver will agree to take me as far as Thawra City, but woe upon woe, the driver said yes without hesitation and agreed to go all the way to Thawra City for me. Ah, would that I had the words to tell you what I was going through from the moment I got into that taxi of ill omen!

Trembling, I said to myself, "What a wonderful gift I'm bringing home to the miserable people of Thawra. People who've never gotten anything from the likes of me, unless you count denunciations and sarcastic remarks, sparing neither the great nor the insignificant! And how do I wrap up my career as a lousy neighbor? I bring home a comrade seeking martyrdom. God grant that it happen before we get to the middle of Maridi Market!"

Should I have said, "Please, I've changed my mind. Could you take me to Mansour or Jadriyah instead?" I don't know! Maybe he would have gotten suspicious and blown his car up there and then? And the fact was, I wanted to breathe the air just a little longer. Life is precious, you know. Dear God, why do the wrong dreams always come true? Where's the short skirt? Where the long hair?

The driver (my hand to God!) was muttering to himself all the while. Maybe he was reciting verses pertaining to the moment that comes before one arrives in paradise. He was calm, though—not at all bothered by all the traffic he had to fight his way through. He was also ignoring me, skipping the usual taxi small talk: "Your face is familiar! Where do you work? Aren't you Fadil's brother? Is your house in Sharika or in Gayyara? Are you on your way home or to work?" etc., etc.

When we reached the Karadat Maryam neighborhood, however, my driver turned to me and calmly asked, "God bless you, brother—where did you say you wanted to go again?" The man had forgotten, or he hadn't heard me clearly, or else the subject hadn't much interested him in the first place!

I was saved! I wouldn't be responsible for escorting a suicide bomber into the middle of Thawra City. I had a brilliant idea and said, "I'm going with you, brother!"

"Is that right?"

"I'm with you, my friend—I'm going wherever you're going."

This could only confuse the driver. "Brother, I'm afraid I don't understand. Tell me, do I cross this bridge, with God's blessing, or not?"

"Cross it, dear friend, cross it!"

"Fine. And afterward, which way do we go, God willing?"

"Wherever you like, brother."

"What do you mean, wherever I like?"

"My brother, only you can find the way to paradise, not I."

"Hey, brother—what's wrong with you?"

"Nothing at all, I promise!" I stammered in dismay, already weeping.

My driver was so stymied he didn't know where to turn. Finally he sped his car across Jumhuriya Bridge, ignoring my sobbing pleas. When we reached Tayaran Square, he veered wildly toward the lines of miserable day laborers waiting for work and . . .

Boooom!

The car exploded with a horrific noise, throwing everything up into the air. A brief pause, and then . . . I found myself—in the company of eight construction workers—partaking of a delicious Ramadan meal to the sounds of angelic music in the eternal gardens of calm, quiet, rest, and happiness. Heavenly virgins surrounded us (one wearing a very short skirt), along with birds, angels, roses, and plenty of perpetual bliss. Goodness me, we had made it to paradise after all!

And as we enjoyed ourselves, the flames of hell were shimmering nearby, grilling a new meal of men in short dishdashas and bushy beards, including my driver, that saintly flower of manhood whose fare I never got to pay.

The smell of cooking meat made our mouths water, and we, the martyrs, decided to press deeper into paradise. It transpired that one of the company of workers was from my very own block in Thawra City. He introduced himself, and congratulated me: "Thank you, Shalash!" he said. "This must be the first good thing you've done in your entire life!"

OCTOBER 29, 2005

Salima on Vacation

Salima's life took a 360-degree turn after her husband, Lafta, brought her along on a brief visit, the very first trip of her life, to the tomb of Sayyida Zaynab (peace be upon the noble daughter of Ali!) in Syria. Salima started carrying her passport around in her pocket and taking it out at every possible occasion—and even without an occasion—as a reminder that she had taken this trip. Likewise, she didn't neglect to remind her neighbors day in and day out that she had traveled on an airplane, which, though it had been expensive, was much more comfortable than making the pilgrimage by car. Moreover, she described how the meal served aboard the airplane had been the most delicious, the most delectable, that she had eaten since the sanctions were imposed upon Iraq in the early 1990s.

The journey from Baghdad to Damascus takes no more than an hour, yet the sum total of all Salima's stories about this trip has already exceeded one thousand hours. As everyone now knows, Salima felt very sad for the stewardess who told her she had broken off her engagement to a cousin. She showed deep sympathy, too, toward the woman in the seat behind her, flying to Syria to meet her son, who had lived in the Netherlands for the past ten years and was married to a Kurdish woman who still hadn't borne him any children. She informed everyone that the singer Abd Falak is currently working in Syria, where things are panning out very well for him. "He's in love with a Palestinian woman, and he probably had a secret marriage, you know, without a religious ceremony." (The manager of Abd Falak's band was on the same flight and told her all about it.) As for the Iraqi national basketball team, it had finished its training camp in Latakia, and was soon to return home . . . (Let's stop there. We don't have the space for all her anecdotes.)

Salima doesn't restrict herself to storytelling. She can repeat, on request, or even without request, and word for word, everything the captain of the airplane said during the flight, for example his greetings to the passengers; she can recite for you the number of the flight, the weather conditions en route, and the exact time of takeoff and landing. What's more, I have personally seen Salima, standing in front of a crowd of women, inflating a black plastic bag the better to explain to them the safety procedures that were followed on board the plane, as well as how to use a life jacket. Salima concluded with a verse from the Qur'an: "Glory be to Him who has adapted all this for our use, when we were not sufficient for it!" Verily, God Almighty speaks the truth!

This is what Salima learned on her fifty-five-minute flight between the Abbasid and the Umayyad capitals.

Perhaps one of you will ask, "And what is it that Salima learned in Syria itself, due to residing for more than a week near the tomb of Sayyida Zaynab (peace be upon her!)?" To which I would say, "Nothing! Apart from perfecting the Syrian dialect, and a knowledge of some ancient Syrian customs." For instance, when her neighbor Qisma asked her, "Could you spare a bowl of your Ramadan lentils?" Salima replied, just like a Syrian, "Why, bless your eyes, sister! I'll bring you the very best lentils in the whole wide world."

Qisma was familiar with Syrian dialect from TV, but why would Salima be using it now? She thought Salima must be making some kind of joke. But after handing over the bowl of soup, Salima kept on talking to her neighbor in Syrian Arabic and with an absolutely straight face. "Anything else?" she asked. "Just say the word, and whatever you like is yours, up to and including these two eyes of mine!"

"What's wrong with this woman?" Qisma muttered as she walked off, throwing her free hand in the air.

123

After breakfast, Salima invited her neighbors around to try some Syrian desserts. The women sat down to partake of what had been so generously provided by their dear neighbor Salima, who was telling them about life in Syria, where everything was so inexpensive and wonderful. Here are some of the pearls of Salima's conversation—all utilizing Syrian pronunciations, idioms, and attitudes—that we were able to glean:

"It's true that life there is very nice, but it's a bit crowded."

"Lafta, just give me a minute, dear! Let me finish my coffee."

"What do you mean, was I talking to Lafta, and not someone else? Yes, of course it was Lafta! Who else? Why shouldn't a husband wait hand and foot on his wife?!"

"At the tomb of Sayyida Zaynab, all the pilgrims were rushing and pushing. Some people—am I right?!"

"Of course, the funny thing is, once you get over there, all the women you meet are from Tawra-Shawadir!" (That is to say, from Thawra City—but in Syrian.)

"My own brother's mother-in-law was over there with her sister, doing tourist stuff. We didn't go out of our way to say hi to them. Why bother? They were there for one thing, we were there for quite another."

"Eat, Umm Jawad, eat! This is the best baklava in all of Syria!"

"The Iraqi women I saw there . . . I can't even!"

"God bless Lafta! He treated me like a queen on our trip. Whenever I asked for anything, he said, 'Yes, cousin! Your wish is my command, cousin!' What a wonderful man I've got! How adorable!"

The recipients of Salima's generosity ate the baklava she had brought back from her trip. They licked their fingers and smacked their lips and studied Salima with looks that mixed envy, uncertainty, disdain, jealousy, and mockery, but Salima took no notice. She went right on describing her time in Syria.

Qisma wiped her mouth with her hand after finishing a fairly large piece of ladyfinger baklava. She got ready to go and said to her hostess, Sayyida Salima, wife of Lafta, in her best sarcastic Syrian, "We're real grateful, neighbor! God willing, we haven't put you out!"

Everyone took this as the signal to retreat—though not before they'd picked the tray clean of everything but a few crumbs and scattered Syrian nuts. Salima's neighbors all took their leave and headed to their various homes—but shortly before parting ways, they had a little chat among themselves.

"She thinks she's all that? God, have you ever seen someone with worse manners?"

"All she had to do was cross the Syrian border and she managed to burn the whole place down! Half their ministers committed suicide, and then, on top of that, the Mehlis Report about Rafik al-Hariri's assassination came out last week and didn't look good for them at all."

"What I want to know is what's come over poor Lafta? He used to keep her in line by hitting her with his shoe every morning!"

"Come on, that baklava was local. She got it from the place down the street. Syrian baklava, honestly? Did you see the flies buzzing all over it?"

"Does anyone believe she even got on a plane? She just saw one on TV and imagined the rest!"

"We have to keep this quiet! You know half the people who visit Syria are only there to buy sex. If that's the deal with her mother-in-law, the whole world might as well give up their morals."

"You hear her talk to her husband lately? 'Lafta, ah, you're killing me!' It's worse than a bad teenage romance. The dirty whore! If only the Angel of Death would swoop down to make it true. And let him shovel crossed-eyed Lafta into the grave too while he's at it, I say."

"Salima used to sell her monthly food rations to get by, and now she's a frequent flier? God, remember how she used to be crawling with lice? All those bugs!"

"She's never seen anything or gone anywhere. If I were Lafta, I'd take her to China and not bring her home till she was speaking Japanese."

And with that last comment, delivered by Qisma, Salima's neighbors parted ways, each to her own house, laughing.

OCTOBER 30, 2005

The Scandal of Shalash Google Earth*

My friends, I made the mistake of a lifetime when I invited Khanjar over and told him, "Hey, I can show you what your house looks like from a satellite!"

At first, Khanjar called me a liar, but then his disgusting mouth gaped open as he followed my clicks on the computer. I zoomed in on our block, then our street, and then Khanjar's

---

* Numerous elements of the trial of Shalash found in this post—including a Kurdish judge, objections to the prosecution, and live broadcasts of poor quality—echo the trial of Saddam, which began on October 19, 2005.

house using Google Earth, now that internet restrictions had vanished along with Saddam. Khanjar saw the roof of his house with his own eyes. After he confirmed it was his house and not anyone else's, he asked me to see Chawadir Hospital, both as a test of my powers and in order to give himself a minute to calm his nerves. In my hubris, I guided Khanjar's eyes to the hospital with a dramatic flourish. Khanjar's jaw dropped as far as was humanly possible. His eyes bulged, his ears quivered. He was dumbstruck, the shock etched into his very face.

And what did he take away from this experience, I ask you?

"Shalash is spying on your women!"

That's the gist of what Khanjar conveyed to the masses, thank you very much. And from a linguistic point of view, ladies and gentlemen, let me tell you that "the masses" should be taken here to mean every specimen of *Homo sapiens* residing in Block 41 of Thawra City.

Ma'suma led the first demonstration in front of our house. It was peaceful and civilized in nature. People raised signs that read, DOWN WITH SHALASH GOOGLE EARTH! as though that were my name now. They sang some patriotic songs and anthems, peppered with a few mild insults touching on the history of my noble family from the time we laid our first brick on this street.

The second demonstration, my friends, could also have been called peaceful, were it not for the fact that they burned some tires in front of my house, together with a pile of old, very old shoes, while some of the big, metal cans used for cooking oil were sent flying in every direction.

The third and biggest demonstration was meant to take place after the conclusion of prayers on the last Friday of

Ramadan. The idea was for the protest to coincide with the annual anti-Israel "International Quds Day" and "Death to Sharon" rallies led by Ahmadinejad, the president of Iran. Instead of the usual rhetoric, cries of "Death, Death to Shalash Google Earth!" went up in the crowd, which now included strangers and all sorts of lunatics and that particular sort of misanthrope who finds no greater pleasure in life than getting people worked up and then watching the sparks fly. Razzak al-Shaykh and Salim Manati, our two representatives in the National Assembly, were also present, in addition to video crews from the stations Al Iraqiya and Channel Euphrates, and some correspondents from the local newspapers. Soldiers from the Mahdi Army took it upon themselves to protect the demonstration, while two American helicopters could be seen circling above the site of the incident.

My family's bid to ensure my continued safety amounted to their piling up some loose household goods against the front door; a valiant effort, but all in vain, since the barricade collapsed at the first gentle kick from the first emaciated protester. After that, the crowds pushed their way into every corner of the house of Shalash, and though I did my best to hide myself in our big tanoor bread oven, they plucked me out by my shirt collar, as though I were a well-dressed rat. Meanwhile, a specialist team of looters, who got their training in the days following the fall of Baghdad, seized our computer and all its accessories after discovering it in my mother's room.

On 60th Street, which separates our block from the neighboring one, people from all over town crowded together to attend the public trial convened to punish the archcriminal

Shalash Sawadi. The judge was Kurdish (and came from the Kurdish district, the cleanest corner of Thawra City, where the most beautiful women live); the prosecutor came from the belligerent Al Iziraj tribe; and the defense team was composed of members of the Bahadil tribe, who are famous for being partisans of justice, equality, and human rights and are often called upon to settle disputes.

What follows are some excerpts from the court session in the square—with apologies in advance for any technical difficulties we might experience, seeing as the broadcast comes to us in very poor quality, for reasons as yet unknown.

The prosecutor: "Revered President of the court, the accused appearing before Your Honor is one of the most dangerous of the brazen criminals roaming our land, insofar as it is clear that he is cooperating, by means of a network of satellites, with parties unknown suspected of using advanced technologies to peep and spy upon the women of Block 41—indeed, upon all the women of Thawra City! I am able to assert, following the testimony of the state's witness, Khanjar, that no woman of unblemished reputation, no innocent young girl, no grandmother in her seclusion has yet escaped his zoom lens. His behavior is not only criminal but a violation of the morals of the block—entirely alien to our customs and traditions! As such, it is only appropriate that we levy the highest possible penalty against the perpetrator. Esteemed sir, my heart will not be calm within me, nor will my mind know peace, until I see the skull of this criminal rolling at the feet of this honorable assembly."

At this, jubilant cries rose up from the honorable assembly, while yours truly gulped audibly.

The defense called out, "Objection, Your Honor! The prosecution must restrict his comments to the facts in the case now being heard."

The prosecutor: "Yes, I'll stick to the point, Your Honor, and ask that the technology in question be brought forward to show the court the pictures that the criminal took of the daughters of our block. Here, here is the evidence!" And he waved a hard drive in the air.

The court was thrown into confusion at this and had to apologize for lacking the technical capabilities, despite its enormous budget—which after all amounted to only 138 million dollars—to access the files. As a means of playing past the general embarrassment, the judge called the previously mentioned star witness.

The witness, Khanjar: "Your Honor, I swear by God Almighty that I am telling the truth. Shalash, son of Sawadi al-Maliki, invited me to his house. After I arrived, but before lunch, he told me, 'Hey, Khanjar, you're my dearest friend, I'm going to let you in on a big secret, something I don't want you to spread around.' 'Shalash,' I said to him, 'I'm a tomb!' So we went into his room, where he turned off the lights, took off his pants, and started up his computer. He pulled up an image of the moon, Mars, and Saturn. Then, through a little hole in the ozone layer, he swooped down onto the earth. He skimmed over the frozen North Pole and moved on to Asia, and from there to the Middle East. Then Iraq, then Baghdad, then Thawra City, then our block, then our street, and then he brought the picture into one house after another. With these two eyes of mine—may God strike me blind if I'm lying to you, Your Honor!—I saw Sabiha,

Nazim's wife, asleep and without anything to cover her up! God's forgiveness, Your Honor! And then I saw Sabriya, the wife of Hajim, Nazim's brother, and she was in this kind of position . . . Oh, sir, your pardon, and may God forgive me! Then I saw Radiya, the policeman's wife—both her and her husband, if you see what I mean. I saw her husband all sweaty and panting! Then I saw Sabiha the Threader as she was waxing Bushra, daughter of Sadiq, the generator man. And I saw Rajiha the teacher, daughter of Agab, the realtor. Oh me, oh my, sir!" said Khanjar, covering his eyes. "Rajiha the teacher, her skin's like buffalo cream, Your Honor. What else can I say, sir? Ah, the word 'honey' doesn't do her justice. God, so cute you want to eat her up! I'd give my soul for the ground she walks on! God, her beauty lit up the satellite the way she lights up a room!"

The defense attorney: "Objection, Your Honor! The witness is letting himself get carried away."

The judge, to the witness: "Khanjar, my son, come to the heart of the matter."

Khanjar, the witness: "The heart of the matter, sir? I can't bring myself to say it! It's too shameful! God! I'm so embarrassed, sir. Forgive me, for the heart of the matter is very, very sensitive, if you know what I mean!"

The prosecutor: "Your Honor, I rest my case."

The judge, to the accused: "Mr. Shalash Sawadi, now that you've heard the evidence, how do you plead?"

I gathered my strength and stood, head bowed before the teeming crowds. "Guilty!" I cried in a hoarse voice. "Guilty as charged, Your Honor!"

Hajjiya Tayyara on a Diet

When the satellite channels arrived in the house of hajjiya Tayyara, the wife of Shnayyin, she discovered that the whole world was in one valley, as the saying goes, while she and the oppressed, secluded women of Thawra City were in another. At first she nearly choked to death on her laughter when she saw old nonbelievers with their hair uncovered, in colorful clothing, and "wearing shoes with little wheels on them, rolling through the streets!"

After a time, though, she came to accept what she'd seen, understanding that it was only a form of recreation for elderly foreigners who had too much free time and nothing to do. Tayyara even saw some foreign hajjiyas swimming in the sea. They stripped off their shawls, abayas, and dishdashas and went into the water wearing nothing but their shorts. Tayyara was dumbstruck at first. Then she gradually got used to that too.

Tayyara spent long months in front of the foreign TV stations. Over that time, much of her surprise dissipated, and she began to fathom many things that would once have been impossible to comprehend. For example, while she used to curse the hajjiyas who "left their husband hajji at home and went on walks with filthy animals," she grew accustomed to the idea of owning dogs as pets. She no longer considered the preoccupation of foreign hajjiyas with beer to be anything unusual. On top of that, Tayyara nearly began to recognize the right of unmarried spinsters to find a "boyfriend hajji" and live with him in peace, without the neighbors feeling scandalized.

Tayyara's sense of the world was evolving. She began to laugh at her neighbors and their rudeness among themselves, their disinterest in keeping their houses or their bodies clean, and their disorganization in the monthly rations line. Indeed, she started to resent the fate that had condemned her to live with such backward neighbors as Fadila, Anayba, and Fakhriya, and all the old women of the block who didn't acknowledge anyone else's personal freedoms. More, she was openly critical of their flabby bodies, for her neighbors never dieted, nor did they pay any attention when they gained weight. "They just stuff themselves without a second thought!"

Day by day, Tayyara began to withdraw from her "backward social environment," as she termed it, and started to concern herself with looking younger than her actual age. She also began paying greater attention to the condition of hajji Shnayyin, her husband and lifelong companion. She bought him an electric razor. She exchanged his traditional dishdasha for striped pajamas, and she accustomed him to wearing a broad-brimmed hat instead of a *shatfa*, his traditional *iqal* with the knots in the cord. She started going for evening walks with him down the main street, hand in hand and eating popcorn, trailed by their beloved cat, Ja'aywa, and the amazed comments of everyone they passed.

The more Tayyara came to rely on her international TV stations, the more her behavior, clothing, and manner of speech transformed. The other hajjiyas, particularly those who had been Tayyara's friends, became inured to her eccentricities over time ("just a mixed-up cat lady"), until they became largely indifferent to them. The criticisms that had been directed her way at the start of her journey—such as, "She's out of her mind," and "That cat of hers is so raggedy it looks like a jinn," and so on—became less pointed. And the farther-flung residents of the block decided not to worry themselves with Tayyara's behavior. After all, they had plenty of other things on their minds.

But look, between ourselves, I happen to think hajjiya Tayyara has taken it all too far. She's not content with making a few simple changes in her life. Just this morning, she marched outside with a new innovation in mind—and a particularly grave one at that.

There she was in athletic attire—shorts, T-shirt, and running shoes—with two small gray braids in her hair. She set off at a quick pace from her house in the direction of Chawadir Street. Immediately, and without any hesitation, all the young children of the block set off behind her, amid an unprecedented amount of noise, commotion, and chanting.

Tayyara had decided to embark upon a weight-loss program, starting today, and she would stick to it come hell or high water. But she hadn't declared it to the whole block, and no one could understand what had gotten into her. Now she's in a real pickle, since once she jogged a good enough distance from her house, the crowds running along in her wake made it impossible for her to get back home again. Every time she tried to turn around, there was her entourage of children, accompanied by hordes of beggars, vendors, busybodies, and of course the professional chanters ready to seize upon the opportunity to try out any of the new, democratic activities guaranteed to them by our constitution.

The distance from the intersection of Gayyara Street to Square 55 isn't at all inconsequential, especially for a hajjiya of a certain age—for hadn't Tayyara been among the first residents of Thawra City to welcome our prime minister, Abd al-Karim Qasim, with her applause when he came to the city a few months before his assassination in 1963? Weren't the words the doomed leader had spoken to her that day enshrined for all time in her memory? Namely, "Well, hajjiya, how's it going?"

Anyway, hajjiya Tayyara began circling around Square 55, with her faithful assembly chanting along behind her. She went around once, twice, three times. Then she took everyone by surprise by flying off toward Fellah Street. The crowd behind her only increased in number, however. There was no turning back.

In the end, hajjiya Tayyara only found out that she had fainted when she woke up, stretched out on her back in the middle of Muzafar Square. A great assembly of photographers and reporters surrounded her, along with representatives of various civil organizations and committees on human rights (women's division). Her husband, hajji Shnayyin, was there too, and everyone was waiting for Tayyara's epic explanation of her jogging procession and all the parties participating in it.

Coming out of her swoon, hajjiya Tayyara stared at the crowd and recognized her husband. She gave him a gentle smile, made an effort to whisper his name, and repeated the English phrase from one of her shows, "I love you!"

Then Tayyara closed her eyes and fell into a delicious slumber, from which she still hasn't woken up.

Khanjar, Minister of the Environment, and the Development Plan

I surprised Khanjar as he was taking apart his RPG-7 to put in a box and bury in a hole inside his house. Khanjar took my sudden appearance in stride and asked me to help. As is my wont, of course I lent a hand to my neighbor. When we finished the operation, Khanjar smoothed out the dirt with his feet and then turned to read my expression. Before he could explain, I asked, "Khanjar, why did you bury your weapon? Didn't you use to call it your honor? What, have you buried your honor?"

"Brother Shalash, we're now at peace, so we'll put weapons aside for a while."

"We're at peace? Who says? Have you driven out the occupation single-handed?"

"No, but our Sayyid Leader has decided to participate in 'practical politics,' and, after all, we're going to be represented in the government."

"A government under occupation, Khanjar? What about all the slogans, the chanting, the cutting, and the flagellation?"

"Who cares about the occupation, brother? We're not against the occupation. We're against a government operating as *agents* of the occupation."

"I'll take your word for that, but didn't you also use to say that participation in government was haram? That it means usurping the authority of the Mahdi (peace be upon him!), and that we must pave the way for his appearance (may God hasten his arrival!)?"

"That's true! But the Mahdi (God hasten his arrival!) seems to have things on hold for the time being. It's been a thousand years, and we've been shouting, cutting ourselves, paving the way, all without any result. Who can figure it?"

"Meaning, you're going to participate in the elections?"

"Yeah! And we've made an alliance with the Hakim organization. Where've you been? Sleeping?"

"Something like that—but isn't Sadr part of the 'speaking *hawza*,' while Hakim represents the 'silent *hawza*'? They have entirely different views about the political activity of the theologians."

"Yes! Muqtada has agreed with them that they should keep quiet and shut up. Not a peep! Only we do the speaking."

"Well done!"

"Indeed, brother. We'll participate in the elections, and we'll take over the government. That's the best way forward."

"Okay! But what about the people who have died and been detained, and the widows and orphans? Where are you going to put them all?"

"The martyrs will go to paradise, and God will give the detained the best of rewards the blessed could hope for: fancy cars from Japan. As for the widows and orphans, well, we'll take care of them ourselves by finding an out-of-the-way spot like Tuwayrij to build them housing complexes. Well, I can see you've got more clever questions for me. Spit it out! You're killing me here!"

"They get paradise, Tuwayrij, and some cars, and you get the political positions and the loot?"

137

"That's life, brother! Were it not for their sacrifice, no one would have bought us for a penny. And actually, we never even got the penny! With God as my witness, even Haeri has withdrawn his support. It's been a year, and he hasn't given us a thing, crying in the face of God that he's a pauper. God only knows where they put the fifth they collect from the people."

"Fine. And what happens if the Mahdi (peace be upon him!) shows up while you're sucking down a meal of *tashreeb* in the Green Zone?"

"Why, we'll pave the way in the Green Zone for him to begin his reign of justice, with a state founded upon integrity and faith."

"Right. But what about you, Khanjar: What are you personally going to get?"

"I'm going to be appointed minister of the environment. Yes! By the soul of my father, minister of the environment and developmental appropriation. Yesterday, we sat down and distributed the ministries equally. We'll buy new suits, ties, and shoes. And next week, we'll finally have enough money to get married."

"What about the poor, who fought with you and were misled by your slogans? You've set them back a thousand years with all this chaos."

"What more do they want? We're going to increase their monthly rations, pave their streets, and pick up their garbage. And God will give them the best of rewards, for they have kept the faith!"

"But Khanjar, I've heard Sadr say a thousand times that we're not to seek high stations."

"You're an ass, man! Our Sayyid Leader just meant that we

shouldn't seek to get high off our stations. You really want us to leave the government to the Badr Legion and people like Chalabi, Pachachi, al-Araji, al-Gubbanchi, al-Majbarchi, and every other fish the Tigris coughs up?"

"Fine, Khanjar. But suppose you don't win the election."

"What the hell does that mean?"

"Just suppose."

"You're crazy, man. If any fool steps up who won't vote for the Mahdi Army (God hasten his arrival!), we'll burn it all down!"

"Come to think of it, I'm not going to vote for you either."

"You're an atheist communist and a loser, and, God willing, your end is nigh! We're even going to nab the two seats Thawra City already has in the Assembly. Any other objections?"

"I really think this is also the end for you. You aren't going to get the votes you're expecting. The people have seen only disaster from you and your people. Those who have been deceived will discover your true intention, which is to buy up cheap positions with their costly blood."

"If we don't win, don't think life will get any easier for you. We'll dig up our weapons and make the streets safe for the Mahdi! (God hasten his arrival!)"

"And the rest of us just go on being pawns in your game?"

"Listen, Shalash, you're taking this too far, and I've put up with you long enough! When push comes to shove, I won't even recognize my own father. You're a friend, a neighbor? Big deal. I've killed my own cousin and then attended his funeral."

"Nice. But what will you tell all those poor people in the sermon this Friday?"

139

"We'll tell them to vote for the party of this world and the next, the party of flagellation and laceration, the party of water and electricity, the party of the Hidden Imam: God hasten his revelation, curse his enemies, and render his children victorious!"

"Which children do you mean? Our guy in the Assembly, Razzak al-Shaykh?"

Khanjar let out a deep belly laugh and said, "Why are you holding onto that poor guy so tight? Let the people do their thing, man. Don't get jealous! You know the envious get a plank in their eye. And now, you old drunk, isn't it enough that we've kept quiet till now about all your shameful deeds?"

I left Khanjar and exited the house. I walked down the miserable streets of the city with all its slain. I looked upon sadness, despair, and destruction, and I raised my face to the sky to scream at the top of my lungs, "God! Do you see the injustice and oppression that fills Thawra? For the sake of your chosen Prophet, and for the pure members of his household, hasten the appearance of your faithful Mahdi!"

NOVEMBER 4, 2005

Salima, Off to Australia under
God's Protection and Care

Salima is going to Australia to marry her cousin, Irhayam, who has Australian citizenship. On this historic occasion, dear to all our hearts, Umm Salima threw a farewell party in her house for her daughter. She invited her female neighbors, who kept themselves busy wiping away Umm Salima's tears over her daughter's marriage and her upcoming journey to the land of kangaroos.

Rasmiya, Salima's aunt on her mother's side, is another world-class satellite-channel addict. She's always looking for music videos by Haifa Wehbe, in part because it's an excuse to tell everyone she was just as gorgeous when she was young. This aunt sat down with her sister's daughter and began offering one piece of advice after another. The first thing she said was that Salima should change her *look*, using the English word she'd learned, by which she meant Salima's fixing her face to make it *moh-doorn*. So she cut off Salima's pigtails and dragged her to the house of Sabiha the Threader for her to do whatever she could do with a thick layer of homemade wax.

When Rasmiya brought Salima back home, she started tattooing the body of the poor girl with pictures and words, both foreign and Arabic. "This is so that Irhayam won't say, 'Who's this ignorant, backward girl they've sent me?!' I'll make you into a human being!" Echoing Wehbe's sexy butterfly tattoo, she drew a black scorpion on Salima's right shoulder; she suggestively inscribed Wehbe's lyric, "A million times, yes!" on Salima's stomach; and somewhere else, she added the most famous line by Abd Falak.

After Rasmiya had finished with this noble task, this loving aunt taught Salima some lessons specific to married life. These ranged from procuring a sixty-watt red bulb to light up her room every day at 9 p.m., local Australian time, to the names of various kinds of bedsheets that were especially soft, to the right sorts of nightgown and incense, and which varieties of baklava must be offered as a crucial before-bed meal. Aunt Rasmiya finished her lessons by presenting Salima with a piece of paper that she had carefully wrapped and tied inside a piece of cloth; the bride was told to put it under her pillow to ward off any Australian jinn or devils.

Then came the turn of Salima's paternal aunt. This aunt advised Salima to submit to her husband and obey his commands, not to raise her voice in his presence, and not to go to the markets or to the local clinic or to visit the neighbors without letting him know first. She also advised her on cleanliness and told her to sweep her front door every day, to spread all the household rugs and blankets on the roof each day ("From the moment the sun rises!"), to be a "clever wife" who would set about baking and cooking from the first light of dawn, to not be picky with her food but rather eat what God had decreed, and to share with her husband in both the sweet and the bitter.

And then, further to the words of these two wise counselors, I can record that the following additional advice was provided by the bride-to-be's dear neighbors:

"My girl, foreigners don't like backbiting and slander and spreading rumors, so take care not to gossip about anyone in front of them."

"Australian women have eyes that kill! Watch out for envy, and each day recite prayers against it before you go to sleep."

"The reputation of foreign women is only so-so. Don't mix too much with them. Who knows whether they might lead you down the wrong path?"

"Don't kiss men on the cheeks like they do on TV. That kind of thing doesn't suit us at all."

"Keep a close eye on your husband. You know what they say about Australian women being home-wreckers!"

"If they say *guud morneeng*, that means *sabah al-khayr*. And if they say *guud eefneeng*, that means *masaa' al-khayr*."

"If they offer you liquor or beer, you can say *thank-yoo berry mach*, but then insist you have a sore throat and pass."

"Don't pick fights with your man. You know plane tickets are way too expensive for a time-out at home with your mother."

"Take along some cassettes of our belly-dancing music so that you'll remember Thawra City."

"If they offer you a Pepsi, don't guzzle it down as though you've never seen one before. Leave a little in the bottle."

"Don't dump your trash in a vacant lot. They'll call the police on you right away."

"If they ask whether you're Shiite or Sunni, tell them we're all Muslims and there's really no difference."

"If Irhayam divorces you, just tell everyone that he's a terrorist and you'll have nothing to worry about. They'll skin him in your honor and bring the bastard's hide to the tannery."

"If someone winks at you, don't tell Irhayam about it, just make out like you didn't see it. Otherwise they might start fighting."

"Don't spit on the ground. That's a fine of two hundred dollars."

Salima listened quietly to this valuable guidance. Then she took her leave to go to bed. The neighbors weren't at all pleased with her abrupt departure, particularly as this was the last time they would be seeing her—her plane left the

143

next morning. They all left in a huff and convened a council in the middle of the street, in which the following was said:

"God! If Salima is this headstrong over there and embarrasses us all, I won't be happy."

"What makes you think a new country will make her behave any differently? She'll stand at the door and wave at everyone coming and going."

"Couldn't this Irhayam have found someone else? If he'd asked me, I could have warned him off with a list of all her shortcomings."

"God! These are the looks worthy of Australia? Why are we sending Salima Big Lips? They need more kangaroos?".

"Well, what about Irhayam? They say that even in Australia he looks old and his teeth are falling out. His face is always red, and he still sells gas from a cart!"

"If Salima doesn't slip away with some blond Australian guy—'Ooh, come, take me away, daddy!'—I'll change my name."

"I hope to God they turn her back at the border for being a gypsy whore."

"I hope an IED blows her up on the way down there."

"No, there's no point hoping things will go wrong for her. That bitch has the luck of a . . ."

Good Morning, Baghdad!

No question about it, winter is the most beautiful of the seasons. Not spring, not fall, certainly not ridiculous summer.

The air today is out of this world! Oh, the delicious sting of the cold with a magnificent morning breaking forth! My God, winter in Baghdad! Oh, the mornings in Baghdad! So it's off to Bab Al-Moatham with you, Shalash! Whenever winter closes me in, there's nothing for it but Bab Al-Moatham, the tea of Bab Al-Moatham, the commotion of Bab Al-Moatham, and all the beauty of Bab Al-Moatham. During the winters in Bab Al-Moatham, Fairuz's songs sound even more angelic, and the rains make you think the very sky is dancing at a wedding.

"What is the meaning of this, Shalash? How has Bab Al-Moatham become so beautiful? What about its dirty ditches, its old cars, the honking horns and the yelling drivers, and all the beggars, burglars, and thieves?"

Don't be so hasty, my brothers! Why must you see only the negative? Have a seat and let me tell you a story in which things work out well for a change.

Bab Al-Moatham is home to a large university campus, which is where you'll find the College of Languages. Within that college is a Spanish department, and at the Spanish department is my girlfriend. The other day, when my girlfriend finished her classes, she walked to the bus stop, where we like to meet. As soon as we meet, of course, she always begins by saying, "I'm really in a hurry," and "My dad's expecting me," and "Mom said don't be late." But was that going to work on Shalash? No way, man, certainly not!

So, a little later, we found ourselves strolling through the neighborhood of Wazireya, where we lost ourselves in our usual loving sweet nothings. There were the traditional ones, such as "Yesterday I couldn't sleep for thinking of you," and "The Eid brought me no joy because I didn't see you," as well

145

as song lyrics, like "Teach me to love you," and "Give me more love," and "God, I die from missing you!" That went on for a quarter of an hour, at which point Mr. Shalash and his sweetheart made it to the Green Café.

The problem, ladies and gentlemen, is that it was only there, at the very door of that august establishment, that your narrator remembered that lunch was completely out of the question. Your beloved brother Shalash is flat broke; he's even out of minutes on his cell phone. I was afraid we would sit down and then suddenly the chick would be ordering a fruit cocktail, or she'd say, "I'm starving—how about a sandwich?" And then, man, we'd be finished! Not that it would be the first time such a thing happened at the Green Café, but what a disgrace, right after Eid al-Fitr, to say, "Put it on my tab." "For shame, Shalash!" they'd say. "Who does a thing like this? I swear, you bring dishonor to us all!"

We sat in a corner, the same corner where it all began. Love, torment, anguish; the late nights, "barred from sleep," as the Fairuz song puts it. Separation, distance, and "No, no! Don't sigh!" as Kadim Al Sahir expresses the pain of impossible love. And then the social differences: she's from the fanciest neighborhood in Mansour, and Shalash is from across the city and a different world in Thawra. She's a Sunni, while Shalash is a Shiite. During the monarchy, her uncle was a vizier, and Shalash's uncle was a corporal. Her mother is a doctor with the Red Crescent, while Shalash's mother was cooking fasolia beans today. There's no end to the obstacles!

"Fine! So what's the solution?"

"The solution is already in your hands."

"So what do I do?"

"Move out of Thawra."

"Move out of Thawra? And go where?"

"Mansour, Harthiya, Jadriyah . . . even Saidiya. It doesn't matter."

"Man, Mansour is expensive, Harthiya is more expensive, and as for Jadriyah, Sayyid Hakim's already stolen the entire neighborhood! How about you move to Thawra City?"

"I don't know, Shalash. Even if my mother agreed, I couldn't live in Thawra City. Oh, my love, my life! How can you stand it?"

"Come on, what's wrong with Thawra? Have you even seen it? They're going to pave the streets and plant sesbania trees and everything!"

"No, my dear Shalash. Please don't be upset with me. Thawra is just unbearable."

"What do you mean, unbearable? Aren't there plenty of people living there comfortably right now, crawling all over the place twenty-four hours a day?"

"No, Shalash. Please, that's enough!"

Enough indeed, my friends. Can you imagine the state she left me in? My confusion, my bashfulness, my hopeless gestures—as I sat there, praying with all my heart that maybe a friend would come and order us a coffee, juice, or tea? I was about to die from the humiliation. Dear Lord, if only you had sent me a friend! And yet, to show that I would neither weaken nor grieve before You, to show that I was a true man of faith, I left my fate in Your hands, O God, and asked her:

"Sweetheart, would you like anything?"

"No, thank you, Shalushi, my life! I'm fasting."

"What do you mean, fasting?"

"You know, fasting-fasting! What's wrong with you?"

"Wait, is Ramadan still going on over in Mamoun? With us in Thawra, even the Grand Eid is over and done!"

"No, Shalash. I'm fasting for the six days of Shawwal."

"The six days of Shawwal? Is that related to International Workers' Day?"

Ah, my Lord, You came through for me after all! Everything worked out, and it didn't matter that I had no clue about why she was fasting! But really, fasting brings out her best qualities. She's the most beautiful person in the world when she's not eating, let me tell you. I'm always saying—not that anyone listens!—that the advantages of fasting are simply without number.

Anyhow, feeling relaxed now, I got up, paid the very reasonable bill for one tea, and we left.

I brought my sweetheart to the bus stop, and she caught one going to Mansour. I got my shoes shined and went back to doing nothing much, dreaming of other mornings, the kinds that might actually exist in some other city: mornings of love, happiness, and leisurely strolls, cool mornings, and safe streets.

NOVEMBER 11, 2005

The Widening Political Divide between Hasuna and Nadima

The heretofore mild differences of opinion fostered by two of my neighbors—Hasuna, the wife of Atwan, and Nadima, the wife of Challub—were exacerbated to a dangerous level recently when Nadima announced her absolute support for Mr. Ahmed Chalabi, one of the Iraqi exiles who returned to run the country after Saddam was deposed, for no other reason than how close his name was to her husband's. Thereupon, Hasuna swore that she would never vote for anyone other than Mr. Ayyad Allawi, another such exile. This despite the fact that the two women had never argued about politics before in their lives—only over some minor enthusiasm like football. In fact, the conflict began as a musical one.

It started when Hasuna decided to adopt the singer Salah Al Bahar as her favorite. At the time, Nadima was known to be addicted, on the other hand, to Hatem Al-Iraqi. His song "O You Who Have Abandoned Me" could be heard playing from every corner of Nadima's house, day and night. Soon, Salah Al Bahar's song, "When and Where Do You Want Me?" was playing on repeat from Hasuna's relatively new tape player. And I should mention too that, by some coincidence, all four of them—the two singers and the two neighbors—came from the same block in Thawra City.

Now Salah Al Bahar drove a Chevy Celebrity, which was why Hasuna developed a passion for that same make. Soon a lust for Oldsmobiles took possession of Nadima, since Hatem Al-Iraqi was the first to introduce one to the block. Next, Hasuna announced her unwavering allegiance to the historical Bahar family, which of course had produced the inimitable Salah; while Nadima considered the Mashhut family to be superior, indeed the finest in the block, because it had produced Iraq's own "dark-skinned nightingale," Hatem Al-Iraqi. This liking extended to Nadima's cheering for the Shurta soccer team since it was Hatem's favorite club. Meanwhile, Hasuna rooted blindly for Talaba FC, the favorite of Salah Al Bahar.

This neighborly feud gradually expanded to include matters that the women themselves didn't care about. For instance, Hasuna's daughter liked to cut out magazine pictures of yet another famous singer, Nancy Ajram, and then paste them to the walls of her room; while Nadima's daughter never came across a photo of Haifa Wehbe that she failed to glue to the covers of her books and notebooks. The fundamental disagreement between the two women kept expanding until it found expression in support for rival politicians.

From there, the breach widened until it came to threaten the block itself. Hasuna began to give vocal support to the American Central Intelligence Agency, of all things, on account of its backing Allawi; while Nadima favored the Department of Defense on account of its backing Chalabi. Now, it's well known that when the CIA and the Pentagon disagree on some matter of international significance, it tends to result in a major catastrophe—at least for the poor people on the ground. So who knows what might happen to our block—on our very street! in just two poor houses on our very street!—if it should be chosen as the ground on which this departmental squabble gets worked out?

See how quickly this story got from silly to deadly? In recent days, my poor neighbors have reported observing certain nighttime delegations approaching the houses of the two women in turn. First a delegation of suspicious foreign types in hats, long coats, and dark sunglasses came to knock on Hasuna's door, after all the entrances and exits to the street had been blocked off by armored cars with tinted windows; and then, as soon as they finished their mission and departed, some four-star generals and marines knocked at Nadima's, escorted by flocks of Humvees and Hummers on the road and circling helicopters in the sky above.

So now it seems that conflicts that couldn't be resolved inside the White House will be sorted out on our street. The warning bells are ringing loud and clear for anyone with ears to hear. Perhaps we ought to be grateful for this increased attention, but it seems to me we risk more than we gain. Rumors are even circulating that Condoleezza Rice and Donald Rumsfeld have made secret visits to the two families under cover of night. And these neighbors of ours once known for their modesty, their amiability, and their affection for this or that pop star, have been seen acting strangely. For example, Mr. Challub, Nadima's husband, has begun wearing dark sunglasses with antennae sticking out of them, while Mr. Atwan goes around in a uniform fit for General Abizaid. When one is out walking, you can bet the other is out too—each on a different side of the street and walking in the opposite direction.

All the houses to the right of the Challub place have now been covered with pictures of Chalabi, beaming his famous smile. Meanwhile, the houses on the far side of the Atwan place have all been decorated with pictures of Allawi, his childlike eyes supervising the movements of us passersby. As for the other side of the street, the houses there were still hung with pictures of the turbaned and bearded Sayyid Muqtada al-Sadr and Sayyid Abdul Aziz al-Hakim. So our whole street is a staring contest between two black turbans and two balding heads, blessed by the US government if not by God.

Of course, each turban has its partisans, as does each hairless pate. And just as the two balding heads are the protégés of the CIA and the Pentagon, respectively, one turban is guarded by the Mahdi Army, the other by the Badr Brigades, and both by the intelligence agencies of the neighboring countries. As if things weren't tense enough, now the common folk passing by have to keep their heads down to avoid giving the slightest appearance of allegiance to one poster over another.

Hasuna put loudspeakers on the roof of her house, and she kept a one-hit wonder from Egypt blaring out the lyrics, "Mama Naima . . . Yes, my dear? . . . Let Allawiye call me." Hasuna found the "Allawiye" of the song, my friends, to be a convenient way to promote Mr. Allawi at full volume, and everyone got the message. Nadima hastened to follow suit when she found an old Iraqi folk song with the heartwarming line, "Rain from Aleppo, fall upon the daughters of Chalabi."

On the other side of the street, a different kind of singing arose. Chanting, to be precise. On one house there were loudspeakers ringing out the phrase, "All the people are with you, Sayyid Ali!" (referring to Sayyid Ali al-Sistani, on whose electoral coattails the followers of Sayyid al-Hakim liked to ride). On the other were loudspeakers blaring, "Terrified are the enemies of the Sayyid!" (referring to Sayyid Muqtada al-Sadr, who considers everyone to be his enemies).

Last Friday, four platforms were erected in the street. Behind the podiums stood four spokesmen: Mr. Entifadh Qanbar, the spokesman for Chalabi; Mr. Rasim al-Awadi, the spokesman for Allawi; Sayyid Sadr al-Din al-Qabbanchi, the spokesman for Sayyid al-Hakim; and Abdul-Hadi al-Daraji, the spokesman for Sayyid al-Sadr. The cries of the spokesmen rose up and mixed with the sounds of the songs and the shouting of the supporters—who were openly bearing different kinds of weapons—amid a conspicuous absence of ordinary people, who all kept to their houses out of fear and only ventured out when they heard the clanging of the gas-seller's cart, drawn by its two donkeys. As soon as the clanging came, out the people rushed, men and women, young and old, raising their voices in chorus to sing out their true allegiance: "Our souls and our blood, we lay down our lives for you, Mr. Gas-Man!"

In the Taxi Van on the Chawadir—Bab Al-Moatham Route

(*Scene: Just after making it through a checkpoint.*)

An elderly man sitting in the front passenger seat: My God! What the hell is this? All these checkpoints and they're pointless! God, they're killing us! When will we ever get a break?

The driver: Checkpoints? You must be joking. They're all robbers, just busy stealing.

An old woman: My son, please hold your tongue. They're our children. What more can they do, standing in the jaws of death?

Another old man: Man, America is truly the mother of all misfortune. They can't capture Zarqawi and set us free already? Really?

A woman in her forties: Solagh is going to get them, every last one!

The old man: Yeah, right! In your dreams!

A young man sitting behind the driver: If Solagh were really that good, he would have kept his sister from being kidnapped!

The old man: Whenever I see Solagh and that other guy on TV, I just say, look out, here come the lies! "We've killed, we've arrested, we've put in place a new security plan, we're going to do this, we're going to do that . . ." But nothing ever happens!

The old woman sitting closest to the sliding door: But tell me, children, isn't Solagh the son of Badriya al-Khanna from Block 33?

Everyone: (*laughter*)

The first old woman: No way, not at all! That Badriya had a husband—may he rest in peace—and his name was Solagh too. But her Solagh had something of the light of Muhammad in him, not like this other guy, the ugly one.

The fortyish woman: Quite right, auntie! It all depends which Badriya we're talking about, no? *This* Solagh came from Iran. And yeah, you can't forget his face once you've seen it—God must have turned it upside down. His name's Bayan Jabr al-Zubeidi.

The old man: No, his name is Baqir Jabr Solagh.

Someone calling from the back: No, hajji! His name is Baqir Jabr al-Zubeidi.

The first young man: No! It's Bayan Jabr Solagh.

The driver: He has two names, but don't ask me why! Pass up your fares, brothers and sisters!

The old man: I swear, I wouldn't make Solagh a police officer, much less Minister of the Interior. Was there ever a picture less suited to its frame?

The first young man: It's no big deal. What's one more ugly politician like Solagh? At least he's better than the Minister of Health. I wouldn't even let him clean the instruments! He looks worse than that singer, Ali Al-Issawi!

A young man sitting in back: What's wrong with the Minister of Health? What have you got against him? Because he's a Sadrist?

The first young man: What the hell, man. When did you hear me bring up the Sadrist movement?

The second young man: Yeah, you better watch yourself. Don't go bad-mouthing people if you don't have the guts to stand your ground. You think things are so bad? Go get yourself a proper haircut before opening your mouth to criticize.

The first young man: Stop the van! I'm getting off! (*He exits the vehicle.*)

The elderly man: He ran away, the poor boy! Oh, what a coward. And here I thought he was a real man.

The elderly woman: What did he say? (*To the second young man.*) You were the one who went and brought Sadr into the conversation. He didn't say a thing, and you just chewed him up and spat him out!

The driver: Pass up your fares, brothers and sisters!

The second young man: No, no, all these punks go around slandering the Sadrist movement, even if they're subtle about it. They better watch themselves and just shut up. That guy with the faded side cut and floppy hair on top—he was just showing off, cockier than a rooster!

The elderly man: There's nothing wrong with that, my boy. All of you are going to wind up in the government. So you'll have to learn to put up with people's talk.

The young man: Hey, mister, you look like you might be one of those people slandering the movement too. Who told you Muqtada al-Sadr was going to be in the government anyhow?

The elderly man: Getting off, uncle! I'm getting off! Fuck this! (*He exits the vehicle.*)

The elderly woman: Now the old man beat it too! He was saying this and that, and then suddenly he can't handle the heat. It looks like the van'll be empty by the time we get to the water tanks.

The young man: Hey, ma'am, are you making fun of me? For shame, auntie! You being an old woman and all!

The elderly woman: Getting off, my son! Stop here! Oh, what a mess! (*She exits the vehicle.*)

The driver: Hey, you! Instead of running your mouth, how about you just help gather the fare for me?

The young man: I'm not sitting up front, little man, so it's not my job! Get it? If you're not careful, I'll have them revoke your license.

The driver: God save me! How will we get out of this? Hey kid, what's the matter with you? What did you eat this morning?

A young woman, silent up to this point: Brothers, for the sake of the Prophet, please take it easy! What's wrong with everyone? You're just riling each other up for no reason. Have you no fear of the Lord's righteous anger?

The young man: God's wrath upon you and your parents! First get a headscarf over those bangs, and then you can philosophize to us!

The young woman: Getting off, please! Thanks so much, getting off! Oh, dear God. (*She exits the vehicle.*)

The driver to the young man: Hey, listen! You've gone too far! What makes you think you can push me around like this? I'll have you know I've sworn this very van to Muqtada al-Sadr's service, and every Friday I use it to take people down to Kufa for the prayers without charging a thing!

The young man: Getting off, sir, getting off! (*He exits the vehicle.*)

The driver: The fare, brothers and sisters! The fare!

NOVEMBER 13, 2005

Nana'a Adopts an American Soldier

Hajjiya Nana'a evacuated an American soldier who was injured in front of her house during the battles for Thawra City that took place between the Mahdi Army and the American forces in the summer of 2004. Because this Mr. Martin Edwards lost consciousness while he was being carried off the field—right after an explosion set his Humvee on fire—he only realized that he was in the house of this noble hajjiya much later, a full two months after his grievous injury. In the end, he only regained consciousness at all thanks to the efforts of hajjiya Nana'a and all the nights she stayed up to provide him with continual care.

For the entire time he was in the bosom of this hajjiya, Martin felt a kind of love, a tender mothering that he had been missing ever since he was five years old, when his parents in America separated because his mother left his father to marry her lover. This form of tenderness, for which our Iraqi mothers and grandmothers are so well known, filled him with reassurance and tranquility. And so his soul clung to hajjiya Nana'a, and his eyes would follow the steps of his *habuba*—the southern Iraqi dialect word for "grandmother" that she taught him—wherever she moved throughout the small house. (No matter that he couldn't quite master the throaty Arabic *haa*.)

Martin—or Abd al-Rida, as the hajjiya called him—became more precious to Nana'a than her very soul. In her eyes, he was a gift from heaven, God's way of compensating her for her son Radi, one of the millions who had been lost in the Iraq–Iran War, especially now that she was all alone after the passing of her husband, Dawway.

In response to this deep tenderness and mothering, Martin—or Abd al-Rida—adapted himself to a reasonably hard life. True, he had lost his all-time favorite breakfast of corn flakes, but in exchange he got a special meal of puffed bread with buffalo cream and honey on the first of the month, when Habuba received her pension—even if the meals over the rest of the month were necessarily poor. His digestion acted up at first, but then he got used to our cuisine. And it's true he also suffered a bit from using the Eastern-style toilet, sleeping on the floor, surviving the frequent power outages during the blazing summer, and so on.

Hajjiya Nana'a hid her American boy from the eyes of her neighbors, keeping the matter a secret until the "police bitch"—that is, Nuwayra, wife of Ghurab—learned about it. She was famous for uncovering the circumstances surrounding any potentially serious situation in a matter of minutes . . . and for knowing her neighbors' secrets better than they did themselves.

"Hajjiya Nana'a, this is so dangerous—for you and for all of us! It's a tragedy in the making! How can you be hiding an American infidel in your house? I swear, if they knew about this, they'd make a sieve out of your house with their bullets."

"My daughter Nuwayra, what else can I do? Please, protect my secret, and may God protect all of yours!"

"How'd you get into this mess? If you were still a teen-age girl, we would have said you were right to do it: he's a beautiful boy and you fell in love with him. But you're just a worn-out sock! How could you do such an awful thing?"

"May God forgive me, daughter Nuwayra! This is my son, God love you!"

"Really? Maybe you're forgetting I knew your late husband Dawway (may he rest in peace)! So how can I believe this is your son, auntie? This boy's a redhead, his eyes are blue, and he's cute enough to gobble up. So where has he come from, this son of yours?"

"Daughter, I'm telling you, he's my son. I brought him up, I tended his wounds, I wore myself out for him staying up night after night. I snatched him from the very jaws of death!"

"How did this son come to you? He doesn't care about his natural mother and father, he's thrown his lot in with you forever? If only you had a house fit for humans instead of half a run-down shack!"

"Nuwayra, please, please keep our secret until we can find some solution. My daughter, my dear soul, I'm kissing your hands! Please, my soul's at your feet!"

"What solution could there be? If the American army knew about this, they'd tear our houses down looking for him. If the Mahdi Army heard about him, well, we'd be in God's hands, quite literally. And if Zarqawi caught scent of the news, it would mean our throats slit on video and an international scandal."

"My daughter Nuwayra, so what's to be done? Please keep it quiet! You're terrifying me!"

Martin, for his part, was stretched out on a mattress, listening with curiosity to this conversation between the two neighbors. He didn't understand much of what was said, however, seeing as his knowledge of Arabic was limited to basic questions about daily needs. He looked to his habuba to find out what was going on. Hajjiya Nana'a, who had already learned a bit of English from him in his clear American accent, gave him a wink as she said, "*Layter, layter*, my boy. *Ay wil tayl yoo* after a while. *Dont worree*. It's not about you, my son, it's nothing."

Martin kept straining his ears to hear what Nuwayra, that peculiar character, was saying. Nuwayra, for her part, kept talking with Habuba even though she was repeatedly distracted by Martin's angelic face.

After doing her best to sow fear and confusion in the hearts of Nana'a and her American son, Nuwayra's own heart wound up softening in the end, and rather than snitch on them, she used all her cunning to save the day. She suggested that hajjiya Nana'a darken Martin's face and hair with the soot from cooking pots. Then she had them get Martin's picture taken by the famous photo guy in Muzafar Square in order to arrange forged identity papers in Maridi Market.

After a few days, Martin Edwards was transformed into Abd al-Rida Dawway. Instead of New Jersey, his birthplace became the remote town of Ali Al Sharqi in Amara. In place of his former Army nickname of Indyk—the US Ambassador to Israel who shared Martin's first name—he chose Al-Izirjawi, which suggested he came from a powerful southern tribe. From one day to the next, he started wearing a dishdasha and tying a *ghatra* around his head. He went out with Habuba Nana'a on her errands to all corners of Thawra City and the other suburbs.

Abd al-Rida started riding around town in all kinds of rickety buses and worn-out taxi vans: the Fords, Reemas, Tatas, Coasters, and Kias. He rode through the different streets and blocks. He watched the American dogs as they patrolled the sidewalks of his city, demolishing all the stuff that had already been destroyed. In short, he grew accustomed to life in Block 41. Roughly a month ago, he began rising with the sun to stand in the main square of Block 55, where he'd join the line of construction workers hoping for work. He'd come back in the evening, exhausted, with a few thousand dinars that he put in the pocket of his habuba— Abd al-Rida had by now learned to pronounce the *haa* correctly—as he kissed her hand respectfully.

Abd al-Rida Dawway became one of us. He lived among us; he moved freely between our homes. And, at last, he complied with the wishes of his new friends on the block and signed up with the Mahdi Army. He started wearing black clothes and attending Friday prayers at Mohsen Mosque in Block 9, the site of historic protests. Just a few days before I started writing this, he was seen at a crowded demonstration being carried on the shoulders of his new comrades, shouting, "Hey, brothers, hey! We take down America for you, O Sadr!" and "America cowers as the Sayyid towers!"

Hajjiya Nana'a saw her son from a distance and called out to him in a mother's tender voice, mixing Arabic and English: "My son! Abd al-Rida! *Bee kayrful! Dont beleef thaym! They aar* all tricksters!"

"I know, Mom! I know!" he shouted back. And with that, he took up the taunt against the American soldiers hiding behind their tanks, chanting at the top of his lungs: "Cowards or men? So come out and fight!"

NOVEMBER 15, 2005

The Marriage of Hurriya, Daughter of Sayyid Jawad

Hurriya, daughter of Sayyid Jawad, was getting sick and tired of walking behind the flock of goats that she tended every day from morning till night. Just the other day, she led the flock out a relatively long way, from Inner Thawra all the way to the outskirts of Al-Ubaidi district. She sat down to rest on a discarded jerry can in Al-Qimama Square, leaning back against a wall and letting her animals poke around for their food. After a few minutes, she slipped into a deep slumber.

When she woke, a venerable round-faced sheikh, of pleasing aspect, clothed in white, stood majestically before her. He was mounted on a palomino mare of a color Hurriya had never seen before. She opened her eyes wide, and her gaze passed over the limbs of the mare and up its neck to its face . . . And from there to its rider's radiant white beard.

"God aid you, Hurriya!" said the sheikh.

"A hundred and one welcomes, uncle! Please, how can I serve you?"

"What, Hurriya, you don't recognize me?"

"No, hajji, I'm afraid I don't. Should I . . . ?"

"I am your grandfather, Sayyid Ali."

"Oh! Grandfather Sayyid Ali!" She wanted to get up, but the sayyid held up a hand as though to say this wouldn't be necessary. "Grandfather, I've never seen you, but I've heard so much about you! How often Mother has dreamed of you, saying each time, 'I saw Sayyid Ali in a dream, riding on a white horse.'"

"Hurriya, I watch over you every day, and every day this blessed mare and I have protected you from all harm. But today when I saw you hungry and asleep, my heart went out to you more than ever. Out of all the young women in this land, why are you so forlorn?" He wiped two shimmering tears from his cheek.

"Please, Grandfather, bless you. What am I to do? These goats don't have anyone to look after them."

"Enough, Hurriya! You are a fatherless girl who has been treated unjustly. All your friends have gotten married. They've settled down and have children now, while you spent your time with goats. When will you get your rest?"

"What am I to do, Grandfather?" Still her burning tears fell!

"Come, get up! Take your goats and go home. Enough! You've endured so much, my dear. Now rest, my daughter."

"What about my living, Grandfather? You know how things have gotten here."

"All will be well. This is the last day you'll see the goats. Kiss your mother and brothers for me. I leave you in God's tender care, my daughter. Pray for Prophet Muhammad and for the people of Muhammad's household."

"Dear God, may your prayer rest upon Muhammad and the people of Muhammad's household . . ."

Poor Hurriya, that spritely daughter of twenty years, awoke from a slumber to find in her lap a purse full of pieces of gold in various beautiful shapes. She immediately recalled the gold her grandmother had boasted of so often, and which had been stolen long ago in the deep of winter, or so she said. The coins, which were surely one and the same, gleamed in her hands, and she occupied herself in turning them over, until she forgot all about her grandfather, who had by then disappeared among the clouds.

Hurriya hurried back home, shooing her small, scattered flock along. As she walked, she kept touching the purse of gold, hidden against her skin under her shawl, to be sure that it was real. Around the district of Orfali, one of her goats rose into the air and gradually vanished from sight among the clouds. A second goat followed it, then a third and fourth, and thus the entire flock evaporated in front of Hurriya's eyes, never causing the least alarm in any passersby. It all happened as I have described it, and then it was as though they had never been.

164

Hurriya got to her house, panting. She was alarmed, joyful, afraid, and exhilarated. Other, harder-to-name emotions washed over her as well. She sat in the middle of the court-yard and opened the purse before the eyes of her mother, who was startled by the sight of the long-lost gold belonging to her own mother, dead and gone these thirty years. Hurriya's mother stammered, went pale, and was finally struck dumb, even as a mysterious smile flashed across her mouth. Hurriya relaxed her exhausted body and leaned against a wooden column in the center of the yard. She closed her eyes and began to speak to her grandfather, Sayyid Ali.

"A thousand mercies upon your soul, Grandfather! You have freed me from torment. May God keep you from the fires of hell! Grandfather, I kiss the ground under your feet!"

The rider on the white horse reappeared before her. He stretched out his hand to Hurriya, pulling her up onto the back of the steed. He set off lightly with her for the distant horizon, rising into the clouds. But no, this time, the rider was not her grandfather, Sayyid Ali, as Hurriya had sup-posed. Instead, it was a handsome young man whose angelic perfume filled the sky. Hurriya looked into his cherubic face, and, with a smile that made her swoon, the man spoke, saying, "Hurriya, daughter of Sayyid Jawad bin Sayyid Ali, will you accept me as your husband according to the laws of God and his Prophet, and the realm of the prince of believers (peace be upon him)?"

Hurriya gave out a gasp so sharp it nearly made the horse-man crash into some stars.

The rider roamed the skies with Hurriya and then brought her down near the earth once more. She cast a quick glance at the city of the downtrodden and weary, and rained cool tears upon it. She dropped her black cloak over the house of her parents. Then the mare carried her off again into the clouds.

Hurriya got married in the distant heavens, not far from her flock, which had preceded her there. The goats rang out with happy songs and pranced joyfully at the approach of Hurriya and her husband, while down below, her mother continued puzzling over the grandmother's stolen treasure.

The Privatization of Da'bul's Oil

Umm Da'bul was a bit taken aback when she discovered one day that her youngest, a child of ten, was peeing oil. Her surprise increased when she discovered that the boy could pee quantities large enough to meet their daily fuel needs, and with a fair surplus even still. She kept the matter quiet at first, especially since it's winter now, and we're suffering from an oil shortage even worse than all the previous ones we've suffered through. In any case, whenever Umm Da'bul needed to light her oven or get the heater started, she would call out, "Da'bul, my son, come here!" And little Da'bul would stand in front of the oven or the heater, and he would begin the process of dribbling systematically into the appropriate receptacles until the fire blazed high.

But Nuwayra, wife of Ghurab, discovered what was going on when she saw the boy peeing on a small garbage fire at the end of the street. Da'bul was laughing with delight as he made the flames shoot up. Nuwayra began her work of prying into this strange phenomenon, particularly since she had just the kind of personality that happened to take particular interest in observing and recording precisely this sort of fascinating anomaly. In the end, Nuwayra obtained a sample of Da'bul's urine and brought it home to her cutting-edge laboratory, where she arrived at an explanation: "Oil!"

The news spread quickly, and soon women were crowded together in front of the house of Umm Da'bul, carrying cans of various sizes. Da'bul found filling their cans to be an entertaining game, one that restored the psychological balance he had lost on account of long neglect by his mother and the rest of his relatives. He began working vivaciously and cheerfully to meet the needs of the block's residents, who were overjoyed at their access to this miraculous child, the solution to one of their most complicated problems, which even our illustrious Minister of Oil, Ibrahim Bahr al-Uloom, hasn't been able to solve with all the degrees he brought back from London.

Then Khanjar showed up with his black cap and his exploitative mercantile mentality. He offered a mind-boggling sum to Umm Da'bul in exchange for a percentage of the yield of her son's bladder for a period of ten years, making clear to her the importance of the deal, which was entirely consistent with the ongoing project to privatize essential national resources. Impressed by Khanjar's boldness and rapacity, Da'bul's uncles on both his mother's and his father's side likewise staked their claims, angling to acquire the lion's share of the dividends of the future arrangement.

The uncles on the father's side said, "Seeing as Da'bul is a boy, he necessarily comes from our blessed line. Therefore, his bladder is an inheritance to which our claim has the greatest legitimacy. We've seen this before, of course, when our grandfather, Shadhan, went through a period of pissing oil back in the 1920s."

"At least two-thirds of the boy comes from the mother's side," argued the maternal uncles, which is to say that they were claiming two-thirds of the profits.

It wasn't only a financial disagreement, for the maternal uncles were party members of the Supreme Council for the Islamic Revolution, which was affiliated with Hakim, while the paternal uncles were in the Sadrist movement. As such, the maternal uncles sought the support of the religious clerkship, which announced that the question, being a wholly political matter, was outside its jurisdiction, always providing that its share of the profits would equal the traditional fifth part. As for the paternal uncles, their backers rejected the notion of any sort of federalist division of the spoils hailing from the boy's bladder and proclaimed that the proceeds were wholly subject to their authority, given that Da'bul and his bladder fell within their geographical sphere of influence.

At last the principal factions—by which I mean the heads of the primary blocs and coalitions in the National Assembly—had to have a sit-down to hash the question out. They decided that any profits originating in Da'bul's bladder were legally the property of all the people of Iraq and would be distributed among them equally. A technical commission was formed to draft the Da'bul Law, and they proposed installing a precise little meter on his wee-wee, which would then be put under rigorous, twenty-four-hour protection by the American forces.

But that only made things more complicated, and the rivalries more intense. With the Americans now involved, international corporate interests came in to study the reserves hidden in Da'bul's bladder, with Halliburton's report stating, "The quantities discovered reach approximately one hundred and twelve billion barrels. Including the probable reserves, Da'bul holds claim to being the number one producer in the world."

Da'bul—held captive in the Green Zone in the company of his mother as well as an American woman, acting as his tutor, and then a team of oil experts—threatened to cut off production if he wasn't set free to go out with his friends to play in the streets of Block 41. When all parties refused to grant this ridiculous and irresponsible demand—since the boy could hardly be expected to administer his bladder on his own—Da'bul made a critical decision. After a few hours of preparation, he began putting his plan into action by loosing the reins on his "tap" and letting a new and refined form of oil gush out. It was believed to be the kind of gas used as airplane fuel. The Green Zone became an inferno, as did the neighboring areas. The fire kept mounting, and all the efforts of the great nations of the world were useless to stop it. So many helicopters filled the skies of Iraq, but they could not put out the fire.

The boy's mother screamed, "Da'bul! My son! Enough! Enough of this cursed black gold!"

Surrounded by flames, Da'bul, that innocent child, laughed as he sang, "Pee on it, pee on it, let it all burn!"

Afghan Iraq:
The Japan of the Middle East

Donald Rumsfeld, that foolish son of a foolish man, says that Iraq lags behind Afghanistan by years! By God, what kind of insult is that to wake up to? I went to bang on Khanjar's door with my newspaper in hand.

"Come on, Khanjar! Open up! Do something, man! The Americans used to tell us, 'We're going to make you the Japan of the Middle East!' So now why do they want to set us behind Afghanistan by years?"

"You scared me, Shalash. I thought something was the matter. What do you care what people say? Now don't you have anything nice to tell me this morning?"

"But listen, man, this is Rumsfeld speaking, not one of the dozen exiled politicians who rode in on his heels."

"Get lost, man! You and this Rumsfeld of yours. Honestly!"

"But Khanjar, this is dangerous talk. Tomorrow they're going to say, 'Just cooperate and we'll develop you until we've made you into another Afghanistan.'"

"And they're right, brother! The Japanese peacekeepers tried to make the city of Samawah like Tokyo, remember? But the provincial governor suggested they take Afghanistan as their model instead."

"The governor suggested that?"

"Yes, my boy. This governor is a member of the Supreme Council party, so in his opinion, Afghanistan is a paradise!"

"My dear Khanjar, would God accept that we are more backward than Afghanistan when our scholars outnumber their mullahs?"

"You're out of your mind. Sure, we have more people in turbans here than they have mullahs. Apart from that, though, Afghanistan is a much more developed and advanced country than Iraq."

"Khanjar, don't believe everything you hear on the news. What makes Afghanistan so advanced—all its rat turds and bentonite clay?"

"Listen, Shalash. The Afghans sat down for two days, had a *loya jirga*, formed a parliament, and held elections, even though they have a hundred races and sects inside their borders."

"A hundred races?"

"Yes, my dear. With the Pashtuns and the Uzbeks and the Tajiks."

"Khanjar, that totally reminds me, we had this awesome jajeek dip at the party yesterday! Man, the place was on fire!"

"Fire, eh? Good. Now they'll catch you and turn you into jajeek."

"No, really, man! We were snapping our fingers and shaking our shoulders until all the guys collapsed."

"Where'd you do all this finger snapping?"

"Everybody was chugging arak, man, and you were pretty much the only guy hiding himself away at home."

"Who were you drinking with yesterday?"

"Everyone. All the guys. There were even some chicks."

"No way! You had girls there?"

"Yes way! Girls! It was all crazy and there was dancing and

singing, 'Who made you upset? Who made you cry? I'll kill the man who made you cry.'"

"What's that? A *latmiya* for the martyred Husayn?"

"No, it's the new song by that singer Hussam Al-Rassam."

"Right, right. You're always letting loose and dancing all night, Shalash, and then you come around asking me what Rumsfeld said and what Condoleezza Rice was talking about! Where do you come up with all this bullshit, dude? You're not turning into a politician on me, are you, you drunk?"

"But Rumsfeld made me so mad! Iraq lags behind Afghanistan?! Really? Not in a million years!"

"Yeah? So what happens if every faction here decides to pull in a different direction? Sadr wants to be known as the Sayyid Leader, Hakim currently *is* the Sayyid Leader, and al-Dhari weeps over this Sayyid Leader. The IEDs, the car bombs, the jail cells, the prison camps . . . We've fucked it all up, no? I'd say there are worse things than being like Afghanistan, dude."

"Even now, our people might be reaching an agreement in Cairo . . ."

"What's the matter with your brain? In *Cairo*? They can't agree in their own country, and you think Fifi Abdou will belly dance them to a deal? Buddy, the only solution is for them just to stay at home."

"How can they stay at home? Who will run the country if they don't go to work?"

"God, you really make me laugh, Shalash! Is there anyone running the place now? What haven't they already ruined in this whole country of ours?"

"So what's the solution?"

"The solution is for the turbans to sit down, take a break,

and leave it all to professional politicians, because fourteen hundred years of conflicts won't be resolved over a weekend in some hotel in Cairo."

"Can you tell me what it is they're all disagreeing about?"

"It's like this: one side insists that Ali ibn Abi Talib was the first caliph, but the other wants to hold him back and call him the ninth—or was it the tenth?"

"Okay, so how did Japan agree on who would be which caliph when?"

"Buddy, from the very beginning, Japan agreed not to get into any fights about their caliphs!"

"What, are they all Sunnis?"

"No! The majority of the Japanese are Shiites and followers of Toyota. Now get out of here, Shalash. You always stay out late, going wild and making yourself crazy, and now you've come to make my head spin too."

"Khanjar, one last question, please!"

"Go ahead."

"Is this Toyota a Shiite or Sunni?"

"Neither, my boy. Toyota is a beautiful Kurdish girl!"

NOVEMBER 21, 2005

I Swear, I'll Make You a Wedding You Wouldn't Believe!

As the Noble Qur'an says: The good are for the good, and the wicked for the wicked . . .

Sayyid Sawadi Irhaymeh is pleased to request your presence at a dinner party in honor of the marriage of his son, Shalash. It takes place at six o'clock in the evening on Thursday, November 24, 2005, in the reception hall at the Mansour Club. Your attendance will complete our joy and delight.

This, distinguished Iraqis, was the full text of the invitation sent out by my grandfather, Sayyid Sawadi Irhaymeh, who currently fills in for the role of my father. It was sent to each and every honored member of the extended tribal clan, as well as to some of our neighbors, acquaintances, friends, and the heads of certain subtribes, along with prominent people from the new Islamic movements, in all their many intellectual hues and varieties.

What follows is the text of the invitation that the family of my fiancée sent to their own acquaintances and relatives on the same occasion:

RU'A & SHALASH

Sayyid Darid Tawfiq Ra'fat and his wife, Kawthar Sami al-Naqshabandi, request the honor of your presence at the wedding celebration of their treasured daughter, Ru'a, which will take place on Thursday evening, namely November 24, 2005, in the reception hall at the Mansour Club. Through you our joy will be complete.

Sincerely,
Darid and Kawthar

* Please note that club policies prohibit children from attending events in the function hall.

You will have noticed, brothers, that Sayyid Sawadi and the hajjiya, my mother—not to mention the noble household of Irhaymeh and the dutiful residents of our block—will be meeting Sayyid Darid Tawfiq Ra'fat and Sayyida Kawthar al-Naqshabandi, along with all their acquaintances, for the very first time, and that the location set for the event is the reception hall at the august Mansour Club, which—I swear, by the Lord of the Kaaba!—not one individual of the Irhaymeh clan has ever entered before.

The event will be entertaining and exciting and will include many performances. The problem is that everything will take place at the expense of my already jangled nerves. From this moment on, given that everyone is absorbed with getting things ready, you'll find me absentmindedly wandering about on my own for hours at a time. I start to imagine the minibuses and the Tata and Kia minivans as they all pull up to the reception hall, crowded with the best and brightest members of our tribe. The women, the sheikhs, the teenagers, and the children of the Irhaymeh clan, together with all their uncles, will tumble out. What will happen when the drums start (*rum ta tum-tum, rum ta tum-tum*), followed by men dancing outside the door and singing ribald songs like, "*We are those who asked her hand, we who drink her purity*"? Or even going inside and taking their seats (if they sit down at all, of course)?

I mean to say, what's bothering me now—a mere three days before the wedding, my friends—are a few little questions that run constantly through my mind. Here's a sampling:

"Is there any black magic in the world I could employ to force my cousin Aliya—called Miss Cheerful—to sit in her chair like a proper person and not go around to meet every single person who comes into the room and exchange cell-phone numbers?

"Is there any argument capable of persuading my brother Fadil and his friends in the Mahdi Army that the female relatives of my fiancée, who will be wearing somewhat revealing clothes, are honorable, faithful, respectable ladies?

"What will my father's cousin, Khamas the Turnipman, think when Ru'a and I cut the cake and then lose ourselves in a slow romantic dance, which Ru'a's aunt taught me only a couple of days ago?

"How will the mother of the bride handle it when my aunt, hajjiya Nasira, embraces her and gives her one of those kisses that never last less than forty-seven minutes and some seconds?

"How do I dissuade my aunt Fatayim from breaking into one of her religious chants and then standing up in the middle of the crowd to make a crude allusion in her hoarse voice, 'Hey, listen, hey! We've brought you this brand-new Brno rifle; no one's yet put a bullet in its chamber!'?

"How will my mother's uncle, Zayir Shalage, react when one of my wife's relatives approaches him, introduces himself, and tries to strike up a friendly acquaintance? How will he hold back from that intrusive and provoking question he's always asking to establish a person's status and connections: 'So, who are your uncles?'?

"How will Lafta the used-clothes-man avoid his habit of winking incessantly at every woman his eye lands upon?

"What force on earth could possibly stop my niece Nuwaysa from taking selfies with the singers, musicians, guests, waiters, parents of the bride, and all their neighbors? To say nothing about making a video that she dedicates to this memorable occasion with her uncle Shalash and his wife?

"By what possible means can we prevent Jaway'id ibn Radi's habit of picking up the biggest plate of meat and rice and just walking off with it, out into the open air, far from prying eyes?

"How will I be able to prevent Cheechan the Mute from putting into operation his belief that the primary duty of a good host is to fill everyone's cup with water from a carafe and then force them to drink while he waits?"

Not that my mind hasn't been occupied by many other things too. But naturally, I'm not letting myself get too upset with all the disparities in clothing, hairstyles, and other adornments that will no doubt be on display at the great event, nor, my friends, the idiosyncratic ways of eating, indeed the slurping, that the blessed House of Irhaymeh would practice in front of the family and acquaintances of my wife.

Likewise, I'm really not thinking too much about the melee of dancers that will crowd the stage, the hallways, and the tables. I just can't get sidetracked by such minor problems as the desire our neighbor, Zuwayd ibn Gadara, will no doubt develop during the festivities to take over from the singer for the band we've hired and regale us instead with songs like the folk classic, "My Little Ali's All Grown Up, Now He's in the First Grade," for a mere hour and thirty-four minutes. Or the insistent wish of Munawa, daughter of Inad, to seize the microphone in turn and launch into a long ululation, finishing, as she always does, with her mindless, "Like that!"

In addition, I'm not the least bit concerned about the group of relatives who will gather around us afterward—my relatives from Block 10, that rough part of town where all the pill-poppers and horny drunks in the family hang their hats. Those crazy guys will dance at funerals, to say nothing of weddings, so what's going to happen when the music starts up with that *shallam-ballam* party song in a hall already half filled with half-clothed women?

Believe me, I'm not interested in all that. However, my friends, the thing that will truly make me sick during the celebration, the thing that will make my grandfather's grandfather roll over in his grave, is when my uncle, Shinawa the Liar, between one minute and the next, puts his hand in his pocket and his mouth to my ear and—politely and respectfully, entirely out of character for him, which makes it even more embarrassing—whispers:

"Shalash, are you short on cash, or should I give you some? Just say the word, and don't worry about it. I even have dollars on me. I'll drown you in money! Shalash, it's all for you. How many Shalashes do we have? Your wife's so pretty, Shalash! Bring her over and introduce your uncle Shinawa!"

NOVEMBER 23, 2005

The Hajji's Third Time through Puberty

I drew your picture by tracing the moon; I lit it up with the moon's own light; I love you, my sweet; you've bewitched my soul.

178

These are the words that hajji Kazim found in a text message on his recently purchased mobile phone after exiting the sunset prayer. The hajji's head began to swim. His mood took a strange turn. His pace slowed so that he could read the message over and over. He was about to send a reply, but he managed to hold himself back.

"This could be my wife, the hajjiya, trying to test me! But the hajjiya doesn't read, she doesn't write, and she doesn't have a phone. No . . . Maybe one of the guys trying to prank me? But who would do that? They're all sensible people, they don't do such things. So who is it, Lord, who is it?"

Instead of heading home, his feet led him to the café near his house. He sat in a back corner and began rereading the message: *I drew your picture by tracing the moon; I lit it up with the moon's own light; I love you, my sweet; you've bewitched my soul.*

"God, it's true—I do look as handsome as the moon! It's not some trick, not some fantasy! Someone has actually fallen in love with me, but I don't know who it is. Poor woman, she must be so hot for me that she'll set the house on fire! My wife's got no interest in all that anymore, so I just spend my time on local tribunals, funerals, and the tribe saying this and proclaiming that."

I drew you a picture of the moon; I lit it up with the moon's own light; I love you, my sweet; you've bewitched my soul.

With these words echoing in his ears, the hajji arrived home. He went to his room without greeting the hajjiya. He stretched out on his bed and pulled close his old tape player, which used to play nothing but sermons and readings from scripture. He took out his tape of "The Desolation of the Grave" and replaced it with "God, I Die from Missing You!"

179

which he had furtively bought on his way home from the cassette shop near the café.

The sparkling voice of the singer Majid al-Muhandis began to fill the corners of the room. The hajji crossed one leg over the other and began tapping his right foot to the music. Outside, the hajjiya uttered a *bismillah* and an invocation of God's forgiveness. She came closer and listened through the door.

"Hajji! Hajji! Hajji Kazim! Oh, Mama, what's happened to him?" The hajjiya waved her hands and withdrew, muttering another *astaghfirullah*.

The hajji took out his phone again and reread the message. He smiled and began to guess. "Maybe it's Hamida, wife of Jabbar, may he rest in peace? No . . . No, maybe it's Fatayim, who was divorced by Inad, and who's been looking left and right for a new man. She's really a beautiful woman, and on top of that, not too old at all. But who knows? Maybe it's Saeeda. No . . . No, God forgive me! Her husband, Hajji Kamil, is my friend. Just today, we were in the mosque together. *Astaghfirullah!*"

The hajji's ecstasy mounted even as the hajjiya's anxiety increased, since her husband was refusing to reply to her repeated calls: "Hajji! Hajji! Hajji Kazim! Hey, hajji Kazim!"

The hajji stayed up late that night, repeating the names of all the attractive women he knew. He woke up early, after only a short sleep. He thought he would abandon his usual iqal headdress today and get his hair cut and dyed dark black. Then he lazily drifted back to sleep.

The hajjiya continued to be racked by anxiety for the hajji, who withdrew from her entirely, barely acknowledging her existence. When the hajji woke up again and ate his breakfast, he didn't say a word to his wife. After that, she kept her distance and stayed in her room, where doubts and conjectures consumed her mind.

After finishing breakfast, the hajji took his phone out of his pocket and read the message one more time. Then he was gone, walking the streets in a daze. He wandered without any fixed direction, as the music of his new and exciting song filled his head: "*God, I die from missing you! I fear I'll die when you're gone!*" He got off one bus and got on another. He examined faces, generously bestowed smiles on all and sundry, and exchanged glances with every woman he saw. He purchased cologne from a street vendor, along with a yellow tin of hair gel, a pair of tweezers, and some Nivea lotion. Then he bought a collection of colorful posters. He returned to his room and stretched out on the bed. He kept reading and rereading the message. Finally, he gathered his courage and decided to call the number from which it had been sent.

"Hello?" he said.

"Hello."

"Who's this?"

"Hahaha!" It was a very feminine laugh.

"Who are you? For God's sake, tell me! Do I know you?"

"Me? I'm Hamida." What a flirtatious tone!

"Hamida? Really? By the soul of my father, I know you!"

"Ummm!"

"Hamida," he said in a soft voice.

"Yes?"

"What are you wearing?"

"My clothes! Hahaha!"

"Hamida . . ." The name rattled in his throat.

"Yes?"

"Is there . . . Is there anything you desire?"

"Yes."

"What?" The hajji's heart had sped up, and his voice was scarcely audible.

"Baklava."

"And after that?"

"After that . . . I don't know!"

"What is it?" The hajji was sweating.

"I can't say."

"Saaayyy it."

Beep, beep, beep!

The hajji's credit had run out. He flew into a rage and dashed his phone on the ground. Realizing what he'd done, he rushed to the hajjiya, still sequestered in her room, and cast himself down before her. He began kissing her passionately and violently, all of which caused the hajjiya to faint into one of those delicious swoons that she'd been missing for twenty years.

NOVEMBER 24, 2005

An Election Assembly for a Hungry Tribe

Before Sayyid Khalf could finish his lecture to our tribe today, he stopped, took off his black turban, and threw it to the ground. His red, sweaty pate shone at us as he yelled, "Hey, what's wrong with all of you? Where's your zeal for the honor of your sect, huh? What are you going to say to Ali ibn Abi Talib when you see him in paradise? Will you tell him, 'We elected the communists,' or, 'We elected a bunch of secular infidels'? What will you tell his wife, Umm al-Banin? Will you tell her, 'It is we who betrayed your stepson, Husayn, at Karbala. It is we who abandoned your son, Abbas, before his hands got cut off. It is we who deprived baby Abdullah bin Husayn of water!'

"Get some sense in your heads! Don't go on being such idiots, such marsh people, such lowlifes! Only one party is blessed by God and his Prophet," he shouted at the top of his lungs. "The United Iraqi Alliance! That's the party of the martyr of Karbala, the party of the Battle of al-Taff, the party of Zaynab, the party of Umm al-Banin and Husayn's son, Imam al-Sajjad, the party of Abu al-Jawadayn!" He kept shouting: "By God! On the Day of Reckoning, you'll still be covering your ears, and the first question will be, 'Who did you vote for?' What will you answer? Will you say you voted for the secularists? If that's how you vote, may God ruin all your luck! If you do, may God curse you as sinners, you marsh people! I'll kill myself right here in front of you, I'll die here and now, I'll condemn my own soul if you don't swear by the head of Abbas that you'll vote for the United Iraqi Alliance. Come on, Hajji Rashag! Be the first to swear by Abbas, and let everyone take the oath after you, one by one."

Under the influence of this shock and awe, reeling from the sharp tone of Sayyid Khalf's rant, Hajji Rashag took two steps forward. His hands shook, his throat dried up, and he started to say, "Uncle, I swear by Abbas—"

183

But someone barked: "Don't you swear!" The words came from Falih bin Ati. "Don't swear! What does Abbas have to do with the elections?" He turned to Sayyid Khalf, who was busy putting his turban back on his bald head. "But I will swear," declared Falih, "and my oath will be by our revered Abbas, which means the oath cannot be false. I swear by Abbas that Sayyid Khalf and his gang are the biggest liars in the world! Where are they all coming from all of a sudden? Where were they during all those years that were so hard for us? Where were they when our own babies were dying of thirst? Where were they when our women went out to beg in the streets? Where were they when we had to sell the very window frames from our houses, when we were forced to cook garbage? Where were they when even a mouthful of bread was a dream beyond imagining? Why didn't anyone come to us then and say, 'We are all one family, our shared beliefs unite us'? They've lived their whole lives in comfort. Their cheeks are rosy; their women gallivant from country to country. Meanwhile, the best of our women went out to sell nuts, while the best of our men sold used clothes from market stalls! Why didn't they say, 'Our people are starving to death, we must aid them!'? Our babies were dying in our hands, and we had no money for medicine to treat them. Our daughters didn't have slippers to wear when going out to the market. Why didn't anybody ask about us? Do none of *them* fear the Day of Reckoning? Is there not one of them who is ashamed before Husayn and Abbas? Are their little ones more precious than ours? Are their women better than ours? Or are their elegant sons better than our children?

"So don't swear, Hajji Rashag! I'll do the swearing today. For example, I'll go on to swear that hell itself is kinder than these people! How many schools and hospitals have they built in Iran with money from the double tithe we paid to the clerkship? How many palaces in London? How many fancy cars follow along behind them while we have to ride crowded Tata minibuses but fear to get on because we lack the fare? Our clothes are falling off in rags. We've seen destruction and injustice. On one side, we had the pain of hunger, and on the other, we had that criminal Saddam. We've been imprisoned, we've been killed, and every illness you can name has played hopscotch across our cities. Meanwhile every one of *their* faces is rosy and fat, their necks puffing out as big as tires . . .

"So no swearing, Hajji Rashag! The elections are not for us—they're for them! So that they might dwell in their palaces, plundering and stealing at their leisure. Didn't we already vote for them before? And what did they bring us that time? What besides more destruction and injustice, and now there's not even a cup of clean water in our houses . . .

"Step outside, Hajji Rashag, and take a look at Sayyid Khalf's car. Look at the Land Cruisers he has for his bodyguards. Just take a look at these so-called followers of Prophet Muhammad and his household! Go ask Sayyid Khalf, 'Where do you live, master? How'd you get two houses in Jadriyah, master? How'd you get twenty cars, master? How'd you get a house in London, master? Where are your daughters, master? Why are they in Iran, master? Why don't they come and experience the injustices our own daughters have suffered? Has God sent down a new *aya* for the Qur'an regarding your daughters, O master?'

"Listen, brothers! God is not concerned with the elections, except to hold the electoral commission to account for a fair vote. Husayn aids the mistreated, not the thieves! Abbas hates palaces and cars bought with the blood of the people. Umm al-Banin protects our children while *their* children are protected by the Badr Brigades!

"No! No, Sayyid Khalf, we won't take the oath. Go find someone else! No one will play us for fools again. You think you come here and introduce yourself to us for the first time today, and we suddenly become your favorite *habibi*? Over twenty years, not one dinar came to us from you. If a single dinar had reached us, honestly, we would have said you did us an honor by coming today. You've played us for such fools, but enough is enough! No longer will we be your pawns.

"Our children don't have shoes on their feet while Hakim's son Ammar has bought up all of Najaf. Our children haven't even made the trip to Al-Suwaira, while your sons and daughters skip from Switzerland to America. Would Husayn and Abbas accept this? Husayn and Abbas were the grandchildren of God's Prophet, but when the swords surrounded them, they did not flee to Iran. When the world collapsed upon them, they didn't go live in London! Husayn and Abbas didn't reach their hands out to the treasury, whereas your children have taken both the treasure and the building that housed it. Listen, Sayyid Khalf, this broken record about mass graves isn't going to work on us anymore. The mass graves are the graves of *our* children, not yours! And when our children were buried in the ground, your children were summering in France.

"Get out, Sayyid Khalf!" cried Falih bin Ati. "Get out! Never again will you play us for fools. We know which path to take. The clerkship too has washed its hands of you. The great imams are our imams: they supported the poor and downtrodden. You remember the thousand pilgrims who died on Aimmah Bridge last month? It was our women, not yours, who were swept into the water. It was our children, not yours, who were crushed that day. Get out! I've had it up to here with you. Out, out, out!"

Trembling, Sayyid Khalf adjusted his turban. His round face was splotched with red that made him look very much like a slice of watermelon. Meanwhile, Falih bin Ati collapsed on account of his skyrocketing blood pressure, and his tribesmen rushed forward to pick him up. They all ignored the sayyid as he went out, cowering, broken, and muttering to himself, "The marsh people are fuel for the fires of hell! The marsh people are monkeys! Water-buffalo! The marsh people are donkeys!"

NOVEMBER 26, 2005

Our Tribe Reaps the Election Harvest

These days, we're living through election season, which is, without a doubt, the most temperate season for our tribal sheikhs and their supporters, those whom Saddam taught all about gifts in exchange for loyalty. That's why they've organized teams to head out and sell their loyalty to the various parties standing for election.

Because there are easily over two hundred parties in the new democratic Iraq, each with their own list of candidates for the various offices, the tribes have divided them up among themselves. Some tribes would sell their claim or give up certain parties in exchange for a reasonable sum. "Selling" here, my friends, means that a tribe agrees to refrain from visiting the party headquarters and offering their loyalty to it following the sale. So, for example, the coalition known as Urgent Defense is sold for ten thousand American dollars, or eighteen million Iraqi dinars, or fifty million Iranian tomans. Likewise, Allawi's list is sold for a similar amount, Chalabi's list for roughly half that amount, and so on, down the line to the smallest lists, some of which get sold for just two crisp bills. In this way, the seller lets the tribe that "buys" the list take that party's generous rewards all for itself.

Now, because I am the poet of our brave tribe, our foremost court panegyrist, without a single rival to the claim, I've been assigned the task of writing poems that will praise the presidents of the fortunate lists. In exchange, I've received a good amount of money, though common prudence during these unsettled times prevents me from disclosing exactly how much.

Our journey began two days ago, and our first stop was the headquarters of His Eminence, Sayyid Abdul Aziz al-Hakim, president of the coalition list that the religious clerkship is supporting. The sheikh of our tribe stood before the great man and swore by Fatima al-Zahra, mother of martyred Husayn, that our tribe, one and all, would vote for this blessed list, known by their official number of 555. After the sheikh of the tribe, the heads of a number of our subtribes took turns giving pompous sermons, all ending by kissing the sayyid's turban and his hand. Finally, it was my turn. I stood before Hakim in my brand-new tuxedo (missing a bow tie), which had cost the tribe eighteen thousand dinars, which would subsequently be deducted from my fee, and I recited my poem, which began:

> Hakim, yes, you, you! Hakim, yes, you, you!
>   (The tribe chants the "you" part.)
> Iraq with its Shiites and all its people sing:
> If we lose Hakim, we lose Islam.
> Your money dawning before our eyes
> Produced the same joy and surprise
> As the Shiites felt at the capture of Saddam;
> Hakim, yes, you, you! Hakim, yes, you, you!

His Eminence, Sayyid al-Hakim applauded freely—no doubt because he didn't know that my verse was adapted from a hit song from the '90s, "The Beloved, You," found on album of panegyrics to our old "Master of Necessity." The tribal sheikh received from Hakim "whatever God provided," as we like to say, and, after a quick count, a smile spread across his lips: we had got what we came for.

Embraced on all sides by God's loving protection, the tribal caravan next set off for the headquarters of Sayyid Allawi, president of the Iraqi National List, who received us with his childlike smile. After sampling an odd-tasting juice, our sheikh rattled off the very same sermons, which the heads of the subtribes followed with their own scripts. Then my turn came. I stood before Allawi in my new tuxedo (now with a shiny tie costing seven thousand dinars, picked up along

189

the way and once again docked from my fee). I improvised a poem then and there for Sayyid Allawi, which also happened to have lines lifted from a famous folk song:

> *Allawi my son is all grown up, and his list is going to win*
> *Despite all danger and threat, dropping you would be a sin*
> *Your face won't put us off, and we won't accept any excuse*
> *Our water is shut off, and the house has blown a fuse*
> *Allawi, give us some dough, for we don't want Azuz*
>> (my way of disparaging our previous audience, Abdul Aziz al-Hakim.)
> *From you we want some generosity, from you we want fuluz.*
>> (You'll no doubt notice that I changed the final S sound in the Arabic word for "money" to a Z, according to the demands of the best poetry.)

Sayyid Allawi laughed his famous laugh, and he named a figure that brought joy to the soul, this time in the form of pounds sterling, which confused our sheikh—God preserve him!—since he wasn't sure of the exchange rate.

Next up, we reached the building of Sayyid Jalal Talabani, the beloved Kurdish leader and current president of the Republic of Iraq—a hop, skip, and jump from Sayyid Allawi's headquarters. The sheikh of our tribe commended His Excellency and praised his administration of the country, extolling the brotherly relationship that had united the Kurds and the Arabs, those sibling peoples. Then he told me to recite my poem. I stood there as I always did, and my throat rang out with some glittering lines in Kurdish that none of my friends could understand.

Sayyid President Mam Jalal saluted me and patted me on the shoulder, saying "I hope you'll recite the very same verses for Sayyid Barzani." Which was his way of indicating that he had no intention of bestowing his generosity upon our tribe: he saw through our BS, and he knew he'd win anyway, thanks to the Kurds and not our paltry votes or hoarse voices. We left His Excellency's office, covered in shame and disgrace, and immediately started talking shit about him at the door: "The stupid Kurdish son of a stupid Kurd: What do you expect? Didn't I tell you we shouldn't bother?"

From the president's office, we headed over to the stomping grounds of the Cadres Party, headed up by Ali Aldabbagh. We reused all our prefatory material, and then I stood up in the aforementioned tuxedo and made my next recitation:

Thawra pledges allegiance to you, Ali!
Both Inner Thawra and Outer, equally!
When the world is harsh economically,
And Solagh slaughters us physically,
The Cadres will back us marginally.
So Thawra pledges allegiance to you, Ali!

With an enviable degree of refined elegance, Aldabbagh removed from his coffers some new Gulf dinars and handed them over to our sheikh. Calculating the conversion this time befuddled him completely, but optimism about the result soon relaxed his furrowed brow.

Gentlemen, we didn't want our journey to continue without stopping to bless Chalabi. As Iraqis see it, Chalabi brings to mind the Barmakid tribe, famous throughout history for

191

its munificence. After all, Chalabi is no stallkeeper in the Maridi Market; he has cash from international banks falling out of his pockets.

Our sheikh recited a whole tome's worth of praise that began with Chalabi's dearly departed grandfather, Abd al-Husayn al-Chalabi; moved down to the father, Abd al-Hadi al-Chalabi (may he rest in peace); and finally reached their venerable descendant, Ahmed Chalabi, who really made America's head spin by wrapping Congress and the Pentagon around his finger. The heads of the subtribes took their turns, praising Chalabi's splendid appearance. Then they left the floor to me. I adjusted my tuxedo, the price of which, including the tie, came to a mere eighty-seven thousand dinars, and I gave a reading in the style of Khadir Hadi, that dearly departed popular poet:

> *When adversity adopted us, we came to you;*
> *Stretch out your hand, and we're with you! (Let's go!)*
> *You are the one who brought America; (Let's go!)*
> *Yes, you, you brought America from across the seas!*
> *O you who deceived Congress (Let's go!) and tricked the Pentagon—*
> *Glory to He who made you!*
> *Cursed be everyone who resists you;*
> *A loser, everyone who opposes you!*
> *Torn out by the roots, everyone who angers you!*
> *Yielding, everyone who meets you!*
> *Our tribe lays down its life for you;*
> *Women and men sacrifice themselves for you!*
> *Show us a bank, sir,*
> *And we'll divide it all with you! (Let's go!)*

Sayyid Ahmed Chalabi laughed heartily and told his deputy, Sayyid Entifadh Qanbar, to do what was right. Their gift was such a healthy amount that our leader got the runs.

Down the street from Sayyid Chalabi's office, we saw a sign reading THE CHALDO-ASSYRIAN PARTY. We'd never heard of them, and so we weren't properly prepared. The question arose as to whether we ought to try our luck anyway. In the end, we put our trust in God and went inside. Our sheikh gave a confused speech, and the heads of the sub-tribes erred on the side of remaining silent. It was up to the great poet to save the day. I stood there in my really quite impressive suit and improvised as follows:

> I am a southern marshlander of Chaldean origin
> Then I became an Assyrian from the Sawa'id tribe
> I don't want cash, just a few bottles of Bashiqa for my brothers
> Hey, brothers, hey: mix the Bashiiiqa! And drink!

I drew out the penultimate syllable of that brand of cheap local arak, and the tribe took up the call: *Mix the Bashiqa and drink!* Everyone cheered, and my cousin Jasim ibn Abid gave me a wink, which was as much as to say that he shared my deep and abiding interest in the subject of cheap liquor.

Before darkness fell and the curfew set in, we quickened our steps to see what the Communist Party might still have in their purse after the collapse of the Soviet Union a dozen years ago. Comrade Abu Dawud received us, and before we even started our spiel, he surprised us with a brilliant speech that clarified the reasons that the party had merged with the Iraqiya list, reiterating the role of the working class in spearheading the work of revolution in our land, which was subject to the dictates of the historical dialectic, same as any other. He concluded his discourse by saying that the Iraqi Communist Party had grown up from the poorest of our people, and, as a result, the party was materially poor, though rich in ideas and programs. Unfortunately, ladies and gentlemen, such ideas and programs do not fall within the purview of our tribe, which has convened this evening to add up its gross income and calculate all the taxes we owe!

The Political Process on Our Block

Khanjar's wife, Saya, is a good and simple woman who knows nothing about the world. She's the kind of woman they invented the word "clueless" for. She's always the last to collect her monthly food ration because she doesn't know that a month has thirty days. Likewise, she's the first to go to the market and the last to leave, without even having bought the thing she came for. She has forgotten her cooking pot on the stove more times than she's fallen asleep in the arms of her husband.

Good faith and neighborliness require me, however, to bear faithful witness here that Mrs. Saya has never meddled in anyone else's affairs, be they neighbors or otherwise. Much less would she meddle in the affairs of her husband Khanjar. The only exception is that Saya was known in the 1990s by the name Umm One-and-One on account of her always wearing one of her own slippers and, on the other foot, not one of Khanjar's slippers, but one of his shoes!

But Saya's amusing eccentricities don't stop there. For example, she was surprised to discover that Abu Hamma, her Kurdish neighbor for twenty years, was Umm Hamma's husband, though they'd always lived together in the same house. When her neighbors confirmed it and swore that the two were married, she laughed a laugh of profound relief and confused us all by saying, "I have to admit, I really had my doubts about them! I thought all their kids were bastards given that Abu Hamma doesn't look like Umm Hamma!"

I happened to meet Saya today as she was carrying election posters and putting them up on street corners. The strange thing was that the posters belonged to a liberal party whose platforms seemed to me rather progressive for a woman who couldn't even find her way to the city center. Saya read the surprise in my face and asked in her most ironic tone, "Well, Shalash, what are you gawping at? Haven't you ever seen a forward-thinking, cultured, liberal secular humanist before?"

"My dear Saya, may God protect the cultured! But oil and water mix better than you and politics."

"Out of my sight, dimwit. You don't even know who Gabriel García Márquez is."

"What the hell are you talking about, Saya?"

"Exactly! You don't know anything at all! Tell me the percentage of nitrogen in the atmosphere. Go on!"

"The percentage of nitrogen in the atmosphere? No, I don't know. Are you telling me that you do?"

"Of course! It's 78 percent. Now, do you know the area of the hole in the ozone layer?"

"No, of course not! Are you telling me that you do?"

"Of course! Twenty-eight million square kilometers. Now, do you know how long the rule of Nebuchadnezzar lasted?"

"No! My God, am I on *Who Wants to Be a Millionaire?*"

"Boy, you are one sad soul. You can't tell your hand from your foot!"

"Are you being serious, Saya?"

"Get out of here, Shalash. Go back home and peddle more of your nonsense online. You're full of hot air and nothing else. And you don't know the first thing about dedicated political work."

"How on earth did you get mixed up in all this . . . ?"

"Look, Shalash, as you know, I'm a deep believer in the role of women in building society. I belong to a women's organization that is working to correct the sexist provisions in the latest draft of the constitution, where, for example, it abolishes the 1978 modification to the 1959 law of personal status, Law 188, thereby allowing the forced marriage of child brides."

While she was talking, Mr. Khanjar, the husband, showed up. He greeted us without the slightest indication that he thought his wife's poster-pasting activities might be out of the ordinary. Indeed, he even offered to help out. Saya thanked him but asked him to go home and prepare lunch. She'd be back as soon as she was done. Khanjar graciously withdrew.

In my surprise and consternation at seeing such a happy family—straight out of Denmark—living in our block, I followed Khanjar and called after him, "Khanjar! Khanjar!"

"What's up, Shalash? But be quick since I'm a little busy. I need to pick up around the house, do the laundry, and cook lunch."

"Khanjar, what the hell is going on?"

"What do you mean?"

"I mean your wife, Saya!"

"What's the matter with her?"

"Nothing's the matter, but Saya's getting all political . . ."

"Brother Shalash, Saya is a civilized lady who is eager to fulfill her social responsibilities, especially since Iraq is passing through a stage of critical transformations that demand the active participation of all segments of society."

I was spinning in circles, dumbstruck by the political consciousness that had descended upon this family. In fact, I couldn't walk a block without finding yet another neighborhood woman putting up election posters that day—while her house-husband in his short shorts was back home exhausting himself in the kitchen, preparing a lunch that was *almost* ready on time.

The strangest thing of all was that although there was such a diversity of posters and slogans being pasted up, the political differences these signaled—religious, liberal, nationalist, moderate—seemed to be making no impact on the harmony of our local social interactions. I couldn't have been more pleased, and I beseeched God in his sublime power to render permanent this blessing of the free exchange of ideas and acceptance of others' views that had descended upon our block, a block surrounded by barbaric neighborhoods where a person gets killed on the spot if he happens to be carrying an election poster that doesn't bear the picture of one of those turbaned geniuses who have been rejected by the clerkship and have formed an alliance to murder whomever does not agree with them.

Happy election season! A thousand happy returns for our block and the people of our block! And down with all political parties!

A Tanta in a Suicide Vest

The truly annoying thing about living under such exceedingly complicated political and security conditions, with death, destruction, and booby-trapped beards all around, is when some *tanta* pops up in your path looking impossibly fabulous. I believe that very few of you, my brothers, will fail to recognize the meaning of the term. In short, I'll tell you that a *tanta* (God lengthen your lives!) is . . . a *tanta*!

In this atmosphere, so confused and degrading on account of our vulnerability, when our Minister of the Interior insists he's in control of the situation, yet on the streets there's a fanaticism running so high that political opponents are liquidated just for putting up party posters; when Hussein al-Tahan, the provincial governor, has been grinding down the mayor's office in Baghdad after having deposed the previous mayor with the support of those angels of mercy, the Badr Brigades; yes, when amid all this loathing and disgust, you run into certain *tantas* on the street, all made up in red lipstick and looking totally relaxed and unperturbed, without a care in the world . . . well, it can really steam you up! How the hell do they do it?

But, look, that's exactly what happened to the so-called Mr. Khanjar in Saadoun Street the other day, when a person of indeterminate sex appeared and surprised him by asking:

"Excuse me, sir, where's the local gym?"

"I really don't know, brother. I'm not from around here."

"How come you don't know? You have the look of an athlete. You must do backflips, your body looks so good! And on top of that, you've got a sweet disposition."

"God's forgiveness! Me, doing backflips? Buddy, I have high blood pressure, and I've had the runs for two days. How in the world could I do backflips?"

"Take it easy! What'd I say to make you so angry?" (The slender youth was writhing like a viper.)

"Brother, really, I'm just hitting the pavement to get a bite to eat. I've never stepped foot in a gym or a bodybuilding club in my whole life. Perfection belongs to God alone!"

"What's wrong with gyms? Do they scare you? They're filled with beautiful young people, so sporty and with amazing bodies."

"Brother, please! I'm from Thawra, and I don't know anything about that sort of thing. Where would we get ourselves a gym? With God as my witness, all we have is radishes, and not even enough of those."

"Whoa, daddy! Thawra, I love it so much! Half of my friends are from Thawra, mostly from Block 69. I'd lay down my life for the people of Thawra! Oh, the radishes they have in Thawra—I love them! Ah, and I'd die for the omelets they make in the main square of Block 69!"

"Thank you, brother, for sharing these beautiful feelings."

"Feelings? Oh, it's good you know about feelings. Why don't you feel anything for me?"

"Feelings for you? What are you talking about, brother?"

"Yes, pay attention here! And you're killing me with your 'brother this' and 'brother that.' What, I'm the son of your mother? The son of your father? If you called me your 'sister,' a guy might go along with it, but . . ." (He smacked his Abu Saham spearmint gum so loudly that it rang in Khanjar's ears.)

"Well, then, I'm telling you, sister, something about this doesn't feel right. Give me some room to breathe! Where do you come from, anyway, popping up first thing in the morning like this?"

"What did I do wrong? Am I getting too close for comfort? What do you think?" (The youth came within the proverbial two bow-lengths to Khanjar.)

"Hey, buddy, what's your problem? Keep your wicked little hands off me! Back off!"

"What's wrong? Oh dear, have I frightened the big man? Come on, there's no need for these theatrics."

"Let me pass, man! Get out of the way! I've got a hundred things to do."

"Like what? I can take care of them all right now with my cell phone, if you like. If I do, will you take me out? No, you look broke, so let me invite you. I've got some cold beer, and we'll get takeout from Oasis Restaurant. We'll go back to my apartment and relax a little. What do you say, baby?"

"Brother, I'm not into cold beer or all that other stuff. Leave me alone!"

"Everyone says that the first time, and afterward, you all

show your true colors! Oh, you're too much! May God knock you down!"

"Are you ever going to stop, buddy?"

"Are *you* ever going to stop? *I'll leave everybody and go with you*," he sang, swaying cutely. "How's this: I'll give you a little breathing room in exchange for you telling me your name and your astrological sign."

"My name is Khanjar, and my sign is pigeons. But after the bird flu, I killed and burned all my pigeons."

"Your name is Khanjar, as in 'dagger'? Oh, no, my dear, 'battle-ax' would suit you better." (The pixie came even closer now, until he was pressed up against Khanjar.)

"Hey, I'll call the police! You're going too far. Get out of my way!"

"The police! Ha! What, are you going to tell them you've stumbled across a *tanta* in a suicide vest?"

"Brother, you're putting my reputation on the line. Don't let anybody see. Get away! Don't stand so close to me!"

"Your reputation? Well, I never. God save us all from your reputation. You're too much."

"God save *me* from you and your kind! By the soul of my uncle, I'll give you a slap you'll never forget!"

"Yes, daddy, slap me! Slap me! That sounds perfectly delicious." (His desire was readily apparent to onlookers.)

"What can I do? Everything I say just turns you on."

"What can you do indeed. You can come to the apartment, and I can perform my duties as host. It's very close, just in Kahramana Square."

"Are you serious? Me, go with you? What, are you crazy? Buddy, I told you, I'm busy."

"Are you serious? Me, let you out of my sight? *Where would I find someone like you, oh, where?*" he sang.

But listen, my friends! Don't believe the vicious rumors going around that Mr. Khanjar went home with Ringaround Rosy (apparently a nickname) to his apartment in Wathiq Square, apartment number 6/9, in the same building where a certain hajji Ta'ma resides. Or that he guzzled cold beer with him and ate grilled chicken. Or that the electricity went out, and that, in the dark, Rosy "realized his desires," as they say. Anyone circulating such rumors is an enemy of democracy and the new Iraq!

And now, don't hesitate! Get out there and cast your vote for Rosy's party!

NOVEMBER 29, 2005

The Day We Rushed toward the Vice President's Procession

When Saddam visited Thawra City one winter's day in 1978, we were just children, and we ran out with all the other kids to welcome him with the slogans that were popular at that time. We reached Block 20, where the then vice president had decided to stop and greet the people of our sad city as they pressed forward to welcome His Excellency. And because we were so small, our emaciated bodies were carried along by the throning crowds into the far corner of the square. From there, we watched that strangest of men, who inspired fear

202

even in our fathers, men we used to imagine were able to kill lions, monsters, demons, and goblins.

Since we were a group of young boys, the thing that most drew our attention was the sight of Saddam's bodyguards, so tall and with such thick mustaches. They surrounded the vice president as if he were the hero of a cowboy movie. The rally ended, and we took the long way home. (I won't describe it. I'm too afraid of our modern-day Saddams to go into any detail about my childhood home.) Hamudi was in third grade at the time, which made him bigger than the rest of us, so he decided he would play the role of Saddam Hussein. That left Muayyid, Hussein, Rahumi, and me—and I think maybe Samir was with us as well?—to play the role of his bodyguards.

We closed ranks around Hamudi as we made our way down the street, shoving aside the crowds that gathered to greet him. The way we ignored the shouted slogans, the steely looks we gave our imagined crowd, the path we cleared through it, our running to keep up with our leader, it was all exactly as the vice president's bodyguards had done it, those men who would abandon said leader more than twenty years later so he could star in a TV show about sleeping alone in a pit.

Anyway, it was after that day, so long ago, that Saddam entered all our lives with a vengeance. After our real-life twenty-minute encounter with the Man Himself in the public square of Block 20, he moved right into our televisions, where he became our entire lives for more than twenty years, occupying our sleeping and our waking thoughts alike.

Over those years, television meant Saddam. How could we forget the days when cursing the television meant cursing

Saddam! War came in the '80s, and we grew up to its anthems and its tragedies. The war took its share and departed. Then another war came in time to eat its fill of our humiliation. Once sated, it too departed. Then the sanctions settled in and transformed us from young men with dreams, striving for life, into street vendors with corner stalls; from excellent students into drivers' assistants on minibuses; from lovers of life into scowling, deeply etched, prematurely aged faces. Our dreams faded, and we married our sweethearts, who had themselves changed from teenagers who graced the streets with their beauty into bewildered women in black, cowering together in the house of some aunt.

We wandered down the streets of life, wrestling with time for the sake of a mouthful of bread. We laced up our army boots and suffered new indignities at the hands of corporals, petty officers, and others too numerous to list.

Out in the street, we would turn to the right, to the left, and back again, fearing the appearance of a car belonging to the secret police, the regular police, or our Ba'athist comrades. We went from dreams of traveling to Europe—that fantasy we all shared!—to long insomniac nights in Harthiya Prison, where armored lice awaited us. Who among us didn't go down to Harthiya for a summer?

The thing is . . . Today was Saddam's trial. The trial of Mr. Vice President himself. So I walked past Hamudi's old house . . . Hamudi, whom we surrounded as his bodyguards, and whom we later left to die near Nasiriyah during the last war.

And I went by Samir's old house. He emigrated with his family to some cold city abroad. He's moved away for good, and we no longer get any news about them. (God be good to you, Auntie Umm Samir! Come back, if the situation improves!)

And I walked by Rahumi's old house. What became of Rahumi? They say he's a tailor in Jordan. My God, friends! Rahumi was the smartest student in the world. Why, dear God? Why should Rahumi be a tailor in Jordan? Give me a minute to wipe away these tears . . . Did you know that, in math class, Rahumi would solve the most difficult equations even before Mr. Fayiq could finish writing them on the board? Rahumi, a tailor in Jordan? Yes, Rahumi now lives as an exhausted stranger, driven by his constant cares. Things will never add up, it's too late for that. Come, Rahumi, you're too good for Jordan. Fuck the world and its sister. Fuck it all!

As for Muayyid, that good-looking kid we envied when all the girls had crushes on him, but whom we couldn't resent because of his morals, his bashfulness, and his humility; Muayyid the Handsome, beloved by all the ladies on the block; Muayyid, who dreamed of becoming an airline pilot and flying over all the continents of the world . . . He is currently serving tea at an internet café that I sometimes frequent—and he turns his face away from me as though he doesn't know me. Turn back to me, Muayyid! I'm . . . well, I'm the one they call Shalash the Iraqi. But still. Turn back to me! Don't be ashamed of your work. It's no dishonor. Muayyid, tell me, what's become of Raja, your sweetheart, whose family heard about your relationship and locked her away at home for many months, until she finally gave up her education entirely? No, don't tell me, Muayyid. Just forget me after all. Forget, just like all the rest have.

As for Hussein, brothers, he now spends his days at the printing press of a local newspaper, and I only see him once a year. Hussein is broken, preoccupied, and full of despair, and because I love him, I don't want to tell you that he has also become touchy and argumentative.

Why, O heavens? These were my friends. This was my slaughtered childhood on the block. I want it all back now. I want them to be children running around Hamudi, their laughter ringing in the air, yelling at the top of their lungs not far from the door of the house of Awhayyid the Reed-Weaver, so that his wife will come out to curse at us, screaming, "Your parents should be beaten with a shoe! They gave you bread but no manners!" God, how I miss that curse now. Awhayyid, a blessing upon your parents! I'm begging you, bring your wife out to curse at us now! Awhayyid, do you hear me, or has the dirt stopped up your ears?

My dear friends—Hamudi, Rahumi, Muayyid, Hussein, and Samir—I remembered you all today when I passed by all of your houses. Did you hear my heart crying and calling out, "I love you"? Why did you leave me out in the street alone? Who will protect me from the dangers I've called down with my writing? (Yes! I've become a writer—indeed, a good one and quite well known.) Do you know why I dropped by your houses today? It was to tell you to have a look at Mr. Vice President. Look at the Comrade Leader who destroyed our lives. Here he is, on trial for murdering a group of our people in Dujail. I also wanted to tell you that His Honor, the judge, is a kind man. He really does seem to be doing his job without remembering that the accused man standing before him did far worse than what's listed on the charge sheet. He murdered our futures. He brought an end to our laughter and transformed our country from a paradise, the envy of nations, into a garbage dump picked over by black cats, as crows caw in the sky above.

The Lake of Light: A Long Story

Today is the fourth full day in a row that Fadila's house has been all lit up. Not that the power has been working for four days straight. What an idea! The electricity has been running sometimes and dead most times throughout the city, as usual, but Fadila's house has never stopped shining, both inside and out, day and night. And I'm not exaggerating when I tell you that we've never seen so much light before. But the thing everyone knows about Fadila's house is that it contains only one poor family made up of one struggling mother and her four children—naked, hungry, and miserable—all of whom have left school, and all of whom have their hands full fighting against poverty itself after having lost their father to an accidental electrocution.

"But where are they getting all that power?" wondered Nuwayra, wife of Ghurab, which is what everyone else was wondering too. But Nuwayra isn't like the rest of God's creatures. She needs to know everything, and to know it now. So she picked herself up and walked over to Fadila's house. She went through the door, which was always open, seeing as the people of Thawra City always keep their doors open to

207

guests, neighbors, and passersby in need of a helping hand. Nuwayra went up to the electricity meter, which included both a counter and a connection point, and conducted a quick investigation to confirm that everything was normal, that there wasn't any secondary, private connection installed.

Having discovered that Fadila's meter was no different from everyone else's, Nuwayra allowed herself to be flabbergasted and so pushed her way into the small house to hunt down the secret—but she was fated to fail. The strange thing was that, in the face of Nuwayra's curiosity, Fadila and her little ones behaved as though the whole matter was eminently natural. Indeed, they were perplexed by Nuwayra's rounds through the house and her surprise as she kept turning over this and that object and finding nothing out of the ordinary. Nuwayra hurried off then to find the generator man to ask him the number of kilowatts that Fadila had purchased this month. The generator man too found it all very strange, given that this family was the last on the block that would be able to bid for any extra power, especially since the cost of a single kilowatt was now around eight thousand dinars. Nuwayra turned the matter over and examined it from every angle. In the end, she reached an indisputable conclusion: Fadila must somehow be tapped into the Green Zone.

And because Thawra is nowhere near the Green Zone, Nuwayra began digging. Maybe there was a secret cable between Falida's house and the Americans. But all her conjectures vanished like smoke in the wind. At last she returned home and hid herself on her roof to keep a close watch. Though Nuwayra stayed up all that night, fighting off sleep as the cold gnawed her bones, she didn't notice anything out of the ordinary. But before deciding to abandon this tedious matter and climb down, she saw a gradual fading of the light in Fadila's house until it disappeared, leaving utter darkness.

Nuwayra rubbed her eyes and renewed her vigil. Yes, the house was completely dark! And then, yes, an enormous ball of light descended from the sky. The closer it got to Fadila's house, the smaller it became, until it was transformed into a tiny point of light so intense it burned the eyes. As soon as it touched the roof, the house was lit up anew.

The next night, the whole neighborhood stayed awake up on its rooftops to confirm the report that she spread so skillfully and with her customary speed.

At the very same hour that Nuwayra had witnessed the incident, Fadila's house was again extinguished and then relit—though, this time, it happened without anyone seeing the ball of light that Nuwayra had described. After the show, they came down from their rooftops and crowded together in front of the house of Fadila and her poor children, who were all sleeping in the warm lamplight that flowed through every corner of their home. It wrapped their skinny bodies in blankets of dreamlike music. Then someone brought a long cord to connect his house to Fadila's, and it lit up instantaneously. Another did the same thing. A third followed suit, and then a fourth, and then all the rest. Soon all of Thawra City was illuminated. From the sky it must have looked like an enormous ship floating through the long, black night of Iraq.

In the streets and avenues of Thawra City, in its squares and buildings, spread reports of the glowing colors that hummed the melody of eternal light. The children of the city threw their skinny bodies into this vast lake of light and

209

swam with the deepest pleasure and delight. All the while, Fadila and her poor children slept with their empty bellies in the dark and the bitter cold. Their desiccated bodies huddled together and dreamed of the return of a father taken away forever by an electric shock.

Shalash: Tongue-Tied and Good Enough to Eat

Today I saw Khadija, the schoolteacher, standing by her door. I decided I would greet her in some novel way. A way, I mean, that would make her think about me a little. But when the time came, I started stammering. I blushed, and, as the poet says, all the words eluded my tongue.

Nevertheless, on account of her experience with kids like me at school, Khadija knew what I wanted. Right away she smiled and said, "Look at you, Shalash! You're so handsome now I could eat you up. Your new job suits you!"

"Thank you, Khadija, but I'm . . ."

"Tongue-tied, my little Shalushi? What's the matter?"

Tongue-tied! I ran away before the embarrassment could kill me. The conversation upset my stomach and made my head spin. Khadija was so beautiful. Wait, *just* beautiful? Hardly. Her beauty could be the death of any man. She shreds you to pieces! And if we have time, later, I'll give you a detailed description.

I continued on my way with a smile this wide. No! On top of that, I was singing in a semi-audible voice. I was walking, yes, but by my soul, I had no idea where I was going. I took out my mobile and saw that it had some credit left. I immediately called Ragab, the man of impossible tasks. And if we have time, I'll tell you later about my dear friend Ragab.

"Hello? Hey, Ragab, how's it going?"

"Hi, Shalash!"

"Where are you? At the store?"

"Yes, at the store."

"Can I come find you? Do you have any bottles of Asriya?"

"Come right over!"

"But listen, Ragab. I might not have any money left since I'm going both ways in a taxi."

"Just come, brother! When do you ever have money?"

"Taxi! Al-Amana Garage, please."

The driver was a young man who looked sporty and modern, but after two hundred meters, he hit a button on the radio. *Click!* It was a latmiya, a religious lament for the Prophet's grandson, Husayn. And what a latmiya! The kind that really gets you! I, being the world's biggest hypocrite, well, as soon as I run into one of those people who are always playing latmiyas, I immediately start sucking up to them.

"This latmiya is really powerful. It's going to make me cry!"

"Yes, it's by Basim Karbalaei."

"God, his voice is so beautiful! Why doesn't he record other songs too?"

"Other songs? What kind of whore do you take him for? The guy has dedicated his voice to latmiyas. He's one of the faithful, a true believer."

"Good for him! The man's going straight to paradise."

"Yes, and may God put us there with him!"

"Now, if only all singers could bring themselves to record some latmiyas, they'd gain both this world and the hereafter."

"What whores!"

"So true! If only Umm Kulthum had recorded a few latmiyas before she died, she would have escaped the fires of hell."

"Satan got into her head and led her astray. Then he left her to writhe in the desolation of the grave."

"If that happened to Umm Kulthum, then what will they do to Haifa Wehbe? Oh, shit, Haifa Wehbe! Especially that new song of hers last month about Ragab."

"About Ragab?"

"Yes, about Ragab."

"A song named after the seventh month of the year? Does she have one for the other eleven too? What does she sing for Shawwal?"

"No! Not the month! Ragab is the name of her boyfriend's friend."

"Her boyfriend's friend? Doesn't sound like any kind of friendship I'd trust, brother. That's nothing but being a very public pimp!"

At that moment, brothers, I realized that Ragab was also the name of one of *my* friends, so Haifa Wehbe could well have been singing about me. Hey, anything is possible under globalization, no? So I started daydreaming about that possibility while the driver babbled about I don't know what, and the latmiya went on playing. We arrived, I handed over the fare, then I raced off to see my Ragab. He was ready with the bottle of strong, local arak in a black bag. I stuck my hand in my pocket for some money, but Ragab said, "Forget it,

Shalash! Consider it a gift." Let me take this opportunity to say that I don't like gifts. But nevertheless, I grabbed the bag, gave Ragab a few kisses, and went on my way.

Over the course of my trip, I'd forgotten all about Khadija and started thinking instead of Haifa Wehbe. Haifa Wehbe is unbelievable, brothers! Have you seen the video of her singing "Ragab," with her long white dress and the butterfly tattoo on her shoulder? How could I not lose my mind watching that? Oh my God! She's no mere woman! She's a bombshell! A nymph of paradise, for sure!

Man, those Wahhabi guys wearing short dishdasha robes are right to blow themselves up. They're already dying from scabies. What good-looking woman would ever check them out? Guys, take it from Shalash, the only way you're ever going to cozy up to a Haifa Wehbe is in paradise, so be my guest and take the express elevator. Go ahead and off yourselves, and may your sin be on my neck! But, please, not by blowing yourself up in the employment line, okay? Go up to a roof instead. Or jump off a bridge. What, you don't have bridges? Fine, go drink some naphthalene then! The Shiites have borne God's wrath for ages, and now they have to put up with you too?

I made it home, set down the bottle, and prepared some jajeek with cucumbers. I didn't make it with any lettuce this time, because you get enough crunch with the cucumbers. By this time my mind was cycling back to our main topic, Khadija. Yes, man, Khadija, the schoolteacher! Khadija is very, very beautiful. But to tell the truth, she isn't more beautiful than Haifa Wehbe. Not the kind of heavenly nymph you'd commit suicide for. But she's worth half a bottle of arak for sure, worth the song "Tricked by Time, Deceived by You," worth a fling in a dead-end alley, worth a poem by the neighborhood poet. And if we have time, I'll give you an exact description of Khadija, the schoolteacher, as soon as I can manage it.

I laid out my meal on the floor and dove into my first glass, then my second. The arak started kicking in. I turned on the TV. Thank God, the power was on! Which also meant we didn't need to endure the noise of the generator down the street. I changed the channel to Rotana and waited for Haifa Wehbe to make an appearance. On my sixth glass, the disaster herself appeared! What's more, it was her song, "Ragab":

Ragab, keep your friend from me
Ragab, your friend drives me mad
Ragab, get close to me
Shalash will drive me mad
Shalash: when he saw me
He said he didn't know me

Haifa was looking right at me, winking and laughing. She assumed I was drunk, and once again I thought I might die from shame. I hid my face, but as soon as she turned her back, I snuck a quick peek. Haifa went on singing for two hours this time. The power went out, and she was still singing. People went to bed, and she kept crooning in my head. No! She was looking at me in this aggressive, half-crazed way, like she wanted to gobble me up. I was paralyzed by shyness. Haifa cried out in frustration. She dropped the mic and jumped on top of me. She was kissing me like mad. Ah, friends, what an

214

old jalopy I turned out to be. All my rust was showing! I was dying! No, oh no! Mommy, come quick! Save me, Nana! Haifa grabbed me by the hand and dragged me to the bedroom. Maybe, if I have time later, I'll tell you what we did.

In the morning, I found the bottle of arak in my lap and my mother standing over me. "Get up, Shalash! You've barely started your new job, and you're already skipping a day? And did you hear, your friend just got engaged! Ragab! No? Now what kind of friend would get engaged and not tell you? But he really deserves it. Not only is the woman beautiful, but she's a schoolteacher too. It's Khadija!"

Hearing that, I went right back to sleep!

The Shalashian Satellite Channel

"The Shalash Media Network, which includes the Shalashian Satellite Channel, the newspaper, *Gooshalash Morning*, and the news radio station, ISHLICH, is proud to announce that it will be providing each of our political parties an opportunity to introduce their platforms on the new program, *You and the Voter*—each being granted a longer or shorter time slot consistent with the given party's status in our hearts.

"*You and the Voter* will be taped live in our studios, so each candidate will have to visit our studios, accompanied by sufficient protection. The network would also like to stress that the following will be forbidden to the candidates and their entourages while on the premises:

- The use of sacred geometric symbols in campaign materials.
- Smoking with a hookah.
- Entering indecent locales.
- Random assassinations.
- Any mention of the Sayyid.

"And now, my dear viewers and honored listeners, we welcome the president of the first party, according to alphabetical order, Dr. Ayad Allawi:

"Dr. Ayad Allawi, welcome to the Shalash Media Network, and its primary channel, the Shalashian Satellite Channel. As I'm sure you're aware, sir, our network is *very* impartial. We do not organize our callers in advance, nor are we acting under any strict orders to prefer the Sayyid Muqtada's Jama'a Party over yours. So once again, welcome, and before we begin our conversation with you, we'll break for two hours for a word from our sponsors. Dear viewers, please don't bother to stick around."

(The break ends.)

"Welcome back, dear viewers! Once again, we welcome our guest, Dr. Allawi, president of the Iraqi National Party. Dr. Allawi, could you give us a succinct idea of your campaign platform? I look forward to hearing your response after taking this call. Hello?"

"Peace be upon you!"

"And upon you, peace and the mercy of God. Who is this, please?"

"Me? What do you care who this is? What's tonight's topic, anyway?"

"Just go ahead, sir, say your piece—but quickly, please! Actually take all the time you need."

"Peace be upon you, as well as the mercy of God and his blessings! With that out of the way, I'm sure you know that Imam Ali (peace be upon him!) said in his letter to Harith al-Hamdani, 'Take what has passed in this world as a lesson for what comes afterward. The one resembles the other, for the latter follows the former.' Now that elections in Iraq are approaching, we call upon you, brothers and sisters, all followers of the household of the Prophet, to participate most vigorously in the process! Know that your votes are a pledge of loyalty. So see whom you are pledging yourselves to! Your vote is a trust. So watch where you are depositing it! It is a victory for our martyrs buried in their mass graves. On a day when neither your wealth nor your sons will avail you aught, you will be asked, 'To whom did you give your vote, noble Shiite?'

"When you are sinking into your grave, dear voter, your ballot will precede you there, into that place where apologies are worth nothing. Then it will be either yes to the three fives multiplied by ten, that amount of good things, or it's seven hundred thirty-one bad things that will blaze in their fire. What a difference between this and that! Remember that, and pick 555, not 731, when you see the list numbers on your ballot!

"And so, in conclusion, I'd like to thank the Shalashian Network, the channel of truth and faith, the channel of the mass graves, for providing this wonderful opportunity for me to be heard! Peace be upon you, as well as the mercy of God and all his blessings!"

"Why, thank you, venerable sir, for your call, and may God give you the greatest rewards of the blessed! I see another call is already coming in. Go ahead, brother, who is this? Go ahead, what would you like to add to this conversation?"

"To be honest, my contribution would be best expressed through song—in particular, my version of the popular folk song by Saadoun Jaber, 'People of Al-Majer.'"

"By all means, brother!"

> "This is the daughter of our master, wearing the dress with
> long sleeves.
>   Too bad, so sad, Allawi! I'm going to vote for our master.
> They're calling me. What do they want from me? I'm going to vote
>   Even if God's wrath were to fall upon me, I'm going to vote!
> This is the daughter of Al-Maksusi; trod, trod on my ribs!
>   I don't want you as my bride unless Azzawi wins
> They're calling me. What do they want from me? I'm going to vote
>   Even if God's wrath were to fall upon me, I'm going to vote!

"That's all I have to say. Peace be upon you."

"And you! We now return, dear viewers, to our dear guest, Dr. Ayad Allawi, president of the Iraqi National Party. Doctor, we were saying—oh! We have another call. Hello? Go ahead!"

"Good evening to you! An evening of love and passion and desire!"

"Whoa, then! And upon you be peace! Who's this?"

"A heartsore poet of the people."

"Go ahead with your contribution, brother."

"You're not to be respected; you're just a silly fool.

It's my fault for loving you, Hiyam, and losing for good Latifa.

You're insincere with your words, while at least she was good.

She was reserved and modest, while you're loose and easy.

You call me a troublemaker, Hiyam? Not a word but a missile!

I'm no troublemaker, Hiyam, I'm just Jawad Lifa.

"So there, you bitch! Your father can lick my shoes, and the chief of your tribe too! Thanks so much for taking my call!"

"Yikes! No problem! Hello? We have a new caller. Go ahead—who's this?"

"Hi, guys!"

"Upon you be peace! Who's calling, please?"

"It's your brother, Faduri, from Al-Kafah."

"Go ahead, brother, please say your piece. Our time is nearly up for the day."

"Brother, yesterday night on your channel, on that blue ribbon that runs across the bottom of the screen, someone on your staff put in the words, 'I shit on the daughters of Al-Kafah, and especially the divorced ones.' And, you know, after seeing that, I couldn't sleep the whole night. I kept calling, but your lines were busy. Can you give me the address of this so-called journalist, so that I might teach him about the daughters of Al-Kafah?"

"Brother, please, this is not the subject of our program."

"No? So what do I care about the subject of your program? This coward needs to be taught a lesson and get to know his own people better, my brother."

"Brother, forgive me, but I'm compelled—"

"What do you mean, *compelled*? Let me tell you that your channel is good for nothing but spurring on religious division and violence. Oh yes! Where do you get off talking about the daughters of Al-Kafah? Why aren't you talking about girls from Najaf? For your information, and in case you haven't heard, but I've gone out with three women from Najaf, all drop-dead gorgeous, and all divorced, okay? You want their names? I have their pictures right here!"

"Oh dear, we seem to have been cut off! But we have another caller all lined up. Go ahead—who's this?"

"I'm hajjiya Nana'a from Amara, from Al-Majer Al-Kaber."

"Welcome, hajjiya! Go ahead."

"I wonder, may I please make a little request . . . ?"

"Please, go ahead!"

"Oh, good. I'd like to request the song, 'Pomegranate, O Pomegranate,' and I'd like to dedicate it to—"

"Hajjiya, we have Dr. Ayad Allawi here with us today, in case you have a question or comment."

"Yes, I do. Doctor, how are you doing? I've missed you! The people of Al-Majer send their greetings and tell me to kiss you for them."

Ayad Allawi: "Welcome! Welcome to the hajjiya! How are you? Please greet your neighbors back for me!"

"But Doctor, I have a question."

"Please, hajjiya, go ahead."

"Doctor, when I walk a lot, I get stomach cramps, I feel dizzy, and I start shaking, and sometimes I even throw up!"

"Hajjiya Nana'a, it's Dr. Allawi who's with us: the president of the Iraqi National Party."

"Oh! I thought he was a stomach doctor. Well, thanks anyway!"

"Thank you, hajjiya. We have another caller. Hello! Who's this?"

"A longtime friend of the program, Hamdan al-Shuwayli. Greetings from the Sheikhs' Market!"

"Welcome, Brother Hamdan! Please, go ahead."

"Could you let me know the topic of the show tonight, so I can participate?"

"Our topic is the elections, and our guest is—"

"Oh, the elections, good! Listen, my friend, our governor is robbing us blind. Can't you think of something we can do about him? Man, he ripped off everything *and* the kitchen sink, but when we tell him, 'We're going to file a complaint with Prime Minister al-Jaafari,' he just laughs. And the police chief in Nasiriyah, both of his brothers are thieves as well. When we tell him, 'We're going to file a complaint with Minister of the Interior Solagh,' he laughs too! And then the director of Sayyid Muqtada's office is getting married every day, so now all our women are gone. We say, 'We're going to the Sayyid,' but he just laughs. I'm telling you, friend—"

"Please, please do go on!"

"What? Are you laughing now too?"

"Brother, I'm sorry, but that's not our topic for tonight. Goodbye! Doctor, you've listened to the calls from our brothers in the audience. Do you have any comments of your own? Ah, but before hearing your answer, I'll take one more call. Hello! Who's this?"

"I . . . I'm Nana'a from Al-Majer. I've prepared something to share with you tonight."

"Why, go ahead, hajjiya."

"I'm your mother, Nana'a, and I've built up my courage.

I want to ignore Muqtada's Jama'a, and I'll vote for Allawi.
They're calling me! What do they want from me, these people
of Al-Majer?

On top of God's anger upon me, these people of Al-Majer!

"Thank you, *merci*, and may God bless you all."

"Now, wasn't that pretty? Dr. Allawi, we have another
caller, and after that, we'll come back to you for your reply.
Hello! Please go ahead. Who's this?"

"I'm Fakhriya, Nana'a's sister. I have a short rebuttal I'd
like to make?"

"Go ahead!"

"Shut up, Nana'a! You make trouble for yourself.

You spoke about the Jama'a, and now Muqtada is upset.
They're calling me! What do they want from me, these
sodden drunkards?

On top of God's anger upon me, these sodden drunkards!

"Good night and *bonjour* to everyone in television land! In all
seriousness, your program is really pretty adorable, you know?"

"Hello? Ah, we have another caller. Hello! Who's this?"

"This is Nana'a, Fakhriya's sister."

"Aha, please go right ahead!"

"Shut up, Fakhriya, and vote for Al Iraqiya!

Your guys are popping pills, and they haven't seen this show.

They're calling me! What do they want from me, those
gambling card sharks?

    On top of God's anger upon me, those gambling card
    sharks!"

"My apologies, Dr. Allawi, it seems like this is really a wonderful day for viewer engagement! We already have another
call on the line. Hello! Who's this?"

"Fakhriya. It's still Fakhriya, my dear, I never hung up."

"Oh, well, you're back on the air. Have you got anything
to add?"

    "I'm your sister, Fakhriya; I've nothing to do with Nana'a.

        By the Seventh Imam, I'm not her sister; she's just putting
        out that rumor.

    You want to take me down, you want to get me in trouble
    with Jama'a?

        They're calling me! What do they want from me?

        They're probably here.

    On top of God's anger upon me, they're probably here!"

"Goodness me, my dear viewers, our phone lines are burning
up! Yet another call already! Please, go ahead."

"It's Nana'a, and I demand my right of response. She's not
being open with you. She's no federalist. You think you're
going to drive the Americans out?"

"Please, go ahead, but please keep it brief."

    "Oh, you filthy Fakhriya! You've become a Muqtada backer

        When you were the biggest Ba'athist in the party branch.

When the luck of the world withered, you joined them
against me.

They're calling me! What do they want from me, you party
member?

On top of God's anger upon me, this party member!"

"And now, my dear viewers—oops! Here comes another call."

"It's Fakhriya, and I demand the right of response to that
response. My heart is burning up inside me!"

"Go ahead! Go ahead!"

"Nana'a, Nana'a, such a big shot, you always talk a big game.

She's the one who was the Ba'athist, the biggest of them all.

Why does she tell lies about me? Lying for her's a habit.

They're calling me! What do they want from me, the Sadr
Army?

On top of God's anger upon me, that Sadr Army!

"*Merci encore* to you and to your kind doctor. He's so nice, it
just kills me! Apologies!"

"And now, my dear viewers, we thank Dr. Ayad Allawi,
president of the Iraqi National Party, for joining us on the
program, *You and the Voter*, and for his answers to all our
questions. Likewise, we thank our viewers for all their valuable contributions. Till next time, my friends—same Shalash
time, same Shalash channel! God keep you all!"

Yesterday's Comrade and Today's Turban: This Is No Way to Live!

The olive-khaki uniform, the pistol, and the stacks of dossiers have disappeared. In their place we have rosary beads, big rings, and a black mark on the forehead from its smacking by the prayer tablet. The purpose of both sets is clear as day.

The old signs terrified us and now the new signs are working just as well. We exchanged Comrade Shinawa for Sayyid Ta'ma. The first was our dear comrade, the second is our exalted master. The ground could hardly support the weight of the first as he walked, while you'd say the second is trying to buy us. The first was held back in school so often it's a wonder he could count, while the second only deigned to sign up for school when his brother got hired as its security guard.

The first one hates me and tells me, "You're bitter about the party and the Ba'athist revolution." The second one hates me and tells me, "You hate the religious clerkship." Between the first and the second, I lived the years of my youth in torment, grief, pain, anxiety, and fear. On your honor, friends, tell me: Is this a country? What kind of country makes you divide your life between Shinawa and Ta'ma?

My brothers in Sweden, Denmark, and Holland, and my sisters in Australia, Canada, Norway, and Finland: On your honor, is this a country? By your conscience, is this any way to live? Why do you keep silent? Why don't you speak the truth? If I were to start swearing now as I tell you all about them, you'd say, "Shalash is so impolite. He uses such distasteful and indecent language." Fine! I'll try it your way. Show me a strong insult without any swearing and let's see if it can quench my burning thirst for revenge upon Shinawa and Ta'ma.

And then I'm afraid one of you will say, "Just let it go! Shinawa's time has passed." No, friends! Shinawa still has his same power, in fact he's now become even more powerful. Listen, Shinawa is a walking catastrophe. He came right back to take charge. He took off the olive-green suit, put on a dishdasha, took out a black rosary with one hundred and one beads, burned his forehead with a grilled eggplant, put big rings on his fingers, and so . . . became our very own lord of the rings.

It's really none of my business. Let him become a minister in the government! I mean, are the ministers now any better than Shinawa? It's a good living, and I don't like to mess around with people's livelihoods. But how about he shows me the same respect and quit dragging me around by the collar?! I wish you'd tell him to just leave me alone and refrain from busting a gut every time he sees me, showing his black teeth and laughing, "Well, if it isn't Shalash the Kiss-Ass!"

On your honor, *me*, a kiss-ass? It makes me want to rend my clothes and go around in sackcloth and ashes. Yes, either let me tear off my clothes or let me swear to my heart's content, please, before I explode . . .

"Me, Shinawa? *I'm* a kiss-ass?"

Fine, fine—I'm going to set aside the subject of Shinawa, and I won't even use any dirty words in the process. But how can I hold my tongue about Ta'ma? It's true that Sayyid

Ta'ma, my brothers, was not formerly a party comrade, but he wasn't a religious sayyid either. Within the space of one year, he has become a sayyid and a religious man, and the people are kissing his hand.

It's okay, you say, since he was just afraid before and had to hide. Fine, I'll go along with that too. But let me ask you something: Why was Ta'ma imprisoned when he was a junior officer? Is it because he was a sayyid? Or did the poor guy get caught praying too much? No. Perhaps it was because he was spying for the squadrons of liberation that entered Baghdad in April 2003? No, friends, Ta'ma was locked up because he robbed an army warehouse. Yes, he plundered a warehouse and spent four years sleeping in the Diyala Prison!

And when Ta'ma got out of prison, the poor guy nearly died of starvation. So where did all the ill-gotten gains from the warehouse heist go? Ha! Didn't he go and buy a yellow semitruck and work the Iraq–Jordan route? Poor Ta'ma! We ought to kiss his hands every day on account of his nice semi. I swear, if not for Ta'ma's truck, all the furniture from the Ministry of Communications would have burned up in the war. But—and may God repay his deed!—he loaded it all up and saved it all from the fire.

So why am I so incensed now? An entire country has been plundered, sure, but what does that matter to me? The problem, my readers, is just that Ta'ma won't leave me alone! Whenever he sees me, he shouts, "Hey, you drunk! When are you going to make things right? Come over here! I'll put you to work driving a fire truck."

I'm not too proud to work. Work is no shame. But, on your honor, have you ever seen an engineer working as a fire-truck driver? Hey, now. Take it easy! I don't want to hear you saying, "Here we go with the lies again! Shalash has made himself an engineer all of a sudden." Come on, I swear! I really am an engineer! What else do you want from me? Do you all despise me like Ta'ma? Why do you want to make me cry? Really, on the soul of my mother, I'm an engineer! Fine, fine. No one believes me. But why don't you take a good look at yourselves as well, my friends?

Let's get down to it! With all due respect to engineers, what's the big deal if some guy's an engineer? These days people just say they're a sayyid, or a partisan, or a Sadrist, and that's enough to make it so, no? So what's the big deal with declaring that you're an engineer too?

Doctors, you say? Doctors are what we need? Ha! Doctors are a dime a dozen! What this country *really* needs are more sayyids, partisans, pious people, Badrists, tribal bards, and self-flagellators in order for us to rebuild Iraq in a modern way. Iraq is the Japan of the Middle East, remember? What's wrong with you? *Wasn't Japan built by engineers?* you ask. Nonsense! I swear by the martyr Imam Husayn, no one but the Japanese built Japan! Engineers had nothing to do with it.

Praise God, today's chapter is shaping up really nice! All in all, I've kept myself under control, and I haven't used any foul language whatsoever, neither about our battling comrade Shinawa, nor about the great Sayyid Ta'ma. Because it would be a shame to sink to their level, right? But, friends, what a relief it would be if you let me sink just for a second! What's that, they have religious significance too, you say? Oh, come off it. One is a comrade, and the other is a burglar. By your honor, let me cuss them out already! What do you say?

Ahh! God, you're destroying me with these morals of yours! Listen—one time in the winter, two months before the regime fell, Sayyid Ta'ma spotted me as I was standing on the corner. He came up to me, and without me asking, he told me a story. Maybe if I tell it to *you*, I'll finally be able to relax. And I promise I won't swear at him afterward.

Well, Ta'ma told me—remember, it's his story, not mine—that when he was coming back in his semi the previous night, he saw a woman near the Sha'ab International Stadium wearing an abaya and flagging down passing cars. "How strange!" Ta'ma said to himself. "A woman out at night waving at my semi." Then he told me: "I made a big U-turn, went back, and pulled up to her. The woman opened the passenger door, and as soon as she got in, one of her sandals dropped off back onto the street because the cab is so high off the ground. So she threw her abaya up to me and got down to retrieve her shoe . . ."

Actually, tell you what, I'm not going to finish the story about what took place in the semitruck's cab because it's just too shameful. But I hope you'll ask Ta'ma's wife all about it, and I'll put her phone number down right here: [REDACTED]. Go ahead and ask her, from Shalash, "Didn't Ta'ma spend the night away from home last summer? Didn't he tell you that his truck broke down in Haswa? And in the morning, after he got back, when you were cleaning the cab for him, didn't you find a woman's purse with ten thousand dinars in it?" Go ahead!

Well, Ta'ma, do you still want to put me to work driving a fire engine? Eh, Sayyid Ta'ma, did you think I would forget? I'm exposing you now for all to see. I'm going to get both the

Nuwayra and Khanjar news agencies tattling about you, and make you more famous than that famous singer, Abd Falak. Oh, Sayyid Ta'ma, you son of a . . .

Whoops! Stopped myself in the nick of time, my virgin-eyed readers. And as for Shinawa, who called me a kiss-ass . . . by God, now that's a pickle! I could tell you all sorts of things about that august gentleman, but I'm afraid that if I start blabbing, you'll just say, "How awful this Shalash is! Airing other men's dirty laundry out of spite!" You'll tell people I've been poorly raised, with the morals of a guinea pig and the scruples of a gangster. Mum's the word, concealment is a blessing, and all that! But, I'm telling you, if Shinawa comes around just one more time with that "kiss-ass" of his, I'll run his filthy shorts up the nearest flagpole . . . how they would catch him in the school bathroom, for example, starting in the fifth grade, and how he kept on doing it until he finished middle school and became a Ba'athist . . .

So tell me, on your honor, what kind of a country makes you spend your life between Shinawa and Ta'ma? When we were in school, instead of teaching us the national anthem, "A homeland has spread its wings to the horizon, etc., etc.," they should have taught us to give praise to "Our Country 'Tis of Ta'ma and Shinawa"!

But be careful, Shinawa: if you say, "Shalash the Kiss-Ass" one more time, you know what I'll do, right?

(I'll do ten push-ups, down my breakfast, and head off to the Bab Al-Sharqi before it rains!)

A Democratic People? What Can You Do?!

Hey, friends, didn't I tell you footwear would ruin everything? No? Well, let me ask you another one: Did you get a load of how lovely democracy is yesterday, what with the people expressing their views in such a sage and appropriate manner as they drove former Prime Minister Ayad Allawi out of the Imam Ali Mosque? Even if it meant using sandals and clogs as weapons? You have now seen our brothers, whose fathers wielded pitchforks and tar maces in peasant revolts down through the ages, raise their very shoes in protest! How proud they made us! What things they accomplished!

Shalash is telling you, we're a democratic people by nature! (You don't believe me?) We're a people who would die for democracy! (You really don't believe me?) Brothers and sisters, I'm telling you, we're a country that's been plundered and torn down around our heads in two days flat, all for the sake of a little democracy and a new Iraq! (But you don't believe that either, do you?)

For hundreds of years, while all the birds of the world were wild, savage, and predatory, the birds of our imams, the ones in the holy shrine in Najaf, have been tame, strutting around the sanctuary at perfect ease. All of you—to be precise, I'm addressing my pious Shiite brothers—do you remember when we were kids, and we would go for a visit to the shrine with our mothers and grandmothers? We would cry, wanting to chase the birds, while our mothers yelled, "Heavens, no! Behave yourselves!"

"Why, Mommy?" we'd ask. "Let me catch them!"

"These are the birds of the shrine, son, protected by the Imam. Don't get us in trouble!"

But these days, the days of a black, turbaned Iraq, the sanctuary birds have emigrated out of fear, and the tomb of the holy Imam has become a trap for careless members of rival parties . . . If the wrong person should enter, people immediately pull out their sticks and knives, along with their sandals, clogs, and flip-flops.

Democracy! A noble contention between varieties of footwear, not only permitted but constitutionally guaranteed! In any case, being raised to fight with shoes is nothing new for our people. All of you remember the famous incident of mutual pelting that occurred in the Islamic Republic of Iran six years ago, when the ayatollah on their side of the border cursed the ayatollah on our side, and then the Iranian followers of the one over here drew their sandals, clogs, and flip-flop weapons manufactured there, and they used them to beat the ayatollah who was over there. Are you confused, brothers, or is all this clear? If anyone doesn't understand, let him raise his hand!

As it says in that song, "I'd tell you what happened, but I'm afraid of what they'll say about me!"

What do I mean? Let me tell you what I mean. Didn't I used to see the "hero of our national liberation" on television all the time, thousands of times, the same guy who's now on trial for dropping a water heater on the people of Dujail one summer? In the holy city of Najaf, I saw him climb onto the roof of his car—with my own eyes I saw it!—and greet the crowds who had come to salute His Eminence, proclaiming their absolute loyalty, every throat reverberating with invocations to His Glory! (God preserve him!) This wasn't millennia ago, folks; it all happened just a few years before the regime collapsed. And, what do you know, these shoe-wielding voters of ours wear all the same faces, indeed they wear all the same shoes! They were here to welcome their leader, who climbed down from his vehicle to rub elbows with his countrymen and pushed his way through with difficulty. How is it no one stepped up like a man, as they did just yesterday, to draw a sandal from its holster and beat the leader silly with it? Well? Is there anyone out there man enough to step up today and tell me why?

I have no doubt that the people who were dancing in front of the leader like monkeys are the same ones who murdered Al-Khoei in the very same spot last year and also those who committed yesterday's crime, the ramifications of which have yet to be seen in their entirety. Those same people plus, maybe (to make a full and complete reckoning), a few of our siblings from our "geographically neighboring countries," as Mullah Ibrahim al-Jaafari likes to put it.

I'm not here to deny the right of people to demonstrate and protest against politicians—there's not a single politician I'd defend, to be frank. Protest is a legitimate right, indeed, a duty! But not with shoes, my friends. What's your deal? So you don't respect the people visiting Imam Ali Mosque. Big deal! At least respect the Imam! Have a little decency! What a shame for you all to be so easily manipulated, such pawns! Besides which, insulting a candidate is an insult to those who vote for him. Be like me! Take a seat way at the back and then criticize and curse to your heart's content!

Ah, I was forgetting who I was talking to! If Salman the Deaf should tell me that Allawi deserved what he got—"You've read his list of candidates: all of them are against the Shiites!"—the tragedy is that Salman can't read, write, or hear. His family doesn't even have a generator to be able to watch what's on TV.

I swear, what's wrong with you people? You just want to let the mob have its fun, is that it? No, no, this is not okay! Would you ever allow some stranger to get up and slap one of your friends around with an old shoe? Tell me! Would you just stand by and accept it?

Elections are meant to be battles waged by throwing pieces of paper into a box, not by launching intercontinental Kurdish slippers at each other near the tomb of the Imam of Truth and Martyrdom.

Brothers, whosoever believes in the democracy of sandals, clogs, flip-flops, and Kalashnikovs either doesn't know what the concept implies, or else has come to us simply to burn everything down—one of the two! He's no politician. Let him sit at home, take it easy, and give the people some rest. Or let him take his wares and go back to his uncles in Iran. God bless you, if you're going to do a thing, do it right! You're making us all sick. You've crossed the line. You shamed us; you exposed us. I don't even know what Iraq has become.

In conclusion: Vote for the Kurdish Slipper Party!

Our Chaldo-Assyrian Brothers

These days, the words that cause me the most fear, the most sleepless nights, the phrase that makes me pray, "God save me!" every time I hear it, is this: "Our brothers." It's taken on so many unsavory meanings, lately. Aggressive, weighty meanings. We Iraqis have lived our whole lives as brothers and sisters, in concord and in mutual love, without ever resorting to such doublespeak. In my entire life, I've never told my parents, "I've received an invitation from our Sunni brothers for tomorrow," when invited by my university friends from Anbar Province to share a meal of their famous dish, *dilaymiya*. Likewise, I've never heard my friends from Mosul say, "We're off to see our Shiite brothers," when they were invited to share a meal of *qima* in the weeks leading up to Ashura. Not, at least, until we became "brothers," rather recently, by the grace of God, who has united our hearts.

From early morning until night, the only thing we hear on television is "our Shiite brothers" and "our Kurdish brothers" and "our Sabian brothers" and "our Yezidi brothers." Give it up already with this brotherhood nonsense! And so that I may be clear with all "our brothers," I tell them that whenever I hear a Sunni say, for example, "our Shiite brothers," what I hear him saying, for my part, in his heart of hearts, is "that lowlife, backwater scum." And whenever I hear a proper Shiite with all his religious rings say, "our Sunni brothers," what I hear him saying, in his heart, is "those Salafi terrorists and enemies of the Prophet's household." And whenever I hear a refined Arab nationalist say, I don't know, "our Kurdish brothers," I could swear he was actually saying, "The Halabja massacre was the least you deserved!" And if I should hear a holier-than-thou Salafi Sunni say, I don't know, "our Yezidi brothers," I am sorry to report that I believe he is adding in his heart, "God's curse upon you and that fallen angel you worship!" And when I hear a Kurd, with his right foot in Iraq and his left in the Kurdistan utopia, say, "our Arab kakat," I'm pretty sure he really means, "those dirty, backward Arabs." And when I hear someone from the Badr Brigades say, "our Sadrist brothers," to me it's as though he's saying, "those illiterate kids God is using to test us!" And when I hear someone from Allawi's coalition say, "our brothers in the other parties," a voice in my head whispers that he really means, "those morons, incapable of administering so much as a market stall!" And as for the tidy phrase "our brothers who 'were away' for the last elections," well, that means, "May God send all their luck away too!"

Whenever they hear the use of this phrase increasing, my brother-readers can be certain that the shit has just hit the fan. This past week, when the phrase "our brothers" was being used more than ever, I put my hands over my heart—that heart of mine, which always knows the score. For more than twenty of "our brothers"—both blood brothers and adopted ones—had fallen as martyrs. Twenty martyrs in Thawra City and its suburbs, and that's just the ones I heard about! Among them were sons of the Sadrist movement, which is a new development in the phenomenon of some of "our brothers" being killed by others among "our brothers."

These days, the term "brother" and its derivations have broken free of their original meanings entirely, flooding into new ones. If someone behind you gives you a push with a lettuce cart because you're blocking their way, and you hear him tell you, "A little to the side, my brother!" don't over-think it, because what he means here is, "Get the hell out of my way, you ass!" And if someone should tell you, "Greet our sister for me," and he means your well-guarded wife, then watch out, my brother-reader, for this might be a kind of signal to the woman, an innocuous "missed call" on her phone, while you're none the wiser! And if someone should tell you, "Yesterday I saw 'my sisters' in Palestine Street," and he's actually talking about *your* sisters, dear reader, well, this means they're being stalked, no doubt about it. And when someone says "She's like my sister" to you when talking about some woman, well, it means the gentleman in question wants to bang the chick, and if you don't know what *that* means, please don't ask me. And when a woman asks you, "Please, my strong brother, how do I get to the local clinic?" believe me, it's time to watch your back. And when someone says, "With God as my witness, you look just like my brother!" then rest assured you're about to get asked for a loan of a few thousand until the first of the month. And, hey, if you read a politician addressing you as "our brother, the generous voter," despite the fact that you know damn well you're the stingiest person anyone's ever met, then just remember that, in the eyes of that campaign, you are no more or less than another piece of paper to be thrown into a ballot box, end of story! On the other hand, my dear reader, to sum up, if you should ever hear your friend Shalash mention that he took your sister on

Seventh: Soft hands intertwined, making up a lovely, mixed-gender circle to dance the *dabka*, all to strains of Kadim Al Sahir's song, "A Joyful Eid That We All Celebrate Tonight."

Eighth: When His Eminence Ayatollah Alqas Yuhanna Dankha came to the celebration, no one ran to kiss his hand or start flattering him, not even the soldiers of the honorable Chaldo-Assyrian clerkship.

Ninth: There were no cheers, no defiant funeral procession, and no call and response with the traditional, "Hey, brothers, hey!"

Tenth: No one was liquidated for putting up posters.

Eleventh: I didn't see anyone passing stacks of money to the voters.

Twelfth: No one recited any vernacular folk poetry.

Thirteenth: They didn't bring up the mass graves, even though their people were the ones found in the first mass grave in the history of contemporary Iraq.

I could go on and on, my dear readers, but I believe that what I've mentioned above is sufficient to remove the label of "Iraqi" from "our Chaldo-Assyrian brothers," even though they were the original inhabitants of our land when Muhammad's people marched upon them and spread inexorably throughout the land.

May God come to your aid, our Chaldo-Assyrian brothers, whenever you hear your Muslim brothers call you a "minority"! It's not because they've bought into progressive ideas about minority rights, but just to point out that they outnumber you by a lot. . . and this, by the current logic, makes for a majority. Which only goes to show that we are *all* minorities in the nation of flies, since, in the new Iraq, the flies outnumber everyone.

Which reminds me. Speaking of flies, when some of "our brothers" in the government come on television, why do the flies always swarm around them? What, don't they have soap in the Green Zone?

High-Octane Political Gasoline

It doesn't matter that Uncle Solagh, our venerable Minister of the Interior, has imposed a curfew ahead of the upcoming elections. I swear by my eyes—by my whole head!—we're not even going to bother leaving the house for a week. That's nothing new for us. We'll watch a lot of TV. No problem at all. Just be sure to keep the electricity running, Uncle Solagh, and you won't hear from us till the curfew is lifted. But can I ask, is *this* your brilliant new security plan? We'll sit right here, and, speaking for myself, I promise not to so much as stick my head out the window. Just a week? Nothing could be easier! But only on the condition, Uncle Solagh, that after this week, I won't have to hear from you ever again. Is that doable? Or is my request too difficult for you because your real goal here is to make us miserable forever? That's not democracy! Under a real democracy surely it should the right of any citizen not to see you if they don't want to? And I personally do not want to see you.

"Khanjar . . . Khanjar!"

"Hi there, Shalash. I'm busy, give me a moment."

"Hey, what are all these barrels?"

"Gas, Shalash, they're barrels of gas."

"What are you doing with gas when you don't have a car or a generator anymore?"

"You'll know soon enough!"

"Come on, man, you're going to burn your house down! You've filled the whole building with gasoline . . ."

"Shalash, don't meddle with politics. Stay just the way you are!"

"Who said anything about politics? I'm asking you about this gas."

"Shalash, my boy, this is political gas, so watch out."

Khanjar rolled the barrels inside his house. He came back out smelling his hands and wiping them off on his dishdasha. Then he came back up to me and said, "Shalash, when are you going to leave politics alone and mind your own business? Listen, son, don't meddle in what doesn't concern you."

"Khanjar, what did I say? I only asked what you were doing with all that gas because you don't have either a car or a generator anymore . . ."

"And I told you, Shalash, that it's political gas. Meaning, it's none of your business."

"But listen, I swear to you, I have no idea what you mean by *political gas!*"

"Well, this gas is a gift from our party to the noble voters."

"Really? But how can you tell which ones are noble, Khanjar?"

"It's obvious who's noble. They're the ones who are going to vote for our party."

"And what about the ones who aren't going to vote for it, Khanjar?"

"They won't get even half a gallon."

"So, Khanjar, we're voting for gasoline . . . ?"

"No, buddy, not just gasoline. Didn't you ever get any food packages? People distributed tomato paste, chickpeas, sugar, canned goods, eggs, date syrup, and macaroni. And then there are candidates who pass out blankets and heaters. They were even giving out mutton! What, have you been asleep all this time?"

"Khanjar, who's giving this stuff out?"

"Ah, many noble Iraqi gentlemen, brother. They've been saving their money for this very day."

"Okay, so if I vote for your gang, how many gallons of gas will you give me?"

"How many gallons? One vote is ten gallons, man."

"What a good and valuable initiative by your party, Khanjar."

"The thing is, Shalash, it's incumbent upon us as good citizens to distribute to each Iraqi their share of our national oil revenue, right? But what can we do for you if everyone has a different party in mind? So that's what's at stake, here. If everyone just joins together to vote for our party, you'll see prosperity in your lifetime, and all Iraqi oil wealth will return to its true owners, the people!"

"Khanjar, I have to say, that doesn't sound much like democracy! You want to buy Iraq for ten gallons a head? That's an insult."

"Just wait for your generator to start to sputter, then come and talk to me about democracy and insults . . ."

"By my honor, Khanjar, I think you're the only Iraqi alive who truly knows how to get by in these strange times."

"Come on, Shalash. Get yourself dressed and come with me. I'll show you the blessings of democracy, because after the elections are over, believe me, you won't get a cent, and nobody will even look at you anymore. Come *now*, while the ordinary citizen is still being respected, while his voice and his vote can still be heard!"

I changed my clothes and Khanjar took me by the hand. We took a stroll to the headquarters of each and every party—religious, national, progressive, regressive, and secular—and came home with a fine haul: food, fizzy drinks (Mirinda, to be exact), and cigarettes (Gauloises!). The president of one of the smaller parties even recognized me. He immediately gave me two forceful kisses on the cheek and told me, "Shalash, your voice has been heard, brother! Give us your support, and find me two bottles of Asriya arak, straight up, and no mezze, please."

On the way home, a line from that new song by Hussam Al-Rassam was running through my mind: "I saw the light from afar and said we've been burned!" And then, my dear readers, we saw that Khanjar's house had burned down because of all his democratic gas. His pictures of his party's candidates burned up because their beards turned out to be highly flammable. And the celebration of democracy on our street? It turned into a lament.

Electioneering in the Street

Hila is a poor housewife who sells vegetables in the market to earn her daily bread. At the crack of dawn, she's out at the wholesale stores in Jamila where she picks up her purchases and goes to the market to sell them. She's been at this work for twenty years, and, thanks be to God, she makes a good, secure living. Her only problem is a small one, namely that her hearing is a bit "slow," which is another way of saying she's deaf, and her whole life she's been yelling, "Eh? I didn't hear you. Speak a little louder!"

By virtue of long experience, Hila has come to understand what her customers are saying by reading their lips. She'll know that this guy wants tomatoes, that woman wants eggplant, this guy wants cucumbers, and so on. In recent days, however, Hila has started seeing strange things in the street: proclamations, rifles, flags, and posters. Sayyids coming and going. Thawra has become packed with visitors and their bodyguards. As a result, Hila has been getting new customers, strangers, people she's never even seen before. And these strangers have come with strange requests, and since she can't really hear what they're saying, she can't begin to make sense of them. She's constantly gawking at some stranger's face, and when she despairs of understanding, she resorts to saying, "Sorry, I don't have any. I'm all out."

Which is all to say that, since the elections are around the corner, all the parties' volunteers are out earning their heavenly reward, and they each think Hila will make for easy pickings.

"Hila, don't forget to vote for Jama'a!"

"I've been all out of ginger since this morning. I'm sorry!"

"Hila, Allawi is the man of the hour, you know."

"No, no, Allawi is the man who married that woman from Kadhimiya, and they have two daughters."

"Hajjiya, pay close attention to Raba'. They are a blessing!"

"I don't sell by the rub', my child: quarter kilos are too little. Only by the kilogram here!"

"Hila, vote for five-five-five!"

"Okay, daughter! Five onions, five cucumbers, and five tomatoes. You must be having people over! Anything else?"

"Hila, start making some noise. Ammar al-Hakim is coming!"

"Cauliflower for Hakim? Yes, how many do you want?"

"Hila, would you mind please distributing this picture of the Sayyid with your onions?"

"I'm not interested. My house is already overflowing with pictures."

"Hila, you're not a Shiite. Give your vote to the Sada Party!"

"I can't afford to give *anything* away, sir. Everything needs to be paid for."

"Hila, don't forget the number of the party!"

"No peppers today. I'll get some tomorrow."

"Hila, support five hundred and fifty-five!"

"Sorry, I don't have any change."

"Hila, Chalabi is counting on you. Don't forget!"

"How dare you call me a bitch? You're the son of a chalab!"

"Hila, there's no other option. Our only real *khiyar* is the United Coalition."

"My child, my khiyar are the Ta'ruzi kind. See how nice these cucumbers are!"

"Hila, vote for Alusi!"

"What! You're always losing your *fulus*! Why are you too stupid to look after your money?"

Hila couldn't get over how weird her customers had gotten. She looked over at the next stall and saw Hamziya the Mute laughing soundlessly. Then she looked at Idan the butcher and saw him laughing too. She went over to the man and yelled, "Idan, what's wrong with all these people? No one's buying anything today!"

Idan put his mouth to Hila's ear and yelled, "Hila, they want you to raise your voice in the elections because your vote is important!"

"Ah!" said Hila, as if finally understanding. Then she looked back to Hamziya the Mute, who was still laughing. "What have you got to laugh about, Hamziya? With no voice to raise, how can you even vote in the elections? And the mayor's office says that if anyone doesn't vote, the municipality will dump their stall upon their head. So there!"

DECEMBER 14, 2005

An Abundant History of Cheering

How long until we are free of the posters, the ads, the cheering, and the noise? How long until we get a break from the hordes of people out there always running with those running, screeching with those screeching, cheering with those cheering, dancing with those who shake their shoulders? How long, O Lord, how long?

The day before yesterday, my aunt Sabiha grabbed her abaya and, without any warning, set off at a run. "Where are you going, auntie? Take it easy! Don't fall down. Hey, aren't you sick?"

As usual, Sabiha didn't reply. She doesn't give a damn about her husband, so why should she give a damn about Shalash? (Not giving a damn about their men is a tradition of long standing among the women in the Irhaymeh clan.) Anyway, my aunt had heard cheering at the end of the street, along with shouts and cries and dancing, and she'd seen dust being kicked up. What was going on? Why, it was a demonstration in the presence of some religious figures. Mind you, I've got nothing but respect for those religious figures, especially the honorable ones among them, and those whose holy turbans will bring us straight to paradise!

I don't ask my aunt Sabiha to stay at home and only make her ballot box decisions after doing some research into the platforms of the various parties. That would never happen anyway, not even in a dream. Likewise, I don't ask her to vote for any specific party, which would be an illogical request, because, as I said, she doesn't give a damn about her husband, so why should she give a damn about Shalash? But I do have a number of other requests, which I believe are legitimate, and which I want to lay before my dear auntie, and before you, and before the international community. These requests can be summarized as follows:

First: It is forbidden for Sabiha to come back from the demonstration after all her running and her jumping and her pushing through the crowds with kids and teenagers only to say, "Those perverts, they put their hands all over me!" (I leave it to my honored readers to guess precisely which sensitive places the mob will have dared to put its hands.)

Second: That, upon returning home, my aunt not grab her side, moan, and cry out, "Ow! I'm dying!" Her blood pressure rises the teeniest bit and suddenly people are yelling at me to take her to Chawadir Hospital! No thank you.

Third: That my aunt refrain from saying, about the brothers she's just seen demonstrating, "Backward savages! They never clear a path for a lady. They just want to get on television!"

Fourth: That she refrain from saying, "My sandal got broken. Bring me another!"

Fifth: That she refrain from saying, "Can you believe it? Abu Shuwan the Kurd winked at me and said, 'Why not come inside my shop for a while . . .'"

That's the sum total of my requests. Apart from that, my aunt Sabiha has the right to participate actively in all demonstrations, all the cheering and running around, in however many different forms and on however many different occasions as she likes. These words also apply to my uncle Shinawa, who does tend to tag along with Sabiha whenever one of these carnivals arrives to kick up more dust. In fact, now that I come to think about it, I had better put in some additional conditions for Sayyid Shinawa, including the following:

That he not come back from the demonstrations and say, "Help! They've emptied my pockets!"

That he not bring some puny sayyid in a turban back to the house and say, "I've invited him over for lunch. Poor thing! He hasn't eaten in who knows how long!"

That he not come back carrying a new camera and say, "It was just lying there on the ground!"

That he not use my shoes to go running around in.

That he not come home, lie down on his belly, and say, "Come on, Shalash! I did my back in. Please walk on it? Your uncle is broken man!"

Beyond that, Shinawa has the right to engage in whatever public activities he desires.

My dear friends, the conditions I've laid out above are not matters I'm only now pulling out of my hat. And they are absolutely not the result of my uncle Shinawa, together with Sabiha, participating two days ago in the lavish local festival to welcome the pipsqueak scion of the holy Najaf seminary, Sayyid Ammar al-Hakim, who graced Thawra with his shining visage, his delicate fingertips, and his almond-shaped lips. Rather, these conditions are born from an agony of long standing that goes back to the autumn of 1990, when Sabiha once put her hand in Shinawa's at six o'clock in the morning, and, without informing any of us of their plans, showed up that evening on TV in one of the streets of our Sister Kuwait, leading the charge to "reconnect the branch to the root."

The whole world remembers Sabiha's heroic stance as she stood in front of the world's television cameras and let out her memorable cry, "Now we reclaim our rights!" She grabbed Shinawa's hand and raised it high in triumph. Then the two of them stealthily repaired to their new villa in the district of Salmiya, one of the upper-class neighborhoods in

249

Kuwait, to spend some time recovering from their heroism in that magnificent house before transporting all its contents to their winter resort in Block 41, so that the estimable and blessed Irhaymeh clan might thereby launch the "era of the VCR," when we were the only family in our block to own such a device.

After that blessed incursion, my dear viewers, Sabiha and Shinawa began participating in all kinds of processions, demonstrations, and celebrations, both local and regional, until they developed quite the reputation for that sort of thing. Perhaps the noble sons of Thawra will remember as well as I that day in the middle of the 1990s when Shinawa went out to the streets with his hair pulled back in a braid, his beard loose, black rubber shoes on his feet, and a Reebok backpack on his back. The sayyida accompanied him, with hair mussed, red knee-high boots, and a Nike backpack. They were carrying a sign that read NO TO GLOBALISM! Which step of theirs sparked the formation of the Organization of Opponents to Globalism down the street in Block 10.

Nor can we forget the demonstration that the two of them led together in 1994 against a disreputable law prohibiting abortion, just as we all remember the hunger strike that Shinawa undertook on his own in Picture Square to defend the rights of homosexuals in the Bataween district and its surrounding alleys.

And I don't believe any of us has forgotten that Sabiha was the first to block the gates of the Ministry of Agriculture to protest the practices of the UNESCO commission searching for weapons of mass destruction. Just as I don't believe any of us has forgotten that Shinawa of the Irhaymeh clan was the first to enter the People's Palaces to protest the threats of old Albright to destroy them, with huge crowds of our noble sons following him to defend our amazing presidential palaces. I'm leaving out many other events that we don't have time to go into. But my point is that the presence of Sabiha and Shinawa at demonstrations to welcome Ammar al-Hakim is nothing more than an extension of this rich and time-honored democratic behavior.

Shinawa and Sabiha are shining examples of how our people still live by that historic Iraqi slogan, "At the sound of the drum, step up, O my feet!"

Merry Elections to all, and to all a Happy 555 Year!

DECEMBER 16, 2005

A Pledging of Allegiance to Our Next President (God Preserve Him!)

We pledge ourselves to you, President Whoever-you-are,
    Not with slips of paper. No! We have put our hearts in
    the ballot box.
Our conscience is what brought us,
    Whoever-you-are, not our legs.
We went out barefoot early in the morning
    Despite the danger; despite the fear, we came.
They even poisoned the water,
    So we resorted to 7-Up.

251

We did today what we had to do—
  If only you knew, sir, how we did it!
We arrived at the voting center, pushed our way through;
  We skipped the line and went right in.
They knew we were with you
  And immediately pulled us close.
We quickly searched the lists
  And put a check against a number.
We pledged ourselves to you, Mr. Whoever-you-are,
  And it was a very good thing we did.
Until breath itself fails,
  We're with you wherever you lead.
The other guys hate us;
  The turbans are furious with us.
We saw lots of hajjiyas,
  Hajjiyas on their last legs.
We can't name a single person
  Who came to vote for the party of 555.
They did not listen
  To hear the words we spoke.
We saw two communists in head scarves,
  Afraid of our mullah leaders.
We saw Shinawa wearing a tux,
  One they probably gave him.
We saw Sabiha walking beside him,
  And said, Now we're truly fucked.
We saw Nuwayra, wife of Ghurab,
  Who came to spy on us.
We saw Mr. Khanjar organizing the people
  And checking our names.

We saw Khadir ibn Inad
    Who came to sell some snacks.
We saw Abbas the Drunk,
    He staggered and lashed us with his tongue.
Though he cursed our whole families,
    We were able to bear it all for your sake.
He took out his spiked club and yelled
    "Black: our chronicles; red: our past!"
Then the shouting began.
    We fled and slipped their grasp.
We quickly escaped, Mr. Whoever-you-are,
    Running through the alleys.
And when it became a matter of shoe-throwing,
    We slipped inside some people's houses.
Did you see how it was, Mr. Whoever-you-are?
    Did you see what happened to us?
Never mention elections again!
    Fool us twice, and we have only ourselves to blame.
We pledge ourselves to you, President Whoever-you-are,
    Not with slips of paper. No! We have put our hearts in
    the ballot box.
O Ali, our Ali, our Ali!

Remember, my people! Were it not for Ali,
    Our ancestor Umar would have fallen.
Now it's plain for all to see
    Our national brotherhood has become our downfall.

So become Kurds for Ali's sake,
    And we'll become Chaldeans for the sake of Umar.

By God, it was a good intention
    That made me call Ru'a my love.
And I hope Sunni Ru'a says yes and
    Becomes poor with a Shiite like me.
She'll pick up her bag and come and
    We'll marry on the first of the month.
We'll have a child who
    Looks like my friend Jabbar.
At my mother's house, he'll be called Ali,
    And at hers, he'll be called Umar.
O Ali, our Ali, our Ali!

JANUARY 24, 2006

A House with Five Doors

Sayyid Ibrahim al-Jaafari, our current prime minister, needs to follow the news carefully in order to know who's coming and going, seeing as Iraq has become as open as a medieval caravansary. People can walk right in without His Excellency knowing a thing. How has this shame come upon us all? Is this a country or the Maridi Market?

Tony Blair is in Basra, Rumsfeld is in Falluja, Dick Cheney is in the Green Zone, and al-Jaafari is sleeping with his head in the sand . . . I know, I know, I could easily take this too far and get everyone upset with me, but listen, brothers: Where are our women? Our women are *inside*. Whoever doesn't know who's coming and who's going in his own house will undoubtedly sprout the cuckold's horns. (Am I right, Umm Ali, or am I right?)

Zalmay Khalilzad sent a request for Jaafari to meet him at the American embassy. Our friend got running and was surprised to find Dick Cheney there. Blair entered the country and turned up in Basra without even saying, "assalamu alaikum." And Rumsfeld is strolling around Iraq so often you'd say it was his parents' house. All this besides the tourists who are permitted to visit and prop up the Iraqi dinar with their Iranian tomans.

By God, of course Sayyid Jaafari is asleep on the job, but what's going on with Solagh? Doesn't he say, "I'm in total control, and if an ant sneezes up north in Zakho, I hear it!" So what's all this, with the presidents of the major powers coming and going, here, there, and everywhere, while he's snoozing? No, this really is a comedy! Even the nightclub shows over in Kamaliyah (God look upon them fondly!) can't match it!

I mean, look, they're welcome. But they should at least give us a ring before they show up, no? If that man, Blair, were to call me up himself and say, all polite and humble, "Mister Shalash, I'm going to be vising Basra if you don't have any objections," I'd reply by saying, "*Yoo ar walcom heer, mister Blair. It iz yoor haws too!*" Not only that, but I'd also sing him that famous song, "He Went to Basra and Didn't Give a Damn" (or something like that).

But it's not just a matter of bad manners. The root of the problem is that Sayyid Strawberry-Blond Jaafari doesn't bother to watch the news. The real news. Our esteemed brother put his trust in God and launched his own satellite

255

channel, which he called, "My Country," though really he should have called it "My Mirror," since he only uses it to watch news about himself. What, did you think Al Iraqiya wasn't giving you good enough coverage, sir? Or is it that, like Uday's papa, our former president, you can never get enough of your own picture, and are starving to see yourself on TV, on every channel, every day?

With regard to the crowded demonstration organized to protest the preliminary election results yesterday, I want to tell my brothers everywhere who are watching the Sunni station Al Sharqiya that the procession was silly and pointless. And with all due respect to the participants, I would say that it was a stupid waste of time.

Which doesn't mean that the election wasn't stolen, mind you.

I'm just saying that the demonstration was pointless because the people who called for it knew perfectly well that the election was being stolen and nevertheless took part in the proceedings. Why even call it an election when rival candidates are being murdered? When even the people who went around putting up election posters are being murdered? Why did they accept the challenge when they realized their opponents would be holding a rifle in one hand and the Qur'an in the other, extracting oaths for this or that vote from the poor electorate, who are caught between the flames of their opponents' threats and the flames of their promises, hemmed in by a fire fueled by their own burning bodies and homes?

So, as for the procession that passed through our street in Thawra City this afternoon, I have no comment because I've seen it all before a thousand times.

And to our brothers lighting the fuse of civil war, let me say to you, in all sincerity: the war you're trying to start won't be fought between factions of the people of Iraq because we are family, we *are* brothers. Instead, it will take place between the militias and the political parties. That's the situation that America is impatiently awaiting, so that they might be rid of all our party leaders and turbans who never wanted America here in the first place.

Now do you see that your brother, Shalash the Iraqi, is a strategic analyst of the first order? I swear, I understand it all, but no one takes me seriously!

And I'm still waiting for the final election results to be announced.

DECEMBER 26, 2005

Habby Nyu Yeer!

Here we are approaching another New Year, and along with it come the harbingers of an imminent crisis emerging on the horizon of Thawra City. The cause of this crisis—God protect you from this manifest evil!—is the conflict arising between the different local factions about the correct depiction of one Mr. Santa Claus.

Everyone agreed that there would be a Christmas tree, and that putting it up would be a shared project, but after that we all lost the Christmas spirit, and now it seems that everyone in the neighborhood is fighting over our understanding of Santa . . .

The Sawa'id tribe believes that Sayyid Santa Claus is of Sawa'id descent, specifically from the house of Zamil. As for our brothers in the Albu-Muhammad tribe, they've resolved that he is a Muhammadian by descent, 100 percent. The Albu-Daraj brothers, for their part, consider that Santa was originally a scrap collector, with his sleigh being the best evidence. Meanwhile, our Azeriji brothers say that Santa is one of them, pointing to his red clothes as a sign, considering that the Azerijis have traditionally been connected with the communist party. As for our brothers in the Kaab tribe, they've sent the tribe's family tree around to everyone, with a red circle around the name of one of their ancestors, Hajji Nowel.

The Albu-Abud tribe says that "Claus" itself derives from the name of their ancestor, Anaus (God have mercy upon him!). The young leader of the Janana tribe says that Santa Claus was a Janani who was born in Amara, whose mother died young, who lived on cans of Guigoz milk formula, and who was called in his time Janani Guigoz, which in time evolved into his current name.

The tribes living on Chawadir Street have all formed a coalition, the National Chawadir Front, while the tribes on Dakhil Street have formed the Iraqi Dakhil Union. Our brothers in the Mahdi Army have made an alliance with the brothers in the Badr Brigades to form what they are calling the United Coalition, by which they mean to keep the other coalitions in line. As for the fourth alliance, it was formed by residents of the Kurdish neighborhood in order to consolidate all possible Kurdish Christmas forces, and this is called the Kurdistan Alliance.

Now, the people of Dakhil insist that Santa was a secularist who has worked all his life to separate religion from politics under the name Comrade Noel. They want him to dress
in a modern suit with a necktie. The people of Chawadir say
he was a Muslim Arab descended from the line of Adnan,
and that he necessarily must wear a red kaffiyeh with an iqal
and go by the name Aliyyan Noel. As for the brothers in the
United Coalition, they say that he was a sayyid descended
from the Seventh Imam, Musa al-Kadhim, that his name is
Sayyid Claus al-Musawi, and that he wears a black turban.
Meanwhile, the brothers from the Kurdistan Alliance insist
upon staying out of the fray, being content with a Mam Santa
of their own. They don't need him to wear Kurdish trousers,
but they do ask that he maybe bring them some new permits
and civil rights in his bag.

So eventually these disagreements turned into open conflicts. There was the usual waving of weapons. The shouts of
the crowds became heated, everyone was jumping around,
and so forth.

"No master to lead us but Imam Ali, and make al-Jaafari
our Santa!" someone shouted.

And from the other side, "By God and his Prophet I swear,
Santa isn't even an Arab—so there!"

At last the members of the United Coalition decided they
would impose their own Papa Noel by force of arms, but then
they too ran into trouble—internecine Christmas conflicts.
The sons of the blessed Sadrist movement wanted to keep the
very same Santa Claus they'd used the previous year, while
their brothers from the Supreme Council's Badr Brigades
preferred Santa's friend, Noel Abd al-Mahdi. In this way, a

hidden struggle began burning within the brotherhood, and we still don't know whether Mullah Noel will come on New Year's Eve in a black turban or a white one . . .

Ah, but the choice should really lie in the hands of the children of our city, should it not? And I'm here to tell you they've already made their choice. For their parts, they'd decided upon a certain Za'ir Chalub as their favored Santa Claus. Why not? He fit the bill exactly. The guy is short, has a round face, and is hunchbacked—and, just like Santa, he sports a thick, snowy beard and a fierce hatred for all children, whom he calls "sly bastards."

And Za'ir Chalub was rehearsing the role of Papa Noel! Walking up and down Fellah Street amid the clapping and cheering of the poor children. They would rush up and tear open his big bag so that some mortar shells and hand grenades might fall out, along with some rifle clips and other ammunition of various calibers.

It was cold and cloudy outside, and there was Za'ir Chalub making his rounds, going back and forth. And then, a miracle: a sudden and heavy snow began falling on Thawra City and its suburbs. It transformed everything to a gleaming white that sparkled with the lights of our fireworks, which flashed in the sky overhead to celebrate the coming of the New Year. At which point an American Apache helicopter descended, filled with marines. They rushed out, seized Za'ir Chalub, and soared up and away with him.

Bereft, the barefoot children in their tattered clothes scattered back to their damp houses to sit and wait for gifts from an American Santa Claus after all.

Shalash the Iraqi: Musician

My cousin used up four prepaid telephone cards—at least, so she claimed—on the TV show *Iraqi Star*, calling in to support one of the contestants. When she came to regret how much she'd spent, after her singer failed to win, she called me up and scolded me. "It's all your fault!"

"What did I have to do with it?"

"It's because the singer was just like you!"

"Just like me?"

"Yes, just like you!"

"Before or after he went and got old in Lebanon?"

"No, no, he doesn't *look* like you, but his voice is like yours, back when you used to sing, back when you used to be fun . . ."

So, as a compensation for her four lost telephone cards, this spoiled cousin of mine asked me to sing for her the song, "I Wish," by Hatem Al-Iraqi. This song, as all of Hatem's fans know, was one of the earliest signs of his greatness—and perhaps, along with his song, "I'm the One Tortured by Love," the beginning of his later popularity. Since it was clear my cousin wasn't going to give up, I was forced to close the door of my room so that no one would hear—seeing as the song was in an embarrassingly high register—and I began to sing:

I wish

I wish! (That's my cousin singing on the other end of the line.)

I wish, I wish

That we were under the same roof! (Her again.)
I wish, I wish, I wish

I finished the song with some difficulty, then I said goodbye to the crazy daughter of my crazy uncle Shinawa, though not soon enough to prevent all my neighbors gathering around my door at the sound of my voice, most of them already assuming that poor old Shalash had gone back to drinking and carousing.

Well, friends, what can I say? Back at the beginning of our acquaintance I somehow never got around to telling you all that I used to be a singer, that everyone tells me I have a beautiful voice for singing in the local style. What's more, I'm one of the best percussionists in Thawra City, sometimes even better than Hazim Al-Asla and Muhammad Lufta, the professionals in Kadim Al Sahir's band.

But the tale of my so-called singing career is a sad, ugly business. All the anti-Shalashians out there who know my story love to harp upon those dark days. And, unfortunately, they started all the way back in my high school days. That's when I got my official start. That's when I got up on an actual stage for the first time, at an event that put a stop to the life of music and drinking with my gang of friends at the end of our street. The occasion—and here, allow me to repeat once more how deep is my regret about it all—was the birthday of our president, the Great Leader, God preserve him! The problems didn't stop there, as I'm pleased to inform my noble brothers in the Badr Brigades, for I sang on *all* our Leader's birthdays, and for nearly all his victories, just as I also sang on various other occasions connected with His Excellency, such as the Day of Dignity, the Day of Fealty, the Day of Total Crossing, and the Day of Days. By the time I hit college, I was pretty well known, at least among my fellow students. I'm sure they still remember my heartfelt nationalistic songs. I'm positive they do, in fact, because, just two weeks ago, one of them got in touch with me and asked me to sing at his brother's wedding reception. When I made my excuses, he came right out and said, without the least hesitation or embarrassment, "If it were the birthday of the Father of Two Lions," using the nickname Saddam got from his two sons, "you'd come running, yeah?"

Through singing, my dear brothers, I attracted a large number of admirers among the ladies, it's true, but for the record, they were all a bit hard on the eyes . . . I wouldn't be seen walking to the end of the street with one of them, I'm ashamed to admit. One of them, sure, one of them wasn't too bad, but her problem was that she was stuck up, she thought she deserved a special song from me over the telephone whenever she was bored or upset . . .

Among the many tragedies that I had to endure during my life as an artist, one came about the time that I was invited to sing in the Al-Ubaidi district, which is located between Thawra and Kamaliyah, at a wedding party that the organizers insisted take place right in the middle of the street. After I arrived with the band, led by maestro Jasim Kassara, we went into a room set aside for the musicians to relax, along with some colleagues of ours, poets in the popular style. We had some arak, beer, and jajeek, and then one of the poets got up and absolutely destroyed me. He began reciting all the popular poetry he could, starting with Muthaffar al-Nawab,

Erian Al Sayed Khalaf, and Kazem Al-Kate, then moving on to Abbas Jijan, Haydar Al-Kaabi, and Hussein Al-Sharifi, finishing up with a selection of modern poets from the era of the tyrannical sanctions that had been imposed on our defiant land.

He was reciting, and I was drinking. He reciting, me drinking . . . he reciting, me drinking . . . until, my good sirs, I was good and drunk, a state that made it impossible for me to perform my set, despite the pleas of the audience and the embarrassment of the groom's family. This forced the uncle of the groom, who is currently working as an ambulance driver, to drive me out of the green room with a series of kicks and shoves. On account of that, the members of my band scattered, as usual, and I staggered home alone, arriving at the end of the night with nothing to show for myself but what remained of my clothes. But my tender mother stood by my side as always, and she protected me from the anger of my older brothers, repeating in my ears her famous insight, "The road to art and fame is a long one, my children."

Another time, two other singers and I were the main event at a pre-wedding henna party for our lifelong friend Abd al-Rida, which was taking place up on the roof of his building. As soon as we arrived, we wasted no time mixing the arak with ice and water, and we began slurping it down to some boisterous tunes. When it was my turn to sing, five people wearing olive-green uniforms erupted onto the roof. I had to jump to the neighboring roof, along with the other singers and musicians, seeing as we were all agreed that getting drafted wasn't going to do our musical careers any favors.

The next morning, it became obvious to me that the people dressed in olive had been Comrade Abu Farqad, the official overseeing our block, with a group of comrades in tow who were there only to offer their congratulations, drink our leftover arak, and suck on sour lemon slices. Given the predicament they had caused, entertainment-wise, it occurred to the comrade in charge that he himself should sing, while some of his squad started playing the instruments that the musicians had left behind. And thus, Abd al-Rida got a wedding celebration for the ages, and everyone danced the *choba*:

> Welcome, welcome, O eagle of the desert,
> You who carry your sword in your hand
> All your people, Saddam, they are your army;
> Yes, Saddam, you whose crescent always shines
> Dance, dance, dance the choba;
> Round again and round again!

It's even said that Abd al-Rida's mother lifted up a picture of Saddam and danced to the rhythm of the song without any self-consciousness whatsoever.

Since that blessed night, Comrade Abu Farqad has been gradually withdrawing from his nationalistic party duties as he transformed into a semi-famous singer. It's said that he now lives in Sister Syria and puts on rowdy concerts for the remnants of the dissolved Ba'ath Party, some leaders of the national resistance, and many of the down-and-out looters who were riding so high in the months after the invasion— God protect them all!

As for me, I withdrew from the spotlight entirely, content to sing "I Wish" over the telephone to the daughter of my uncle Shinawa, imploring God that her knight in shining armor might come quickly so that I could retire once and for all from the world of crooning and music. Then I would put on my own hijab and sit respectfully at home, helping the hajjiya, my mother, until my own shining knight arrives.

Documents from Maridi Market

The connection between the Maridi Market and forgery extends, as far as I can tell, back to the mid-1980s. It started with the forgery of forms granting short leaves from the army, pieces of paper with which AWOL soldiers could purchase their lives. The brave souls down at Maridi Market were ready to comply with requests for such valuable papers, the prices of which depended on the length and nature of the leave being granted. For instance, a long-term illness was more expensive than a normal leave of seven days. Accompanying these major forgeries were other, less formidable varieties, such as student IDs or cards proving that the bearer was a player on a team of one of the big sports clubs. Each of these was a get-out-of-jail-free card, no matter how hard the hearts of our military policemen.

In the 1990s, the forgery profession became more sophisticated and expanded its reach. The forgers undertook to confer honorable discharges from the compulsory military service, and they even forged logbooks documenting successful completion of military service! Little by little, the profession advanced to forging passports for those who had grown weary of living in Iraq, the "fount of civilization," and for some reason preferred exile. Among these exiles-in-waiting were those who advanced strange requests to the "forgers' guild" in Maridi, such as a special order for a document confirming that the person here named is among those sought by Saddam's security services, or indeed that the bearer is being pursued because of his courageous defiance of the regime. Others wouldn't accept anything less than a confirmation that Saddam himself will be going without sleep until this dangerous member of the opposition, Da'ir Thajil Shalaga, currently residing in Copenhagen, is arrested. Perhaps I need not spell this out, but such proofs were an excellent way to expedite requests to the United Nations to grant asylum, on personal or political grounds, in Europe, America, or Australia.

Given the high demand, the professionals of the Maridi Market became quite inventive in their forgeries of the stamps used by the security service, the intelligence service, the city leadership, and the courts of Thawra—even managing a fair approximation of the signature of Saddam himself.

In the post-Saddam era, of course, tastes changed. New orders were received by the venerable artisans of the Maridi Market, for example for confirmations of the damages people had suffered under the former regime, including confiscation of their assets, liquid or otherwise, or their dismissal from some position on account of their sympathy with the Islamic Dawa Party or the Badr Brigades, and so on. That would be for the sake of obtaining plots of land or jobs or any of the imaginary distinctions offered by the parties that have emerged from the trenches of our national struggle. It even got to the point that a minister would say to his nephew, "Go, graduate from the Maridi Market and then come back for a job."

(Indeed, the forgery business has grown and diversified until it's become impossible to regulate or in any way to keep tabs on its operations. What you'd need would be an organization dedicated precisely to that task. A Forgery Regulatory Commission, if you will. And perhaps such a group will form in the future? Hopefully taking into consideration, however, the fact that our noble forgers never sought to establish a guild or a trade union to guard their legitimate rights, as did the other slices of civil society that started multiplying within a week of the fall of the regime . . .)

And it's not just bachelor's degrees, oh no! Over the past three years, we've heard about higher degrees—the very highest!—being forged so that someone could be appointed to a particularly sensitive and important position. The title "doctor" has become just so much garbage here. Even the guy who used to run the liver-and-heart stall became a doctor and is now a ministry official. I'd venture to say that, by the end of the past year, the art of forgery has reached so advanced a stage in our country that no other nation on the planet could possibly compete. Namely, in the first democratic elections of their kind, an entire new Iraq has been forged, from the north to the south, such that we needed an international committee to ferret out the evidence of this many-headed crime, from which will sprout our first elected National Assembly!

Still, my friends, let me say, up till now, even this state of affairs has seemed reasonable. The development of the art of forgery in our land has been both gradual and justified. But the latest catastrophe is that our counterfeiters, no longer content with forging earthly distinctions, have begun filling orders for tickets to heaven as well!

Everyone knows we have spurious as well as authentic pilgrims plaguing our land. Yes, even pilgrimages to Mecca can be forged. For instance, my aunt Sabiha and my uncle Shinawa (God protect them both!) are now in the Guesthouse of the Merciful, imploring the Creator Most High to preserve Iraq, its people, and the government of its strong and trustworthy leader, and they will bring home the papers to prove it. (Oh, sure, we have some real pilgrims too, such as Fakhriya and Nana'a, who made the harrowing pilgrimage to the Baghdad International Airport for the first time in their lives, and then returned to their families after an acceptable sojourn, as decreed for them by the Merciful One. Either way, our actions, as we've been taught, are judged by their intentions—not to mention a million-and-a-half Iraqi dinars, which has got to be the first bribe in history a government has offered to its people for making a pilgrimage to God's Inviolate House in Mecca.)

And when our spurious pilgrims return tomorrow, will we call them liars? Not at all! We'll go along with their forgery, kiss their hands, and say, "A blessed pilgrimage and an acceptable endeavor in God's eyes!" We'll bring large cans of cooking oil to "hajjiya" Sabiha and "hajji" Shinawa as gifts to commemorate the occasion of their safe arrival, with praise to God for his providence. For their part, they'll give us kaffiyehs, iqals, prayer beads, and Indian perfumes in recognition of our affection—even though the greatest scientists in the world would have great difficulty drawing a connection between God's House, on the one hand, and cans of cooking oil and Indian perfumes on the other.

But it's about to get a lot easier for the spurious pilgrims, my brothers and sisters, for last night I ran into a group of professionals from Maridi Market making plans to forge papers that would confirm for Munkar and Nakir, the angels of the afterlife, that the bearers of said documents were pious believers who had completed the pilgrimage to God's Inviolate House. Thus, the road to everlasting paradise will from now on pass through Maridi Market, where certificates will be issued that attest to lifetimes of prayer, almsgiving, enjoining good, forbidding evil, and every other pious deed on the menu.

Not that there aren't precedents for this, I suppose, in the forgery of religious titles, such as "His Eminence, the Authority on Islam and the Muslims," or "Most Sublime and Excellent Sheikh, the Very Height of Holiness," or "Committee of NASA Scholars to Research the Universe of Islam," or "President of Pilfering the Blameless Shiites and Sunnis," or, of course, "Our Jihadi Sheikh, the Prince of Preachers and Throat-Slitter of the Apostate Shiites."

O Lord! Send your miraculous flock of swallows to level Maridi with their stones! And may God make us all pilgrims to the Ancient House in Mecca. What was it the Prophet said? He who does not deceive us is not one of us? Something like that!

A Blessed Eid and Many Happy Returns!

Should I let my beard grow or shave it off for Eid tomorrow?
I swear, I can't decide. If I shave it, I'll have to get up early every
day to procure a little water and then heat it up in order to
keep my beard shorn to the roots, just like Muhammad Saeed
al-Sahhaf, who got so famous declaring Saddam's victories
over the Americans on live TV. And if I let it grow, I'll start
looking like the fundamentalists, and I'm afraid the gorgeous
schoolteacher Khadija will start giving me dirty looks. What
to do? A beard is a complicated problem. Either you attack it
every day with a razor and look brand-new, out of the package,
or you leave it alone and—God forbid!—look like a goat.

"Shalash, what's wrong with you? So you've solved all your
real problems and have nothing left to worry about besides
your beard? Shave it, man, shave it! Tomorrow's Eid, and
the people are all celebrating. At least let them wake up to a
decent face for once!"

"Okay, okay! I'll shave it. No need to yell!"

So I shaved my beard and went to the end of the street.
People seemed to be doing all right, coming and going from
the market. Salaries are good, and Jaafari has been giving out
gifts of one hundred thousand dinars to the voters—a great
mercy, and may God bless him! People have been buying
clothes from Palestine Street and from Khayam Street. Some
people were even shopping at Cornerstone Market, while
others were content with their clothes from the last Eid—
nothing wrong with that, still as good as new! And some

271

genuine Arabian horses were being released from their carts and gotten ready for making the Eid rounds, since young people prefer them to riding on donkeys. Likewise, gallows were being erected in all the public squares.

"Wait—what gallows, Shalash? These are all swing sets! Are you drunk?"

Swing sets, sure, and even just some round scraps of metal at the intersections for the children to play on tomorrow. These games, along with the donkeys, the horses, and the carts crowded with kids, are the same amusements that have been swallowing our Eid money for many long years. I can say that Kareema, the hajji's daughter, who will bring her son to the square tomorrow, used to play and have fun with the same games herself. Faces change, the world has been transformed, yet our own private Disney World is just the same as ever.

The amusement park is close to Thawra. Indeed, we're the closest district to it. But it's not really safe enough for children, so it's left to the young adults and some teenagers, who bring their drums and fill the place with a beautiful racket. The rides are somewhat old and expensive. All the new ones have already been worn out in the cities of neighboring countries and brought in by our brother-merchants for the sake of a poor Iraq. (By the way, friends, if someone wants to go to the amusement park and ride "The Flying Plates" for free, my uncle Shinawa works there. Just tell him Shalash sent you and he'll let you go on. Really, he told me: "Just send your gang over, and I'll treat them well!")

The world is cold—very cold!—and our brothers who have moved to Canada over the years write to tell me that the streets there are covered in snow. I tell them that the dead of winter here is turning ears red as slices of watermelon, and that the dark combined with the cold makes our depression levels soar to the heavens. Believe me, if arak weren't readily available, Abd al-Rida, Abbas, Jaafar, and Hamza would all have killed themselves by now. What's wrong with you, friends? What do you have in Canada to whine about? At least you have electricity and running water, and your elections come off without a hitch!

The weather was better yesterday. A little better, even though it rained. But at night it was so cold you could die! And poor Jabbar, son of the policeman, loves Yusra the Basran. He stands on the corner and stares at her house in case she happens to take out the garbage and he can catch a glimpse of her. Jabbar is dying from the cold, and Yusra is sitting in front of her stove! Poor Jabbar still believes in love. How old-fashioned! Man, what is love, anyway? Even love has lost its flavor. It's become voice messages, missed calls, and dedications posted on the bottom of the screen on the Rotana channel. Go, brother Jabbar! Go, stand at her house as long as we have electricity, and send some messages over the local channel. Mix in some English, including a translation of her name, so that no one else will read your sweet nothings. "*Froom the son uf the poleesman,* to *Left* the Basran: When will you realize how I feel?" I promise, Yusra is reading the message right now and will reply with a dedication of her own, "Poor Jabbouri! But I swear, there just wasn't any trash to take out today. Love, Y-s-r-a."

What more can I say? I was hoping to finish this entry without politics, because politics aren't good for anything. First, because nobody reads, and second, because it turns out that even the people who do read my stuff just laugh at me.

It's true! An important official—very, very important—sent me an email, saying, "Shalash, whatever you do, don't stop writing. I'm so totally entertained by it, you know, and every day you make me fall off my chair laughing." So it turns out that Shalash is entertaining the government! And here I was so proud of myself, thinking that whenever I wrote about a politician, he would be too embarrassed to even show his face on television. Laugh, my dears, laugh! Aren't I the laughingstock of the degenerates? Well, their day will come. How long will you go on tricking the people, Mr. Official? Yes, your day will come.

I know half of you couldn't care less. You can always abandon ship and head back to your homes in London, Iran, and the Himalayas—especially that Doctor Mowaffak al-Rubaie. He'll be the first to skip town, mark my words! If Mowaffak al-Rubaie remains in Iraq, my name's not Shalash. You know why? Because our brother, the doctor, got his share in advance. As soon as he arrived in Iraq, he sold military production factories to Iran for parts and got paid millions of dollars for it. After that, he collected his share of the telecom company MTC. I'm not pulling this talk out of thin air: even Mam Jalal Talabani knows it. Mam Jalal, on your honor, you're a lawyer, a good and decent person, and you don't tell lies: Aren't I speaking the truth? If it's a lie, revoke my citizenship and send me to New Zealand. I swear, I'll take it in stride and won't get mad. Please, ship me out and I'll kiss your hands. I'm that fed up!

I'm asking you: This Mowaffak al-Rubaie, why do the Americans love him? Why did they appoint him as a consultant for national security for the whole length of his stay in Iraq? Why does Sayyid Sistani also love him, such that al-Rubaie can go see him without an appointment anytime he wants? Why is everyone so afraid of him? How'd he bring that about? Or was it all arranged from the start, and we just didn't know? Everything is possible in this world of ours.

Nevertheless, I love Mowaffak al-Rubaie. At least he laughs. And he's the only one who really knows how to suck the juice out of a place like Iraq. Damned Mowaffak, you're behind it all. Laugh, Jackalman! Hey now, didn't we say we wouldn't talk politics? Come on! Okay, but just about Doctor Mowaffak. We're not going to talk about anyone else today. The man's not a sayyid; he's no ayatollah: talking about him is permitted! Still, easy does it. Just a little at a time.

Mowaffak, on my honor, you live up to your name, "prospered by God." And with your help, I see that God is prospering your brother as well, in the new Iraqi deal. Don't read my posts and laugh. I'm at the end of my rope, and still you laugh! This is what we've come to? We've become a laughing-stock to one and all! But God is generous, Mowaffak, isn't he? If the good times had lasted for Saddam's brother, Barzan, they wouldn't have arrived for you when you took Barzan's place in the security apparatus.

It's all so depressing! What's more, they're going to cut off the electricity soon. What do you say, my Canadian brothers? Should I go slam a half bottle of arak with the guys, or should I stand on the corner with that giddy lover, Jabbar, son of the policeman, in case Khadija comes out to greet me? I swear, Khadija's shoe is better than Abu . . .

A blessed Eid and many happy returns! May each year find you well—and Iraq too! I'll see you after the holiday.

At the President's Table

Good morning, Mam Jalal! What, are you a racist now too? You invite Masoud Barzani over because he comes from Irbil, but you don't invite me because I'm the scum of the earth? Why, my dear brother, why? Aren't you called Abu al-Jamee'a, the Father of Everyone? Nevertheless, I approve of the way you've brought together brothers who are usually enemies. Honestly, it was a good opportunity for us to see all these groups as they sat at the president's banquet, overflowing with good and pleasing things. Perhaps they will grow closer to one another. Perhaps they will develop some mutual understanding and grant some relief to the millions, the hungry, oppressed, bereft millions—all those suffering from their scheming and their conspiracies.

As you know, most of the people lined up on both sides of the president's table are the least significant of the political elite who succeeded Saddam's gang. Even so, their monthly salaries, as you'll also know, sir, combined with the salaries of their assistants and their relatives, would be enough to build a residential compound for at least a thousand people. That isn't some random guess but a reasonable estimate, and perhaps even shy of the real number.

And if I add to these brothers the members of the National Assembly, together with their bodyguards and attendants, the compound would become bigger and even more beautiful, with every comfort and with services that rival the best gated communities in the world. All these people—and you among them, Mam Jalal—are responsible for three years of destruction and death, murder and torture, outages of electricity and water, lack of security and civil services, and manifold other disasters. If they continue in this way—and setting you aside for the moment—their place isn't at the president's table, oh no, but in the jail cell with Saddam Hussein and his seven assistants. Their place is not at the table of the president, Uncle Jalal! They are a shameful extension of Saddam, not a divine mercy that has descended upon the people, as they like to think. I swear to God, they are thieves and burglars who commit their thefts in public, and the best evidence for that are these palaces they now inhabit, the property they possess, and the money they have seized.

Mr. President, these honored guests at your table, who wolfed down red and white meat, tashreeb, biryani, and hummus, which they followed with baklava, jalebi, and lady-fingers, they are all happy to agree on a unified national government, even if they differ on the distribution of the sovereign ministries, which they see as the Ministries of Defense, the Interior, Finance, and Oil.

As you can see, my dear Mam Jalal, at least two of those ministries are all about power, ruthlessness, prison cells, and torture, not about defending the borders of the country, which have become a revolving door for the Iranians and who knows what others anyhow. Meanwhile, the remaining two relate to theft and embezzlement. The desire to oppress, terrify, and humiliate others is a sovereign concern, I guess. And the desire to plunder, siphon, and smuggle is yet another sovereign concern, and the very highest priority

277

of that worthless member of the National Assembly, Abbas al-Bayati—a good-for-nothing starling if ever there was one. As for the Ministries of Higher Education, Electricity, Water Resources, Health, Child-rearing, Human Rights, Women, Civil Society, and Science and Technology, these are trifling administrations, not at all worth arguing over. (Oh, and don't forget the poor Ministry of Culture, which some people call the Ministry of the Bearded Vulture!) Have you ever seen so many sovereign ministries in a country occupied from one corner to the other?

I'm very sorry to say, Mr. President, that half your guests are monkeys, and the other half still need some time to reach that level! No fewer than four of them are competing for the position of prime minister. The first is Ibrahim al-Jaafari, and the last thing he wants is for anyone to ask how this time will be any different from his first stint at the big desk, reminding him of where we all were a year ago, with all the murder, destruction, sectarian convulsion, and failure that he left in his wake. We didn't understand a thing that came out of his mouth, aside from all his talk about investigative committees, I guess, which became little more than jokes anyway. On top of that, he insisted on smooth-talking us into our graves with his hollow, foolish speeches, whose only measurable effect was to piss us all off.

Next comes Hussain al-Shahristani, a nuclear physicist who left the world of science last year to become a class monitor in the unruly elementary school that is Iraq! And whenever Hajj Hajim al-Hassani, speaker of the National Assembly, disappears to solve the world's problems at Davos and so on, this atomic physicist sits down and says, "Brother, don't talk without raising your hand first. Show some respect before you say, 'Fuck the atom, yes, by God!'"

Third up, the poor doctor, Nadim al-Jabiri. He shared in the hunger and privation of those eggplant years—ha! You haven't forgotten the '90s, have you, my strawberry-loving brothers, when all we ate was eggplant? This fellow seems to think that having endured with us the injustices and cruelty suffered by the oppressed in those days is sufficient quali-fication for the power brokers emerging from the corridors of Iran to grant him the position of prime minster. But they waste no time in placing before his eyes a folder of everything he wrote in praise of Saddam. It all goes to show the truth of the motto, "Your skeletons are safe with us, but only if you keep with us."

The last is Adil Abdul-Mahdi, a Sorbonne-trained econ-omist and the calmest of the four. He just needs to come out from under Hakim's abaya in order to gaze upon us as fellow citizens with a pure Iraqi spirit. As I see it, he's the best of the bunch.

Mr. President, I've been away from Iraq for the past few weeks, and the progress, prosperity, and income that I've seen others achieving in this modern era terrifies me. I'm still trying to recover from the shock of it, even as I write. I beg your pardon, but may I send an enormous gob of phlegm at your guests, bigger even than the kind that people saved up for Saddam? Saddam didn't live in the West like these fluttering bats did, so all he knew about civilization was that we were barefoot, and he was the one who would give us shoes. These thieves, however, have lived in the West and in the East, yet all they learned was the best way to laugh at us and plunder our wealth. In the space of three years, their friends and relatives, and the friends and relatives of their wives, have been transformed from nobodies, sprawled across sidewalks in the cities of the West, into big names on the playgrounds of the rich and famous. Meanwhile, all us unfortunates here have just moved from one misery to the next.

Do you want numbers, Mr. President? Don't be in such a rush! I'll provide you with all the numbers and documents you need. But what are you going to do with those numbers and documents when you don't have any power or authority?

My dear Mam Jalal, the hungry poor deserve the country's banquets and the country's blessings more than these scumbags at your table!

FEBRUARY 8, 2006

A Distant Childhood in a Black Dishdasha Robe

On a day just like this, wearing black dishdasha robes, perhaps the ones we received the previous year, we would drag our childhoods over toward the Thawra Dam, with the older teenagers in the lead. It was something we would do on the night before the tenth day of the month of Muharram, a day we called Hijja, meaning pilgrimage.

Our mission was to collect old, discarded tires. The older boys would roll the heavy truck tires, while we younger boys would root around for ones that better suited our childhood sizes. Filled with an unaccustomed, conflicted gladness, we would return to our block, where we'd pile our tires up on top of each other and then guard them, for they would be fuel for the long cold night, the eve of the tenth of Muharram, when our parents would let us stay out, unsupervised, till morning. Before the darkness fell, the fire of the first tire would rise, with its black smoke that touched the old clouds above. We'd form a circle around the fire as our mothers and sisters began their tour from house to house. They would let down their long hair and go running, sobbing and crying out their lament, led by Mahdiya, the hired mourner:

The star has disappeared over the bank, Abbas
They say it's time to get up and ride, Abbas

The fire rose. One tire followed another, and our childhoods inhaled black smoke, the smoke that still lingers in our nostrils. It was Hijja Eve:

Hijja: no sleep till morn
Hijja: eyes wide, no sleep

The girls of the neighborhood were all dressed in black, fluttering like sad butterflies. They jumped around with their mothers, learning the ritual practice of beating themselves, wailing, crying, and pledging devotion to Zaynab (peace be upon her!), the heroine of the longest night in history. I would steal away from my friends to follow the crowd of women, searching among them for the face of my mother (may she rest in peace!). Her cheeks would be wet with tears, her voice choked with crying. My mother, who forgot about me for the whole night and wouldn't check up on me, her child

281

passing those late hours beside a heap of burning tires. My mother, whose devotion to Husayn made her forget about her own son, cast aside by the fiercely rising fires as sadness penetrated the night.

The fire scorched us, so we moved back a little. Then the cold of the old days stung us, so we returned to the circle of the warmth. Karim, son of Hajji Jabbar, came up to me, carrying an old tape recorder. He pressed play, and a voice blared out. Karim turned it down to keep it as one of that night's many secrets:

> O Husayn, in our heart of hearts.
> We cried, "We believe in you!"
> Not a cry of emotions, this.
> Not a prayer, no mere opinion.
> One of our founding principles, this.

As far as we were concerned, Husayn wasn't a political figure. He wasn't the property of any one party or side. None of them could snatch him away. He belonged to all of us. He was Husayn, something bigger than could be contained by an organization. All the sky was Husayn, and all the earth too. Husayn meant us, because he was Husayn. We didn't need a meaning of our own. We didn't need slogans or signs. We didn't need anyone to guide us to a path that arrived at love for Husayn, a black dishdasha, and sorrow, forever renewed, year by year, descending with the umbrella of memory.

The night passed slowly. Sleepiness snuck up on us and the conversations faded. A numb weakness stole into our tender bodies, and we sought refuge from drowsiness in drowsiness. The sun had to dawn upon our vigil so that we might fulfill our duty without falling short. The older boys would have nothing to lord over us. Only he who surrendered to sleep on the night of Ashura would suffer from shame.

Dawn began to creep timidly out of our night of sadness. Pale, bitter, and sick, it came. Lame and hobbled, it came! Our gathering broke up, and we went to our separate houses, leaving behind the last flame on the last tire to burn alone and lonely. We stretched out near the heating stove and listened to a distant voice of the muffled radio:

"When dawn came upon Husayn on the day of Ashura, he performed the morning prayer with his companions and then addressed them. May God praise him and extol him!"

It was the voice of the deceased Abdul Zahra al-Kaab reading the story of the Karbala Massacre, which still wrings tears from the heart. The story lasted two hours or a little more; it ended with bitter weeping and a strange cry. Husayn, stained with his pure blood, raises his hands to the sky, and in a moment when time has stopped dead in its tracks, he says, "O God, break them into manifold factions, with whom no ruler shall ever be pleased. O God, turn their might against each other, and place in power over them one who shows them no mercy."

Yes, O Sayyid Husayn! We, the sons of those who killed you, have become manifold factions; dozens of parties, movements, and organizations, and see here, our might has been turned against ourselves, and our blood is shed every day by our own hands. Every day, O Sayyid of the Martyrs, we kill each other. We bring you good news, O son of the daughter of the Prophet of God! For no ruler is ever pleased with us, and we are never pleased with our ruler! God has answered your prayer and placed one to rule over us who shows us no mercy, one who laughs at our naïve goodness.

The prayer came true, O Sayyid. We killed you, and here we are, filling the world with crazed regret for you, a stinging regret that is scattered like the blood that our clubs and swords draw from our scalps. Look at us, O son of the daughter of the chosen Prophet, and see how cruel are our hearts! We've begun slicing the skulls of our children with our swords so that fountains of blood spray up before our very eyes. It is as though God has made us to be like those who kill us: devoid of compassion, mercy, and human feeling.

O Sayyid, I implore you, by our bitter childhoods, which the sad nights filled with the tears of our mothers, with the mourning of our fathers, that you accept our regret and hear our apology, we who love you and have been afflicted by your kidnappers. They all claim you as their distant grandfather, while we have no grandfathers apart from those peasant farmers who died by tuberculosis and typhoid. We have no grandfathers, O Sayyid, and no fathers. We've lived our whole lives as orphans, the children of orphans. They've stolen even our innocent sorrow for you. They want to transform it into a political sorrow so that our blood flows out in rivers. They want to turn you into the president of a party, the leader of a tribe.

Your name has been kidnapped, O Sayyid, and we've been exiled from our childhood in its black dishdasha. They've reduced you until you've become merely the household deity of this or that house or family. No, worse, they've gone so far as to make you, O Sayyid of the Free, merely another black turban, a turban that leads us first to the right and then to the left. We beat ourselves, but they don't join the ceremony with us. We tear the skin on our heads and the heads of our sons, while their heads and the heads of their sons are healthy and whole. With rosy cheeks and turbans on their heads, they live at ease in the warmth of their palaces. They have made a paradise on earth and wear silk brocade, drinking water mixed with camphor. Their entire lives consist of bunches of fruit, hanging low and within reach, while we are still as we were, poor and haggard in short dishdashas. O Sayyid of the Martyrs, in the name of your noble cry, the cry of Karbala, palaces were erected, wealth was plundered, virgins were given in marriage, and the hands of the thieves were kissed.

O Sayyid of the Martyrs, I'll go alone to the dam this year to roll a big tire and stay up late as it burns. I will cry alone as I watch for the face of my mother. Perhaps she will come with me tonight. Perhaps nostalgia for my childhood will grip her. I want my mother. I want an ancient black dishdasha. I want to cry, Husayn. My country is wounded, Husayn. Iraq is groaning, Husayn, from one end to the other. Iraq is dying, Husayn. Iraq is bleeding its sons, Husayn. And we poor unfortunates have nothing but Iraq. We have nothing but Iraq, O Husayn!

MARCH 5, 2006

To Iraq's Health!

My friends, I was invited, together with a group of my cousins and neighbors, to join with a great crowd of people from our city for a shared prayer service. We went, and they welcomed us with their customary kindness and affection. We fell deep into conversation with each other, and some of the brothers who were men of religion talked about the necessity of holding these kinds of heart-to-heart meet-ups from time to time.

Such meetings, dear sirs, are not social events, not mixers, not opportunities to get to know each other, not reconciliation sessions between two opposing sides. Instead, in my humble opinion, their real usefulness is as an object lesson, an important message we send to those who work in the shadows to pollute the deep brotherhood we've inherited from our fathers and grandfathers and beyond, a means of survival in these lands taught to us by those first human beings on earth, huddling together in the Euphrates–Tigris valley.

At the end of the joint prayer service, we embraced. Our tears flowed, and God sent his mercy and reassurance upon our hearts. Lord! How beautiful is our affection and our brotherhood, which diminishes our enemies and renders their way of life so difficult. I rejoiced at my tears just as I rejoiced at the tears of others. I realized the sublimity of our hearts. Iraqis, my friends, possess hearts that are good and merciful in their intentions, but these criminals want to kill our sweetest and most beautiful qualities. God curse them and return them to their burrows across the border!

On the way back, my uncle Shinawa was with us, unfortunately, in the same bus into which more than thirty passengers were packed. In the middle of this benevolent crowding, Shinawa shouted over to me, "Hey, Shalash, did you hear how beautiful the prayer was? I swear to God, wasn't this meeting so much better than all that other stuff?"

286

Everyone understood, of course, what "all that other stuff" meant. Some passengers let out a loud laugh, while others just smiled; some muttered an invocation against Satan (may he be pelted with stones!); others turned toward me to enjoy the embarrassment that this terrorist uncle of mine would no doubt provoke.

And, indeed, I hung my head in shame, and my cheeks went red (well, not really). Shinawa's words kept ringing in my ears, for I was thinking back to "all that other stuff," meaning arak, beer, chickpea soup, jajeek, and all the rest. And I thought back to the splendid days of the bars, and how we arak drinkers were Iraqis in every sense of the word. For we had spent our lives in a great, communal, and nondenominational drunkenness, every faction and formation equally welcome, without discrimination. After the first quarter bottle of Asriya arak—the brand with the black stopper—we'd all start exchanging hugs and kisses after the inevitable and wonderful prelude, "Don't I know you from somewhere?"

To those who never honored their noble kin by entering those bars, let me say only that we used to love each other as brothers. We didn't know who was a Sunni, a Shiite, a Sabian, a Kurd, or a Turkoman. Everyone was an Iraqi, nothing more, and the proof is that there weren't Shiite bars and Sunni bars but just *bars*. Mikha'il was the bartender at our local, the one who stayed up to serve us drinks and make us feel at home, who loved us all and would often stand us a round on credit. He didn't know anything about any of us apart from the fact that we were nice people, we didn't lie too much, and we tended to keep our word. We would get drunk together and sing together. We'd listen to the stories jilted lovers told when they approached our table to ask for a light. Then we'd invite them to take a seat so that the broken record, broken in perpetuity, could begin once again:

"I loved her for sixteen years, and then she married her cousin, the car mechanic."

He'd sit there smoking and heaving horrendous sighs until someone else broke in to say, "Sixteen years? That's nothing. Me, I practically grew up with mine, then I found her with another man on the roof."

The stories would continue, true ones as well as fantasies, until someone would break out with a song from some corner of the bar:

> Someone who knows nothing of my problem
> He tries to comfort me, tells me it will be fine
> What is love? If it turns your hair gray from the start
> What is love? Who can say how it all will end . . .

All our fingers would start keeping time with the traditional Iraqi finger snap. Bring me a quarter of arak! I'll nurse a quarter bottle till midnight. I'm here, my noble sirs.

Mind you, I'm not calling on the national government to build big bars for Iraqis in order to preserve our brotherhood and our national harmony, for our brotherhood and unity are present and strong, God willing! But I do want to say . . . well, everything in due time.

Anyway, on this noble occasion, let's drink to the health of Iraq the magnificent, the father of goodness and generosity: the Iraq of affection and songs, the Iraq of crazy lovers, the Iraq of beautiful Iraqi women! On this occasion, I raise my glass in greeting to you all, the sons and daughters of beautiful Iraq, wherever you are. Getting together with you was nice, but I need to go! Curfew starts soon, and our house is quite some ways away . . .

Having Made It onto the Map, Sabah El Khayat Square Now Enters History

The singer Sabah El Khayat became famous in the second half of the 1980s and the early '90s. He launched his career with the song "I'm Torn," which he followed up with a song of truly epic social dimensions, "She Came with Her Girlfriend." El Khayat was cut off from his audience for a certain amount of time when Iraqi troops entered our elegant, sisterly neighbor, Kuwait. After that, in the early years of the unjust sanctions upon our long-suffering land, El Khayat felt an obligation to join the advance guard of the cavalcade preserving the traditional music concert. He inaugurated a new era of popular music with his hit song, "The One with Apricot Cheeks," on the occasion of the wedding of his nephew, who was known as Ali Jali.

During the wedding of one local guy, Sabah El Khayat looked amazing up on the stage that was set up especially for the occasion—and which, for the record, consisted of the horse cart belonging to our neighbor. Sabah El Khayat found an opportune moment to drop his latest artistic bomb, for which, as usual, he wrote the music, and on which I was honored to accompany him on the *zanbur* drum. It goes, "Hey girl, riding in the Celebrity, you don't know how lost I am . . . She has thrown off her abaya, hands dotted with henna." (We'll translate the song into Latin on some future occasion.) This resounding hit was as good as a train of glory that carried El Khayat to the summits of enduring fame, which the singer Sa'id Abd Rambo (of blessed memory) had nearly snatched away from him.

Friends, so that we might enter the heart of these historical events and really get inside the political environment from which this towering artist sprang, let me describe the social and geopolitical manifestations of that time. Samir al-Shaykali, Saddam's fearsome Minister of the Interior for Thawra City, launched a campaign against the *breekiya* groups, or breakers, who took their name from the English term "break dancing" and were famous for their black pants, called "Bermudas." As a result, these playful and more-or-less peaceful dancing groups were scattered, and all traces of them nearly wiped out. They would have been lost entirely if virtuous remnants had not rallied, wearing black *sirwal* trousers this time, to form new groups, which were called *khoshiya*, meaning "the good guys."

To our brothers from the neighborhoods of Drage, Daoudi, Harthiya, and Jadriyah, and likewise my brothers from the Iraqi colonies from Toronto to Malmö, I must say now that the khoshiya are violent punks who have abandoned meekness, art, and beautiful dancing in favor of savagery, pill-popping, and the machetes and razor blades they carry as weapons. Instead of dancing at our weddings, usually conducted in the streets or up on the rooftops, now *they're* the ones who break up these celebrations two hours before any proclamation that the deed has been done. They draw their machetes and scream into the faces of the noble members of the audience their famous challenge, "Step up, if you're man enough!" Allow me to translate this peculiar sentence, especially for our brothers from Ziyouna; to you I say that the literal meaning might be construed as "Raise your hand if you want your mama to rend her clothes and cry your name aloud in the street."

I'm sorry for this digression—necessary though it was to satisfy the demands of serious scientific research—and I now return to the topic of today's episode, which is the progression of that eternal artist, Sabah El Khayat. But before I get to the heart of the matter, I want to remind my brothers watching at home that the aforementioned khoshiya groups, which were formed from the last remnants of the breakers, are the very ones who became the "soldiers of Al-Mansur Billah," referring to our deposed leader, whose nickname declared him to be "he who is made victorious by God." That is, by first dressing all in black and then changing into a dreadful white, they turned into the Fedayeen of Saddam. And more recently, ladies and gentlemen, it is these same people who have started to call themselves the "soldiers of the Imam Mahdi" (God hasten his appearance!). And believe me when I say I think they are indeed the ones paving the way for the appearance of the Hidden Imam, now dressed in black, now dressed in white! Because if the Imam doesn't show up soon and scatter them to the wind, there'll be no point whatsoever in his sublime appearance.

Sorry, sorry, in any case, let's come back again to that epic artist, Sabah El Khayat, who set himself apart from the rest of the singers from Thawra City by being the first to carry, along with his oud, a machete, which he used to terrify the khoshiya and prevent them from ruining his concerts. In his venerable presence, the very flanks of those cowards would tremble at the splendor of his might! And when you told them, "Come on! Do it, if you're your mothers' sons!" they would say to you, "No, we love Sabah El Khayat! We could never offend against his refined art." These were his greatest fans, and the intensity of the terror they felt at Sabah El Khayat would make them pee their black pants when the singer so much as glared at them. They were so afraid that they memorized his songs, which they went on to sing at every suitable occasion, or even without one. They stopped cheering for that eternal artist, Abd Rambo, who gave up singing to join the Sadrist movement and went on to don a turban and receive instruction at the seminary . . . (Let me add, however, for the historical record, that the man maintained his limpid artistic spirit, and nothing has yet escaped his lips that might grieve either the honorable men in his movement or the sons of his oppressed native city.)

Sabah El Khayat (God preserve him!) was mighty of stature. That is to say, he was enormous. He had a big head and broad shoulders, and he bore a strong resemblance to Shabth bin Rabie, one of the infamous criminals who murdered Imam Husayn on the day of Ashura. He wore no mustache, had thick hair, and his skin tone tended toward bronze. He sometimes had his cheeks threaded by Akram the Barker, while at other times he'd go to the "Friends Barber Shop" on the other side of Thawra.

Among his defining characteristics was that he would wear white shoes on all occasions. Also, in an era when all musicians would pluck their ouds, El Khayat had a way of striking his strings that gave his songs a powerful resonance and set his music apart. People tried to imitate him, but nobody could manage it, not even his brother, the not-so-famous Turki Jabbar, or rather "Turki al-Rihani," as his name was written on his second cassette. The testimony of history also records that Sabah El Khayat was the very first person in all of Thawra City and its suburbs to ride a Royal Supercar—his was red and had a Baghdad license plate, number 949488. That car has maintained its place at the pinnacle of the car hierarchy in Thawra, even now, after we've entered an era when so many cars are being imported that the registry can't keep up.

Sabah El Khayat got out of his Supercar, feeling cocky and proud. How could he not, when a singer as good as Hussin Albasry, who'd preceded him only by a handful of years, never even got to own a donkey? So when El Khayat continued to glitter and rise to greater fame, and the suburb of Ur was built next door to Thawra, Sabah El Khayat had the honor of being the first to walk its newly paved streets. Just as it was our great ancestor who was the first to enter the historical city of Ur, Sabah El Khayat entered the modern Ur as a liberator, not a conqueror. It was there that he launched his art to even greater heights, if such could be imagined, and encroached upon the boundaries of the empire that Abu Ammar's records had established in the city of Sha'ab next door. Though in turn, a bit of Sabah's own artistic luster and glow faded when that suburb subsequently insisted on celebrating its native son Basem Al Ali, who composed the famous aria, "Look at her, so cute! O Fatin ... Crying with henna on your hands ... O Fatin!"

Why this masterful introduction to Sabah El Khayat, you may ask, O zealous Iraqis, wherever you may be? Well, it was in the neighborhood of Ur that the body of the Saddam's lawyer, Khamis al-Obeidi, was strung up from one of the electrical poles after his assassination this past week, in the very square that bears the name of Sabah El Khayat. It was an obvious challenge to the authority of Prime Minister al-Maliki and, in equal measure, to the international community, on the part of the breakers, who became the khoshiya, then the Fedayeen, and finally the Mahdi Army, as I previously explained. This terrifying spectacle wasn't all that different from the things Saddam would do, like the time in the mid-1980s when he had the body of a courageous political opponent thrown to the dogs in Square 55. And these local heroes of ours have confirmed that they are "Soldiers of the Leader," even if one leader has been exchanged for another. Indeed, they are soldiers loyal to any leader, as long as they may remain sheep for someone to herd off toward death whenever that someone can see some benefit for the nation in doing so.

These audacious killers have offered Saddam Hussein the very best gift in his captivity, confirming for him that his crimes against the people were also done for the benefit of the nation. What else could you expect a man leading a nation like ours to do with us?

Finally, let me put in a request for Sabah El Khayat's song, "Hey Girl, Riding in the Celebrity," which I'd like to dedicate to Ali Jali, Muhammad Salman, Muhsin Al-Lami, and Abu Hussein al-Hilfi, the heroes of the blessed struggle. Just as I congratulate the Sayyid Leader (long may his might endure!) for this unambiguous victory. May he proceed from one triumph to another, God willing!

JUNE 28, 2006

A Discourse on National Reconciliation

On this occasion of national reconciliation meetings, I want to know why Umm Hussein is so angry. What's wrong with me? Am I some fundamentalist, terrorist, or Saddamist? Believe me! I swear, my hands aren't soiled with anything besides Iraqi mud, plaster, and cement. I deserve reconciliation more than anyone, Umm Hussein, because, as you know, I'm a simple citizen who has no problem with anyone. Indeed, I run away from problems, even though they come chasing after me.

By God, even when I see our occupiers, those dogs, up on their tanks or Hummers, I draw myself up, raise my hands in the air, and say, "*Halloo, Mistir. Yoo welcome heer. Bee free. It iz yur kantree.*" And our Ba'athist brothers, I don't have problems with them either. Every day I play backgammon with Comrade Maghamis, and sometimes I lend him some money when he needs it, saying to myself, "Poor guy, you really have to take pity on a comrade who's gone from riches to rags." As for our brothers in the militias, you can trust by the affection I bear you that despite their comments and the way they laugh at me, I love them too, because they're so unfortunate and don't have a clue about what's really going on—that other people are just tricking them and taking advantage of their pea brains.

The big politicians? Well, look, I never run into them, and they never run into me. We don't run in the same circles! Thank God for television, so I can at least have an idea what they look like! And sometimes, despite their administrative corruption—their public thievery, that is—I say to myself, "Poor things! Let them eat! Iraq doesn't belong to anyone!"

So after all that, you're still mad at me? But why? What do you want, for me to beg? I'll do it! To apologize? I'll do it! To hit my head against the wall? I'll do it!

Umm Hussein, you're an intelligent person. Life's not worth fighting about, and we're family. Our national reconciliation will unite the group on this side with the one on that. I promise, after just a few months, you'll find them together like hummus and tahini. They'll probably even be in-laws by then, with one guy marrying the other's aunt. I'm not against that, Umm Hussein. I swear, I'm all for the national reconciliation, heart and soul. If only you'd be content, life would be easy! As the poet puts it, "May God never bring discord between us!" Or as Hussam Al-Rassam sings, "Someone upsets you and makes you cry? I'll beat the father of the man who makes you cry!" And likewise, let's remember Kadim Al Sahir's famous ditty: "Who made you mad? It was I who made you mad? By God, I'll make the world mad so long as nothing bad happens to you. Now watch me count to ten!" If you don't reconcile with me, Umm Hussein, just watch! I'll

Gate. Then when we get home at night, happy and singing, we'd even find the electricity working! All it takes is a little luck. But, then again, who says we have even that much luck to spare if even you, Umm Hussein, are turning against me and can't spare me a "How's it going?" when we pass in the street. No, let me revise my previous statement—luck isn't the way. It's only by force that things happen. Us, lucky? When have we ever been lucky? But you are a true Iraqi, I know, and your heart won't let you stay angry with me. I respect you and value you too much for that. You deserve all the respect in the world!

Anyway, I don't remember anymore what it was I was going to tell you. Wait, wait, now I remember! Regarding national reconciliation, I don't think it can be found in talking, in speeches. National reconciliation is in good intentions, in realizing the seriousness of our situation, and in surmounting our silly differences. Yes, most of our differences are silly! Not so much the murdering, and not so much the religious intolerance—but, leaving that stuff aside, what I mean are the disagreements between ordinary Iraqis who've nurtured a bit of hatred in their hearts for each other. The reasons for this anger are trivial, unworthy of so much animosity! After this long connection we've had for thousands of years, does it make any sense that we would start labeling each other "Grudgin' Sunnis" and "Refusin' Shiites" because some Muslims held a grudge against Ali and others refused Ali Bakr and Umar as the Prophet's successors some fourteen hundred years ago? Does that make any sense at all, my fellow Iraqis?

I swear, I've gone to Umm Hussein's father to ask her hand in marriage on at least twenty occasions, and he's refused me every time! Yet not once have I called him a Refuser.

Let him refuse me; it's his right! I mean, what sort of father would marry his sweet, educated daughter to a guy named Shalash? Ha! Just imagine, Umm Hussein, someone marrying his daughter to a guy named Shalash. I swear, if I had a *goat* I wouldn't marry it to someone named Shalash, much less if I had an educated, pretty daughter. No, and that's the tragedy: this guy is named Shalash, one of his uncles is Shinawa, and another is named Shinshul. Yes, on my honor, his name is Shinshul al-Iqabi! What, you've never heard of him? And on top of that, Shalash and both his uncles never have anything to say except "Who's got the arak?" and "Who brought the mezze?" And yet, and yet! Despite all that, I've never called Umm Hussein's father a Refuser.

As for the Grudgers, look, one day a certain commando from the Ministry of the Interior exercised his grudge against me at a checkpoint in Karaj Amana. He had me take my clothes off and then run around in the afternoon sun. But I swear, even after that, I didn't call him a Grudger! He made a laughingstock of me in front of everybody, and you know Iraqis: when they get someone to laugh at, they can't believe their luck; they'll drop everything for a good laugh. The crowd started chanting, "Make him run! Make him run!" Even the old women started in with their trilling. And yet, all the same, I just say, "It's his right. The man's bored, and he's burning up in the sun. Let him put his grudges into effect upon me. What else can he do? He can hardly go and act on his grudges against those poor soldiers who are occupying us."

Well, Umm Hussein! I've said my piece. Is there any hope that you'll reconcile with me, or should I go to the café and spend the day playing backgammon? It's your decision!

Will God judge us, Umm Hussein, for spending an hour together when the rest of the country is coming together?

Greet your father for me! Give him my best and tell him I'd die for him, okay?

I'm an Iraqi

I'm an Iraqi. Yes, by God, an Iraqi! I swear to you, brothers, I'm an Iraqi. Not on account of my having a certificate of Iraqi citizenship, nor because I come from two parents who are Iraqi by birth. No! I'm an Iraqi because I'm Iraqi. When I sleep and when I rise, when I eat and when I drink, when I sit and when I walk, when I cry and when I laugh, and when I stand and when I ponder, I'm an Iraqi. Anyone who sees me, who sees the pain, the sadness, and the tear perched in my eye, immediately says, "Here is an Iraqi."

Look at me, dear reader. See how I smoke, and hear the sighs and groans rising from my breast. Take a good look in my eyes. Come closer and look at me. Do you see the grief of cruel years, the weariness of bitter days? On your honor, is there anything within me that isn't Iraqi?!

I'm an Iraqi, which means I'm sick. Sick of everything called Iraqi. I love the Iraqi Kurd, and I'd die for the Iraqi Turkoman. If an Iraqi Sabian gets sick, I'm the one who fills his cup with water. If a Christian cries "Help!" I come running as soon as I find the way. If someone should ask me, "Shalash, are you Sunni or Shiite?" by God, I feel as though he's swearing at me. Actually, not just swearing at me, but pulling the very nose off my face: that's how insulted I feel. I don't know why, but there are readers who even ask me sometimes, "Shalash, by the soul of your mother, are you with us or with the takfiri jihadists?" I'm telling you, I'm an Iraqi! Why do you make me yell and lose my composure? I mean, why do I have to become sectarian? No! Even if all of you died, I would say nothing besides I'm an Iraqi. I'll never be anything other than an Iraqi.

I'm an Iraqi from Anbar Province. Believe me, I'm from Anbar. But I don't allow takfiri jihadists into my house to wait their turn to detonate a suicide vest in the midst of our grandmothers and our children. No, I don't do that! I'm an Iraqi from Anbar, but I don't use the pretense of resistance to blow up markets, restaurants, bus stations, and worker lines. I'm an Iraqi from Anbar, but I don't stop people at roadblocks to say that Sunnis will stay and Shiites must go.

I'm an Iraqi from Diyala. Believe me, I'm from Diyala, but I don't cut off the heads of our countrymen's sons and put them in banana crates. I'm an Iraqi from Diyala, but I don't launch mortars into the mosques and Husayniya prayer halls. I'm an Iraqi from Diyala, but I don't let strangers enter my city and kill my people.

I'm an Iraqi from Saladin Province. Yes! From the cities of Tikrit and Samarra and Baiji. But I don't blow up power stations and gas pipelines. I'm an Iraqi from the northern city of Irbil, but cherished Baghdad remains my capital city, the Iraqi flag flutters above my house, and I don't think only of myself.

I'm an Iraqi from Thawra City, but I don't go around forming militia gangs to kidnap people and kill them for disgusting

301

sectarian reasons. It's not right, Hajji Muhammad! Why do you do such things, Abu Maryam? I'm an Iraqi from Al Shuala, but I don't attack my neighbors in Ghazaliya and kill people for no reason. It's not right, Sayyid Shinawa! By God, what a stain on your honor, Sayyid Shinawa! I'm an Iraqi from Dora, but I don't wear half a dishdasha and incite others to cross the river and attack Rusafa because the people up there aren't from my sect.

I'm an Iraqi from Basra, but even so, if Abu Kisra, or Rostam, or Beheshti, or Bilshati, or Esfahani, or any other Persian should come and want to enter Al Ashar without permission from its people, by God, I'd break his legs and those of his parents! I'm an Iraqi from Amara, an Iraqi from Nasiriyah, an Iraqi from Kut, from Diwaniyah, from Samawah, from Hillah. I'm an Iraqi, and I'll take whichever province you want to put me in.

I'm an Iraqi, and I'm ashamed that my people are wandering in Jordan, Syria, Egypt, and the rest of the surrounding countries. I'm ashamed that our young men and women are breaking their hearts at the borders, that our beautiful daughters are strangers in the capitals, looking here and there. I'm an Iraqi, and I'm ashamed that our intellectual assets plead for a job from the most foolish of people. I'm an Iraqi, and I'm ashamed that my government is number one in the world for corruption. I'm an Iraqi, and I'm ashamed that our National Assembly consists of people who are illiterate, regressive, sectarian, racist, and seething with envy of each other.

I'm an Iraqi, and I'm ashamed that when I visited a government ministry and applied for a position in my own country, they told me to go ask for support from one of our major political parties, such as the Islamic Call, the Supreme Council, or Fadila—which should really be named Calamity, the Blind Council, and Fadila the Milk Lady. I'm an Iraqi, and I'm ashamed that America is occupying us: its tanks come and go in Palestine Street, Beirut Square, Bab Al-Sharqi, Saadoun Street, and everywhere else in Baghdad. I'm an Iraqi, and I'm ashamed that the fate of my country is in the hands of an ayatollah in Tehran. I'm ashamed and embarrassed for the martyrs of Iraq, fallen at our borders, only for those borders to open now to dogs who spy, commit crimes, and traffic in drugs.

I'm an Iraqi. And because I want to remain an Iraqi and die an Iraqi, I will take part in the independent people's campaign for a day of national unity on that theme. I'm not just saying that I'm an Iraqi, but that from this moment, I will behave like an Iraqi.

It's not just me who's an Iraqi. You, dear reader, are also an Iraqi. And because I'm Iraqi and you're Iraqi, let's listen to the call of the noble youth, and in one voice, let us cry out with them, "I'm an Iraqi!"

OCTOBER 24, 2006

Not Everyone Who Shakes His Shoulders Like You Is a Pro!

Happy Eid! May all your days be happy! I want to thank all my sisters and brothers who have filled my inbox yesterday with Ramadan greetings and letters every bit as outstanding and beautiful as the good Iraqis who wrote them. Honestly, I'm torn between joy and embarrassment on account of these messages, and in light of these feelings, I can only say, "May God return your Iraq to you, just as you dream it, an Iraq of harmony, affection, brotherhood, and understanding, an Iraq of 'How are you, my dear, and how are your parents? Greet your father for me, and tell your mother that tomorrow she's having dinner with us!'"

To the brothers who have missed out on eating pastries and buffalo cream, I say to you, "Don't worry! Today, Shalash has eaten enough for twenty men." Believe me, I'm not kidding! Today, I ate buffalo cream and pastries as if I've never seen them before. Even my aunt, Sabiha, said, "What's the matter with you? You have a hollow leg or what?"

And yesterday, all my dreams came true, and I slammed a quarter bottle of arak. The guys invited me over, and I said, "It's a generous invitation. I totally deserve it, and I have no choice but to comply." Just like every year, I get hungry, tired, and thirsty during the month of Ramadan, and then I get a little sloppy during the Eid. Our session yesterday was truly amazing because the guys who were in charge—God love them!—prevented any talk about politics. Whenever someone wanted to bring us around to a political discussion, Wisam would go over and crank up the volume on the television. Those songs yesterday! Each one touched us where it hurt.

There was one song I liked by a singer whose name I'm not remembering, but the cool thing about this singer is that he looked a little like me, and he was also a bit of a scoundrel like me. His song went, "Not everyone who shakes his shoulders like you is a pro." As he was singing, he was flirting with one of our gypsy dancing sisters who were romping around in front of him, whipping their hair back and forth.

The subject of this song caused the strategic thinker in our group, Abd al-Rida, to burst out with one of his dramatic explanations. "By God, it's true! Not everyone who shakes his shoulders like you is a pro in his work!" He went on to say, "Professionalism and experience, brothers, are necessary in every field, particularly in politics. The cause of our tragedy is that the brothers in charge of political matters here are not politicians! Not even close! And they work according to the motto, 'I give you nothing, nor do I let God's mercy find you!'"

"Hey, man!" Razzak interrupted. "Didn't we say, no politics? By God, if anyone starts talking politics, I'll throw him right out!"

Razzak was known for his criminal record of throwing out his friends. He even threw us out of the house once in the middle of the night. But this time, if he threw us out, where would we go? The roads are blocked, there's a curfew, and unfortunately, we're all Iraqis, so it's forbidden for us to walk in the streets. Only the Americans can come and go through our streets as they please.

On top of this oppression, our poor brothers in the police these days have never seen a drunk in their whole lives. They have all come straight from the seminary in Najaf out to the street, and if they catch a drunk, they'll immediately say, "He's a Wahhabi-Salafi! He's a fundamentalist terrorist! He's a Saddamist!" Whereas in reality, any brother who loves arak couldn't be further from all those descriptions. Indeed, we are

305

the nicest people! I challenge you to find a single arak-drinker willing to blow himself up or join a militia or say whether he's a Sunni or a Shiite!

May the bars of bygone days rest in peace! They truly were a tent for national unity. Inside them, we were one big loving family, back in the days when we hadn't heard about federalism or national reconciliation, and we didn't need any Meccan Concord to fix this mess. Back when the blood and wealth and virtue of Iraq were haram and not to be touched. Unfortunately, the time has come when our country, our blood, our wealth, and our virtue are all halal. In what world would they grant permission to devour all these things, while arak, beer, gin, and mezze remain haram?!

OCTOBER 26, 2006

Shalash and the Adoption!

Today the weather was so nice! Clouds and light drops of rain. But as usual, Thawra City is not enjoying the beautiful day. Its fate remains black and its luck is spotty! Rather than living life and celebrating the Eid like the rest of God's cities, the pickpockets of Abu Dara' and the house breakers of Hajji Muhammad and Abu Maryam have spread through its streets since early morning to face off with the American helicopters, their armored vehicles, and the marines, who have come to arrest Abu Dara'.

God have mercy on bygone days! I swear, four offices would be enough to block off the alley, and no one would dare say a word. Whereas now, the biggest empire in the world has come to get Abu Dara'. Such crazy things we've seen! Anyway, that guy took off, feet pounding through the side streets. Dumb Filayyah gave directions to the bold fighters and cautioned residents about what would happen if they came out of their houses. There was a random firing of guns. People died, people were injured, and it all ended with a crowded public celebration led by our two representatives in the National Assembly, Razzak al-Shaykh and Salim Manati.

Chanting cheers, jumping around, wailing, denunciations, and pictures of the leader. It's a familiar scene I've witnessed a thousand times, ever since the days of the dictator. And here I am in the middle of the chaos, not having had anything to eat or drink. I just want to relax a little and write a few lines, but no one lets me do it! You'd think I was sitting on the frontlines, not at home. What have I done, O Lord? Why's it like this? Can't I just rest a few days? Why do we live our lives passing from one oppression to another? An entire year of beating our chest! Now the Eid has come, and Muqtada and his people have turned it into lamentation and oppression too!

Now, why was I even born in this blessed corner? Meaning, did it have to be Thawra City? Why didn't God make me Chinese, Filipino, Mozambican, or even French—it makes no difference to me! Listen, man, I'd even take Malawi! At least in Malawi, Madonna might come and adopt me. Imagine Shalash having Madonna for his mother! Every day, I'd get up early in the morning, wash my face, brush my teeth, comb my hair, and give Mama a kiss, "*Hai, mammy, haw ar yoo tooday?*"

Mama would smile, place her hands on my hair, and speak from the bottom of her heart, "*Hai, baybee!*"

Baybee? I swear, she really said *baybee*. I didn't do it, so why are you jealous? What's wrong with you, haven't you seen foreigners before? *Baybee* this and *baybee* that, whether you like it or not! Don't think *baybee* is more than I deserve, you marsh-dwellers! If my luck pans out and I live under Madonna's wing, I swear, that's a million times better than the wing of Hajji Irhaymeh. Where would he get a wing, anyway? Hajji Irhaymeh doesn't even have a sofa!

God! Just let me dream a little, and don't wake me up! Mama's going to Paris, and she's taking me with her. She's going to Mexico—so there!—and she's taking me along. She's making the pilgrimage to Karbala, and she's bringing me. She's going to the market, and she's taking me. Wait, shut up! Why would Madonna be going to the market?

I mean, what would happen if Madonna adopted me for real? Shakira would become our neighbor, the house of Julia Roberts would be in the back, and the house of Jennifer Lopez would only be a short distance from the roundabout. Over on the right side, as soon as you turn, you see the house of Britney Spears. And at the end of the street, close to the samoon bakery, you have the house of Cameron Diaz. On my honor, brothers—on my honor!—if Madonna adopted me, I'd give each one of you a crisp greenback, a full hundred bucks! I'd give one to each of you, because money be damned! Why do I need it? Money is what makes our world so dirty.

Madonna, by your honor—and you have more honor than the National Assembly—why did you go to Malawi to adopt a baby? You should have told me! I'm an innocent baby too, and I don't have anyone. I swear, I'm an orphan, and life has totally worn me down. Why, Madonna, why? How could God allow this!

Hey, man, it doesn't even need to be Madonna. Isn't there some singing, dancing gypsy girl who could come adopt me and save me from Abu Dara'?!

OCTOBER 29, 2006

Shalashian Feelings

The peaceful demonstration put on by Muqtada's people came to an end, and everyone parted ways. It wasn't a work-day, but even if someone wanted to go out for a while, the roads were filled with checkpoints and inspections, and the Americans were everywhere. They had lost someone and were turning the world upside down to look for him. All these patrols for just one soldier? What's the matter with you, haven't you ever seen a soldier before? Hey, put yourself in our shoes: What would you do if you had lost your whole country? You'd probably dig up Mars! The problem is that this soldier of theirs who's missing was one of us. Poor guy, he escaped to America, but he couldn't take it easy there either and went and joined the army.

Why in the world would anyone from America put on military fatigues? Why not go to Hollywood and become a singer instead? In America, nothing's easier than singing. You sag your pants, you tear some holes in your clothes, and you get yourself a few chicks from Qayyara. When you get up on stage and yell, "*Ai luf yoo!*" they'll put you in a band called "*Feeftee Sant.*" Come on, man, it doesn't even need to be "*Feeftee Sant.*" I'll make you a band called "Fifty Piasters," and if they don't accept Iraqi currency, just call your band, "Fifty Bucks." I mean, couldn't you find anything to do besides becoming a corporal in the army? Then you come here and get lost, and look at the trouble we're in because of you!

It's been a week now that the Americans have surrounded Baghdad. The people are sitting in their homes without a peep, not moving a muscle. They even moved the national reconciliation summit to London because of you! At least the roads are open there, they say. But isn't it funny how we battle in Abu Sayfayn and Al-Fadl, and we reconcile in London? Hey, the politicians went to the Kaaba in Mecca to reconcile, but we didn't get anything. You think in London, we're going to patch things up? Brothers, if someone is angry with me, have him meet me in London so we can reconcile! Seriously, let him come to London, and he'll find me under the bridge. But only on the condition that he won't wrong me again!

Anyway, I put on my pants and a shirt, and I went out to sit in a corner near some cinder blocks. Who knows? Maybe a friend would be passing by, and we'd kill some time in chit-chat. Suddenly, my heart started racing, my face went pale, and my hands felt clammy. Khadija the Schoolteacher was coming! She had taken her students to the demonstration today, and now she was walking back, poor thing! I pulled myself together, thought of a few nice things to say, and got ready. Khadija got closer . . . she arrived . . . she stopped in front of me. Face-to-face. My heart nearly fell out of my chest, and I was shaking all over. Someone hold me: I'm about to die! But then Khadija passed on without showing me the least regard. Not a word! Not a greeting!

She walked by with her nose held high. Why? I don't know! I sat there trying to think: Had I done something wrong? No, I swear! I've been behaving well for two months. No drinking, no carousing, no singing at the top of my voice, and not even picking a fight with her brother's wife! So what's the matter with her? Why did she ignore me like that? Well, let her go. Is there any shortage of women? Shalash, what's wrong with you? There are a thousand women out there who want you! Besides, Khadija's not so pretty. She's not that beautiful. And she's a little arrogant. Why am I working myself up so much? As the recently departed Saadi Al Hilli says in his song, "My dear, your mother won't let me talk to you." But why didn't she even greet me? Maybe she didn't see me. But how could she not see me? Am I a gecko? No, I'm a man! See how big and strong I am!

Come on, let her go! She's not the only woman in the world. All the times I've stayed up late for a girl, going out on the town, neglecting my homework, disregarding my family, and forgetting the future; all the times I went AWOL from the army and endured humiliation from the corporals; all the times I got tired and stood at the end of the street, putting up with trouble and rain; all the times the sun roasted me and the cold froze me: What did I get for that? Anytime someone catches our eye, and we say she's a girl from a respectable family, it turns out she's gone out with sixteen people, and she ends up marrying one of the looters who got rich after the invasion.

I have to forget Khadija and her father. Their whole family are such lowlifes. Her father is the biggest terrorist, her brother is a spy for assassins, her uncles are sailors who stole oil from the gas depot. Besides, Maryam, daughter of Hajji Fares, is a thousand times prettier. She looks like the singer Myriam Fares, and the name even matches! You know Myriam Fares? You don't, on your honor? You really don't know her? Is there anyone who doesn't know Myriam? If Nancy Ajram is a rocket, Myriam Fares is an aircraft carrier! Her hair alone is worth a thousand Khadijas.

I'm going to turn it up today. I'm going to get sloppy and scramble my brains. I really am going to forget Khadija and her whole tribe, and I'll do it with a shoe! I wouldn't give a damn for her if she kissed my shoe. Let her know who her betters are and not think that I'm killing myself over her. Dignity above all! Resistance is a holy right for all people!

Really, I'm telling you, I don't pay her any mind except to say, "Poor thing!" Sometimes I feel bad for her, and I give her a compliment, when actually she isn't the girl of my dreams. No, really, man, who's Khadija? She only crosses my mind because I'm bored and have nothing to do when the electricity's out, the phone lines are down, the internet cafés are closed, and I can't find anything to entertain myself. But quiet! Shut up! Khadija is coming. On my honor, it's her! I know her by the sound of her footsteps. Yes, by God, it's her! She came back! She came back! I'd lay my life down for that walk. She's arrived! Quiet!

"Oh, Shalash, how are you? Why are you sitting here? I've really missed you. I haven't seen you in forever! Shalash, my life!"

What in the world is this? My temperature's up, I've got a fever. I'm going to die! "Shalash, my life!" It's more beautiful than any song in the world! My Khadija, you're my everything! You're my life! My whole tribe will lay down their lives for your shoe! Hey, man, didn't I say that Khadija didn't see me the first time? Poor girl, she was tired.

Khadija is the prettiest girl in the world, I swear. If the Americans saw Khadija, they'd immediately abandon their lost soldier and follow her instead. Khadija is the queen of beauty for the universe. She's the moon over our block, and the electricity that powers our neighborhood. Khadija is a 700-watt generator: she pumps us full of sensations and feelings. The whole Rusafa neighborhood lights up when she laughs, and when she cries, all of Karkh across the river shuts down. I swear, her footsteps are musical. Compared with her, Maryam, daughter of Hajji Fares, is a hunchback. Old Maryam, twisted and twitchy Maryam. I beat her and her father, Hajji Fares, with a shoe! She's always out, and she's so stupid. She doesn't measure up to Khadija's shoe!

"Shalash, my life! Shalash, my life!!"

Listen, did you hear her say, "Shalash, my life," or am I not paying attention? Maybe she did ignore me, and I'm just imagining things! If she ignored me, I'll murder her grandfather, that bitch! No! I also ignored her! You saw me, how I turned my face away and didn't respond to her? I don't give a damn for her. What, is there a drought of women? There are thousands of women!

Shut up! Quiet! My dear Khadija has come back!

Masters of the Elephant

When Naima's elephant appeared in our street for the first time, people finally believed what Nuwayra, Ghurab's wife, had been saying all along regarding the annoying patter up on the rooftops, which is that it was caused by a small elephant that Naima recently acquired. But Nuwayra, despite the precision of her intelligence reports, did not advance a satisfactory explanation for how Naima acquired this elephant, and she was just as confused as everyone when asked where this elephant had come from.

And because we are a city that readily mixes fiction with reality, some people believed Rahi bin Hanun's words when he claimed to have seen a small elephant with wooden wings descend upon Naima's roof a year and a half ago. Similarly, others believed the tale of Mr. Flea the Cheetah, who declared that Naima's husband, Bajay, had not actually gone to Syria, as Naima claimed, but had been transformed by God into an elephant on account of all the false oaths he took in the names of prophets and imams.

Anyway, what I'm trying to say is that there are many stories about Naima's elephant. Personally, I'm not interested in all that gossip. What does interest me is the entertainment afforded by the presence of an elephant in Thawra City. Our deprived children thronged around it. This elephant was their own roaming zoo, and in their delight, they bubbled over with songs, whistles, and jokes. As for Naima, despite the relatively high cost of the elephant's living expenses and the difficulty of her own conditions, she insisted on taking care of it.

If we had known that Naima's elephant was an armored vehicle that couldn't be scratched by the largest bomb, we would easily have found an excuse for Naima's decision to raise this gigantic animal. The elephant began wandering around Thawra City from ten in the morning until four in the afternoon. Then it would go out again at six in the evening and stay out until curfew, and sometimes even an hour or so past curfew. After all, the police were afraid of it, and no one could prevent it from doing so.

In her annual visits to shrines during this past month of Sha'ban, Naima was seen riding in a howdah on the back of her elephant amid crowds performing the collective rites of marching. The elephant stretched out its trunk to clear a path, while Naima drifted off to sleep on its back, as comfortable as if home in bed. The clashes between the terrorists and the pilgrims on that occasion became known as "The Battle of the Elephant," since people sought cover behind Naima's elephant, which blocked the bullets. A few other times, Naima was also seen boarding her elephant for shopping trips, visits to friends and relatives, or whenever she went to the local clinic. There are eyewitnesses who saw IEDs exploding under the feet of the giant elephant without Naima suffering the least harm. Such explosives would have destroyed the strongest American Hummer, but the elephant didn't even notice.

The government got word about the elephant, and it sent a delegation to negotiate with Naima about making use of its services to transport some officials who were deprived of seeing their people. In the face of everyone who raised the subject with her, Naima repeated a single sentence. She declared that this elephant was a divine providence to protect her from the danger of terrorism, which was harvesting the souls of everyone.

President Jalal Talabani offered Naima, her family, and her animals a stay at his splendid resort at the Dukan Dam up north if she would just let him use the elephant for one month to stroll among his people like any elected president. Naima agreed and went to live for a time at the resort. The elephant entered the Green Zone amid the jealous envy of the speaker of parliament, the prime minister, and all the other officials toward crafty Talabani, that fox who was able to obtain the services of an armored elephant.

Prime Minister Nouri al-Maliki went to Talabani's house, which was not far from his own, and begged to accompany him on the elephant's back for a joint tour through the streets of Baghdad. Speaker of Parliament Mahmoud al-Mashhadani heard about the arrangement, and he went and made the same request to Mam Jalal. And because Talabani has a generous heart, he agreed to both requests. The three of them mounted the back of the elephant, and when it took them across the bridge into Jadriyah, Sayyid Abdul Aziz al-Hakim saw them. His heart was filled with such envy at what he saw that he offered to cede his goal of a federalist state for the center and south of Iraq in exchange for getting up behind them.

The other three agreed to the deal, and Hakim joined them on the elephant, where they sat encased in a box of bullet-proof glass. The elephant set right off, and the four of them toured the Rusafa district on the east bank of the Tigris amid the surprise and confusion of the people at this strangest of things they were seeing. The greater part of their surprise was not on account of an elephant in the streets of Baghdad, but that the four evangelists had left the Green Zone and come among the people without their bodyguards!

During this blessed tour, Mashhadani asked his brother Talabani about the direction he had given this elephant. Talabani laughed and said, "This is a Kurdish elephant! It used to fly above the mountains of Kurdistan, hunted by members of the Peshmerga." Mashhadani laughed, as did Maliki. Hakim heard Talabani's words and laughed as well, which the elephant found disgusting. It raised its trunk up high, spread its wooden wings, and flew into the sky amid a crowd of onlookers, whose eyes followed that marvelous sight until the elephant disappeared among the thick clouds that were rapidly gathering in the sky above the city. The people did not disperse until a severe thunderstorm, the likes of which Baghdad has never seen before, broke out.

On the morning of the next day, after the rain had stopped and the sun rose once again, Dr. Ali Aldabbagh, the government spokesman, went on Al Iraqiya to announce the elephant's flight and the disappearance of the founding fathers of the nation. His statement opened with a noble verse from the 105th sura of the Qur'an, "Have you not seen what your Lord did to the masters of the elephant?" He concluded by saying that the joint forces were investigating the suspect, Naima, Mother of Elephants, on a charge of plotting a coup against the democratically elected government.

317

This Is Not the Problem

Greetings and peace! The court has sentenced Saddam to death, and I believe that you, my dear readers, might have some ambiguous feelings about this event. I'm right there with you, alternating between contradictory emotions. It's as though I were standing in a big new garbage dump, and they want me to try to smell the old one. I've forgotten all Saddam's crimes in the horror I feel at the savage crimes we are living through today. I'm choked with death all around, and they want me to remember the death of my ancestors!

To be honest, I'm afraid. Afraid of people exploiting the opportunity and creating imaginary heroic deeds. Saddam fell because of America, he was arrested by America, and he was prosecuted under the supervision of America, and with America's protection, desire, and timetable. Maliki is not the hero of our liberation. Hakim wasn't the flag-bearer of the armies that brought down his regime. If Maliki wanted to become a true hero, he has other criminals right in front of him that he can prosecute and send to court, yet he holds them closer than his own jugular.

We don't want the enemies of national unity to exploit this occasion and kill our people in the name of revenge for Saddam Hussein, even though they don't love him or feel any sorrow on his behalf. Nor do we want others to dance for joy at his sentence. They could be faking it, right? What have we gotten from his fall apart from death, death, and more death? Fear, fear, and more fear?

I don't deny that Saddam was a dictator, but show me a single democrat in the Green Zone—and no, I don't count the ones on television!

I don't deny that Saddam was cruel, terrifying, and perplexing, but are the brothers in the Green Zone such angels of mercy, overflowing with compassion, affection, and tenderness?

Saddam promoted his relatives and members of his party. Fine. Must I slap my face in despair?

Saddam stole the wealth of the people. Fine. Must I rend my clothes?

Saddam was an agent of foreign powers. Fine. Must I rip out my soul and bury it in the basement?

Saddam was a sectarian—no! I can only laugh at that one!

Brothers! I used to want to see Saddam brought to trial before the people, but I wanted to see it at a time when construction increased, freedom spread, joy filled the streets, and Iraqis would stay up all night till morning on the banks of the Tigris. Our schools would compete with those of Japan, our streets would be cleaner than a vessel of buffalo cream, our riches would be obvious before our eyes, all our exiled brothers, scattered under all God's stars, would return to their families and loved ones as everyone rejoiced together.

Our schools: come and have a look! They are ruins and animal sheds. Our streets: given the daily curfew, I can't figure who it is that goes about every night pissing in them. Our families are scattered, with some of them in poor countries and the rest living in tattered tents that would break your heart. There are ever more beggars in the streets; the poor squat amid the ruins of houses; and who can describe

319

the despair, the sickness, the drought, and the terror? Now that my friends and relatives have departed, I'm left alone in this desolation, and some idiot who doesn't even know how to write his own name yells at me, "Hey, Shalash, why aren't you happy? Come out to the demonstration!"

Yes, man, of course I'm happy. Delighted! I'm just afraid to show it since people will envy my good fortune! We've escaped the long night of Saddam only to tumble down a well. How long till we get out?

Our problem is not Saddam. It is not his codefendants, Barzan or Taha Yasin Ramadan. Our problem is who will be dragged off today, away from his children and his family, only to be found tomorrow morning as a corpse without a head. God willing, it won't be me and it won't be you, dear reader! God willing, may the sectarians be consumed in a fire of their own making!

NOVEMBER 11, 2006

Each Day Worse

The national government elected by one-quarter of a fatwa from the religious clerkship has closed down two satellite stations, Al-Zawraa and Salah Al-Din, on the pretense that they were provoking sectarianism. This dangerous step suggests that our government is clipping the fingernails of the media, bit by bit, and is well on its way to adopting the theocratic rule of an imam like they have in Iran. Next they'll come for the internet and say it corrupts the morals of the youth because of the porn and the terrorist sites! Next, they'll be banning satellites and cut us off entirely, like a dog cornered in a mosque. This Maliki has turned out to be a real trickster, and step by step, he's submitting to the orders of the turbans.

Personally, I've never watched Salah Al-Din, and I'm not even sure a station by this name exists. Sometimes, to tell the truth, I do watch Al-Zawraa because it has music, dancing girls, parties, and news about its founder, the controversial politician Misha'an al-Juburi. But—thank God!—singing and dancing are not sectarian deeds. In any case, most of the singers and dancers are our own people, and I don't believe they would dance to the tunes of Abu Ayyub al-Masri, the beats of Abu Qadama al-Tunisi, or any of the other top al-Qaeda terrorists. No way! These girls only dance to songs from the central and southern federalist regions.

If there were sectarian channels to make us throw up, they would be Channel Euphrates and Al Iraqiya. The former calls us followers of the Prophet's household. But we are all Iraqis, whether we are followers of the Prophet's household or admirers of Ibn Taymiyyah! Those channels are shameless frauds, trying to stir up division between Shiites and Sunnis. What does it mean to be followers of the Prophet's household? By a rough classification, there are millions of Indians, Pakistanis, and Iranians who are followers of the Prophet's household. Indeed, all Muslims are followers of the Prophet's household. Otherwise, how could they be Muslims? Our problem isn't the classification of Muslims, but rather the reunification of Iraqis. What this term is really about is tricking the minds of the poor by saying: you are followers of the Prophet's household, and everybody else is an enemy of the Prophet's household.

In my humble opinion, that man who stole the neighborhood of Jadriyah—it hurts me even to mention the name of Hakim—his son Ammar, and all their Iranian retinue and bodyguards are the enemies of the Prophet's household because they commit their thefts in the name of that pure household. The Prophet's household, by the way, are not the Tabtaba'iyin tribe in the south, who claim descent from the Prophet's grandson Hasan. The Prophet's household don't work in oil-trading, and they don't live in Jadriyah. The gang that wants to snatch us all away from Iraq in the name of the followers of the Prophet's household are a group of takfiri terrorists who are no less depraved than al-Qaeda and all those taking up its mantle.

One of Maliki's followers says these two channels were broadcasting demonstrations in support of Saddam. The way I see it, the demonstrators who came out to support Saddam have been created by Maliki because his government has turned the days of Saddam into a golden era compared with the tragedies we are living through now. Back then, at least we had a country for a dictator to rule! Now we don't have a country, but a brothel for political prostitution, throwing open its doors to everyone and his brother. Mortar shells tumble down on our heads, suicide bombers prowl our streets, and, according to a statement from the Ministry of Health, we've lost one hundred fifty thousand Iraqis—a trifling sum compared to the actual numbers.

We may have been sheep during the days of the dictator, but we've become flies in the time of Maliki. We've forgotten about water, electricity, sewers, and other services, and all we want is to still be alive when the sun rises tomorrow. What kind of life is that? Nevertheless, they want us to keep our mouths shut. "You're a Saddamist!" they tell anyone who dares to object. The truth is, they're the biggest Saddamists, and were it not for Saddam, we'd never have seen their rotten, disgusting faces.

Today, Sistani used his spokesman to demand that Saddam's execution take place between the mausoleums of Husayn and Abbas, as though Saddam were the one who murdered the Prophet's grandsons at Karbala. Sistani is a man who has rejected Iraqi citizenship, so I don't know why he even gets a say in these matters, which come down to Iraqi law and Iraqi courts.

Poor Saddam! First he was detained by the Americans, and now Sistani wants to execute him beside Husayn. Both claim to be taking vengeance upon him in the name of Iraqis. It's such a farce! Why aren't there Iraqis judging him? Where are the men of Iraq, the ones who made the ground quake under their feet, whose marching steps, echoing down Saadoun Street, made the pavement in Tehran and Isfahan tremble? The men whose strong arms and dignity provided refuge for all Arabs, from ocean to gulf?

And now, alas, we've ended up as prisoners, with jerboas and lizards for our jailers. Our wealth is stolen, our oil is smuggled, our Iraq is divided, and our people are cringing and scattered. Our scholars and professors are murdered. We've exchanged Iraq's glory, our scholars, for experts on ablutions, ritual impurity, and the nine steps you take to cleanse yourself after peeing!

I swear, Saddam—even though you haven't even asked me to take an oath—you deserve to be executed. Not for what you did to us in the days of your rule, no! But for your ridiculous end and the way you surrendered Iraq, this wide expanse of humanity, into the hands of a good-for-nothing sayyid, the lowest of the low. Don't let anybody say Shalash is drunk! On my honor, it's not the bottle of arak knocking me over, but the fire burning in my head, and were it not for your kindly faces, I would already have abandoned this garbage dump we formerly called our homeland.

But don't fear! Our homeland will be a homeland again. Iraq has weathered plenty of disasters throughout its history, yet it has remained Iraq. What of Maliki, Jaafari, Hakim, Zuba'i, and Hashimi? This is Iraq! So don't worry. Iraq will get up, shake off the dust, and chase them like vagabond slaves across the open borders to the dazzling palaces they own on their cousins' land . . . if they can even make it that far.

Sleep well!

NOVEMBER 15, 2006

Tomorrow Things Will Be Clear

Forty cars came and armed men got out in the middle of the sensitive neighborhood in Baghdad. They seized more than a hundred men and then took off. After that, the Ministry of the Interior came and set most of the kidnappers free. All this happened, and yet the prime minister demands a search for the perpetrators, and the Interior sets about looking for them. What is this, a Pakistani film? Because even the Indian movies coming out of Bollywood have a plot that makes more sense than that.

Mr. Prime Minister, let me tell you something. The "perpetrators," as Ali Aldabbagh calls them, are the members of your government. They are your agencies and the parties in your coalition government. You are the perpetrators because you have risen to power to the beat of their drums. Young and old know the perpetrators; everyone knows them except you, and I don't know what's wrong with you that you don't. God, I really don't know!

To explain this country of yours even more, sir: today at the university I discussed the terrorists, the Saddamists, and the heretics, and when I got around to al-Jama'a, I called them the free militias. You want to know what I mean by free? What I'm saying is that there are regulated militias: militias that don't move except under orders, don't kill except under orders, and don't commit major crimes except under orders. We call these militias regulated because they respect the word of the Sayyid, and thus they are able to move freely, even in the vehicles belonging to the Ministry of the Interior or of Defense.

My dear Prime Minister: a killer is a killer, whether he be free or regulated, and whether or not he lines up to pray behind a fake sayyid. A criminal is a criminal. There are no ranks and titles within crime, and according to the Qur'an, the person who kills a single soul kills all of humanity.

Tomorrow we are going to see what you'll do! Are you really going to reveal the killers and bring them to justice?

325

Or will you form investigatory commissions that will just vanish into thin air like all of Jaafari's commissions? Be strong, man! Do you want to rule a country, or do you want your speeches and appearances on television? The state, Mr. Prime Minister, is not cameras and microphones. The state is a real state, and it needs strong, resolute men. There's no state whose affairs are run by prayers, incantations, and holy rings. The word "shall" is good for nothing in a country like Iraq, which is making the world dizzy. Forget "shall" and show us deeds. It's been a year that you've been crying, "No weapons outside state authority!" Yet the advanced weapons that have recently entered Thawra City are enough to arm the entire state.

For shame! It's been years since we've remembered what our lives were like, or the neighborhood of Karkh across the river. We can't recognize Kafah Street and don't even know how to get there anymore. Everywhere we walk, we're looking over our shoulders in terror. Either solve that problem, or say, "Brothers, forgive me. There's no longer any hope. We've entered the void. Death is the only way out." The only way out? Death has become a hobby, a habit! Our children see more corpses than living people these days. Generations of sick, complicated, and hostile people have started propagating among us. Find a solution, please! You see, we've started vomiting from speeches, promises, and words, from the political process, the national reconciliation effort, and all this nonsense. If you have what it takes for this country, please show us. And if you don't, don't be ashamed. It's not a game. Your grandfather wasn't Napoleon; you weren't weaned for positions of leadership.

I'll tell you what, Maliki. Have you heard of the newest thief, Radi al-Radi, or not yet? You see, we've known about him for a long time, but he had a conflict with Muqtada's people and they exposed him. What a shame! For the past four years, all we've wanted was one noble man in government, and there's none to be had! What's happened to the Iraqis who feel an ounce of shame? Why have we been brought to thievery by day and night? Thievery? Tell it like it is and call it administrative corruption. I've never seen the likes of our government, these people who have no conscience. No! And the real problem, the biggest tragedy of all, is that our people also feel no shame at calling these gangs a government!

JANUARY 25, 2006

Emigrating to Jordan

The family of the Irhaymeh clan crowded together in the early morning of this bitterly cold day to bid farewell to their dutiful son, Shalash the Iraqi, who had decided to travel to Jordan. Thus, since the early morning, they thronged together in the house of the pillar and founder of the family, Hajji Irhaymeh, may God preserve his life!

Those present stood together in a moment of despondent sadness, and when the moment of farewell drew nigh, Hajji Irhaymeh stepped forward in his full, towering height. His appearance was splendid, and his steps as dignified as though he were processing to the sound of a military marshal.

327

He ascended two steps on the staircase of the crumbling house, cleared his throat, swallowed hard, and fought back his tears so that his words might not lose their way at this moment when the grandson dearest to his heart and closest to his soul was departing. A stubborn tear burst from his eyes, his lips trembled, and he struggled to utter a single word. That caused my grandmother to lose all composure and launch herself noisily in my direction: "O my Shalash! O dear beloved boy! Who will reassure me? Where will I go? O Shalash, my child!"

At that, each person present gave voice to the emotions they had been bottling up. Tearful lamentations rose even from those who couldn't care in the least whether Shalash was near or far. They remembered their own loved ones who had departed from the beloved country to live as strangers across God's broad earth. Hajji Irhaymeh wiped his eyes with an ancient kaffiyeh and said something to soothe the dismay of the women. Then he addressed the assembly:

"My brothers, sons, and grandchildren: it is appropriate for me to declare before you in all honesty that today I am losing my honor and my dignity now that the grandson dearest to my heart, my precious Shalash"—(here he was interrupted by a sob)—"has decided to leave me all alone and travel away. I declare before God and before everyone present that this boy was dutiful to me and to his sick grandmother."

My grandmother cried out again, "O my Shalash! O dear beloved grandson!"

Hajji Irhaymeh interrupted her as he went on to finish. "There was never a day, not even one, when Shalash fell short in his duties of respect and obedience. What's more, he took primary responsibility for taking me to the doctor and arranging the medicine for my treatment. Oh, what exile and desolation I'll feel when he's gone!" (When his eyes sought me out at this point, I could not hold back my tears.) "Who do I have besides you, Shalash? Death is easier for me than our parting!"

Hajji Irhaymeh stepped down, trying to hold himself together. Next, my uncle Shinawa stepped up to take his place, even as Sabiha, his wife and my aunt on the other side of the family, pressed herself to his side as though taking a commemorative photograph. Shinawa cleared his throat and said, "Ladies, ladies!"

Sabiha clapped her hands, a big smile stretched across her heavily made-up face, and she did not stop posing until Hajji Irhaymeh scolded her to step away so that the depraved Shinawa could resume his charade, in which we heard the following:

"What a surprise your journey has given us, Shalash!" (Of course, he was the first person to know about it, and he was the one who booked the flight to Amman.) "When your aunt Sabiha informed me of these tidings, you could have found me trembling from the top of my head down to the bottom of my feet." (Sabiha nodded vigorously to confirm his words.) "The news struck me like a thunderbolt, and I said to her, 'Don't joke like that, Sabiha! Did you really say Shalash is emigrating? Oh, what a catastrophe for us! We're ruined! We're lost!' I even started beating my head against the wall." (Sabiha laughed and looked out at the crowd to catch as many eyes as she could.)

"So it is, therefore, O moon of the House of Irhaymeh," Shinawa went on, "that you are leaving us for the Hashemite

Kingdom of Jordan, which I got to know when I was working there from 1996 until the year 2000. Yes, my brothers!" Shinawa went on. "I worked there. And where exactly did I work there, my good sirs? Don't get carried away with your doubts! Don't believe the ugly rumors that I stretched out on the ground with Sabiha, and that we sold ragi-oil soap in Hashemite Plaza! No! A thousand times, no! By the honor and virtue of Sabiha, by her virginity!" (Sabiha laughed.) "I was working in the splendid royal palaces. Sabiha here can testify to all that, and God is my witness to everything I've said!"

Before he got down, he said in a voice that all could hear: "Shalash, don't worry if the days there weigh you down, or if some lout assails you. Just call the office of the monarch and tell them, 'I'm here with Shinawa the Soapman,' and you'll be fine." (Sabiha gave him a shove to push him out of the way, and he followed her down.)

After that, brothers, came the turn of my friend Abd al-Rida, my lifelong friend who would stay up late with me and party. The poor man stood up to read a poem he had written to lighten the mood of this occasion. He broke off after reading just two lines, when shoes began raining down on him from every direction.

Shalash, O candle of the house, O disturber of the people!
   O half-night vagabond, you are a whispering devil.
You're going to plant yourself in Amman, you burglar,
   you housebreaker! You pickpocket, you drummer! You
   drunkard, you murderer's waterboy!

As for Khanjar, that chameleon neighbor I've told you so much about, he arrived wearing an abaya lined with heavy fur. He stood on the stairs and thanked and praised God at length, calling for prayers on behalf of God's chosen Prophet, Muhammad, and the pure people of his household. Then he said, "Moving on, O my brothers: Verily, our blessed side street—nay, our holy block!—has not produced, in all its history, a son as devoted as Shalash the Iraqi. This noble man has supported me; indeed, more than a brother. He stood at my side when I opposed Saddam's regime and his oppressive agencies." (This was a reference to Khanjar's time as a communist.) "There are so many times that he reinforced my strength and my resolve by repeating his famous words: 'Press on, Khanjar! We're right behind you!' Now, in my own name and the name of my trustworthy and believing brothers, I greet his nationalist spirit at the moment he departs the religion, the sect, and the homeland. In this man, I have met someone virtuous, noble, and pious, one who was bold and fearless in defending the right and his family. He does not deserve to be abandoned in this conflict, such that he choose to settle in Jordan. But after having despaired of turning him back from his decision, we can do nothing more than to say, 'May you enjoy Jordan, O Shalash the Iraqi, both the government and the people!'"

The light rain that had been falling grew harder as Khanjar's words rose higher, and the drops wet the heads of a celebratory, angelic scene of a kind rarely seen before. The gathering broke up, and Khadija the Schoolteacher moved away with tearful eyes after pushing into my pocket a cassette tape with Hatem Al-Iraqi's sad song of farewell, "I'll See You Wherever You Go, Just Tell Me the Country." At the

went dry, and my lips cracked. O God! Is this really a city? Or is it a giant monument to gloom? Is this Amman, where my friends rotted for so long before emigrating to far-flung continents, out under God's distant stars? A hot tear fell from my eye onto the strange sidewalk, and I thought it would burn until the day of resurrection. A single eternal hot tear that, one day, would say, "O, you merciful sky! Remember the torment of the Iraqi people!"

An Iraqi Goodness

In the entire world, there's no one better than the Iraqis. That's not an exaggeration. It's not racism, not bias, not anything else. It's just the truth! Here in Jordan, I've run into friends, acquaintances, neighbors, classmates, some of whom I haven't seen for years. Oh, how good to run into someone who embraces me, kisses me, invites me over! Someone as happy to see me as if I had just dropped from the sky with a parachute.

There's no one better than the Iraqi people, and anyone who doesn't like what I say can go drink from the Dead Sea. By God, I spent three days wandering without a clue. But then, for someone who would come running when he heard me approach! I know how bad they have it here, but what can I do when they generously insist on playing the host?

Tomorrow, I will bid you farewell and continue my journey, and my tears have already started to fall. How does a person say goodbye to the likes of you? Here you are in the heart of exile, and you drive gloom from the hearts of your friends. It's right for the world to envy us. Not for the oil, not for the Tigris and the Euphrates, not for the date palms, not for our green mountains. No! We are envied for our goodness, our love, our sympathy, and our affection. Envied for our pure hearts, envied for our attentiveness, our intelligence, our devotion, and our diligence. Envied for everything! But unfortunately, we have politicians who are the dregs of the world. Actually, we don't have politicians, we have thieves, cheats, swindlers, traders in conspiracies, orations, and lies.

In my hands I hold an elegant monthly magazine published by the office of the mayor of the great city of Amman. Look how elegant and pretty it is! It describes the capital and its programs, its plans, and its activities. Great Amman has an elegant magazine, and Godspeed great Amman! But what made Baghdad deserve its fate? On top of God's subjugation, we get a whole council instead of a mayor, and they're a herd of half-witted bulls.

One of you is going to say, "What's the deal, Shalash? Why do you go on and on about the mayor's office?" Why, brothers? Because what does this revered council in the Baghdad mayor's office do? They just came together and dedicated one week for the environment and another week specifically for the trees. They picked a day for the sparrows and a day for the butterflies, a day for the date palm, and a competition for the most beautiful damask rose. Having discharged all their duty to transform Baghdad into a garden of paradise, do you know what the council of the mayor's office did? They launched an international initiative, gigantic and unprecedented, to make Eid al-Ghadir an official holiday, because God knows we don't have enough national holidays!

Why is Eid al-Ghadir an official holiday, you ask? Well, when the Prophet (prayers and peace be upon him!) was on his way back to Medina after his farewell pilgrimage, he sat down at the stream called Ghadir Kham and entrusted Imam Ali (peace be upon him!) with leadership of the community. But the Prophet's companions (may God be satisfied with them!) failed to carry out the instructions in a perfectly correct manner, and they messed up the order of the caliphate. So now, fourteen hundred years later, the council overseeing Baghdad is determined to set things right, even if that means the right is situated upon heaps of garbage and the trash piles of Baghdad, where the sewers overflow and turn the place into something that looks like a cattle pen in Rwanda.

Imam Ali (peace be upon him!) personally ruled Kufa for four years, nine months, and three days, making it the capital of the Islamic state. Yet not even he (peace be upon him!) declared al-Ghadir a national holiday for the noble sons of Kufa.

The Day of Ghadir is undoubtedly a blessed day. But rather than celebrating this day, I beseech you, O Council of the Capital's Betrayers, to visit the neighborhood by that name in Baghdad. Have you even heard of the place? Could you find someone to take you? Go and see what the rain does to its people, and how the sewage seeps into the bedrooms. I know exactly what you are going to do. The only thing you know how to do is stir up sectarianism. You don't think there's enough of it, so you pour on a little gasoline to make it burn to the heavens.

I rolled up the Jordanian magazine with shaking hands as Rahman yelled from the kitchen, "Finish your drinks, guys!" The gang was back together again, sharing mutual affection and cherished memories. We spoke about our high-school days, about al-Mustafa, Port Said, and Qatiba; about the falafel in the city; about the bookshop of Abbas bin al-Ahnaf and the tripartite Alexandrian theft; about the fall of Baghdad and everything that came before it; about the pain of the Iraqis in the barren hills of great Amman; about those who moved on and emigrated yet again; about those who returned to Iraq; about all those who were driven from their homes and settled here.

Sitar and Hatem are knocking at the door. They've brought two bottles of Haddad arak and a bit of mezze, and they apologize for being late. It's a day for singing and drinking and talking till morning!

By God, we're the best people in the world! We're the best people in the world, and—God willing—this is all just a bad dream that will pass.

When I get back, friends, I'll ask you what's up!

NOVEMBER 25, 2005

I'm Shalash, or Shalash Is Me

When I woke up this morning, I found Shalash the Iraqi looking uncharacteristically gloomy. He had a deep scowl on his face and turned away as he clipped his finger-nails.

"Hey, Shalash, is everything all right? You don't seem yourself. You doing okay, I hope?"

"Just leave me alone!"

"What's the matter?"

"I'm so fed up! I can't live this role you've put me in any longer. What kind of person are you, brother? Have you no compassion? Why do you put me in harm's way every day while you comfortably hide behind me!"

"How can you complain when you've become so famous that people have started writing about you? Did you see the Kitabat website yesterday? Look what they wrote!"

"What does it mean to be famous? Who am I, anyway? And why am I part of this whole mess?"

"You want me to change you? No problem. There are a thousand other aliases out there, you know."

"Yeah, right. Now you're the Lord of the Universe! Having created me, you now want to wipe me away? If you change my name, see if anyone respects you. It's me the people love, man. I'm Shalash the Iraqi! Who the hell are you?"

"Then what do you want, brother?"

"Damned if I know! But I'm embarrassed that the people sympathize with me and respect me while I have no power, no strength, and am just an illusion. Just a name with no referent behind it. A borrowed name."

"Isn't that better for you? The people honor you. They write you hundreds of emails. They speak of you in glowing terms and pray for your good health!"

"Don't forget the curses and threats! I was even insulted a couple times in the Friday sermon: Shalash the Unbeliever, Shalash the Infidel, Shalash the Traitor!"

"Don't worry, Shalash! You're not a mother or a father, so you bring no shame on your family and leave no one behind if you are killed. You're just a figment of somebody's imagination, so let them revile you at their leisure."

"What a hypocrite you are! First you tell me, 'The people honor you and pray for you.' And when it comes to the curses, you tell me I'm a figment of somebody's imagination. But listen. You need to know that's not true. I'm a real thing with a real existence. The people love me because I'm their conscience. I speak on their behalf without the least personal interest. I'm a hero. My name resounds every day. You're just a coward and a cheat, hiding behind my name like a mouse!"

"Watch yourself, Shalash!"

"I am watching myself. You watch yourself! Write your real name and leave me alone!"

"Write my name, Shalash? Fine. And, God willing, it will all turn out okay. I'll write my name, but you know, from that moment you'll disappear forever."

"I won't disappear. I'm the people. I'm the poor. I am the truth. I'm a scream of protest in the face of crimes. Without me, you're just going to be another flattering hypocrite. You'll be writing what the powerful want, not what you want. Without me, you aren't worth two pennies."

"Shalash, now you're just insulting me."

"Sorry. I apologize. But isn't it the truth? The brave man fights in broad daylight, not under the cover of darkness. Don't you feel ashamed when you sit with your friends, family, and other people, and they're talking about Shalash the Iraqi, and you make as though you don't know me? You laugh with them and pretend you're affected just like them by posts that you yourself have written. Not just that! Sometimes you swear at me and make fun of me in front of them!"

"But I never mean it, Shalash."

"Yeah, yeah! Just be a man. Face yourself and the people! If you believe what you say, why are you afraid? A noble writer is never afraid."

"You've gone back to insulting me, Shalash."

"Sorry, but it's the truth."

"I love you, Shalash, and from the time we've met till now, I haven't known who you are, or who I am. Which of us is real, and which is imaginary. Are you me now, or am I me? Or are you and I both me? Are both of us me, and both of us you?"

"What's all this about? Don't get me mixed up. You're making things so difficult!"

"I love you, Shalash, and I can't give you up. You've protected me from danger. You've liberated me from myself, from my fear, from the people, from hypocrisy, and from flattery. You're so much better than me. Sometimes I'm afraid, and you just laugh. I'm weak in the face of temptations, and you give me strength. There are so many times I've felt crushed, and then you pick me back up by yelling in my ear: 'Stay where you are! You haven't been beaten. Life is about the conflict! Sit down and write!'"

"It's okay! Don't get upset! Let's agree on some new and fair principles."

"Say what's on your mind, Shalash."

"First, let me know who you really are. Second, tell me where you're taking me, and what my future is with you. Third, can we agree to share what the people say, both the compliments about me and the curses against you?"

"Yes, Shalash, we can agree on all that."

"Come on, then. Tell me who you are."

"Me?"

"Yes, you!"

"Here." I handed Shalash my state-issued ID.

"Haha! It was you all along? No—inconceivable! God, I was expecting it would turn out to be anyone besides you. Never would have occurred to me! Goddamn! Haha! For real? No, inconceivable!"

"Now are you satisfied?"

"Yes, completely satisfied! Because you are an upstanding chap, a good guy who gets along with everyone. But—and don't get angry with me—you're a bit of a coward."

"Haha! Just a bit?"

"Yes, just a bit."

"And now, Shalash?"

"Tell me who is married to Ru'a: me or you?"

"Hey, cut it out. Don't go there."

"But the wedding the other day was the marriage of Ru'a and Shalash."

"Watch yourself, Shalash. Honor's not cheap."

"Dude, let's ask Ru'a and let her choose between us."

"You're crossing the line, Shalash!"

"I'm just messing with you! Why are you so dim? You and I are one soul, and I'll stay with you to the death. Put it there!"

I reached out my hand and gave Shalash's a powerful shake. Then we sat down to write today's post. But I don't actually know which of us is the so-called Shalash the Iraqi, writing this post for you.

TRANSLATOR'S NOTE

Even when it was beginning, my yearslong journey of translating *Shalash the Iraqi* struck me as improbable, important, and impossible in equal measure. In the first place, after discovering a passion for the Arabic language in my twenties, my connection with Iraqi literature occurred as a fortuitous happenstance: a teacher of mine knew an Iraqi author looking for a translator at the very moment I felt inspired to approach this field. Other opportunities followed the publication of that first book until I found myself drafting a few pages by Shalash as an audition to send to the author. Then, too, as a citizen of a country whose policies have had such a devastating impact upon the lives of the Iraqi people, I couldn't help but feel a responsibility to understand that country's history and the experiences of its people. Reading *Shalash* allowed me to see the story beyond the news headlines that dominated my attention for years. It drew back the curtain to show how life is lived there, how people relate to each other, the stories they tell about themselves and the world.

More than any other text I have approached, however, *Shalash the Iraqi* resists translation. The first challenge was to establish the text to be translated. When writing these posts, their author did not plan to publish them as a collection in Arabic, much less in English. He didn't even save copies, and since the website that first hosted them has long since gone defunct, Iraqi scholar Jamal Ameadi had to search out the entries from various other websites and Facebook pages where they had been reposted. Shalash then selected and ordered his work in a way that he felt made a cohesive whole out of episodes that were never originally conceived as a unified narrative (as the attentive reader may have gleaned, for example, from our humble narrator's marital status). Indeed, when I set about trying to provide historical context for the posts by researching when each one had first gone "live," I discovered that Shalash had chosen to present several episodes outside of their initial order of composition. (To better echo the conventions of blog writing, then a genre in its infancy, I included the original date that I found for sixty-four of the posts, inventing a date for the remaining six—entries 25, 29, 30, 32, 45, and 48.)

The next challenge in translating *Shalash* was linguistic. While the narrative passages of the book are written in Modern Standard Arabic (MSA), the dialogue is written in Iraqi dialect. The standard convention of using MSA for writing dialogue works fine for many Arabic stories and novels, but in this text, it is the spoken dialect of Thawra City that brings these scenes vibrantly alive. Since Shalash's choice would be an immediately striking feature for Arab readers, I considered possible ways of representing it in my translation. In the end, I attempted to capture the energy of the source text through tone and diction, rather than a distinct dialect of English, leaving the ways that Shalash plays with linguistic register as one of the many riches to be discovered by anyone who ventures beyond the translation to explore the original text.

The cultural specificity of the text made for a third challenge. Elements of Iraqi, Arab, and Islamic culture fill each page, and I initially envisioned a translation with an encyclopedia of footnotes that would open up this world to the reader. In the end, I decided that such an approach would erect more barriers than it removed, and I chose the other extreme of no footnotes at all (well, maybe two), allowing the humor of the situations, characters, and dialogues a chance to connect directly with readers who have arrived with an openness and curiosity to engage with a different world and a unique literary voice. Shalash's characters and scenes are imaginative and wickedly satirical creations, even as they reflect the rich perspectives of a specific culture at a specific and most perilous moment in time. The brief summaries I've added to the table of contents are Fielding-esque attempts to frame the reading and ease the reader's way. Where I judged further information was essential, I've added contextual clues within my translation, with Shalash's explicit permission.

Beyond those concessions, I warmly invite the reader to consult YouTube, Wikipedia, and Google Maps—essential tools for my own reading of the text—to learn more. To aid that search, I have, whenever possible, chosen the most common English spellings of names and other Arabic terms.

Every translation begins and ends with gratitude. As the translator of *Shalash the Iraqi*, that gratitude runs especially deep.

Gratitude begins with the author, the person who created a work that fills me with curiosity and delight and a renewed sense of the power of literature. I am indeed grateful for Shalash, for his creativity and energy to produce the work that has filled so many of my days in reading, thinking, learning, and laughing. I am grateful for Shalash's permission to translate his work, and his generosity in replying to every question I sent.

My deep thanks go as well to Kanan Makiya, who invited me to share in his vision, going back a decade and more, of making *Shalash the Iraqi* available in English, and who worked with the Diwan Kufa Foundation to fund my efforts.

I am filled with gratitude for two others as well. I would not have attempted this translation without the help and encouragement of Yousif Hanna, who, despite his busy weeks as a medical student, met with me on dozens of Sunday mornings to improve my reading of the text through his linguistic and cultural expertise. Beyond the enduring debt I feel, I will always treasure the friendship we forged over a shared love for Arabic literature.

I think with gratitude of many others who contributed to this project, either directly or else by supporting my journey in the field of translation. One who must be named is Jeremy Davies, my editor at And Other Stories, who believed in the importance of this work and suggested countless ways to improve the text. His ear for humor and a well-turned phrase touched nearly every page of this book. Working with Jeremy confirmed my understanding that a good translation involves good writing, and he has inspired me to keep striving for both.

LUKE LEAFGREN
October 2022
Cambridge, Massachusetts

THIS BOOK WAS MADE POSSIBLE
THANKS TO THE SUPPORT OF

Aaron Bogner
Aaron McEnery
Aaron Schneider
Abbie Bambridge
Abigail Gambrill
Abigail Walton
Adam Lenson
Adrian Kowalsky
Ajay Sharma
Alan Raine
Alastair Gillespie
Albert Puente
Alec Logan
Alex Pearce
Alex Ramsey
Alex von
  Feldmann
Alexandra Kay-
  Wallace
Alexandra
  Stewart
Alexandra Webb
Alexandra
  Tammaro
Ali Riley
Ali Smith
Ali Usman
Alia Carter
Alice Toulmin
Alice Wilkinson
Alison Hardy
Aliya Rashid
Alyssa Rinaldi
Alyssa Tauber
Amado Floresca
Amaia Gabantxo
Amanda
Amanda Astley

Amanda Dalton
Amanda Fisher
Amanda Geenen
Amanda Read
Amber Da
Amelia Dowe
Amitav Hajra
Amy Bojang
Amy Hatch
Amy Tabb
Ana Novak
Andra Dusu
Andrea Barlien
Andrea
  Oyarzabal
  Koppes
Andreas
  Zbinden
Andrew Kerr-
  Jarrett
Andrew Lahy
Andrew Marston
Andrew
  McCallum
Andrew Place
Andrew Rego
Andrew Wright
Andy Corsham
Andy Marshall
Angela Joyce
Angus Walker
Anita Starosta
Ann Rees
Anna-Maria
  Aurich
Anna French
Anna Gibson
Anna Hawthorne

Anna Milsom
Anna Zaranko
Anne Carus
Anne Edyvean
Anne
  Germanacos
Anne Kangley
Anne-Marie
  Renshaw
Anne Withane
Anonymous
Anonymous
Anthony Cotton
Anthony
  Fortenberry
Anthony Quinn
Antonia Lloyd-
  Jones
Antonia Saske
Antony Pearce
Aoibheann
  McCann
April Hernandez
Arathi
  Devandran
Archie Davies
Aron Trauring
Asako Serizawa
Ashleigh Phillips
Ashleigh Sutton
Ashley Marshall
Audrey Mash
Audrey Small
Aurelia Wills
Barbara Mellor
Barbara Spicer
Barry John
  Fletcher

Barry Norton
Beatrice Taylor
Becky Cherriman
Becky
  Matthewson
Ben Buchwald
Ben Schofield
Ben Walter
Benjamin Judge
Benjamin Pester
Bernadette Smith
Beth Heim de
  Bera
Beverley Thomas
Bianca Jackson
Bianca Winter
Bill Fletcher
Bjørnar Djupevik
  Hagen
Blazej Jedras
Brenda
  Anderson
Briallen Hopper
Brian Anderson
Brian Byrne
Brian Conn
Brian Isabelle
Brian Smith
Brianna Soloski
Bridget Prentice
Briony Hey
Buck Johnston
  & Camp
  Bosworth
Burkhard
  Fehsenfeld
Caitlin Halpern
Caitriona Lally

James Leonard
James Lesniak
James Portlock
James Ruland
James Scudamore
Jamie Mollart
Jan Hicks
Jane Bryce
Jane Dolman
Jane Leuchter
Jane Roberts
Jane Willborn
Jane Woollard
Janis Carpenter
Janna Eastwood
Jasmine Gideon
Jason Lever
Jason Montano
Jason Sim
Jason Timermanis
Jason Whalley
Jayne Watson
Jean Liebenberg
Jeanne Guyon
Jeff Collins
Jen Hardwicke
Jenifer Logie
Jennie Goloboy
Jennifer Fosket
Jennifer Higgins
Jennifer Mills
Jennifer Watts
Jennifer Yanoschak
Jenny Huth
Jenny Newton
Jeremy Koenig
Jeremy Morton
Jerome Mersky
Jerry Simcock

Jess Wood
Jesse Coleman
Jessica Gately
Jessica Laine
Jessica Mello
Jessica Queree
Jessica Weetch
Jethro Soutar
Jill Harrison
Jo Keyes
Jo Pinder
Joan Dowgin
Joanna Luloff
Joao Pedro Bragatti Winckler
JoDee Brandon
Jodie Adams
Joe Huggins
Joel Swerdlow
Johannes Holmqvist
Johannes Menzel
John Bennett
John Berube
John Bogg
John Carnahan
John Conway
John Gent
John Hodgson
John Kelly
John McWhirter
John Purser
John Reid
John Shadduck
John Shaw
John Steigerwald
John Walsh
John Winkelman
Jolene Smith
Jon Riches
Jon Talbot

Jonas House
Jonathan Blaney
Jonathan Fiedler
Jonathan Gharraie
Jonathan Harris
Jonathan Huston
Jonathan Paterson
Jonathan Phillips
Jonathan Ruppin
Joni Chan
Jonny Kiehlmann
Jordana Carlin
Joseph Camilleri
Joseph Darlington
Joseph Thomas
Josh Sumner
Joshua Davis
Joy Paul
Judith Gruet-Kaye
Judith Poxon
Judy Davies
Judy Rich
Julia Foden
Julia Von Dem Knesebeck
Julie Greenwalt
Juliet Swann
Jupiter Jones
Juraj Janik
Justine Sherwood
KL Ee
Kaarina Hollo
Kaelyn Davis
Kaja R Anker-Rasch
Kalina Rose
Karen Gilbert

Karin Mckercher
Karl Kleinknecht & Monika Motylinska
Katarina Dzurekova
Katarzyna Bartoszynska
Kate Beswick
Kate Carlton-Reditt
Kate Shires
Kate Stein
Katharine Robbins
Katherine McLaughlin
Kathleen McLean
Kathryn Burruss
Kathryn Edwards
Kathryn Hemmann
Kathryn Williams
Kathy Wright
Katia Wengraf
Katie Brown
Katie Cooke
Katie Freeman
Katie Grant
Katy Robinson
Keith Walker
Kelly Hydrick
Ken Geniza
Kenneth Blythe
Kenneth Masloski
Kent Curry
Kent McKernan
Kerry Parke
Kevin Winter

Kieran Rollin
Kieron James
Kim Streets
Kirsten Hey
Kirsty Simpkins
Kris Ann
   Trimis
Kristen
   Tcherneshoff
Kristen Tracey
Krystale
   Tremblay-Moll
Krystine Phelps
Kurt Navratil
Kylie Cook
Kyra Wilder
Lacy Wolfe
Lana Selby
Laura Ling
Laura Murphy
Laura Newman
Laura Pugh
Laura Rangeley
Lauren Pout
Lauren
   Rosenfield
Laurence
   Laluyaux
Lee Harbour
Leona Iosifidou
Liliana Lobato
Lily Blacksell
Lily Robert-Foley
Linda Jones
Linda Lewis
Linda Milam
Linda Whittle
Lindsay Attree
Lindsay Brammer
Lindsey Ford
Lindsey Harbour
Linnea Brown

Lisa Agostini
Lisa Dillman
Lisa Hess
Lisa Leahigh
Lisa Simpson
Liz Clifford
Liz Ketch
Lorna Bleach
Lottie Smith
Louise Evans
Louise
   Greenberg
Louise Jolliffe
Louise Smith
Lucinda Smith
Lucy Moffatt
Lucy Scott
Luise von Flotow
Luke Murphy
Lynda Graham
Lyndia Thomas
Lynn Fung
Lynn Grant
Lynn Martin
Madden Aleia
Madison Taylor-
   Hayden
Maeve Lambe
Maggie Humm
Malgorzata
   Rokicka
Mandy Wight
Marco
   Medjimorec
Margaret Wood
Mari-Liis
   Calloway
Maria Ahnhem
   Farrar
Maria Lomunno
Maria Losada
Marie Cloutier

Marie Harper
Marijana Rimac
Marina
   Castledine
Marion
   Pennicuik
Marja S
   Laaksonen
Mark Bridgman
Mark Reynolds
Mark Sargent
Mark Sheets
Mark Sztyber
Mark Waters
Martha W Hood
Martin Brown
Martin Nathan
Martin Eric
   Rodgers
Mary Addonizio
Mary Angela
   Brevidoro
Mary Clarke
Mary Heiss
Mary Wang
Maryse Meijer
Mathias Ruthner
Mathilde Pascal
Matt Carruthers
Matt Davies
Matt Greene
Matthew Black
Matthew Cooke
Matthew
   Crossan
Matthew
   Eatough
Matthew Francis
Matthew Gill
Matthew Lowe
Matthew
   Woodman

Matthias
   Rosenberg
Maura Cheeks
Maureen Cullen
Maureen and Bill
   Wright
Max Cairnduff
Max Longman
Max McCabe
Maxwell
   Mankoff
Meaghan
   Delahunt
Meg Lovelock
Megan Taylor
Megan Wittling
Mel Pryor
Melissa Beck
Melissa Stogsdill
Meredith Martin
Michael Bichko
Michael Boog
Michael Dodd
Michael James
   Eastwood
Michael Floyd
Michael Gavin
Michael
   Schneiderman
Michaela Goff
Michelle
   Mercaldo
Michelle
   Mirabella
Michelle Perkins
Miguel Head
Mike Abram
Mike Turner
Miles Smith-
   Morris
Miranda Gold
Molly Foster

Mona Arshi
Morayma
  Jimenez
Moriah Haefner
Nancy Garruba
Nancy Jacobson
Nancy Oakes
Nancy Peters
Naomi Morauf
Nargis McCarthy
Natalie Ricks
Nathalie Teitler
Nathan
  McNamara
Nathan Weida
Nichola Smalley
Nicholas Brown
Nicholas Jowett
Nicholas
  Rutherford
Nick Chapman
Nick James
Nick Marshall
Nick Nelson &
  Rachel Eley
Nick Sidwell
Nick Twemlow
Nicola Cook
Nicola Hart
Nicola Mira
Nicola Sandiford
Nicolas Sampson
Nicole Matteini
Nicoletta
  Asciuto
Nigel Fishburn
Niki Sammut
Nina Todorova
Nina Nickerson
Norman
  Batchelor
Norman Carter

Odilia Corneth
Olga Zilberbourg
Olivia Clarke
Olivia Powers
Pamela Tao
Pankaj Mishra
Pat Winslow
Patrick Hawley
Patrick Hoare
Patrick
  McGuinness
Paul Cray
Paul Ewing
Paul Jones
Paul Munday
Paul Nightingale
Paul Scott
Paul Stallard
Pavlos
  Stavropoulos
Penelope
  Hewett-Brown
Perlita Payne
Peter Edwards
Peter and Nancy
  Ffitch
Peter Gaukrodger
Peter Griffin
Peter Hayden
Peter McBain
Peter
  McCambridge
Peter Rowland
Peter Wells
Petra Stapp
Phil Bartlett
Philip Herbert
Philip Warren
Philip Williams
Philipp Jarke
Phillipa
  Clements

Phoebe
  Millerwhite
Phyllis Reeve
Pia Figge
Piet Van
  Bockstal
Prakash Nayak
Priya Sharma
Rachael de
  Moravia
Rachael Williams
Rachel Adducci
Rachel Beddow
Rachel Belt
Rachel Carter
Rachel Van Riel
Rachel Watkins
Ralph Jacobowitz
Raminta Uselytė
Ramona Pulsford
Rebecca Carter
Rebecca Moss
Rebecca O'Reilly
Rebecca Parry
Rebecca Peer
Rebecca
  Roadman
Rebecca
  Rosenthal
Rebecca Shaak
Rebecca Starks
Rebecca Surin
Rebekka
  Bremmer
Renee Otmar
Renee Thomas
Rhiannon
  Armstrong
Rich Sutherland
Richard Ellis
Richard Gwyn
Richard Harrison

Richard Mansell
Richard Shea
Richard Soundy
Rita Kaar
Rita O'Brien
Robert Gillett
Robert Hamilton
Robert Hannah
Robert Weeks
Roberto Hull
Robin McLean
Robin Taylor
Rodrigo Alvarez
Roger Newton
Roger Ramsden
Ronan O'Shea
Rory Williamson
Rosalind May
Rosalind Ramsay
Rosanna Foster
Rose Crichton
Rosemary
  Horsewood
Rosie Ernst
  Trustram
Roxanne O'Del
  Ablett
Roz Simpson
Rupert Ziziros
Ryan Day
Ryan Oliver
SK Grout
ST Dabbagh
Sally Baker
Sally Warner
Sam Gordon
Samuel Crosby
Samuel Stolton
Samuel Wright
Sara Bea
Sara Kittleson
Sara Unwin

Sarah Arboleda
Sarah Brewer
Sarah Lucas
Sarah Manvel
Sarah Pybus
Sarah Stevns
Scott Astrada
Scott Chiddister
Scott Henkle
Scott Russell
Scott Simpson
Sean Johnston
Sean Kottke
Sean Myers
Selina Guinness
Serena Brett
Severijn
  Hagemeijer
Shannon Knapp
Sharon Dilworth
Sharon
  McCammon
Shauna Gilligan
Sian Hannah
Sienna Kang
Simak Ali
Simon Clark
Simon Malcolm
Simon Pitney
Simon Robertson
Stacy Rodgers
Stefano Mula
Stephan Eggum
Stephanie De
  Los Santos
Stephanie Miller

Stephen Cowley
Stephen Pearsall
Stephen Yates
Steve Clough
Steve Dearden
Steve Tuffnell
Steven Norton
Stewart Eastham
Stu Hennigan
Stuart & Sarah
  Quinn
Stuart Grey
Stuart Wilkinson
Su Bonfanti
Sue Davies
Susan Edsall
Susan Ferguson
Susan Jaken
Susan Winter
Susan
  Wachowski
Suzanne
  Kirkham
Sylvie Zannier-
  Betts
Tallulah Fairfax
Tania Hershman
Tara Roman
Tatiana Griffin
Taylor Ffitch
Teresa Werner
Tess Lewis
The Mighty
  Douche
  Softball Team
Theo Voortman

Thom Keep
Thomas Alt
Thomas
  Campbell
Thomas Fritz
Thomas van den
  Bout
Tiffany Lehr
Tim Kelly
Tim Nicholls
Tim Scott
Timothy
  Cummins
Timothy Moffatt
Tina Rotherham-
  Winqvist
Toby Halsey
Toby Ryan
Tom Darby
Tom Doyle
Tom Franklin
Tom Gray
Tom Stafford
Tom Whatmore
Tracy Bauld
Tracy Birch
Tracy Lee-
  Newman
Trent Leleu
Trevor Wald
Tricia Durdey
Turner Docherty
Valerie
  O'Riordan
Vanessa Baird
Vanessa Dodd

Vanessa
  Fernandez
  Greene
Vanessa Heggie
Vanessa Nolan
Vanessa Rush
Veronica
  Barnsley
Veronika
  Haacker
  Lukacs
Victor
  Meadowcroft
Victoria
  Goodbody
Victoria Huggins
Vijay Pattisapu
Vikki O'Neill
Wendy Call
Wendy
  Langridge
Will Weir
William
  Brockenborough
William Richard
William
  Schwaber
William Orton
William Sitters
Yoora Yi Tenen
Zachary
  Maricondia
Zoë Brasier
Zoe Taylor
Zoe Thomas

SHALASH THE IRAQI is the Iraqi author of *Shalash the Iraqi*. He probably lives in Iraq.

KANAN MAKIYA was born in Baghdad. He is the author of several books, including the best-selling *Republic of Fear*, *The Monument*, *The Rock*, *The Rope*, and the award-winning *Cruelty and Silence*. He was the Sylvia K. Hassenfeld Professor of Islamic and Middle Eastern Studies at Brandeis University until his retirement in 2015. He lives in Cambridge, Massachusetts.

LUKE LEAFGREN is an Assistant Dean of Harvard College. He has published six translations of Arabic novels and received the 2018 Saif Ghobash Banipal Prize for Arabic Literary Translation for his English edition of Muhsin Al-Ramli's *The President's Gardens*.